JULES LERMINA

HUMAN LIFE

TRANSLATED AND WITH AN INTRODUCTION BY
BRIAN STABLEFORD

THIS IS A SNUGGLY BOOK

ISBN: 978-1-64525-128-6

HUMAN LIFE

JULES LERMINA (1839-1915) was a radical journalist arrested more than once for subversion; he was in prison when the siege of Paris began in 1870, but appears to have been offered release if he would join the National Guard; he agreed, and was sent out of Paris to fight the Germans, thus being unable to join the Commune and avoiding subsequent transportation to New Caledonia. Chastened by the experience, he returned to Paris and journalism, becoming a successful writer of action-adventure *feuilletons*. When his daughter Marie-Pauline married the occult bookseller Henri Chacornac, Lermina became involved with the Occult Revival, writing several stories based on ideas fed to him by Papus. Lermina introduced occult elements into numerous stories, usually for purely melodramatic purposes, but his prestige as a writer was sufficient to prompt Papus to ask him to chair the Congress of Occult societies that he assembled in 1889.

BRIAN STABLEFORD's scholarly work includes *New Atlantis: A Narrative History of Scientific Romance* (Wildside Press, 2016), *The Plurality of Imaginary Worlds: The Evolution of French roman scientifique* (Black Coat Press, 2017) and *Tales of Enchantment and Disenchantment: A History of Faerie* (Black Coat Press, 2019). He has translated more than three hundred volumes from the French, mostly in the genres of *roman scientifique, contes de fées* and Romantic and Symbolist fiction. His recent fiction includes the visionary science fiction novel *The Revelations of Time and Space* (2020) and its sequel *After the Revelation* (2021); the last in his long series of "Tales of the Genetic Revolution," *The Elusive Shadows* (2020); and the comedy fantasy *Meat on the Bone* (2021), all published by Snuggly Books.

CONTENTS

INTRODUCTION

MOST of these stories by Jules Lermina (1839-1915) appeared in book form in *La Magicienne*, published by Chamuel in 1892. One novella from that collection, "L'Héritage des Zippélius" has, however, been recently translated elsewhere as "The Zippelius Secret," so I have substituted three other stories for it in the present collection: two shorter occult fantasies written in the same period as "La Magicienne" and the humorous novelette "La Naufrage de la *Rigolette*," written as part of an earlier set of "*nouveaux contes drolatiques*." *La Magiciennne* is a mixed bag, combining material from different phases of Lermina's remarkably checkered career, the initial occult fantasy and an item of *roman scientifique* being followed by three psychological studies of obsession, one of which, "Le Sacoche"—of which an 1894 translation appeared as "The Money-Bag"—is framed as a detective story, while the others feature accounts of the unfortunate effects of pathological jealousy.

Because Chamuel was a specialist occult publisher it was natural for the collection to be titled for its only occult fantasy, which was also the only story original to the collection, but that decision had the side-effect of placing the stories out of chronological order of composition and obscuring the fact that they belonged to markedly different, but not unrelated, phases of the author's mercurial development. The present collection retains a structure akin to that of the original, but it is worth taking note of the initial dates and places of publication of the stories because those data help in understanding the evolution of Lermina's work in the wider context of his career. The invaluable bibliographical work done by Jean-Luc Buard and published in *Le Rocambole* 43-44 in 2008 has permitted that reconstruction, so far as it is presently possible.

La Magicienne was the fourth collection of short stories by Lermina and the only one to be published by Chamuel, *Histoires incroyables* (1885), *La Vie joyeuse, nouveaux contes drolatiques* (1885) and *Nouveaux histoires incroyables* (1888) all having been issued by the downmarket publisher L. Boulanger, who also published the book versions of most of Lermina's many *feuilleton* serials and marked his rather lowly situation in the hierarchy of the Parisian literary community. By the time they appeared Lermina was already branded as a *feuilletoniste*, and hence as a purveyor of ephemeral popular fiction, but his work is actually very varied and often enterprising, especially at the intermediate length of the novella. His continual experimentation and changes of direction, often forced by changes in circumstance, enabled him to become a pioneer in several of the modern genres of fiction that were then in early development, although his versatility and constant desire to do different things—and to do them differently—was not conducive to building a reputation as a genre specialist. Such ventures into occult fiction as "La Magicienne," reflective of a genuine but conscientiously skeptical interest in contemporary "psychic research," presumably alienated some readers while rendering him suspicious to true believers in one or other aspect of the contemporary Occult Revival. "Chamuel" (Lucien Mauchel, 1867-1936) might have preferred to issue a collection consisting entirely of occult fantasies, but the priorities of publishers and authors are often at odds, and authors are understandably eager to take advantage of the few opportunities they get to follow their own inclinations rather than those of their gatekeepers.

For whatever reason, Lermina did not take the opportunity to supplement "La Magicienne" with other works of the same kind—as I have done here by adding translations of "La Vie d'un mort," which appeared in the occult periodical *L'Initiation* between June 1891 and January 1892, and "L'Envouteur" (*L'Initiation* July 1892)—although "L'Héritage des Zippélius," an early example of what Maurice Renard subsequently dubbed "scientific marvel fiction," belongs to a neighboring genre. His own priority was to include—perhaps "conceal" would be a more apt term—three novellas that had earlier appeared as feuilletons in *Le Temps*, "Le Sacoche" between 29 November and 18 December 1887, "Histoire d'une nuit" between 28 November and 17 December 1888, and "Vie humaine" between 26 April and 9 May 1890, which constituted a different phase of his work, much more ambitious in purely literary terms—perhaps too ambitious. No more novellas appeared in *Le Temps* after "Vie humaine," which he probably held in high regard—although Lermina did publish two further novels of a different kind in the feuilleton slot—*Reine* (*Le Temps* 1 November-26 December 1890) and *Alise* (Le Temps 24 August-22 September 1892)—before vanishing from its pages, perhaps having tested his crowd-pleasing brief to destruction with the stubborn esotericism and downbeat quality of his work for the paper.

If that is what happened, it was surely not the first time. Jean-Luc Buard was unable to identify a prior feuilleton version of the salacious comedy "La Naufrage de la *Rigolette*," although internal evidence suggests that it was composed in sections for an intended serial publication that might have been aborted for diplomatic reasons. *La Vie joyeuse* is one of numerous Boulanger publications now reckoned to be "*introuvable*," and the brief phase in Lermina's career represented by its contents has been virtually forgotten, but the story was reprinted as a serial in the literary supplement of *La Lanterne* in 1891, and the present translation was made from that version, reproduced in the Bibliothèque Nationale's *gallica* archive. It was during the 1880s that the notion of "pornography" was repopularized in journalistic debate in Paris, and its limitations significantly redrawn by multitudinous satirical examples illustrating and challenging the notion of the "unmentionable." Lermina was by no means the only writer of the era who tried the limits of the conventionally acceptable, but he did not manage to find a method of procedure that would enable him to place work on that particular edge of the marketplace.

The feuilletons that Lermina published in *Le Temps* were of particular significance in the context of his long journalistic career, which had begun in the hazardous climate of the Second Empire, when his path from such radical papers as *Le Soleil* and his own fervently anti-Imperialist *Le Corsaire* to the relatively respectable liberal daily *Le Gaulois*, had been distinctly thorny. The even-more-respectable *Le Temps*, edited under the Third Republic by Adrien Hébrard, who went into politics and eventually became a center-left senator, was a much more pretentiously-ambitious and politically-moderate paper whose circulation had grown steadily after a slow start during the Second Empire and was reportedly in excess of 30,000 by the mid-1880s. The novellas that Lermina serialized there, printed under the feuilleton on page one, were by far his most ambitious works, particularly in terms of their heavy emphasis on the unusual psychology of their protagonists, which sometimes took up and elaborated themes first explored in his earlier work for the literary supplement of *Le Figaro*.

One of those novellas, "Le Centenaire" (*Le Temps* 18-23 October 1887; tr. as "The Elixir of Life"), was a serious exploration in occult fiction, but it was not that aspect of his narrative experimentation that first claimed his sustained attention. He became temporarily fascinated by the idea of obsession, in terms of its psychological role in human affairs and its potential as a generator of interesting narratives. That preoccupation prompted him to make a remarkable contribution to the embryonic genre of detective fiction in "Le Sacoche," and then inspired an early experiment in the use of "stream-of-consciousness" narrative technique in "Histoire d'une nuit," which makes innovative, albeit slightly awkward, use of what critical jargon would later call an "unreliable narrator."

The moral question posed in the first and last lines of "Histoire d'une nuit" is dramatically re-emphasized, from a more distanced but still skewed viewpoint, in "La Vie humaine," which is an intense study of the limitations and eccentric propensities of a "scientific mind"—or, more precisely, a scholarly mind that would nowadays be characterized as afflicted with "high-functioning autism" or "Asperger's syndrome." Without those notions available, and without very many literary models for comparison, it must have been difficult for contemporary readers to appreciate the story fully, but nowadays readers with appropriately-educated sensibilities—fans of such recent US TV series as *The Big Bang Theory* and *Scorpion*, for instance—will have no difficulty recognizing the personality-type to which the unfortunate protagonist of the story belongs.

It is arguable that all three of those stories are flawed: that in attempting to do something new, each of them bit off a little more than the author could chew, and as studies of perversity go, they are certainly more than a little perverse themselves, but that only helps to emphasize their originality and their achievements. It is a trifle difficult, in retrospect, to understand why the editors of *Le Temps* published a story like "La Vie humaine," given that it is so alien to the normal expectations of readers of popular fiction, but *Le Temps* also issued a separate version as a pamphlet extract from the newspaper, and subsequently did the same with *Reine*, so the probability is that the paper's literary editor simply appreciated their merits and decided to publish them in spite of the fact that they were not the usual fare of feuilleton serials. The editor in question might not have been so generous in respect of other material, however; "L'Héritage des Zippélius," which first appeared in the fortnightly *Revue politique et littéraire* as "Le Secret des Zippélius" between 26 November and 28 December, 1889, can be regarded as a part of the same set of novellas and might well have been planned and initially written with *Le Temps* in mind, during the gap that separated the appearances there of "Histoire d'une nuit" and "La Vie humaine." If "L'Héritage des Zippélius" was rejected by *Le Temps*, though, it was presumably on the grounds of its exoticism rather than any lack of quality, and the disappearance after 1892 of Lermina from the newspaper was surely due to the fact that his work simply seemed too adventurous for its humdrum readers, given the anodyne quality of so much feuilleton fare designed for the consumption of the bourgeois audience.

If Lermina did, in fact, suffer banishment from *Le Temps* in 1892 for being too innovative in his work it was probably not the first time something similar had happened to him, and it was certainly not the first or the last time that something similar happened to one of his contemporaries. Lermina probably regretted the loss of the market, and regretted too that in order to have "La Vie humaine" and its companion novellas reprinted in book form, he had to take advantage of a marginal publisher like Lucien Mauchel, but he must have felt that any such publication was better than none and that, following the dictum of the heroine of "La Naufrage de la *Rigolette*," one must do what is necessary, however embarrassing it might seem when viewed from a different point of view. The fact that he did not simply give the collection to Boulanger is, however, surely of some significance.

*

Jules Lermina was born in Paris in 1839, during the reign of Louis-Philippe. His father was what his fiction would often refer to as a "functionary": a civil servant in the rapidly-expanding bureaucracy of government, with a post in the Ministry of War. While Jules was still a child, however, his father lost that employment when the revolution of 1848 overthrew Louis-Philippe and introduced the Second Republic, the political affiliations of the elder Lermina apparently being too royalist. Jules finished school during the turbulent and economically-difficult years before and after the coup of 1851, which eventually made Louis-Napoléon Bonaparte the second Emperor of France.

When Jules Lermina left the lycée he initially continued the orthodox career path of the sons of functionaries by "doing his law," but he did not find that tedious study to his liking and soon abandoned it. He was a voracious and omnivorous reader, and he maintained literary interests on the side while he searched for another vocation. He appears to have tried his hand at various employments, working for banks and insurance companies as well as undertaking more adventurous enterprises, founding a workers' co-operative in the Compiègne and spending some time in England, but his employments did not last and his entrepreneurial ventures failed. He appears to have been more comfortable working as a freelance journalist, although that labor cannot have been profitable, and when he married in 1861 he had to pay more attention to the practical possibility of sustaining a household. He settled into a position at the newspaper *Le Soleil*, eventually progressing to become its editor-in-chief in 1866.

Censorship of the press had been very severe during the 1850s, but as the 1860s progressed and the Empire came to

13

seem secure, the censors gradually slackened their grip and a measure of political dissent was tolerated, although never free from hazard. In addition to *Le Soleil*, Lermina resurrected the title of one of the radical Republican papers that had enjoyed a precarious existence under Louis-Philippe, *Le Corsaire*. It was quickly suppressed, but, just as the original *Corsaire* had briefly fused with the even more radical and fiercely satirical *Le Satan*, Lermina began issuing a *Satan* of his own, whose sheet of newsprint was folded in four rather than the usual two, so that it could be "hidden" inside a conventional news-sheet. Not unnaturally, the ploy did not save it.

The attempted suppression of the press often tends to sharpen its satirical inclinations, especially if it drives the opposition "underground," forcing it to have recourse to clandestine printing presses—of which Paris had a very long and active tradition going all the way back to the age of Louis XIV. Jules Lermina was not a docile person, and it would probably not be unjust to describe him as inherently "bloody-minded." His anti-Imperialism became increasingly active, and he became a popular orator at public meetings, his speeches becoming increasingly violent. It was inevitable that he would eventually exceed the limits of tolerance in his new position on the staff of *Le Gaulois*, which he joined in 1869, the year in which he also published his *Histoire de la misère ou Le Proletariat à travers les ages*.

That employment was relatively respectable, but Lermina also associated socially and professionally with the staff of the far more radical *La Marsellaise*, owned by Henri Rochefort and edited by Paschal Grousset. That personnel included Yvan Salmon, who adopted the provocative pen-name Victor Noir; it was in his company that Lermina was arrested and jailed for the first time, following a small political demonstration. Victor Noir became an important symbolic figure for opponents of the regime after being asked by Grousset to serve as his second when he challenged Prince Pierre Bonaparte, a cousin of the emperor and a pillar of the imperialist newspaper *Le Revanche*, to a duel in January 1870. The prince's response was to refuse the duel contemptuously and shoot Noir dead: a murder for which he was not held to account because of his family connections. The outrage caused by the death of his friend in such circumstances must have influenced Lermina's decision to make an incendiary speech on 28 April 1870 at a public meeting at the Folies-Bergère which concluded with a war-cry demanding that a sentence of death be passed on the régime and its ruler. Lermina was arrested, charged with insulting the emperor, and sentenced to two years in prison, plus a fine of ten thousand francs and the revocation of his civil rights.

As things turned out, Lermina did not spend long in prison, although he offered colorful accounts of his time there in newspaper articles that might not be entirely accurate. In June, suffering from poor health, he was transferred to a sanitarium, but when the Prussians invaded France in September, he was enlisted in the Army in order to help fight the invasion. He was sent out of Paris to fight, and allegedly engaged the enemy on at least two occasions, although he somehow avoided being killed; an "eye-witness account" of the battle of Buzenval "by a volunteer" that he published in 1872 might well have employed a certain poetic license in its description on the action and a measure of sarcasm in its by-line.

Lermina's conscription might have been something of a blessing in disguise; it ensured that he was not in Paris at the end of 1870, when the Commune de Paris briefly took control of the city before being brutally suppressed by the French Army when the Prussians withdrew, acting in the name of a new national government. Many of his friends and associates had accepted positions within the Commune's organization and were shot, transported to New Caledonia, or, like Paschal

Grousset, forced to flee and live on the run for several years. Lermina, having been released from the army following the French surrender, was able to return to his wife and children and resume his career, albeit carefully, seemingly cured of incendiary rabble-rousing as well as whatever ailment had sent him from the Mazas to the sanitarium.

Lermina remained on the political left of the Third Republic, and was quite content during the *fin-de-siècle* to be described as an Anarchist (in fairness, there were few members of the literary community who were not), although his closest affiliation was with the député who proclaimed the Third Republic, Léon Gambetta—who had not participated in the Commune because he had been driven into temporary exile in Spain. Lermina stood with Gambetta's hastily-reconstituted party as a candidate in the election of 1871, but the radicals suffered a heavy defeat and Gambetta's provisional Republic was inherited by the far more conservative Adolphe Thiers.

Lermina had begun publishing items of pseudonymous fiction in *Le Soleil* and *Le Gaulois* before the war, but his production of such work increased massively and rapidly afterwards, although some time passed before he began to use his own signature, much of his early fiction being by-lined "William Cobb" and feigning an American origin. A great admirer of the work of Edgar Poe, he published several imitations of his work and initially represented the novelette "Les Fous" (1869 in *Le Gaulois*; tr. as "The Lunatics") as Poe's work before confessing to the hoax in a letter to the editor signed "William Cobb." "Les Fous" was the first of many stories by Lermina developing an intense interest in contemporary analytical accounts of abnormal psychology, whose later products include the stories in the present volume.

Lermina had published work of that kind as early as 1861 in the short-lived literary periodical *Diogène*, in connection with which he formed several significant friendships. The writers associated with the periodical had included Jules Clarétie, who provided a preface for *Histoires incroyables* and was long associated with Lermina in the Societé de gens de lettres, and Marc Fournier, in collaboration with whom he wrote a feuilleton novel and a dramatic adaptation of Nathaniel Hawthorne's *The Scarlet Letter*, "La Lettre rouge" (1874). It was in 1871, however, in the pages of *Le Gaulois*, that his fiction gained impetus, particularly with the publication of "Le Clou" (tr. as "The Nail") and "La Peur," both signed William Cobb, the former influenced by Poe's accounts of the deductive prowess if Auguste Dupin, and the latter by the America author's classic psychological melodramas. The hero of "Le Clou," Maurice Parent, reappeared later in "Le Sacoche," translated in the present volume as "The Satchel," in which the different argumentative accounting-schemes employed by the narrator and Parent are carefully contrasted, foreshadowing what was to become a standard relationship between master detectives and their observationally-challenged sidekicks.

"William Cobb" also began publishing short stories in other periodicals in 1872, but in the next decade Lermina concentrated his efforts on long feuilleton serials, published under various pseudonyms. He began to use his own signature far more frequently after 1879, though, when "William Cobb" faded away for a while, mostly employed thereafter for the more bizarre ventures in the series of *"histoires incroyables"* that Lermina delighted in producing. In the 1880s, however, a new boom in newspaper production began, enabled by technological advances in automated printing and paper manufacture, and newspapers proliferated rapidly in Paris, engaging in fierce circulation wars that led to considerable experimentation in quest of reader-pleasing material. The market in popular fiction issued in cheap volume formats also boomed, and offered an invaluable resource for Lermina and several of his friends, including Paschal Grousset, who repackaged himself as "André Laurie" and Yvan Salmon's brother, who renamed himself "Louis Noir" in his sibling's honor.

Although feuilleton serials retained their importance in the popular newspapers during the boom of the 1880s, there was also a much-increased demand for short fiction, and Lermina took advantage of both kinds of opportunity. That economic shift and its effects, which extended to the end of the century and beyond, determined the shape of Lermina's subsequent career. It was in 1880 that he began working prolifically for L. Boulanger, a somewhat obscure figure—Jean-Luc Buard was unable to discover his forename when he wrote a brief account of him in *Le Rocambole* in 2008—who became his principal publisher for the next two decades. Lermina did a great deal of hackwork for Boulanger's various publication lines, in numerous genres of fiction and non-fiction, and he edited two of the four periodicals that Boulanger founded in 1890 as cheap imitations of established titles, *La Revue pour tous* and *La Terre illustrée*; Lermina wrote much of the contents of the latter publication, a vehicle of Vernian "travelogue fiction" that was eventually absorbed by its model, the more successful *Journal des Voyages*, for which Lermina continued to write routinely into the early years of the twentieth century.

Lermina's move upmarket in the feuilletons featured in *Le Temps* happened in parallel with his routine work for Boulanger, and must have seemed to be somewhat in contrast with it. Although *Le Temps* reviewed some of Lermina's action-adventure novels in its pages, along with more ambitious works, it would not be surprising if the newspaper's literary editors had decided that his presence there, while he was churning out pulp for Boulanger, was not entirely conducive to the image of relative sophistication that they were trying to present, even though there is no lack of narrative sophistication in his experimental novellas—quite the contrary. In fact "Histoire d'une nuit" was also serialized in *Le Temps* in parallel with the longest of Lermina's stories in the occult periodical *L'Initiation*, "À bruler, conte astral" (October 1888-May 1889; tr. as "Burn This"), making a rather curious juxtaposition. The coincidence resulted from the fact that it was also in 1880, the year he formed his association with Boulanger, that Lermina had become interested in occultism: an interest greatly encouraged some years later when the eldest of his three daughters wanted to marry Henri Chacornac, then a *bouquiniste* with a stall of the bank of the Seine, who specialized in occult books.

Lermina helped Henri Chacornac move into an actual shop, which quickly became an important nucleus of the Parisian Occult Revival, and the site of a publishing enterprise that initially rivaled Chamuel but eventually merged with that publisher. In the early days of his operation, Chacornac's principal publication was *L'Initiation*, founded and edited by the neo-Martinist "Papus" (Gérard Encausse), for which Lermina wrote several stories, including two translated herein. When Papus organized a pioneering conference bringing together the various occult societies of Paris, in an attempt to find a common spirit, he persuaded Lermina to chair it, with the difficult task of trying to minimize conflict between warring factions of Spiritists, neo-Rosicrucians and Theosophists.

Following Lermina's disappearance from the front page of *Le Temps* he did not make any conspicuous bids for a more respectable situation within the Parisian literary community in the pattern of his fiction, but he did continue to produce more ambitious works of non-fiction. He was also a very active member of the Societé de gens de lettres throughout his career, and while serving as its secretary he compiled several reports for the society on the progress of various campaigns to secure authorial property rights, especially in an international context. Several of his non-fiction projects fell by the wayside, however; among other items of interest he published a volume of translations of Shakespeare in 1898 with illustrations by Albert Robida, but it was issued by Boulanger and seems to have been very poorly distributed, absent even from the Bibliothèque Nationale collection.

Perhaps feeling that he had no practical alternative, therefore, Lermina effectively settled after 1892 into being a fluent mass-producer of offbeat action-adventure stories in the same vein as his younger *alter ego* William Cobb. The psychological role of obsession still played a part in his plotting, but it was reduced to casual measured proportions rather than taken to the intense but idiosyncratic extreme of "La Vie humaine." He was skilled in that sort of mass-production, and he was certainly more intelligent than much of the work he churned out in the last two decades of his life, but he never gave up the edge of originality and distinction that his best work possessed, perhaps because rather than in spite of the fact that he was always working in market circumstances that were hostile to his unusual and somewhat changeable interests.

Henri Chacornac's publishing operation was eventually inherited by Lermina's grandson, Paul Chacornac, who became the curator of the author's surviving manuscripts—a collection that greatly assisted the bibliographical work eventually carried out by Jean-Luc Buard when interest in Lermina was renewed in the early twenty-first century. That renewal of interest was stimulated by scholars and readers interested in the history of popular fiction, especially Vernian travelogue fiction, detective fiction and analogues of what would later be called "science fiction," in all of which fields Lermina laid down important milestones, alongside those he established in the slightly-displaced field of occult fiction. The author's versatility did not work to his advantage in reputational terms, though, making him seem even more of a butterfly than he actually was, and it did not help that his few story collections were a trifle lacking in coherence. The present volume, alas, only adds to that confusion. It might have been more satisfactory to make a single volume out of the novellas from *Le Temps* and to compile a companion volume consisting entirely of occult fantasies, putting the author's exercises in *roman scientifique* in a third volume and his detective stories in a fourth (although the assortment would have been afflicted by certain ambiguities), but the order in which I made and published the translations did not permit such reorganization with the aid of hindsight—*mea culpa*.

In spite of that less-than-fortunate confusion, however, I hope that my translations of Lermina's works do demonstrate that he was a very interesting writer, whose failure to make a better reputation for himself was due to circumstance rather than any dearth in the quality of his imagination. He produced work in such quantity that the quality was bound to be somewhat uneven, but he was a hard worker and a relentless researcher, putting solid labor into such projects as his *dictionnaires* of argot and Anarchism, which probably deserved more attention than their poor distribution permitted. It must be admitted that some of the more eccentric products of the reckless opportunism of his later years are distinctly caricaturish—"L'Effrayante aventure" (*Le Plein Air* 22 July-2 December 1910; tr, as *Panic in Paris*) is one example—but others, including "Mystere-ville" (*Journal des Voyages* 4 December 1905-26 March 1906; tr. as *Mysteryville*) are almost magnificent in their surrealism, and there is some cause for regret that the mammoth feuilleton about a future world war that he planned to write for *La Terre illustrée* as "Le Bataille de Strasbourg" (23 April 1891-11 February 1892) had to be curtailed in a rather brutal manner. In his shorter works, however, as well as his more earnest historical and romantic novels, he was far more stylish. The recent resurgence of interest in his works, as reflected in the celebration of it in the pages of *Le Rocambole* is entirely justified.

For most of the twentieth century Lermina's works were the almost-exclusive province of collectors of rare books but that situation changed dramatically with the advent of the internet and the Bibliothèque Nationale's establishment of the *gallica* website, including the newspaper archives that have made access to much of the author's work easy again, not only individually but collectively, facilitating comparison and analysis and providing rich fodder for hobbyist scholars like myself. The present volume of translations follows four volumes published by Black Coat Press,[1] and there might yet be more if I live long enough, or if someone else cares to continue the project of making a small but significant fraction of Lermina's rich and very various body of work available (albeit belatedly) to English readers. Within that body of work, however, the present volume includes a substantial part of the cream, and is well worthy of interested and sympathetic attention.

—Brian Stableford, August 2021

---

1 The four volumes in question contain the novels *Panic in Paris* (2009, supplemented by the novella "The Elixir of Life"), *Mysteryville* (2010, supplemented by the novella "Twice Dead"). *The Battle of Strasbourg* (2014) and a collection that I titled *The Zippelius Secret*, but which the publisher rendered mistakenly as *The Secret of Zippelius* (2011) and refused to correct because, he said, he could not see that it made any difference. (I can.) I would still like to add a further collection of *Incredible Stories* and a translation of the occult novel *Comtesse Mercadet*, but, contrary to the wise advice of the Blue Oyster Cult, I fear the Reaper and the plan might not come to fruition. Black Coat Press has also published a translation of a Lermina novel made by Georges T. Dodds, *To-Ho and the Gold Destroyers* (2010).

HUMAN LIFE

THE MAGICIENNE

To Maître Lebanon, notary[1]

MY dear friend, it is to your old and sincere affection that I confide the story of the most marvelous adventure that happened to me during my long career as a physician. I beg you urgently not to communicate it to anyone before my death.

Why do I refuse to publish it before my death? I am too old to confront the polemics that it might excite. I would suffer too much from the outraged denials that would be addressed to me and the compassion, even more insulting, of those who would lament my senile credulity. I have passed the time of struggles and disappointments, but I do not recognize the right of the egotistical Fontenelle and, holding a verity in my hand,[2] I shall at least allow it to escape from my dying fingers. It will be for newcomers to pick it up and enable it to bear fruit.

With you, my dear friend, I shall not lower myself so far as to reiterate the affirmation of my absolute sincerity. The

---

1 Probably not an actual name but a pseudonym borrowed from Masonic lore.

2 The reference is to a well-known quotation from Bernard le Bovier de Fontemelle (1657-1757), which translates as: "If I held my hand full of truths, I would be careful how I opened it."

observation that follows is as exact as that of an intern beside a hospital bed. I have seen, and I am giving evidence.

I have retired, as you know, to the little village where I was born. Fatigued, older in body than in mind, I was pleased to return to the initial point of my life in order to leaf through once again the book that I had lived. To make the synthesis of my entire existence appeared to me to be a task worthy of a man who has loved science above all else, but who, through the vicissitudes of the struggle for the life of others has not been able to spend the time to add up the sum of his efforts. Of all my studies and all my endeavors—some of which were qualified in their time as audacious—would any certainty emerge for me in one direction or another? In short, having searched so much, had I found anything?

I shut myself away in an almost absolute solitude and I absorbed myself in a classification of notes, which soon impassioned me. However, I did not play the hermit. A few old friends, former comrades of childhood, had knocked on my door, and I had not kept it obstinately closed. I deem that even at the end of one's career, it is still necessary to mingle a little in the lives of others. Two or three times a week I went to spend my evenings in homes where the cordiality of the welcome compensated for the remorse of a few hours stolen from the work. Certainly, the conversation did not revolve around very transcendent subjects, but it was not unpleasant to indulge in gossip devoid of malevolence about the infinitely petty episodes of provincial life that are often elevated to the level of important events. In that society everything is proportionate, and the speck of dust that causes an aphid on a leaf to stumble is as terrible as a colossal iceberg is to a polar explorer.

As you know my sentiments of a penitent bachelor remorseful of the solitude he had made for himself you will not be astonished by the pleasure I experienced in seeing around me the children of people I had known a long time ago at

the local school: one-time scamps and mischief-makers now
fathers and grandfathers, proud of being surrounded and
fêted, thanked in a way for the life they had given. I too, if
I had wished, could have had grown-up boys close at hand
who might have confessed follies injurious to my purse, ambitions that would have made me pale with anxiety and days of
examinations whose fortune outcome would have singularly
compromised my impassivity, and daughters who might have
proved to me that in matters of beauty atavism is only a word,
fortunately for those who, like me, have had an amiable reputation for ugliness. I loved that activity of youth, its laughter
and blushes. Gradually, having initially been feared as a very
scholarly and utterly boring old monsieur, I conquered the
sympathy of that small society, and, from one concession to
another, I came to remember that I had once played the piano
and sat down, without being begged too much, on the stool
to which the convicts of the polka and the waltz are shackled.
And it was a veritable joy for me to hear the rustle of dress-
es and the murmur of voices behind me; from all that true
pleasure an atmosphere was disengaged that soothed me and
rejuvenated me; and in unrepentant analysis I asked myself
whether there might not be some truth in the ancient theory,
so widespread in the Middle Age, of the prolongation of the
life of old men by the frequentation of young people radiant
with vitality.

One evening, while swaying to the rhythm of my
pseudo-musical improvisation—fulfilling a task that had become almost quotidian—I saw, looking at me over the piano,
scarcely surpassing it, a thin, jaundiced face with brilliant and
feverish eyes. In the surprise that that unexpected apparition
caused me, the first idea that occurred to me, imposing itself
upon me with the clarity of a powerful imprint, was that the
head and eyes belonged to an absolutely unhappy man, but
one deserving of his misfortune. It was an entirely instinctive

impression, perhaps communicated to my gaze by an unsympathetic expression—for the man had suddenly disappeared, leaving me with a sensation of unsatisfied curiosity.

When I was free of my chain I searched for the person with my gaze; he was no longer in the drawing room. Having had the habitude for a long time of not being a hypocrite, even in my own regard, I made enquiries of the master of the house.

"Oh, I know!" he said. "That's Monsieur Lambert" (a fictitious name, of course). "The poor man! He adores his daughter, and she's dying . . ."

"Why did he come to such a joyful gathering, then?"

"Don't get annoyed," he said. "What do you expect? One drags the cannonball of one's renown everywhere. He learned of your presence here; he knows that you've accomplished near-marvelous cures in Paris, and if he had dared, he'd have asked you . . ."

I interrupted him abruptly. "Never!" I exclaimed. "I'm no longer, and never have been, a physician." And I added, laughing dryly: "I have enough murders on my conscience; I shan't augment the number."

The other continued: "That's what I told him. So he wasn't bold enough to speak to you. He's very unhappy. His daughter is sixteen or seventeen year old; her mother, it's said, abandoned her when she was very small. The father has raised her but, unhealthy since infancy, she has never been able to vanquish the malady undermining her. She's growing weaker by the day . . . in short, she's dying. All manner of physicians have been summoned, the most knowledgeable and the most renowned. They haven't understood. The most honest have admitted that, the others have treated her anyway. The father, desolate, has even had recourse to charlatans, to magnetizers . . . can that be considered a crime? All that has been obtained is an amelioration of a few days, Now it seems that, although the adorable child has no evident organic lesion—I've seen her—her death is only a matter of days, perhaps hours. That's what he would have told you had he dared to speak to you. His appearance isn't sympathetic, in common with all those who suffer continuously . . . you'd have refused him . . . he thought it better to abstain . . ."

"Send him to me tomorrow," I said, abruptly.

In truth, I didn't know how those words, contrary to my will, had sprung from my lips. I wanted to take back what I'd said; in my turn, I dared not. And yet the most serious reasons militated in favor of my non-intervention. The physicians who had not prevailed had been named to me. They were colleagues, masters, even my pupils, and not the least valuable. Was I so proud as to believe in a possible success, after such failures? No, sincerely, that was not what I was thinking. Let us admit that I had obeyed a banal impulse of humanity, of pity.

I went home preoccupied, discontented with myself, irritated that I had put myself once again—doubtless uselessly—in a position to observe the inanity of our pretended science. I had never, as so many others had, attained the fortunate port of absolute insensitivity. I suffer the pain of my patients; I become angry at my impotence; I feel the remorse of their death!

I slept badly, and in the morning I had almost decided to withdraw an authorization that I deemed imprudent and dangerous for my repose. But it was too late. My maidservant introduced the previous evening's stranger, Monsieur Lambert, into my study. I was trapped. It only remained for me to put on a brave face.

Monsieur Lambert was small, sickly and ugly, wedged tightly into a black frock-coat. He gave an impression of suffering, and yet of something false and peevish in his appearance and his gaze. For me, first impressions are always translated into a sensation of color; I saw him as a yellowish, almost dirty, gray.

However, I could not dissimulate from myself that his physiognomy bore the traces of a profound despair, a kind of rage against fatality; he was suffering, and that was enough for me to set aside all prejudice. I invited him to sit down and explain himself.

He did so in a low voice, repeating exactly the explanations given to me the previous evening, passing rapidly over his conjugal misfortunes, although I divined a profound rancor in him—quite justified, in sum.

When I asked him, being slightly hard of hearing, to speak a little more loudly, he said: "Excuse me, but with my poor daughter, whom the slightest sound seems to hurt, I've acquired the habit of speaking that way."

"So," I said, "your wife abandoned you abruptly? She deserted the conjugal hearth without any concern for her daughter?"

He nodded his head affirmatively.

"And she has never sought to see her child?"

"Never," he said.

He seemed to me to have been gripped by a hesitation, but I thought I might have been mistaken.

I enquired then from a medical viewpoint about various details, which he gave me complaisantly, even anticipating some of my question. He had brought the prescriptions left by the various physicians he had consulted. I examined them attentively. The diagnoses had varied, reaching ill-defined conclusions, but it seemed to me that everything that it was humanly possible to do had been attempted.

As I had lowered my head in order to read, the idea occurred to be to raise my eyes suddenly in order to surprise the expression of my interlocutor, against whom I felt an inexplicable suspicion. But I had to admit that I was mistaken; the anguish was real, the expectation dolorous. The doubt had only been stubbornness.

To recuse myself was impossible; I had taken responsibility for his last hope, and I did not have the right to evade the consequences of my weakness. However, I did not feel the slightest confidence in myself, and what followed was to prove how right I was not to believe in my science.

"I'll go with you," I said to him.

He made a movement as if to throw himself into my arms. We went out together. He lived in a magnificent property half a kilometer from mine. A carriage was waiting for us at the door, but I manifested the desire to go on foot. Monsieur Lambert walked beside me, striving to match my long stride, He seemed like a schoolboy next to me. We did not exchange a single word on the way, but I examined him slyly from above and saw that he was impatient to arrive.

At the gate, a domestic in livery opened up to us. In our very simple region, that luxury was somewhat out of place; I was evidently dealing with a snob. The fault is not great when it cannot be satisfied. The garden—or, rather, the park—was admirably kept and rich in flowers. Taste was, however, lacking; it was the work of a gardener to whom it had been said that expense was no object and who had surrendered to the inspirations of the supplier.

Before going into the house, a heavy construction in the style of the first empire of almost manorial aspect, I stopped Monsieur Lambert and leaned toward him.

"One word," I said, in a low voice. "Does your daughter ever speak to you about her mother?"

He started. "In what regard, since she never knew her?"

"What have you told her to explain your solitude?"

"That that woman was dead."

He had pronounced the words *that woman* in a hateful tone, which struck me. He had put all his rancor into them, all the bile of a deceived husband. Did I have any right to deem that a fault? The mother who has abandoned her child merits even less pity than the adulterous woman. Christ would not have lifted her up.

I shall not dwell on the interior disposition of the house; they were of solid luxury, heavy and costly, with a certain false preoccupation with art that gave me the impression of a bitter fruit bitten too hard.

In the vestibules the walls were covered with huge paintings of hunting scenes of the most odious mediocrity. And as I gazed at them with an intimate shudder of protest, he said, as if responding to an unformulated question: "Yes, I'm something of a painter." And in that "something," as there had been a little while ago in "that woman", there was a world of hidden meaning, an enormity of self-satisfaction beneath the verbal modesty. It was only childishness, though, and I had not come as a valuer. I contented myself with a nod of the head that he was free to translate as he wished. I was in haste now to see my patient. I was already thinking of her as "my patient."

In a bedroom hung entirely in white, a silken nest that my Parisian habitudes would have permitted me to sign with the name of the upholsterer on the spot, in the midst of pretty bibelots highly prized as New Year's gifts—saxe or biscuit trivia created for display—a young woman with black hair and a pale complexion was lying on a chaise longue, her eyes closed, who appeared not to have heard anything.

The luxury of the bedroom matched that of the garden; it must have cost very dear, but with an odor of artificiality; everything was lacking that gives life, grace and charm. Muffled and quilted, that bedroom was cold. I had an impression there of emptiness, of absence, as if I were entering an atmosphere deprived by some chemical operation of one of the elements necessary to life. My sensation is poorly explained because it was inexplicable to me then.

The curtains were lifted and from the window in front of which the young woman was lying the park was visible, scarcely marred by yews stupidly shaped into balls and cottages but superb in their green foliage, outlined against a superb blue sky.

Monsieur Lambert advanced first, on tiptoe. He leaned over the invalid. I saw his narrow back, his pointed shoulders and his bald head with a crown of reddish hair, rebellious to combing.

"Marie!" he murmured, softly.

She opened her eyes, without a shudder. She smiled—a mortal smile—at her father, who took her bloodless hand and raised it to his lips,

"This is . . . a friend," he said, turning to me as if to excuse the lie, "who would like to talk to you. He's knowledgeable . . . very knowledgeable."

Marie—since that was her name—turned her eyes toward me: blue eyes, marvelous in form and limpidity, but possessed of a strangeness that wrung my heart. One might have thought them the eyes of a blind person, empty of gaze. She could see quite well, though.

"Come, Monsieur," she said,

The voice also made me shiver; although it was soft, it seemed to me that I heard an echo coming from far away, very far away. That voice—how can I put it?—was also empty of sonority.

I drew closer, trying to prevent my heart from beating faster. On my honor, I had never been so emotional. I took her hand, and once again I felt the bizarre impression that I had before my eyes nothing but an appearance, something like an empty shell, an envelope with nothing inside.

My very astonishment rendered me my sang-froid; in confrontation with the unknown a seeker stands up straight, like a soldier before danger.

The father had withdrawn discreetly, in order not to inhibit my ministry. I would rather that someone had been there, though—a woman—in order to make my examination more thorough. I acted with all possible precision, however. The child—for, in truth, she was only a child—lent herself meekly to my observation. The most attentive ausculation did not reveal the slightest lesion, and I did not observe any of the phenomena that accompany anemia or consumption. The condition of the lungs set aside any hypothesis of pthisis. The invalid was not experiencing any pain, of whatever nature, and as I pressed her a little, desirous that a word might escape her ignorance instinctively to enlighten my pseudoscientific consciousness, she said;

"Oh, I know what you want to know . . . there's nothing wrong with me. It's life that I lack."

Life! Yes, she was right; it was that unexplained and invisible, but real, force; that influx of power come from who knows where, that was lacking in that organism, otherwise normally organized.

Immediately seized by confidence, she told me that when she was smaller she had felt much stronger, but that it was like a reserve that had been gradually exhausted without ever being renewed.

"What do you expect?" she added. "I didn't bring enough life in being born, that's all."

She said that resignedly, in her empty voice, caressing me with her empty gaze. And I sensed, without comprehending it, that it was true.

Life! Life! But where to discover that inexhaustible reservoir in order to steal a parcel to reanimate and resuscitate that charming creature? Oh, wretched and stupid physician, here you are, with your ever-impotent aspirations! You have invented blood transfusions, and you have been very proud, but they have only given an aliment to life, without creating it. Life! That Lambert was a millionaire, and he would have given his last louis to acquire an atom of it . . . and after that people mock the efforts of the alchemists, who had the audacity to stick to the veritable problem! We crush them with our ridiculous palliatives instead of struggling, like them, with the Sphinx, martyrs to the true science, and dying next to a crucible from which the splendid and vivifying flame might one day spring forth.

What could I say to that father when he interrogated me?

I was ashamed of my ignorance, and I veiled it with the habitual formulae: an initial examination was insufficient; I would come back. I was more cowardly still; I wrote a prescription . . . yes, I scribbled a few cryptographic words at random for that man who had had some confidence in me. I recommended the most rigorous exactitude in the execution of my prescription. I was ashamed of myself!

When the man shook my hand, enveloping me with the gaze of a damned man who still believes in a possible redemption, I was on the point of shouting at him: "Slap me, then! I'm lying! I'm lying!"

I went out, half mad. I ran to shut myself in at home. I wanted to find myself face to face with my ignorance, with my stupidity. I shook my fist at the library for which the Académie is impatiently waiting the royal gift.

I, the great physician, the master so often acclaimed, fell into an armchair and sobbed, because a poor eighteen-year-old girl was dying and I could not do anything—anything at all—to save her.

I knew that I was vanquished in advance, and yet I wanted to continue fighting. For an entire week I spent long hours with the moribund, trying to deceive her, playing the role of an obliging grandfather while my eyes searched that cranium, that chest, seeking to plunge all the way to the most intimate fibers of that being, who kept repeating to me: "I know . . . I know . . . it's life that I lack."

On the eighth day, I had lost all hope; the physical decline was hastening with a despairing rapidity. I knew, and that was the only and horrible privilege of my science, that in our entire medical arsenal there was no weapon that could drive death back by a single step.

I had let a demi-confession escape. The father's face was atrociously contracted. He had ground his teeth, crying at me: "Like all the others! Like all the others!"

I fled. I ran like a madman along the roads and over the fields. I insulted mute nature, the deaf heavens and the life that radiated everywhere but which only revealed itself by its implacable impassivity. I dared not go home; I was now afraid of being alone with my despair, with my remorse.

A storm had burst, without rain: one of those burning tempests in which it seems that the earth is being shaken in the claws of some gigantic fire-breathing monster.

At midnight, I climbed my perron and opened my door, enervated and exhausted. My maidservant was waiting for me, candle in hand.

"Monsieur le docteur! So late! When there's a lady upstairs who has been waiting for you for more than three hours!"

"A lady! I don't want . . . I can't see anyone . . ."

Then I saw a black form appear on the stairs, over which shone the whiteness of a face illuminated by two glittering eyes, and without knowing why, I said: "Here I am! Excuse me, Madame, here I am!"

And I went up.

The unknown woman preceded me; I went into my study behind her, and closed the door carefully behind me.

Then, going to my desk, I picked up the lamp and, returning to the woman, I raised it to the level of her face.

She was very dark, with a mat complexion and a high forehead, and blue eyes that shone like diamonds,

"Who are you, Madame?" I asked her, stammering.

"My name is Madame Lambert," she said. "I'm the mother of the child who is dying."

Strangely enough, that reply did not astonish me. It was as if I were expecting it.

A word before continuing: it might be, my old friend, that in spite of your confidence in me, you are inclined to doubt, not the sincerity of the story that follows, but the sang-froid of the person who is writing it. A long time after this happened, I have re-read and transcribed these pages, and I have not found a single word therein to change. I am sixty-eight years old. A month ago, I addressed a *mémoire* to the Académie on a technical question that had the honor of a public reading, which attracted the felicitations of my colleagues—which tells you that I am in full possession of all my faculties. What follows is true.

Madame Lambert sat down facing me; I had removed the lampshade in order to examine her more closely. She was a woman scarcely forty years old, whose beauty was exceptional, not merely because of the impeccable regularity of the features, but perhaps most of all because of the intelligence that brightened her physiognomy. And yet, once the first moment of surprise had passed, I recalled that the woman had abandoned her child and I wanted to constrain myself not to admire her. I could not do it, but at first I exaggerated the dryness of my welcome to the point of impoliteness.

"What do you want, Madame," I said, "and why have you come here?"

"My daughter is dying . . ."

"That's true, Madame. What does it matter to you?"

She had a strange smile, almost proud; then, without responding directly to my question, she said: "I've come to save her."

"You?"

"Me."

As she pronounced that word, she had raised her head, staring straight into my eyes, as if challenging me.

I stiffened myself against all pity.

"I hate grandiose statements," I replied, harshly. "You cannot save your daughter, who is doomed, any more than I can. I have done my duty. Why have you come to me? Do you think that you have some reproach to address to me? Even if I had merited it, it is not from you that I could accept it . . ."

She interrupted me. "You do not merit any reproach, since you do not know of what she is dying."

"Perhaps you do know?"

"Yes. She is dying of not having had a mother."

I burst into angry laughter. "You can say that! But in that case, it's you who is guilty of that murder, you who abandoned her . . . odiously, inhumanly . . ."

She had risen to her feet, but without anger, slowly, extending her hand toward me.

"I did not abandon my daughter. I was expelled, thrown out like a servant, like the worst of enemies. I fled a torture more horrible than death."

"It was necessary to take your child!"

"I could not."

"It was necessary to demand her, to take her, to steal her."

She put a piece of paper before my eyes, and with amazement, I read: *Death certificate of Marie, daughter of Jacques Lambert and . . . died at the age of two years on the . . .*

"This document is fake!" I cried.

"This is the letter by which her father addressed it to me."

It was a note of a few brutal lines announcing the death of the child, forbidding the mother the threshold of the house. They did not contain a single positive fact. They were hateful and furious, nothing more. According to the postage stamps, the forgery had been made abroad. What means had Lambert employed to deceive the authorities? I never found out. As for the past, the woman revealed it to me, very simply, without anger, with a striking breadth of comprehension:

A marriage imposed by an infamous intrigue; her father was a seeker, a sort of Balthazar Claes,[1] in quest of alchemical secrets. He had devoured his entire fortune; a dishonest steward had engaged him unwittingly in orations of dubious honesty and he had found himself delivered to Monsieur Lambert's father, a small town usurer, an ambitious rogue who had given him the choice of marrying her to his son or seeing his father dishonored.

"Above all," she said to me, "don't blame my father, who was honest among the honest, good among the good. If he was searching for the most hidden secrets of nature, it was certainly not with an egotistical objective, but on the contrary, because he hoped to realize by means of science the wellbeing of humanity entire. He knew nothing of practical life, and I, habituated to losing myself with him in the regions of pure justice, divined nothing of the odious web that was being woven around us.

"I ought not even to have hesitated, and yet, when the horrible truth was revealed to me I was terrified at first by those abjections of the soul. I knew that it was that Lambert, the executioner's aide, the factotum of the torturer, whose every gold coin sweated a tear . . . Before the threats shown to me by my father, suddenly snatched from his generous dreams and plunged into the inferno of criminal prosecutions, I resigned myself . . .

"The strangest thing is that the Lambert son, the man whose name I can still bear, was said to have artistic tastes, proclaiming himself a poet, musician, painter . . . what do

1 Balthazar Claes is the protagonist of *La Recherche de l'absolu* (1834; tr. as *The Quest for the Absolute*) by Honoré de Balzac, who is ruined, along with his family, by pouring his resources into an obsessive alchemical quest; the novel is the archetype of the literary subgenre to which several of Lermina's novellas belong.

I know? No mind as false was ever encountered with such a stupid pretention. I had consented. I was doomed. Fatality pursued me doggedly. I had scarcely accomplished the horrible sacrifice than my father died, leaving his work unfinished.

"Then a life commenced for me so terrible that I would seek in vain to enable you to fathom all its horror. I have told you that, raised by my father, I had received an education superior not only to that normally given to girls but even to that of many reputedly knowledgeable men. With his narrow ideas, his nullity of conscience and moral sense, with his arrogant pretentions to talent, to genius, not the least seed of which existed in him, Monsieur Lambert, jealous of me, came to hate me. In vain, knowing that I was about to become a mother, I strove, even at the price of lying, to soothe and flatter that envious and hypocritical man. He suspected my most intimate thoughts, spied on me all the way to my soul, analyzing my gaze, the sound of my voice—what can I tell you? Sensing himself to be despicable, he accused me of being scornful of him; and when our child . . . my child . . . came, the perpetual persecution became crueler, more torturing. I swear to you that I resigned myself to it with an absolute passivity; I never contradicted him.

"Without the slightest irony I admired his paintings and his musical compositions. He shouted at me that I was lying, that I was deceiving him, that I denigrated him behind his back. What can one do against a malevolent madman? I protested in vain, I curbed myself to all baseness; he hated me all the more the more harm he did me. I had wanted to nurse my child myself; he had opposed it, and when I insisted he accused me of wanting to poison her because, he said, she resembled him. I had the pain of seeing a stranger give her breast to the poor child while mine was swollen with milk. And without reason, without the slightest pretext, that man, that lunatic, made me lead the existence of a torture victim for two years. I supported everything, for the sake of my child. Then he separated her from me and sent her away, with the nurse. I wept, I begged . . . Why so many words? One day, he tried to kill me, and so terrifyingly. He attacked me, and for the first time in my life I was frightened. I fled.

"The next day, I came back. The house was empty. I ran to the village where my daughter should have been. He had abducted her, taken her away. For a year, a frightful martyrdom for a mother, I searched everywhere—everywhere! No trace . . . until the day when I received that document, with that infamous lying note . . .

"And for sixteen years I have been lamenting that lie!"

"But how did you finally discover that your daughter was alive?" I exclaimed.

She looked at me for a moment without saying anything, as if she were trying to read in the depths of my mind.

"Do you know John Harvey Schmidt?" she said.

"Certainly," I said. "The great American chemist is not unknown to anyone, myself least of all. Look," I added, turning toward my bookshelves, "all his books are there and I've often leafed through those pages, imprinted with a veritable genius. I only regretted that he allowed himself to be drawn . . ."

She interrupted me. "Here," she said, presenting me with another sheet of paper, "is a letter that accredits me to you."

"To me? But he doesn't know me . . ."

"Read it anyway."

The note really was addressed to me. Harvey Schmidt appealed to my benevolence, to my conscience; he begged me to lend my cooperation to Madame Lambert, his pupil and collaborator.

"You're Harvey Schmidt's pupil?" I asked, with a sincere surprise—for everyone knows the heights to which the vision of that man has been raised, of whom it is said that he has forced the door of the unknown.

"My father knew him when he was young," she replied. "Hazard put us in communication. In my solitude, without a child and without a future, I was seized by the desire to devote my existence to the research that had cost my poor father his life and of which I had understood, if not the developments, at least the first principles. I spoke about it to Harvey Schmidt, who took an interest in me and in my studies. You know the result of his experiments, contained in the book *Studies in Superhumanity*, so widely attacked and misunderstood. It will soon be sixteen years that I have not quit him."

"He calls you his collaborator . . . are you, then, the woman of whom he speaks in his book with whose aid he has seen amazing phenomena produced? In a word, meaning no insult by the term, are you the woman called mockingly in France the *Magicienne*?"

"That's me," she said, simply.

Thus, I had before me the strange creature who had accomplished veritable miracles, inexplicable by all known laws, in Harvey Schimdt's laboratory, in the presence of witnesses and, it is affirmed, under the rigorous control of absolutely precise instruments of verification.

The great majority of French scientists had greeted with burst of laughter those astonishing manifestations of an unknown force: apports of flowers or material objects in a locked room; the apparition of fantastic lights; arms and hands, contact with which frightened the spectators; and above all, which surpassed the most audacious hypotheses, the evocation of a being simultaneously spectral and alive, who spoke, walked, allowed herself to be touched, and who gave herself the name of Laurie Queen.[1]

---

1 The "spirit" reportedly evoked during investigations conducted by the English physicist William Crookes in collaboration with the teenage spiritualist medium Florence Cook between 1871 and 1874 was reportedly named Katie King.

I had been one of those who, without opposing to his extraordinary revelations an anger, unjustified in my opinion, had nevertheless formulated the most express reservations. But my politeness was due, above all, to the competence and the superior value of Harvey Schmidt, who, at the same time as he proceeded with his extrascientific experiments, continued to astonish the world with practical discoveries of an incontestable utility.

All those thoughts and memories had traversed my brain with lightning rapidity. At the same time, a brutal, unpardonable suspicion imposed itself upon me. The emotion that had overwhelmed me during Madame Lambert's story had disappeared completely before the perfectly natural dread of being nothing but a vulgar dupe.

With an undissimulated bitterness, this time, I said: "It's very late, Madame, and I confess that I feel very tired. Will you please reply in a few words, without elaboration, to two or three questions. You have come from America?"

"Indeed."

"When did you depart?"

"I can't reply."

"Why not?"

"Because I wouldn't have the right to prove to you that I'm telling the truth."

I made an angry gesture. "Isn't it rather because I could convict you of deceit?"

She extended her hand toward me. "Today, at seven o'clock, my daughter said to you: "I know, I know . . . it's life that I lack."

I uttered a cry; those words had been pronounced, and yet I was perfectly sure that we had been alone.

Was I so certain, though? The woman might have been hiding in an adjacent room.

Decidedly, I was playing a ridiculous role. I avenged my-self with an almost insulting insinuation: "In truth, Madame, if you want to prove to me that you are a magicienne, I am at your disposal. We're alone. Accomplish here, in my study, some miracle . . . the simplest possible. Here—displace this pen-holder by mean of the sole energy of your gaze . . .

In a voice that was still even, she replied: "No, Monsieur, I shall do nothing of what it pleases you to call a miracle."

"It's always thus when you and your kind find yourselves confronted by a skeptic with sang-froid, ready to unmask you."

"I shall neither do nor attempt to do anything, because I don't have the right to expend even the thousandth part of the force that is in me, and which is necessary for me to save my child."

"Again! Enough, Madame. You can't suppose that I will lend myself to a sacrilegious comedy. I know nothing, and don't want to know anything, about the differences that have arisen between you and your husband. I only see a father who has protected and raised his child, and is dying of her death . . . I only know him. If you want to see your daughter before she dies, go and knock on his door . . ."

Her face contracted dolorously. However, she appeared to make a great effort to retain her self-control.

"I cannot," she said, "precisely because I want my daughter to be saved. You distrust me, you're prepared to insult me, to throw me out. I can't hold that against you; you don't know. I'm only asking you for a few minutes of attention. After that, if you reject me, I shall attempt to accomplish alone the ma-ternal task for which I have come."

She took her head in her hands.

"But no, but no! I'd kill her . . . I know that full well! Listen," she continued. "I only ask this of you. Tomorrow, at the earliest hour, go to Monsieur Lambert's house. Tell him about me, tell him that I've returned, that I affirm—do you hear?—that I swear to save his daughter. I only ask to remain with her for an hour, with you, the physician; that I will not do anything that you have not approved personally, and that, once my work is accomplished, I shall disappear forever. Tell him that, beg him, use all your influence as an old man, an honest man . . . But you don't know him. You'll see! You'll see . . . ! And if he refuses, what shall we do then? Oh, unfortunate that I am . . . !"

She was not weeping. Around her there was a kind of atmosphere of despair, which penetrated me poignantly. I repented of my harshness. Even culpable, was she not a mother? Was she not imploring me in the name of her child?

"I'll go," I told her.

She stood up. "At what time shall I return?"

"Be here at ten o'clock . . . but the darkness is profound; I'll accompany you."

She made an indefinable gesture. "Oh, I have nothing to fear. Until tomorrow . . . I have your word."

She left, without my making the slightest effort to retain her, I was so troubled.

In reality, there was a chaos of contradictory thoughts in my mind: scorn, sympathy, hatred, admiration; I did not know what that woman inspired in me.

When she had disappeared, having dismissed my maidservant in spite of her objurgations—she divined that I was not going to bed—I took Harvey Schmidt's book and meditated all night.

At nine o'clock in the morning I presented myself at Monsieur Lambert's house.

The invalid was still in the same state; as soon as I approached her, however, she shuddered in a manner that was not habitual to her. When I took her hand she drew me toward her—oh, so gently; the poor thing was devoid of strength—and with a singular curiosity she palpated my garments, passed her fingers over mine, gazing at me with her eyes devoid of any gleams, in which I read I know not what surprise. She breathed out deeply, smiled and rested her head on her pillow. She was so pale that I feared a supreme crisis; I was mistaken. The lamp was not extinct. I even thought that I distinguished a minute acceleration in the movement of the almost-insensible pulse—doubtless an illusion.

As usual, the father was waiting for me on the threshold. I drew him into the garden.

"You know," I said, "that in spite of our efforts, the danger is increasing every day . . ."

"Alas!"

"I have given you enough proofs of my sincere interest for you to permit me to speak to you . . . as a friend."

As, at that word, he made a gesture difficult to explain, I believed that he was protesting, and I went on: "Far be it from me to emerge from my role to mingle in your private affairs; however, my age entitles me and imposes a duty on me to communicate an idea that is haunting me . . ."

This time he raised his eyes upon me, abruptly, which resembled those of a cat and lit up with a malevolent gleam.

"What idea?" he demanded, in a tone that was less than courteous.

But my theme was already prepared and I had no intention of departing from it.

"It is from your own mouth," I said, "that I learned of the sad events that followed the birth of your daughter. Her mother . . ."

He started, as if bounding on both feet. "Her mother! That woman! It's about her that you want to speak . . ."

"Perhaps she is still alive."

"Well, what is that to me? What can that matter to me?"

"I beg your pardon for insisting . . . but no matter how culpable she has been, it appears excessive to me to refuse to let her see and embrace her daughter and, at the supreme hour . . ."

I could not finish. Seized by a fit of fury, which rendered him hideous, the man cried: "I'll kill her! I'll kill her . . . Oh, she scorned me! Oh, in her eyes I had neither intelligence nor talent! Oh, that scholar resigned herself to her fate, as if I were not worth a hundred times more than her . . . a thousand times! You know where she is . . . tell me! I demand that you tell me . . . I'll cry to her that her daughter isn't dead, but that she really is dying this time . . . reawakening her dolor in order to render it more irreparable! I'll see her weep, sob . . . ah, that will amuse me . . . and then she'll see that I wasn't the imbecile she thought . . ."

Was the man mad? In that furious incoherence there was the rage of a brute . . . and he went on without interrupting himself, evoking no other grievance against the absent woman except for her supposed scorn for his genius. Oh, she had not dared to show it, but he divined it . . . and he had thrown her out . . . yes, thrown her out like a servant . . .

It was an incredible and stupid hatred, made of wounded vanity, base jealousy. He execrated her beauty, he admitted, because he was ugly, her intelligence because he felt stupid, and the grandeur of her conscience because he knew himself to be abject. And he spat out all of that in a vomit of cynicism. His hypocrisy, suddenly bursting forth, was displayed in a repulsive wound.

That man was a monster.

But at least, did the monster not adore his daughter?

"Listen," I said to him, seizing his shoulders and approaching my face close enough to his to touch it. "What if I told you that your daughter might be saved by her mother?"

"But if I want her to live," he cried, "it's because I enjoy knowing that her mother believes her to be dead!"

How I didn't slap him, how I didn't spit in his face, I don't know. A revolution took place within me. I understood that honesty, right and truth were on the side of the woman that that man hated bestially. And, obedient to a will as-yet-obscure, I had the courage to lie brazenly.

"There, there," I said to him. "What's the point of getting carried away? I beg your pardon. In making a supposition that nothing justifies, I didn't believe that I would irritate you so much. I have no idea whether that woman is alive or dead . . . and I scarcely care. Let's talk about your daughter. She appears to me to be a little better this morning. I'll come back this afternoon, Adieu."

I shall pass over my impressions; they can be divined.

When I arrived home I found Madame Lambert, who was waiting for me. She came straight to me and said: "Now will you help me to save my daughter?"

One might have thought that she had witnessed our conversation, but I did not have time at that moment to debate any particular circumstance. Her question saw the situation clearly. I responded to it with a nod of the head.

When Madame Lambert told me what she wanted me to do, however, I jibbed. She wanted to get into her daughter's room that very night. How could I introduce her? She claimed to have no need of my assistance, but it was necessary that I be there, by her daughter's bedside, to witness the scene that would be produced and to intervene in certain conditions that she would indicate to me in due time.

All that was very confused, quite inexplicable, but I experienced such an anger against the wretch; I had understood so clearly that what I had called paternal love was only a perverse egotism; his exasperations had been so clearly confirmed; his wife's story had inspired such a compassion in me for her and her daughter, that I made no further resistance by virtue of the obstacles that opposed the realization of her desire.

And then, I wanted to know.

I did not forget that, as a physician, I had a considerable responsibility. We admit neither mysterious remedies nor the methods of bone-setters. It is necessary that everything be explained within the limits of acquired knowledge. I summoned Madame Lambert to explain her plan to me. I admitted her good faith, her real maternal love, but what guarantee did I have of her competence, of the utility of her intervention? On the contrary, might it not provoke a crisis that would accelerate her daughter's death?

This is what she said to me then; I have transcribed her words as exactly as possible, and I am certain, not only of not having omitted anything of importance, but of not having added a single idea of my own. Unfortunately, what I cannot render is the tone of ardent conviction and the simplicity of the language, the logic of which gripped me and triumphed over me in spite of all my resistance.

"My daughter," she said to me, "is dying of not having had a mother. It isn't only the initial life that a child receives and ought to receive from her; at the maternal bosom she acquires a quantity of force that gives her the vital energy necessary for a relatively short period, but that force needs to be renewed incessantly—which means that to the initial effort in which the mother detaches, in a sense, a part of herself, and animates her child with her own existence, it is necessary that further efforts be added continually, which maintain and augment the power of that organism, incapable of self-sufficiency. It is only later, much later, that the definitive separation of the mother and the child occurs. The bond that you physicians believe to be severed at the moment of birth subsists and forms a sort of channel by means of which the substance of the mother comes incessantly to aliment that of the child.

"You talk about magic; substitute for that word "unknown force" and you will understand that there is no magic more powerful than maternal magic. If a child is suffering, the mother places a hand on the head, on the heart, on the limbs and the pain is eased—but impatience and ignorance compromise many cures. The mother who wants, with all the force of her will, to expend herself to the profit of her child can double the child's vital resistance. Don't you know the story of the Princesse de Ligne saving her dying child by lying over her, body to body, and infusing her with the strength to live?

"Even in normal circumstances, a child is nourished by absorption of the maternal atmosphere as a plant is by the solar atmosphere. My daughter said to you: 'It's life that I lack!' That life can only be given to her by her mother. The father might have been able to substitute for her, although in an inferior condition. That the latter has not fulfilled that duty, but has, on the contrary, almost killed his daughter, is what I shall explain to you shortly; but my dear child, I know, had the effect on you of an empty shell . . ."

I was amazed to hear my observations enunciated in the same form that they had taken in my mind. She went on:

"That is really the case; she is only an envelope, fashioned by nature at birth, which only her mother can fill with its interior aliment. Those effluvia are familiar to the child who asks a mother to pass her finger over gums that ache, to kiss a spot that has been bruised, and say that it no longer hurts. For sixteen years my daughter has only lived in the initial impulsion that my maternity gave her, with the augmentation of a little vitality that she received from a stranger, a careless nurse without any desire to abandon anything of herself except for a few drops of milk. The mother that nurses does not only nourish by way of the breast but with her entire being. That is why so many children separated from their natural nurse die. Well, the vitality that the man whose name I bear stole from my daughter by chasing me away from her, I can restore in its entirety with, so to speak, the interest of the capital of vital force of which I am the debtor. What will become of me you will find out when we are near her—for I do not want to deceive you.

"A word about her father: he is wicked. No other word can qualify him. Within every man there is a source, without every man there is a radiation, of good or evil. Each one has around him an atmosphere made of his virtues or his vices. Evil poisons at a distance. Where there is a wicked man, even though he does not commit crimes in the family environment, that environment is saturated by venomous effluvia. Whoever lives with a wretch is corrupted and dies. The poison that is killing my daughter is the evil atmosphere emanated by her father, a latent criminal and all the more dangerous for it. If I had always surrounded her with my healthy atmosphere, like a suit of armor, she would have resisted and we could have vanquished the aggression of evil, or at least neutralized it. Her personal reaction has been insufficient; she has asphyxiated, like a bird under a bell-jar of carbon dioxide.

"You don't understand yet what I can do—or, rather, you divine it without being able to explain it. You shall see. I swear to you that I can save her. What will become of me? What will become of her father? You shall see. For myself, I am not preoccupied with him. Between that man and me it is war, the fight for the life of my child . . ."

I do not know whether those theories will appear to you, as to me, to have a simplicity that is logical and sublime. I had no thought of trying to refute them. I confess without shame that the woman had conquered me, and I obeyed her.

Following her instructions I returned to Monsieur Lambert's house and, without making the slightest allusion to our strange conversation, of which he did not remind me, contenting himself with launching sly gazes at me, which I sustained boldly, I declared to him that after mature meditation I believed that I had found a means of opposing the malady of which his daughter was dying. A potion that I showed him might work marvels, but it had to be administered in doses so scrupulously measured that I could not leave responsibility for the treatment to anyone else. As time was pressing and it was necessary to act without delay, that very night, I desired, if he would consent—and that was his duty—to spend the night with the young woman, serving as her nurse.

He did not resist for long, having no suspicion and supposing that the suggestion I had made that morning had no precise cause. It was therefore agreed that I would come in the evening to install myself beside Marie's bed. I demanded that I not be disturbed under any pretext, alleging that the slightest disturbance, even the sound of a door opening, might compromise the success of that supreme attempt. I no longer know what other arguments I employed, but I succeeded fully.

Marie was neither astonished nor alarmed by that solicitude. On the contrary, it seemed that since the morning, my presence brought her a kind of comfort, almost of joy. Was that because I approached her impregnated with a parcel of the maternal atmosphere about which the magicienne had spoken to me?

At nine o'clock I was at my post. Everything around me was still and silent. Marie, lying in her white bed, had her eyes closed . . . was she asleep?

Madame Lambert had told me that she would be in the room at ten o'clock. How she would get in I did not know, but I did not doubt that she would keep her word. She had recommended insistently that I keep the lamp turned down, to the extent that I could only distinguish the silhouette of the lines of a book, not the form of the letters. She would give me the final instructions.

Certainly, it seemed very strange that I, an official scientist imbued with the obligatory skepticism that our intolerant entourage imposes on us, was lending myself to practices that would previously have smacked of heresy. That was because a host of details in my conversation with Madame Lambert had awakened in me the passion for research that had possessed me in my youth, when I had had a holy confidence in the triumph of verities, whatever they might be. Since then, like so many others, I had curbed my shoulders under the Caudine Forks of prejudice. I straightened up again—but too late, alas, and I would not have wanted anyone to see me. Such is our petty human cowardice.

At ten o'clock precisely, the lamp no longer giving anything but the glow of a hooded lantern, I was waiting impatiently.

Suddenly, a cold breath passed over me, as if a window had been suddenly opened, and I saw a form a short distance away, confused with the curtains of the bed, indistinct at first, which then became clearer, more vivid . . . Madame Lambert was before me. She beckoned to me.

I drew nearer; it was not a matter of a spectral apparition; she was quite real.

She spoke to me in a low voice, but I heard it quite distinctly, not with my ears, but throughout my being.

"Take my pulse," she said to me. "Listen to my heart. Assure yourself that I am in an entirely normal state. I need to know that in the most positive fashion."

I obeyed. No nature was ever healthier or better equilibrated. I told her that. At that moment we heard the young woman agitating, with slight moans.

"It's necessary that she is asleep," said Madame Lambert. "I don't want her to see me. Who can tell whether she might divine me? She might kiss me, and in a kiss I would expend too much force."

She had extended her hands in the direction of the child, whose voice died away.

Then, at length, in a contained voice, Madame Lambert spoke to me, revealing to me in all its sublime strangeness the sacrifice that she was about to accomplish. She handed me a flask of ether, of which I was to make use in conditions indicated, as well as a little steel blade with a sharp point.

Then, having explained the precise moment at which my intervention would be necessary, she said: "Let's go. I'm counting on you, and I only ask that later, you will not speak too ill of magiciennes."

I inclined over her hand and kissed it. She withdrew it, inviting me with a gesture to place myself beside her daughter—which I did, no longer curious or anxious, but penetrated by a respect against which I could no longer defend myself.

I saw Madame Lambert lie down on the chaise longue where I had seen her daughter for the first time. It was about two meters from the bed. The lamp was only projecting a bluish light, which scarcely allowed objects to be distinguished; however, I could see the black form of the mother distinctly, now motionless, the head tilted backwards. The stillness and the silence were absolute. As for possible phenomena, I neither believed nor doubted; I waited.

During the night I did not measure the time, so I do not know how many minutes had gone by when I heard Madame Lambert's voice, very faint at first, intoning a halting, trailing plaint, and then rising, as if with a painful effort; the clamor that precedes deliverance, on a small scale. It was suddenly extinguished; then, after a silence, it resumed. More emphatic and more poignant, and yet so low that perhaps no one except me, whose senses were excited to an unaccustomed acuity, could have perceived it. The moans became more rapid, condensing into a long sigh, as if in a time of repose, soon to recommence.

At the same time, around Madame Lambert's body, still motionless, I saw something like a fine mist, which I could only compare to the dilute fog surrounding a jet of water. It was something other than a smoke, a juxtaposition of infinitesimal dots, innumerable in quantity, incessantly in motion. That mist became a vapor. At the same time, little sparks sprang forth in the air one by one, like fireflies, reddish in color, the nuclei of microscopic comets with trails of violet smoke.

I am so made that nothing astonishes me, and I observed those phenomena with a mind as free as if I were in my chemistry laboratory. The productive apparatus was a human being; there was no other difference. I did not forget Madame Lambert's prescriptions, therefore I took the flask of ether, opened it, and, as one does with a vaporizer, I projected the liquid in droplets from the place where the mother was to the daughter's bed. Again in accordance with the order received. I dipped my finger in the ether and touched the sheet at the level of the invalid's heart.

The cloud that surrounded Madame Lambert had thickened, now resembling a breath in cold weather, enveloping her and hiding her from me completely—except that, at a point that also seemed to me to be at the level of her heart, a thread of vapor sprang forth, advanced through the air, undulating, as thin as a little finger, stretching more and more, following the line I had traced with the ether. The dilution was augmented to the point of only leaving a ray of light, which slid over the bed and came to pose at the exact place where I had put the drop of ether over the young woman's heart.

At that moment Marie uttered a faint, abrupt cry, as if she had been stung. I saw her body rise up in the form of a bow, presenting—offering, so to speak—its breast to that light. In the cloud that surrounded Madame Lambert, luminous dots were rising and falling. Suddenly, all that agitation calmed down. The luminous line that linked the two beings at that moment resembled a sunbeam in which mobile corpuscles were frolicking, and in which there was something like a flow of atoms of an inconceivable tenuity, going in a vertiginous current from the mother to the child, as in an operation of transfusion.

I stood up and I took Marie's pulse, counting attentively, as I had been told to do. That pulse, the beats of which had been scarcely perceptible in the morning, awakened under my fingers, was vivified, the intervals recovering their normality; I heard the lungs expand, and the invalid, who could not even raise her head, slowly stood up, without aiding herself with her hands.

Then I took the pointed blade that had been given to me, and at the moment when I judged—how did I judge it?—that the transfusion of the mother's vital fluid into her daughter was sufficient, I interposed the metallic tip in the luminous line. The line suddenly broke; I felt my hand enveloped by a warm vapor . . .

I dropped the knife; that was the instruction. And, running to Madame Lambert, I bent over her. She was inert, as pale as a corpse; I blew violently on her eyelids, which opened abruptly.

"The lamp!" she said. "The lamp!"

I revived the wick swiftly. Madame Lambert was standing behind me, looking over my shoulder at her daughter, who was sleeping profoundly. She said: "She'll sleep like that until tomorrow; she's drunk on my life . . ."

In truth, I no longer recognized Marie; blood had flowed into her cheeks; a flame was circulating in her waxen face, the lips were red, the hand that had previously seemed to be melting in mine had recovered the consistency of life . . .

I felt Madame Lambert leaning on me. I turned round. She was now the pale one, the condemned, the dead woman—but so smiling, her eyes illuminated by a joy so profound and so adorably maternal!

"The magicienne has accomplished her miracle," she murmured. "I owed it to her for such a long time . . . I've paid the debt . . . I've given myself to her entirely, once and for all. I entrust her to you. Love her . . . that she might be glad to be alive!"

"Kiss her!"

"No, no . . . that would be egotism. I don't want to take anything from her."

"But you're suffering yourself . . . it's necessary to react, to live . . ."

"Me, me . . . you haven't understood then . . . it's me, now, who lacks life . . ."

Then she gave me a few recommendations; she had no fear of the father, without giving any further explanation . . .

Then she asked me not to look in her direction for a few minutes. She headed toward the curtains, in which she seemed to me to wrap herself. I turned away.

When I looked again, she was no longer there.

✳

What more can I tell you? After that story, that witness statement, nothing can astonish you any longer. Marie Lambert lived, in that inexplicable resurrection.

Singularly, as soon as he saw her strong and full of health, her father experienced an evident repulsion in her regard. The healthy and honest atmosphere that enveloped his daughter was antagonistic to his life. If he approached her, he suffered, like the damned in the *Divine Comedy* who approach the Elect. He hated her, and now wanted to avenge himself on that living purity, which irritated him. I understood then the profound philosophy of Nathaniel Hawthorne's story of Rappaccini's daughter, born in a milieu of poisons, saturated with their venoms, and dying on the day when she was enabled to breathe broad and healthy air.

Under the pretext of completing the cure of my protégée— who had almost become my daughter—by means of a sojourn in the Midi, I obtained permission from her father to confide her to one of my old friends. He consented, even with a kind of urgency. That departure was a relief for him, but what he did not understand was that when the healthy influence of his daughter ceased to combat the evil effluvia that enveloped him, he would be poisoned by his moral pestilence, rebounding on him.

Marie departed for Nice, Six months later she was an orphan—an orphan because, the day after that admirable night I had found on my desk a note signed by the failing hand of Madame Lambert, which said:

The maternal magic has accomplished its work; the magicienne is dying . . .

I have spent the final years of my life playing grandfather . . . and of the Magicienne's daughter I have made a happy wife and a devoted mother.

THE SPELL-CASTER

ALTHOUGH curious about the occult sciences, I am not naïve, and if my imagination sometimes carries me away, I am able to resist its traction by hanging on with all my strength to the sane affirmations—retrograde, if you wish—of cold reason.

Today, not daring to formulate a conclusion myself, I want in what follows to take the reader for a judge. I will not hide anything nor add anything to the strict truth, without omitting any detail; then I shall leave to others the care of conclusion—which is to say, of responding to the question: was the man of whom I am going to speak a madman or a criminal? Not only a criminal by intention—that would be a subtlety—but a criminal in fact; or to put it another way, although it is certain that he thought of a crime, did he actually commit it, and was he able to commit it?

First of all, who was the man?

I did not know him well, not having had with him any other relations than those sketched between young men who encounter one another in society. However, I cannot say that I had not noticed him; he was one of those who, for anyone slightly endowed with a spirit of observation, would have had difficulty passing unperceived.

His name is unimportant; I shall call him Gérald. He was very assiduous in the home of an important and very rich businessman, Monsieur Solmes, whose greatest pleasure was hosting quasi-princely receptions.

That millionaire was very affable, although I did not request any service from him; he testified a real amity to me, and a certain confidence, perhaps for the very reason of my independence.

One evening, after a concert that was prolonged rather late, he retained me, and after asking me to follow him into his study he said: "I'd like to ask a favor of you; I deem you to be a man of honest conscience and good advice, and I beg you to respond to me in all sincerity. What do you think of Gérald?"

Rather surprised by that interrogation and hesitant to assume a responsibility still ill-defined, I took refuge behind banalities. Gérald was a man of exquisite distinction and eccentric physiognomy, perhaps trying a little too hard to compose a physiognomy that the old romantics would have qualified as "fatal," but, in sum, intelligent and good company. The few words that I had exchanged with him had revealed to me an inquisitive mind, passionate for labor. Finally, without knowing anything positive about the matter of his pecuniary situation, his entire lifestyle indicated an ease almost amounting to fortune. Of his occupations I knew nothing; he seemed to me to be undertaking experiments in chemistry, or at least high mathematics. I had come across him several times in the street carrying books with old-fashioned bindings under his arm, dating from a previous century.

The millionaire interrupted me.

"Regarding those details," he said, "I'm almost certain. Gérald is rich—a consideration of only mediocre interest to me, my own fortune leaving me complete freedom of action in the present matter. I know that he leads a very regular existence, that he has installed a laboratory in his house in which he devotes himself to research in the natural sciences—or supernatural sciences," he added, with a half-smile. "Who knows whether he might not find the philosopher's stone? Much good may it do him . . . In truth, that ardor for the crucible will pass, and he might make a fine figure in the scientific world. All that, I repeat, is secondary . . . but . . . have you looked at his eyes?"

"His eyes?"

"Yes, his eyes, and to speak frankly, it's on that very particular point that I wanted to consult you. I deem you to be a good physiognomist, having sometimes collected observations from you of great accuracy. So what do you think of Gérald's eyes?"

I had difficulty in remaining serious. Do you see me called to make a profession of checking passports? His eyes . . . ? Evidently, they were . . . singular, which is to say, not exactly like commonplace eyes . . . let's see . . . wide open, with slightly raised lids, allowing the sight of a golden pupil—spangled, even—and a white circle . . . sometimes tarnished like a metallic oxide, sometimes, on the contrary, bright, as if a light were shining behind. Also, those eyes were not absolutely rectilinear; under the empire of an emotion they lost their normal axis instantaneously, as if afflicted by an intermittent squint. At those moments a kind of flash escaped from them, like—I'm explaining myself as best I can—the impact of two rays whose interference would have constituted an incandescent source.

As I was speaking, I realized that I had attached to those eyes much more importance than I had thought at first . . . and that I thought even more than I was saying, for, I don't know by virtue of what association of ideas, the words of the second Faust were resonating in my ear with a hoarse monotony: "The vision looms up, hollow-eyed, like a bizarre specter that troubles life and the mind."

All Monsieur Solmes said was: "Those eyes frighten me."

That radical formula did not astonish me unduly, but I attempted to protest . . . the eyes were neither crossed nor squinting; there was an unimportant singularity about them. "In any case," I said, not without a certain impatience, "what is the point of these questions?"

"Gérald has asked me for my daughter's hand."

I could not suppress a shudder; for at that moment, it seemed to me that everything in me was proceeding by revelations. I loved Camille—yes, I loved her, without ever having admitted it to myself. How could that be? Not that I was surprised by loving her, for she was certainly the sweetest and most interesting creature that I had ever encountered: as delicate as a winter flower, but not frail—robust, on the contrary, and almost indefatigable, as I had seen her in the interminable games of lawn tennis that we had played in summer at her father's provincial château.

Why had I not declared myself yet? Because I had not known that I loved her amorously and it had been necessary for me, in order to read my own heart, to learn that someone else . . . !

"And what have you replied?" I asked, in an almost imperious tone.

"I don't recognize the right to exert the slightest constraint over my daughter . . . however, I have, you understand, some influence over her, and I reserve that of directing her choice. I would, I admit, immediately have given some hope to Gérald . . . if it were not for his eyes . . ."

"Demonic eyes!" I exclaimed, involuntarily.

Monsieur Solmes looked at me, doubtless astonished by the facility with which I now found the characteristic epithet.

"Demonic," he said, shaking his head. "Certainly, for us, as skeptics, the expression is hazarded—and yet, it springs to my mind, as to yours."

"You've rejected him . . ."

"Between men of the world, one doesn't proceed expeditiously . . . I want to consult Camille. Women have ways of seeing different from ours. I've put off any response; that seems wisest . . ."

I breathed out, like a man who has just escaped a grave peril. Monsieur Solmes smiled, without my seeking to understand why. I have found out since. He let me go, thanking me, and announcing that he would take some time before coming to a decision.

I left his house absolutely metamorphosed; I was prey to a complicated sentiment, compounded of anger, joy and I know not what vague hope that I had never conceived before. At the same time, however, a hatred rose into my brain against that man, that Gérald, whose audacity had almost compromised the happiness of my entire life—as if my timidity and my insouciance were not the only culprits.

Oh, he permitted himself to love Camille! Who was he, anyway? What was he hiding behind his strange eyes, which now caused me both horror and terror?

I started to spy on him, with a tenacity that nothing deterred; I spied on his life. He almost never left his house, but I bribed one of his domestics and I soon knew that the studies to which he devoted himself were confined to those mysterious sciences whose secret seems lost, but which are today reinscribed in the register of human curiosity. I obtained from the valet that he would copy the titles of the works that Gérald consulted most frequently, and I was not astonished when, through the orthographic fantasies under which Latin words hid, I recognized the most evil works of the necromancers of old from the *Minerva Mundi* to the *Enchiridion*, and from the *Pimander* to the worst works of Paracelsus . . .[1]

---

1 *Minerva Mundi* is one of several titles attached to an apocryphal work attributed to "Hermes Trismegistus" and thus belonging to the *Corpus Hermeticum*, whose first item is *Poimandres*, or *Pimander*. An Enchiridion is a brief treatise or handbook; with a definite article the title usually refers

He was a madman, and his eyes were those of a madman!

Monsieur de Solmes was absent; I was not belated in revealing those facts to him, before which a father had to hesitate. One does not give one's daughter to an insane man! And I still want to believe, in spite of the horrible misfortune that has struck me since then, that that appreciation of my reason was accurate. I want to believe that Gérald was a madman, and an impostor, above all . . . oh, yes, an infamous liar!

A few days later, I received an invitation from Monsieur de Solmes; I was careful not to be late, and I was one of the first to arrive.

"My friend," he said to me, "I've reflected at length, and I've also interrogated Camille . . ."

"And . . . ?"

He had the smile again that I had remarked before.

"That husband," he told me, "cannot suit my daughter in any fashion. Like me, Gérald's eyes frighten her, and your expression *demonic* appears to her to be absolutely accurate . . ."

"So that . . ."

"So that I shall signify to Monsieur Gérald today, with all the customary regrets, that he will have to address himself to another house . . ."

In an irrational impulse, I seized Monsieur de Solmes' hands and shook them forcefully.

"Good, good," he said, still smiling, "we'll talk about all that later. For the moment," he went on, more seriously, "I confess to you that the necessity I am in of confronting that evil gaze troubles me slightly. I'm not a nervous girl, but I'm in haste to be finished with that individual . . ."

"A madman who devotes himself to sorcery, to black magic . . ."

---

to the *Enchiridion* of Epictetus, a manual of Stoic philosophy. The "worst" works of Paracelsus are presumably the magical treatises falsely attributed to the physician in question.

"In any case, who is not at all the husband that I desire for my daughter. I ask you not to lose sight of him . . . I can't say that I'm anxious about the consequences of my refusal, and yet, it seems to me that those eyes might cover stubborn rancor . . ."

"Count on me."

Gérald arrived; he was, in truth, very handsome, pale, with his long thin face, his blue-tinted black beard, and his thick hair, which a habitual gesture threw back in a flicker of flame.

We found ourselves beside one another, and chatted; he seemed at ease, as if he had nothing to fear that might thwart his projects. Toward the middle of the night I saw Monsieur de Solmes take him aside; I would have liked to hear the words exchanged, but I could scarcely see the two of them, half-hidden by a door-curtain.

Finally, they separated, and as Gérald went to the door his eyes met mine . . . a flash sprang forth. I felt something like a burn. In the distance, Monsieur de Solmes had addressed a furtive signal to me, as if to remind me of my promise.

I arrived in the vestibule a few seconds after Gérald. At first I did not see him, but as the lackeys were helping me to put on my overcoat, in a corner where other groups were nearby, I saw a singular scene in the mirror: on the steps of the perron Gérald was receiving something from a valet; an envelope that he slipped rapidly into his pocket, giving a handful of gold in return. Then he left.

I ran after him.

The night was cold, very bright under a white moon.

He was twenty paces ahead of me and marching quickly. I slid alongside the houses, muffing the sound of my footsteps.

Suddenly, at a street corner that the moonlight was blanching more brightly, he stopped, holding in his hand the envelope that he had received a little while before.

A shadowed covert permitted me to approach more closely, and I got close enough to touch him . . .

And I saw that he had opened the envelope and taken out
a cardboard square: a photograph in album format.

Boldly, I leaned over his shoulder . . . and I uttered a cry
of rage. Camille! The man had stolen a portrait of Camille!

I extended a hand in order to snatch it from him. He
stepped aside abruptly, turning round, and we remained motionless for a moment, face to face.

"Monsieur," I exclaimed, in a voice in which I strove nevertheless to retain a note of courtesy, "explain to me why you
have bought from a lackey the portrait of that person . . ."

He said nothing, keeping his eyes fixed on me: eyes that
were sparkling like red-hot coals. Never have I seen in a human face such an expression of hatred . . . of ferocity . . .

"You have stolen that portrait," I went on, my anger rising
to the point of rage. "That's a dishonest action . . . a disloyal
action, for no one has the right to possess that image except
the man whose name she will bear . . ."

"And you know that that isn't me . . ." he said, in a voice
that hissed between clenched teeth.

"Yes, because it will be me, if it pleases God!" I said. "And
I demand that you return it to me . . ."

As he sniggered, my hand rose to slap him . . .

What happened then? Today, I still ask myself whether I
was not the victim of a hideous nightmare . . . and yet . . .
and yet . . . !

I felt the pressure of his fingers on my wrist, circling it
like an iron bracelet. Then it seemed to me that under that
constraint, I was dragged away and lifted up. Around me,
the streets, the houses and everything else passed with a vertiginous rapidity. Then walls opened up to give us passage,
closing again behind us, silently . . .

I found myself in his home, in that man's home, in his laboratory . . .

Upright—magnified, it seemed—his face pale and his mouth contracted, he lifted above his head the adorable portrait of Camille, of my Camille . . . and he said: "You have believed, have you not, that one can toy with me with impunity. I have been rejected like a lackey. In his pride as a millionaire, that man has insulted me with his refusal. You are his accomplice. I know everything: your espionage, your calumnies, and your illusions too. That man is mad! Mad! Listen to this: I hate that arrogant father, I hate that daughter, and I hate you. I want to avenge myself on all three of you, at a single stroke . . ."

I did not reply; I would not have been capable of pronouncing a word, any more than of making a movement, as happens in dreams where the limbs are paralyzed and strength abolished . . .

But I saw around me all the grimacing apparatus of necromancy: retorts, furnaces, the athanor of the philosophers . . . And then, what attracted my attention most particularly were little figurines with human faces, which had needles in the form of swords stuck in their hearts.

He took one of them, and then, in a sneering tone, like that of a schoolmaster giving a lesson to little children, he said: "This represents to you a professor of mine, a grotesque incapacity who permitted himself, one day, to doubt my science. I tried out on him the antique practices of spell-casting. You must have heard mention of Ruggieri,[1] who accommodated so well in this fashion the enemies of the great Catherine de' Medici. I've restored them in their perfect exercise. I bewitch, torture at a distance and kill those I hate. I killed this man,

---

1 Cosimo Ruggieri (?-1615) was a favorite of Catherine de' Medici, who was arrested more than once for allegedly practising murderous sorcery, and thus acquired a great reputation as a magician.

but the effort of casting spells by means of wax images is too violent and dangerous for one's own security—which is easily understandable, since it's by an effort of will that one has to transport into inert matter the vivifying force on which the maleficia must be exercised . . ."

I have not forgotten a single one of the words pronounced, and, strangely enough, they seem as clear to me, and as true, as if I were myself an adept of the criminal magic.

"I want now," he continued, "to act with less risk. I shall kill your Camille, in order that both of you, father and husband, will weep bloody tears over her grave, but I shall have no need to model a figurine, nor to infuse it, by borrowing from my intimate energies, with an artificial life, for I possess a parcel of her own life, of her vitality, in this . . .

"You believe, do you not," he continued, "that there is nothing, in this reproduction of a form, of a physiognomy, but a play of light? Ignorant fools! Between the body that places itself before the objective lens and the sensitized plate a current is established, removing from the being, as in a galvanoplastic operation, innumerable particles of its own matter, of it substance, of its life . . . Chemistry fixes them, nothing more, and—understand me well—between that representation, which seems dead to you, and the distant living being, a bond exists that can never be broken . . . between one and the other, innumerable threads subsist, like a network of electric wires. And when I strike, when I wound, when I lacerate that image, blows, wounds and lacerations, like a telegraph signal, like a voice on the telephone, will reverberate on the living being . . . who will not understand why she is suffering, why she is moaning, why she is dying . . .

"Yes, with this simple photograph, I have the right of life or death over your Camille, and I want to use it. No one knows that, no one has divined it, except me; I have understood that in nature, no bond is ever broken, and what is fixed on the glass is the vital dust; and it is on this that I am going to avenge myself . . ."

Suddenly, it seemed to me that the bonds that were holding me had just broken, and, in a paroxysm of fury I rushed at Gérald in order to snatch from his accursed hands the image of the woman I loved . . .

But he escaped me . . . and I saw that, leaning over the adored image, he was slowly plunging a point into the heart . . .

Then everything disappeared, and when I came round I was in my study with a volume by the necromancer Éliphas Lévi open before me.

It was broad daylight. I shook off the torpor that was oppressing me, and, remembering, I forced myself to laugh at what could only have been—I wanted to believe—a horrible nightmarish fantasy.

Someone rang my doorbell; a domestic came to look for me on behalf of Monsieur de Solmes.

Terror and dolor! During the night, Camille had died, as if struck down by an unknown malady.

I ran . . . and I fell into the arms of the sobbing father. He permitted me to see the adorable young woman, with her pale virginal face, and her hands folded over her breast.

Gérald! The assassin! Oh, I needed his life! I rushed to his house.

There I was told that he had not returned home; I cried that it was a lie; I knocked down the domestic who opposed my passage. I half-broke down the door of his laboratory in order to get through it more rapidly. He was not there, and yet, I recognized the vast room, with its retorts and its athanors . . . except that the wax figurines were no longer there.

And since that day, I have never seen the infamous Gérald again.

Camille is dead . . . dead . . . and I, shivering with anguish, wonder whether that man was mad . . . or whether I myself . . .

THE LIFE OF A DEAD MAN

WHOEVER possesses a verity in himself ought to produce it in the light, so I ought to tell this one. I was able to hesitate, however, because I know unsupportable and stupid quibblers, eager for objection, who would contest the rising of the sun because it could not be explained.

They will not fail to ask me from whom I obtained the story—or rather the revelation—that follows. They will be spiteful because, persuading themselves that they could not have an identical notion, they will affirm that no one could conquer it. With their limited senses, they constitute the inviolable limit that no faculties ought to surpass.

I shall not even attempt to explain to them all that I have seen, heard and perceived, none of it in the conditions admitted by their narrow and negatory sciences. If I tried to formulate that it penetrated me by an endosmosis, by an imbibition of the unknown, without any point of contact appreciable for the most delicate registering instruments, without conductive wires establishing communication between the physical and psychic planes, having been able to reveal itself tangibly, or even intellectually, in the restricted sense of human comprehension. What took place between the being that is me and the astral being of whom I am going to speak was a sort of precipitation analogous to what happens in a galvanoplastic bath, all proportions retained between the ponderable and the imponderable; the people for whom 1 + 1 can only make 2, never more nor less, would look at me with a bewildered amazement, while in their imagination of stupid logicians the silhouette of a padded cell would be evoked, equipped with straitjackets.

In fact, let the possessors of finite science stop here and not go beyond this line; there are glimmers that their Daltonism cannot conceive; stubborn in reason, crusted with common sense, impenitent ignoramuses, let them remain in their impeccable and stupid mollusk existence; it is for the madmen that I am writing, for those who stand up, elongate and stretch, in a sublime attempt at levitation, above and beyond . . . above the visible, beyond the lie of life . . .

So, beloved madmen, listen.

The man had killed himself stupidly, like an animal, in a moment of cerebrospinal insanity; his story was despairing in its banality. His name was Maxime Durand, and in truth he was the Maximus of all possible Durands: a null, flat being, male in the fashion of the goat of Mendès, large in appetite, robust in health, hungry with bourgeois hypocrisy—inferior beatitudes and vulgar satisfactions.

A congested imbecile, he had wailed in his time, sucked at the teat normally, gained good marks at the fair in calculation and orthography, copying when necessary the homework of others, reached puberty soon and actively, served in his modest tartufferies by a complexion that nothing blanched, and had finally acquired, thanks to solitary sedations, the renown of an orderly young man ripe for a serious life; he had soon put on the gray jacket of a salesman, properly equipped with lustrine sleeves, combing his rebellious hair—but vanquished by oleific grease—every morning into a rectified and rosy line, reputedly careful of his person, well-dressed, and even distinguished.

His accounts, superbly aligned, with titles in capital letters and reports in italic, testified to the probity of a castrate. He was not one of those coxcombs who derange themselves and commit follies over women.

In truth, he was nothing but a coward. In his vigorous organism all the trumpets of furious erotism sounded the charge, and while, correctly, he received a female client in the absence of the department head and he asked mellifluously "Anything else, Madame?" without even looking at her, he saw her, with his inner eyes, with the fury of a faun in rut, tearing off her garments and, having laid her bare, digging his fingernails into her white flesh.

He was a very polite salesman.

On settlement days, the fifteenth and thirtieth of the month, when wads of banknotes formed a silky mattress at the corner of his desk, tapping them with his middle finger in order to count them, he devoured impassively with his eyes the bare arms of Industry and Labor, hunched over stockings of blue-tinted paper; he tore away their peplum, saying: "987, three per cent discount for cash," he had in his mouth the taste of secret devourings.

And that honest man stole frightfully, in potential if not in action, having at the tips of his fingers, stuck to gold coins like the suckers of an octopus, inexpressible bulimias.

Now, it happened that the summer was hot and stormy, and the wife of the owner of the shop where he worked, struck by a surge of feminine bestiality, thought about curing that Joseph's innocence. The success was prompt, and from her first interviews with Maxime she emerged both delighted and alarmed. Never, in such bourgeois familiarities, had she divined such vigor and such avidity. Stout and robust, she was able to sustain them, like the women of Brest on the return of the crews of cruisers. Then nature weakened, cried out, became disgusted and horrified, and for her deliverance the unfortunate woman appealed to a discreet adorer, in whose bosom she wept, imploring protection.

The other placed himself in Maxime's passage in one of the galleries of the vast four-story department store, and brutally, with punches in the face, enjoined him to cease his assiduities if he did not want his back broken.

Maxime was so frightened that he took two steps back, and, the door of the elevator being open, he fell from the full height of the shaft and fractured his skull on the edge of the cubicle where the lady was enthroned.

Bloody splinters sprang from the fractured skull over the rich bosom, while droplets dotted her rice-powder. The lady uttered a loud scream and then, her arms suddenly tight to her body, began to ululate in a nervous crisis . . .

Fundamentally nothing was more correct: an imprudence, an accident, and the regulation attack of the sensitive woman . . . it was a minor incident in her crude dalliance, concluding with the impotence of all the means employed to recall the individual to life.

In fact, Maxime Durand was dead, as Durand, a dull personality with red cheeks, bulging eyes, waxed moustaches and thick lips; dead, the Durand who, every morning, got up at six o'clock, and breakfasted on bread dipped in a milky coffee, read a one-sou newspaper, curious about anything—a murder, a suicide or a moral transgression—that a headline brought to his attention; dead, the Durand who, opening the door of the shop, smiled at the owner and glorified in the hand of the owner's wife, held out to him . . . empty, his leather armchair; widowed his bone pen-holder; orphaned, his blotter . . . dead the Durand with the beautiful handwriting, so proud of his impeccable penmanship.

That idle aggregate had come apart; that shell was broken.

But was all of him dead? Or, to put it better, was nothing of him still alive? Was that dead man, entirely and forever, inert?

✳

At the moment when, the beast being still alive, his foot having slipped on the iron rim and where, in spite of an unconscious contraction of the arch, the sole had turned on the smooth rod, the man, sensing his shoulders fleeing, had twisted in an instinctive need for equilibrium, pointing his head forward in a crazy intention of counterweight.

But, lacking any point of support, he had fallen, and in the void another instinct had come to him, to hang on with his fingernails to the wall. He had, in fact, touched it, and the shock had enabled him to recover the vertical momentarily, but at the same time, the fall being more rapid, he had twisted, corkscrewed, as if he wanted to fold up into a ball . . .

Surprise had choked him at first; then he had begun uttering gurgling sounds.

In that second—which the bewildered spectators had not evaluated as long—interminable and multiple sensations, and innumerable thoughts had passed through his mind, created by the various forms that his eyes perceived, then instantly deformed, amplified or specialized by cerebral labor in a kind of tenfold multiplication of the imaginative faculty.

Thus, the silvered gallery that bordered the cage of the elevator at every floor reminded him of the curls of waves that he had seen one day in Le Havre, and he had thought about a long voyage beyond the oceans, with the gold from the cashbox in his pocket . . . The banisters of the staircases had taken him back to the Place de la Concorde, before the legislative body, where députés and ministers were disappearing though tall glazed doors . . . They had money and nothing to do! And women, and honors, and crosses . . . A furious envy bit him.

He collapsed. The atrocious shock extracted a gasp from him. There was a crack in his entire being, followed by a sensation of tearing, and then of unsticking, as if his bones were being torn out of their periosteal sheaths . . . an intense heat, a shower of sparks . . . the frightening and heroic din of a fanfare in his ears; then a metallic click, a sharp stabbing pain like that of a chipped sword being withdrawn from a wound . . . a dull thud . . . perceived in the epigastrum, like a blow launched from the interior toward the periphery . . . and finally a sudden, stifling, crushing immobility, and silence . . .

It was a very short interval, however, a provisional escape from movement, death having as one of its phases a reestablishment of equilibrium by oscillation.

Our languages, deflected from their sensational principle to the consonant skeleton disfigured by the massoretism[1] of a fantastic vowelization, lend themselves with difficulty to the enunciation of events that occur on a plane other than the one where our illusions progress; it would be necessary, in order to bend them to the positivity of things to strip them of their futile and superfluous pulp in order only to conserve the expressive musculature.

Their virtuality does not bend easily to the scientific description of the unknown and the beyond, where there is sometimes nothing adequate; only their substratum, as Fabre d'Olivet[2] has proved in his translation of *Genesis*, responds to

1 The Masoretes (Lermina always credits related terms with a double s) were Jewish scholars working between the fifth and tenth centuries A.D. who compiled handbooks of grammar and pronunciation to assist the compilation of definitive versions of the Hebrew texts that became the basis of the Bible. Because written Hebrew only reproduced consonants to begin with, the "vowelization" of the text by notations added by Masorete scholars enabled its pronunciation, sometimes controversially.
2 Antoine Fabre (1767-1825), who preferred to style himself Fabre d'Olivet, was a poet, composer and linguist whose unorthodox hermeneutic studies of the Hebrew language and investigations of neo-Pythagorean philosophy

the eternity of principles; the approbation of words to insignificant details, to the arabesques of vital caricature, forbids
them the algebraic precision that linear verity requires.

Hence the great difficulty that I experience is translating
what, from that humanly dead being, penetrated into me by
purely intuitive revelation. It is not easy to say what has not
been spoken.

Pardon me, then, for an absence of conciseness of which
I am the first to suffer, and remember that it requires words
to render, even on our inferior plane, the idea that, in an infinitesimal fraction of time, all these contingencies can spring
forth complete and, so to speak, fully armed.

First, know this well: Durand, dead in human eyes, declared a cadaver by the physician who was summoned, was
not yet dead. It is an error to believe in the instantaneous-
ness of death. Decease—a more accurate word—is a departure with phases of distancing. The doctor who leaned over
Durand said: "There is an immediate and profound lesion of
the brain. See, no reaction can any longer provoke the slightest movement. The heart is no longer beating, the pupil is
not subject to the influence of light; no breath emerges from
the breast to tarnish the polished surface of this mirror. He is
dead!"

People hastened; a nun was made to respire salts; her body
struggled, in a sort of reflexive revolt against the violation of
that fog, which penetrated her without really touching it,
placing strange and inexplicable reflections before her eyes.
She shuddered and sighed, straightening up in the resistance;
her astral body, which had abandoned her, an accomplice of
its colleague, violently attracted by her reawakened vitality,
recovered its normal state; she opened her eyes, resuscitated
in a way, rejecting Durand, who lurched under the shock of
that expulsion.

---

had an enormous influence on many of the leading figures of the French
Occult Revival, including Lermina's associate Papus.

But at that moment, the owner's wife, who had come round, summoned by her female generosity to help the nun, came in holding a bottle of vinegar.

Durand, who was floating in his astral intoxication, perceived her, impregnated by the femininity that the catastrophe had activated, and in his disequilibrium he fell upon her, rediscovering the brutal affinity of past desires; the other collapsed, in the habitude of a rediscovered sensation. Durand searched the known coverts, insinuating himself into the shaken fibers of a remembrance, and the owner, having run in response to the cries of fright that the writhing had drawn from the spectators had a momentary perception of an anomaly injurious to his dignity as a husband. Too stupid to struggle alone, he cried: "Monsieur Oscar!"

Monsieur Oscar was the other, the newcomer who had chased away the predecessor, vigorous by nature, especially muscular, who loved the owner's wife with all the ardor of his as-yet-unfatigued senses.

He arrived and saw her, her nipples erect, her legs quivering, inhaling through all her pores the ferocious amour of the dead man who was devouring her. He did not understand, but that attitude stimulated all his contained erotism, and from him also the astrality sprang forth, saturated with vital force. And the two astral bodies found themselves, in the narrow space of that room, where the air was heavy with rustic effluvia, in confrontation with one another, one palpitating with the fatigue of the lethiferic effort, the other robust with true vitality, which gave it a point of support. They stuck to one another, mingling their psychic gyrations, biting one another with their dental potentialities, tearing one another with nonexistent fingernails, insulting one another with their mute wills, which were diluted as they vomited unexpressed epithets . . .

Oscar, very pale—exsanguinated, so to speak—was holding the hand of the owner's wife, already almost liberated, who was shaking with the quivering commotions of a dying bird . . .

Durand resisted the living pressure that dominated his residue of mortal energy, but now the lady's astrality, in a surge of fury, rushed in her turn with the rage of hatred against the one who had wearied her with amour. And the two astralities of her and Oscar fell upon Durand, twisting him in their rhombi, strangling him in their coverts and perforating him with their impacts, while elementals, their appetites stimulated by that tearing apart of morbid residues, attached themselves to the wretch like crabs to a cadaver, and ate him so gluttonously that he experienced the terrors of those bites and fled, stretched in a long-drawn-out thread, far into the indefinite elongation of an escape.

※

Night, a profound, enveloping obscurity in a cone of luminary shadow between two straight walls, beyond which is the abyss, the luminosity of which has the appearance of unfathomable depths . . .

In his momentum, projected as if by a spring, Durand has arrived there, in the *in pace*, devoid of hope, devoid of radiance.

A sickening laxity puts in that impalpable and flaccid thing an ignoble insipidity.

It is not alive, it does not feel; it drifts, floats thither and yon without any breath pushing it: a drunken coming-and-going that has no reason for being, no beginning or end, a rotation without a circle and without impacting angles.

Something like the sensation of a drunkard collapsed in the angle of a boundary-marker on a rubbish heap, save for the feverish fibers of a brain. He turns, turns, turns.

Every time the projection sends him toward the limits of the cone of shadow, without any experienced shock; he swerves in a soft collapse, hesitates momentarily, and then departs again plunging into the denser night, only to emerge again into the crepuscular glean inhaling, so to speak, in the fashion of fish, a mouthful of that light, which is his air.

Not a sound.

Other astralities, more or less diluted, more or less purified of animality, are also turning. Strangely enough, they do not move aside to let one another pass; they traverse one another, transpiercing one another without the slightest sensation alerting them to that perforating conflict. They seem to be nothing, but when, after being mingled momentarily, they find themselves outside the collision, they have their individuality, only to be confounded a moment later with other individualities.

In that perpetual evolution, though, Durand has the sensation—without sensing the perception—of a heaviness that, whenever he tends toward the light, plunges him back into the night.

There is a weight, however, that gradually becomes lighter, in thousands and thousands of gyrations, like that of a prisoner who, by virtue of going back and forth dragging his chain along the pavement of his jail, wears it away, thus rendering it less weighty by infinitesimal disaggregation.

Then there are tendencies of escape, as if by virtue of the effect of an unappreciable attraction. That astral entity, which a single vocable, a neutral IT might qualify, obeys influences that it cannot comprehend or define.

The cone of lunar shadow is limited by lines, At each instant (what is an instant in what no longer has the time measurable by our numbers?) the astral liquescence overflows, reentering without being aware of it the sphere of terrestrial attraction, toward which a sudden but uncomprehended attraction draws it.

Now, in the living sphere of life as we know it, banal and submissive to the action of the kamarupa,[1] this happens.

Full, laughing, misshapen, in one of the taverns of the Boulevard Rochechouart, a man has emerged, drunk on three absinthes and six beers swallowed at the counters of various drinking-dens.

Intoxicated, having a notion of the rotundity of all things, unconscious of angles, he lurched, clamoring the words of an idiotic song, stumbling and rebounding, opposing a stupid laughter to the hardness of street corners, cheerful at the inter-sections that leave him complete liberty . . . to say everything, a radiant drunkard having had his fill and surpassed the limit of his means of operation.

He was drooling contentedly.

He is absolutely honest, and does not permit anyone to say that they are more honest than him. For, in sum, he knows himself well! For conscience he has no peer, and if anyone ann . . . oys him he will tell them so. One knows one worth, not so?

He was not walking very straight, and that's a fact; but provided that he arrives at Louison's—a lovely girl—who ought, at eleven o'clock, to be in bed . . .

Only that was difficult. In which direction did Louison live? There was certainly a wall . . . but where was that wall? It's odd that there are walls that are never there when one searches for them. It's true that there are other walls, but they're not the right wall . . .

The worthy alcoholic was in search of a point of support when he bumped into the threshold of a café. The step is dry,

---

1 Kamarupa was the name of a state in the north-east of the Indian subcontinent, which was gradually fragmented after the twelfth century A.D. It was represented by some historians as a descendant of the mythical kingdom of Pragiyotisha, featured in the Mahabharata, and the name was mystically redefined during the French Occult Revival as a trivial noun, especially in the context of Theosophy.

and that's a fact. Another silver coin. Louison doesn't need as much money as that, earning her living in the laundry. And then, when one is thirsty, it's necessary to have a drink.

Very dignified, with the consciousness of a man condescending to satisfy the beast, the drunkard goes in. What to have? Syrups, that's the thing!

"Two greens in one glass, and fresh water."

That isn't to be refused.

And, his gaze seized by a little white dot darted by the zinc counter, Julot downs the two greens. But it needs a party of four, or there is no amour.

And the four sisters kiss one another in his stomach

He goes in. It's cold, a dirty temperature that the rich call a little dry: damnation!

It's bizarre; there's something that escapes him. He would like to think, to reason, to remember. There's Louison, there's a house somewhere, with a sixth floor, a hovel, under the declivity of a roof pierced by a skylight. One goes to bed there, one curls up, one sleeps. Sleep. But where is it?

Then, suddenly, there is a crack in the brain, something like a fissure abruptly opened.

From that impotent body, where alcohol has killed the will, the astral body escapes, a captive that nothing any longer retains. It oozes out as if from a cracked vase, stretches out above the collapsed beast, drifts in the air, striving to detach itself, to tear away, to break the bond with which reflexive vitality still knots its fluidity.

But although a prisoner, the astral body of the drunkard is free; it elongates in space, it looks over the wall of the human plane, it glimpses the frightening and superb visions of the beyond, and it intoxicates itself with a commencement of infinity.

Durand, through the slack gyrations of his errant vacillation, devoid of thought, will and instinct, nevertheless experienced—without instruments of perception—a ferocious, brutal desire to live again. There was something like a penetration, an absorption by of magnetic forces that attracted him in furious inhalations. He could not remember what life was, but he had a dull, obscure but powerful appetite for it. What was hanging after him of as-yet-undiluted matter constituted for his astrality a ballast that he could not resist, like an aerostat recalled to the ground by a rope. What remained in him of animality sought a refuge, an implement of resurrection, of enjoyment: monstrous pollen in quest of a pistil.

He rolled through space, sometimes escaping from the lunar shadow and rushing toward the terrestrial light, into which he plunged with the anguish of a blind owl, sometimes drowning again in the cold darkness, in the vermicular fluidic swarming of innumerable astrals, which carried him away in their tortuous and mute serpentations.

Now, in one of those crazy peregrinations, Durand brushed the place where the absinthe-victim lay.

Abruptly, he stopped, as if nailed.

A polarity was imposed. The bodiless astrality sensed the body devoid of astrality. He wanted that.

The astral of the drunkard, in its flight out of the brute that no longer retained it, went further and further, only connected by a thread of vapor to that mass, whose mechanisms were no longer active.

Durand understood that: an empty house. He precipitated into it, via the nose, the mouth and all the orifices of the skin, by means of a general and savagely abrupt absorption; sliding like water through the porosities of a sponge, he took possession of that rag.

When he had it, like a dog that has just stole a bone, he started bounding within the prison in which he was contained, rushing, bumping into the walls, penetrating with searching rage into the least coverts, hanging on to the most secret fibers.

And the drunkard, under that formidable and macabre pressure, first shuddered intensely, and then tried to straighten up, making a bridge between the heels and the nape of the neck; then there was a convulsion, twisting the torso and drilling the legs . . . the man was now rolling on the pavement, his face, stretched into a Japanese mask, had utterly bizarre displacements of the eyes and mouth. The forehead shivered in abominable wrinkles that made the hair stand on end.

A frightful sensation, as if millions and millions of wood-lice were swarming within him, sticking to his muscles, burrowing in his flesh, active and sucking . . . he grimaced entirely, in the face, the belly and the back. Then, in the brain, the overexcited lobes started playing like a musical instrument in the paws of an ape; into the Aqueduct of Silvius, in the Fissure of Rolando, Durand's astral dived, wandering joyfully . . . and from the twisted mouth of the drunkard cries and words were ejaculated, hideous and stupid, so hurried and hoarse that they brought saliva from the throat that foamed and drooled over the chin . . .

Around that grunting clownery, an idiotic crowd gathered . . . other astrals enlaced with the astrals of those stupid curiosity-seekers and maddened them with terror and disgust, and also cruelty. Some cried: "He's rabid! Kill him!"

Another, who had a clean-shaven face like an actor or a priest pronounced the phrase *delirium tremens*. A reader howled: "Vieux Coupeau!"[1]

Someone ran in search of policemen.

Meanwhile, the astral of the drunkard, suddenly recalled by the reflexive will of its normal proprietor, was striving to reenter its domain and to expel the intruder that had usurped its place . . .

---

1 "Vieux Coupeau" is a character in *L'Assommoir* (1877) by Émile Zola, who descends from sobriety into violent alcoholism; his story is presented as a kind of case-study, including an account of *delirium tremens* cited as exemplary by the physiologist Claude Bernard.

But Durand held firm; he had in his favor the right of conquest and he intended to use it, all the more so as the erotic appetites of the alcoholic were becoming overexcited and beginning to satisfy the voracity of the dead man . . .

"Oh, the swine!" shouted a child. And he threw a stone at the denuded cynic, which stuck him in the face and drew blood . . .

The shock had an unexpected effect; Durand, avid for blood, threw himself on the red place, and in that movement cleared the issue of regular penetration momentarily . . . and the astral of the drunkard, lying in wait, was suddenly reintegrated, expelling the stranger in a furious struggle that caused the man to shake horribly, having become the battleground of the two psychic entities, which attacked one another like two duennas pulling one another's hair.

Vanquished, Durand fled . . .

Discreet, muffling their footfalls and rounding their backs like churchwardens entering a sacristy, meeting two by two at the black coaching entrance and tightening their lip before ringing, then, the cordon having been lifted, passing through the courtyard striped with dirty rays of gaslight, passing under the mocking curiosity of the stout concierge, whose plebeian face was stuck to the panes, then going upstairs, almost respectful of the creaking of the steps and kneading the handrail with ecclesiastical grips, taking a breather on the landings, as if oppressed by the god, worthy men came, troubled, twice a week, to the home of the lady on the fourth floor, whose name they only pronounced with vocal tremors, pharyngeal signs of respect.

Although impatient, before knocking on the door, they leaned toward one another and in a murmur congested by contained emotion one said to the other: "Provided that the dear spirits . . ."

"Oh, as the last time, Saint Vincent de Paule . . ."[1]

"Do we dare disturb him again?"

The noise rose from down below, in the dark stairwell, of the door of the vestibule closed again by two new arrivals.

He first two knocked, the door opened, swallowed them, and closed again, while, magnified as the ascent was effectuated, women's voices intoned sentimental trivia.

"This time, I want to speak to my little Adèle . . ."

"Pardon me, but I've promised to see the captain . . ."

"The dear spirits will have pity on us both. Shall we have Monsieur le Comte? What a delightful man . . . !"

"And so polite. Have you heard him conversing with Jean-Baptiste? Truly, one might think they were brothers . . ."

And the door, swinging on its hinges, ingests new arrivals, and then others, and then more . . .

In a drawing room furnished in garnet velvet, with protective crochet-work on the chairs and armchairs, the Lady of the house is standing, chatting to Monsieur Frédéric, thin and dark with hair back-combed over his ovoid skull. Monsieur Frédéric has dark eyes with pronounced rings, a broad mouth and thick lips. His fingers are very long, with short, black-bordered nails. He is grave; his is lamenting that Madame, too indulgent, has allowed incredulous individuals to penetrate.

"What do you suppose our dear disincarnate will think," he says, severely, "if we extract them from their spheres of light to expose them to insult?"

"But Monsier Frédéric, no one is permitted . . ."

"I tell you, Madame, that Fénelon was very discontented, and Saint Siméon declared that he would never set foot in your home again . . ."

"Monsieur Frédéric, I beg you to tell Saint Siméon . . ."

---

1 It is not obvious why Lermina's character misrenders the name of St. Vincent de Paul—or, indeed, how she indicates the difference in speech—but the addition of the extra e to the text is soon revealed not to be entirely superfluous.

"But Monsieur Frédéric is no longer listening."

A robust woman with a prominent bosom has just come in, accompanied by a specter: a pale nocturnal thread.

"Ah, dear sister," cries Monsieur Frédéric, "how good of you to come, and your dear child . . ."

The specter is a young woman, perhaps sixteen years old, pale and thin, with a diaphanous cranium and immense eyes devoid of a gaze. She cannot see Monsieur Frédéric, but her dead voice interrogates: "Is my beloved master not here?"

Monsieur Frédéric's zygomatic muscle twitches nervously. "A thousand regrets. But we have not yet seen Monsieur le docteur D***."

The robust lady and Monsieur Frédéric have exchanged a wink.

"It's necessary to be careful, my dear child," murmurs Monsieur Frédéric.

But she blasts him with her suddenly-illuminated eyes, saying in a harsh voice: "Monsieur le docteur is my master."

Languidly, a woman of about thirty, pale with chlorosis, undulates toward Madame and takes both her hands in her own moist clutch. "Monsieur le Comte?"

"He has just arrived. Come, my dear, let me place you . . ." Then, in the pale lady's ear: "Don't forget to speak to him, on behalf of the dear spirits . . . he's so generous."

Around the drawing room everyone has sat down, the armchairs close together; there are heaps of skirts and legs . . . Madame, content, has sat down next to the fireplace, smiling— she is very dark, her lips shadowed by a moustache—and she says: "Monsieur Frédéric, do you think that our dear spirits will be favorable to us?"

Seriously, having covered his eyes with a lorgnon with smoked lenses, in order not to be distracted by mundane contingencies. Monsieur Frédéric has approached the side-table, after having lowered the wick of the lamp slightly.

"Spirits, dear spirits," he says, in a solemn, throaty voice, "forgive our temerity, but we are people of faith, and our supreme joy is to enter into communication with the beloved dead. Speak, be manifest, if it pleases you to come to us . . ."

A loud crack is heard from the table.

"Mademoiselle," says Monsieur Frédéric to the young pupil of the absent doctor, "will you please help us to interrogate the spirits?"

Immobile and livid, she seems at first not to have heard, but her mother whispers in her ear; she shivers, gets up and comes to the table herself. She sits down next to it without touching it.

"Extinguish the lamp," she says.

Monsieur Fréderic blinks his eyes significantly; phenomena are about to be produced . . .

On the order of Monsieur Frédéric, everyone forms a chain; hands are joined; the lamp is extinguished; the silence is absolute, the darkness complete.

In all those people, slowly, a disequilbrium is produced. Respirations are retained, contention pushes the liberated astrals outside each being. In the room, overheated by those breaths, an atmosphere forms, made of morbidities and neuroses, which elementals in quest of temporary revivification—elementals avid for vital effluvia—sense from afar.

And under the low ceiling there is, invisibly, the gyration of psyches floating in the beyond, dragging their passionate cannonballs, entities of this side, hateful in non-being. The astrals of the living wander unconsciously, deserting part of the shell that is their domain; in the doctor's pupil the emergence is complete . . .

From his sinister corner Durand has scented that virgin flesh, macerated by enervating practices, and he has slid thereinto, attentive and avid . . . the extinguished light liberates him from the redoubted torture. Still heavy with vices, he is stronger than the others, jostles them aside, extends himself toward the young woman's heart, and drills into it . . .

Suffering sighs are heard, something like spasmodic gurgles . . .

"The spirits are here," announces Monsieur Frédéric.

The hands of the chain clutch more forcefully; there is erethism everywhere.

The orgiastic gasps are accentuated.

"Dear Sister," pronounces Monsieur Frédéric, "Have the spirits come to us?"

A silence, then something like a cough.

A blue gleam rises into the air and vanishes in a flocculent dilution. The subject is moaning now; Durand is eating her being.

"Respond to us, dear sister. Evoke a spirit . . ."

In an utterly changed voice, grinding her teeth, she responds: "Yes, I see a spirit . . . there, above us . . ."

"Ask it who it is."

"Spirit, who are you?"

She repeats the question twice, and then: "It's Victor Hugo . . ."

There are prideful gasps in the audience.

"Ask the soul of the great poet to say something to us . . ."

In the same strangled voice, the young woman says: "I can hear him clearly . . ."

"What is he saying?"

"*Merde.*"

Little exclamations in the chain. Monsieur le Comte is offended, but Monsieur Frédéric has understood.

"Remember," he says, "that our venerated poet wrote that word in *Les Misérables* . . ."

Now the young woman speaks, with an alarming volubility . . . odious, obscene words are spat out by her lips . . . Durand is unleashing all the filth still contained in him

. . . Madame has given an order, the lamp has been turned up and rapidly relit . . . The young woman stiffens, her legs stretched, her hands on her shoulders, her head tilted back, still mouthing indecent argotisms, recalling the attitude of the worst convulsionnaires; Monsieur Frédéric takes her in his arms and carries her into another room, followed by the mother, whose nipples are erect with terror.

"There are spirits who play practical jokes," says Madame, smiling at the comte.

He, who has a stammer and is half-deaf, utters halting words: "I don't . . . like . . . peo . . . ple . . . making f-fun of me . . ."

The pale lady protests: "Perhaps there are incredulous . . ."

"An occultist?" Madame threatens, parading her moustached gaze over the audience.

"Let's return to the table," says a small voice. "Perhaps Saint Vincent de Paule . . ."

"After that," says Madame, "for the great saint to come . . . that cannot be . . ."

"Let's try anyway . . ."

Monsieur Frédéric returns, very animated.

"There are people—I'm not judging anyone—who are greatly culpable . . ."

"The doctor . . ."

"I said that I wouldn't name anyone . . . but don't worry, no such scene will be renewed . . . henceforth it will be me who completes the education of that young woman . . ."

Madame has a shudder of delight, and nudges Monsieur Frédéric's elbow.

"You've got there, you old rogue!"

Meanwhile, order is reestablished. Durand has exhausted himself in brutal effort . . . the light is obsessing him; however, he still wants to remain. Everyone has sat down at the table, which is meekly tapping its eloquent feet.

"Spirit, are you there?"
Toc, o.
"Ah! Who are you?"
"Saint Vincent de Paul."
"De Paule . . ."
"Come on, let's not quarrel with the spirits over spelling. Great Saint, say something to us, if only a word."
The table moves.
"One, two, three . . . eight . . . ten . . . twelve, thirteen . . ."
"It's an M. Second letter?"
"Fiv . . . that makes *Me* . . . The third.
The table taps five, ten, fifteen; it reaches p and then q . . .
"Let's stop," says Monsieur Frédéric. "The spirit jokers haven't departed . . ."
This time, Durand, unable to support the light any longer, is violently attracted by the cone of shadow, which reabsorbs him, leaving the field free for the elementals, which, with remembrances of sniggers, await the question . . .
"My sisters," says Monsieur Frédéric, "let us recall Saint Vincent de Paule . . ."

✳

Drop by drop, as from a sack the bottom of which has a fissure, the shameful appetencies of Durand, the brute, have escaped from his astrality, whose form, stretched thus far by the weight into an inverted pear-shape, is normalized in its tendency toward the mathematical ideal.

Thus lightened, the shell, like an aerostat freed of its ballast, is no longer crawling, buffeted by all the passionate attractions and the terrestrial affinities. Durand is emptied of evil; the residues of his senses atrophy and his desires are extinguished; he forgets the charms of bestiality, which fade away, are distanced and disappear. He is no longer oscillating;

he rises, and then, as is normal, his fluidity is seized by the spiral, embryo of the perfect form . . .

He has escaped the light, but in the curve, with several revolutions on the same plane, there are still dark corners; it is the last, but the longest phase of weighty suffering; the spiral condenses for the resistance, going toward its asymptote, which is the circle . . .

Of the shameful animal that Durand was, nothing any longer subsists but the tendency toward physical altruism; the will expands his life in the life of others; he rolls toward the height, gradually penetrated by the light, stifled, supremely vitalized, ripening for the decisive combustion that will reject his atoms into the circulation of worlds . . .

And much, much later, the spiral, drawing away further and further from the point, equally modeled by cosmic forces, is resolved into a sphere, into an incandescent ball, an infinitesimal sun of humanity, which throws back its fecundating heat into humanity, a renaissance followed by a further purification, until the long-awaited hour when the luminous sphere, possessing a heat adequate to the sublime chain, is reabsorbed and melts into itself, an element become infinite in the infinite light . . .

THE WRECK OF THE *RIGOLETTE*

"D OWN with the topmast! Yare! Lower! Lower!"

"Bring her to try with main-course."

"Lay her a-hold, a-hold! Set her two courses off to sea again, lay her off."

Those lines are extracted from *The Tempest*, by the divine Shakespeare.[1]

Why that citation? For several reasons, the first of which—the most topical—is that a quotation from the "divine" Shakespeare always produces a good effect and gives a writer weight.

As for the second, it is more complicated . . .

Can you imagine, Madame, that I have an absolute need to describe a frightful tempest to you?

Now, if I simply wrote: "The weather was awful" you would think me a trifle dull.

On the other hand, to explain appropriately the wind that was blowing—whether it was coming from this or that direction or another, to delimit precisely the degree of latitude and longitude at which the ship found itself, and finally to put into the mouths of sailors, along with their plugs of tobacco,

---

1 I have used Shakespeare's actual lines, spoken by the boatswain in Act One, Scene One, rather than back-translating the slightly different lines employed by the author, which might come from a French translation or which might have been improvised by Lermina.

the exact terminology of mizzen, jib, reef, abeam, pitching, etc.—I would need a science that I lack completely.

I have never regretted so much not having been taken aboard a ship when very small and not having had my ears boxed many a time thereon. My nautical education has been direly neglected.

Now, not wanting to admit that, and refusing to spend six months of my beautiful existence infusing myself with that science, which I qualify as admirable but perfectly useless to my future, I am falling back with mischievous romanticism on the aforementioned Shakespeare, and answering all demands by means of that brief prefatory citation.

In sum, you will be able to see perfectly from now on.

In simple terms, the many-decked ship, which bore the amiable name *Rigolette*[1] was dancing the most frightful saraband, jig and Hungarian czarda on the angry waves. Its keel

---

1 The French adjective *rigolette* is the equivalent of the English "funny," in the sense of humorous; the word has a different meaning as an English noun. It might be relevant that Giuseppe Verdi's licentious melodramatic opera *Rigoletto* (1851), based on *Le Roi s'amuse* (1832), an ironic tragedy by Victor Hugo, was premièred in Paris in 1857, and that the name of the opera would have been perfectly familiar to Lermina and his readers. The original title of the opera, *La Maledizione* [The Curse] had been replaced when it had problems with the Austrian censors, then dominant in northern Italy, to that of the main character, the Duke of Mantua's hunchbacked jester, derived ironically from the French term. The ill-fated jester had originally been called Triboulet, the name of the parallel character in Hugo's play, and the actual court jester of François I. *Le roi s'amuse* was banned after its première, because the censors took the view that it contained parodic references to Louis-Philippe and it was not performed again until 1882. Lermina would have been keenly aware of the likelihood of his story running into difficulties with the censors of his own era, although it is politically anodyne; it is collected in 1885 in *La Vie joyeuse, nouveau contres drolatiues* and internal evidence implies that must have been written in the same year, but the evolution of the story suggests composition in sections for a newspaper *feuilleton*, although no such previous appearance is identified in the 2008 *Rocambole* bibliography of Lermina's works compiled by Jean-Luc Buard.

and its prow delivered themselves to a frantic two-step. I don't know what Neptune had eaten that day, but he had almighty hiccups.

The *Rigolette*, which liked the joke well enough, had begun by sketching gracious steps on the crests of the waves, like a girl knitting with her little feet while shaking her apron, but the god of the winds did not hear that tap-dance, and started to fidget, and beat time.

On the ship, which was a frigate—unless it was a brig (cursed ignorance)—there were a certain number of people playing different roles in life but who, at that moment, were worth no more than one another.

Captain Van Crack—an old sea-dog, naturally (anyone who has encountered an old sea-dog raise your hand)—was standing on the bridge, howling bizarre things into his loud-hailer, which were doubtless intelligent orders.

The sailors were running around like demons; some were high up on the masts, or astride cross-pieces—are they called yard-arms? I don't know—working on the sails, which were flapping like giant shirt-tails and making disagreeable whis-tling noises . . .

A little imagination, damn it!

The wind . . . the rain . . . the darkness . . . the howls of nature . . . the sky collapsing . . . the water bounding . . .

In short, it was ten or twelve minutes past four in the morning when the *Rigolette*, having received a large wound in her side, sank slowly into the gigantic salty gulf . . .

Horror!

And Neptune uttered an infernal laugh as he swallowed the ship like a hard-boiled egg.

Perhaps you think that it was all over, but you'd be utterly mistaken. This is only a drama; the tragedy is about to begin.

✷

In what region, at what exact point of the globe was the *Rigolette* when that misadventure overtook her?

I'd like nothing better than to be able to tell you, but that detail was only known to Captain Van Crack, and as he is doubtless occupied at present talking to the fish, who are asking one another whether they are going to eat him with green sauce or capers, it would be difficult for me to interrogate him.

Anyway, you will see shortly that you have no need to resolve that geographical problem, which is of secondary importance in the circumstances.

Besides which, I beg you to leave me to my emotion—which is poignant—and not to trouble me with annoying questions.

✳

Here I must insert a further description, and I confess that I could not be more perplexed.

I have in a notebook, thus catalogued, "description no. 127: Shipwreck; cries of agony," but I am forced to admit that it is absolutely romantic—which is to say, passé. Imagine my embarrassment: in order to be perfectly and conscientiously exact, it is at least necessary to have witnessed a shipwreck; in order to render the cries of agony suitably, mingled with the whistling of the tempest, it is necessary to have heard them, and I have never had that chance: an education more and more incomplete. Fundamentally, it is evident that it would have been a hundred times better not to have embarked on the narration of this marine adventure. At every word I risk being frightfully inexact and, in consequence, covered in shame . . .

In truth, too bad! I'd rather confess to you right away that I'm the last of ignoramuses and carry on.

※

In sum, the sailors and the passengers of the *Rigolette* had to go through what is known, in the noble style, as a bad quarter of an hour.

Think about it. One finds oneself on a good plank, which is moving a little, but which offers resistance. Then, suddenly, a break-up, and one plunges into the cold water. That kind of Russian bath is one of the most painful, and I associate myself with all my heart with the protestations of the victims of the shipwreck. Futile protestation, though, because, for a long moment, in the utter chaos of the waves—which I could compare poetically to a gang of hooligans coming out of a *barrière* ballroom, all drunker than one another and giving one another the most violent kicking in the world—the human eye was unable to perceive anything.

However, with some attention, one could have ended up distinguishing half a dozen black dots on the glaucous waves.

Those black dots were simply victims of the shipwreck.

Certainly, in the presence of such a catastrophe, anyone who loses a pint, or even half a liter, of good blood is very unfortunate; but in truth, those victims of fate found themselves in a rather ludicrous situation. One of them was clinging on to a cage full of chickens, which was delivering itself to frolics of an academic choreography; another was astride a vigorous section of mast prancing madly on the liquid plain. There was one is a barrel, which was maintaining its equilibrium the devil knows how.

The wind was blowing violently, but the theory of compensations has not been invented uniquely for the clients of Monsieur Pasteur,[1] and what had doomed the *Rigolette*—be-

____

1 Probably a reference to the application of the so-called Pasteur Effect in brewing beer, where yeast-cells are multiplied in aerobic conditions but

tween us, an old nag of a boat, which wasn't worth a nail—was to save the unfortunates who were splashing around in the salty swell . . . those, at least, with whom we are occupied, for I have no idea, at the moment, what became of the rest.

In order not to feel remorse and to be able to recount with an appropriate calmness the adventure that follows, let us persuade ourselves that all the other navigators had also found barrels or chicken-cages to their taste.

Now, it was scarcely an hour after our interesting shipwreck-victims had quit—involuntarily—the sinking ship when the wind, having seized them in a turbulence that lifted furious eddies on the surface deposited them, or rather threw them like a catapult on to something very hard.

To tell the truth, they did not argue or protest. It was hard, but it did not shift, and neither did they. They had fallen in a heap on top of one another, without even saying *oof!*

Oh, they embraced the land—rock or soil, it did not matter—on to which they had fallen, with an instinctive kiss that was no less cordial than prolonged.

As it was dark, we shall wait, before introducing them to our readers, for the hands of the clock to rotate, and let us say a few words about the terrain on which they had found refuge.

It was neither more nor less than an archipelago. Look in any treatise on geography and you will find that an archipelago is a group of islands. Well, it was not entirely a matter of islands, for in the same manual you will find that an island consists of land surrounded by water.

Now, of land there was hardly any, but there were stone, rock and silicates of every provenance by the shovelful, pro-

---

the subsequent fermentation is stimulated by oxygen deprivation.

vided that the shovel was very large and its handler equipped
with vigorous biceps. And those groups of rocks separated
from one another by a few cables (I say cables in order to
avoid an exact measurement; "cables" signifies everything and
nothing) formed the archipelago in question.

✳

At dawn, the castaways stirred.

It was no easy matter to undo the inextricable tangle
formed by the arms and legs of our characters.

The sun rose radiantly, putting a gentle warmth into their
backs.

Yvon Cloarek, the cabin boy, was the first on his feet. He
was a pretty boy of sixteen or seventeen, a trifle thin and weak,
but attractive in his muscular slenderness.

He shook himself like a bird in the first rays of the sun and
looked around.

"Nice shipwreck!" he said, laughing.

It is necessary to say right away that in Brest, from which
he had departed, he had not followed courses in *gaminesque*
argot with Parisian comrades. It was not necessary for him to
do so; he knew it as well as you or I.

"A thousand thunders and a thousand herrings!" howled a
stentorian voice.

And Pierre Laramé, known as Tête-de-Loup because of
the formidable profusion of the pilosity that enveloped his
cranium, occiput, sinciput, face and neck like the spikes of a
hedgehog, stood up on the enormous tree-trunks that served
him as legs.

From below, that man was shaped like an ogive. His feet
were so large that they could have served as bases for society.
And that torso—what a torso! A thicket on two tree-trunks. A
vigorous man, his friends said that he had the hide of an ape,

and a few ladies assured that he had a chest like the lid of a trunk—the trunks of our forefathers, that is, who wore wigs.

Under the excessive development of the beard, moustache and hair one perceived with difficult, by persistence, profound dark eyes, fleshy lips, a nose that resembled by virtue of its form, and a little by its color, a Mumm White Label champagne cork.

Next to Yvon, nicknamed for his part Fil-d'Acier, that colossus had ogreish proportions. It seemed that he could have swallowed the cabin boy like a cutlet. Fortunately, he was a good fellow, with only three faults—who has none, alas?—summarized in the famous chorus of *Le Chalet*:[1] "wine, amour and tobacco." Oh, tobacco first of all, and then, almost *ex aequo*,[2] amour.

Tête-de-Loup was amorous by nature and had no peer for formidable pub-crawls on returning from a long voyage. As he put it, when he had spent a few months at sea, he was ready to explode. A terrible drunkard, as violent as a wild beast and as brutal as a bulldog, he was otherwise the most charming fellow in the world.

Like his comrades, and in spite of his formidable stature, he had, as they say, quite a mouth on him, and when he came round his first reaction was a frightful anger. He cursed the heavens, the sea, the *Rigolettte*, the captain and the whole upheaval with a luxury of oaths that would have disarmed a *carabinier*.

Finally, Tête-de-Loup grabbed Fil-d'Acier by the ear and said: "Damn it, little wretch, will you tell me where we are?"

With an abrupt twitch that seemed familiar to him, the gamin disengaged his ear and then, leaping backwards, said: "Down, helmsman; we're no longer aboard now . . . no more jokes, no more familiarities . . ."

---

1 *Le Chalet* (1834) was a well-known *opéra comique* by Adolphe Adam, with a libretto by Eugène Scribe and Mélesville.
2 "equally placed".

"Eh! What are you saying?"

Tête-de-Loup took a step, lifting the mighty leg-of-mutton that served him as a hand.

"No need to get heavy," riposted Fil-d'Acier. "If you annoy me, you understand, I'll be off, and I'll leave you alone to sober up."

"What! You'll run away!"

"Of course. Two strokes and I'll be on another rock. To each his own. And then, Tête-de-Loup, you won't like that at all, you know—and you won't be sorry to have me here to catch fish—and that will be necessary if we're not to die like dogs of starvation, I warn you."

It appears that that reasoning penetrated easily enough into the passably obtuse understanding of Tête-de-Loup, for he nodded his head and only responded with a grunt. Except, as he still had his anger to discharge, he launched a mighty kick backwards, at random, to which a howl of pain responded.

"Sainte Marie! Jesus! I'm dead!" ululated a plaintive voice.

"Who's that?" clamored Tête-de-Loup.

And, bending down, he picked up in his enormous fist something that he lifted off the ground: a bundle of wet rags, but a moaning, tremulous bundle.

"Don't hurt me!"

"Ah, it's Petit-Corbeau," cried Fil-d'Acier.

Aboard the *Rigolette* that was what they had called a certain passenger, a kind of apprentice seminarian in his twenties, tall, thin and pale, always praying, with his arms folded over his breast and his eyes lowered. Fil-d'Acier had the disastrous habit of mocking him, hiding ham in his soup on Friday and other little jokes that drove the nice young man to despair.

"Nice young man" is perhaps excessive, for, on the contrary, the fellow had the air of an abominable little hypocrite.

"There!" said Tête-de-Loup, depositing him on his feet.

Petit-Corbeaiu—whose real name was Onésime Bardurot—then showed to the face of Heaven the sickliest expression and the slickest hair—in brief, the most seminarian physiognomy—imaginable. And as he still had in his blood the blue funk that, by a singular phenomenon of reaction, rendered him green, he started shivering and tried to kneel down in order to plead with the imaginary enemy that he might have mistaken for a sperm whale desirous of swallowing a new Jonah.

Tête-de-Loup kept hold of him firmly. Onésime, whose feet quit the ground as his knees bent, spun like a puppet.

"Hold still, monkey!" cried the helmsman.

"Monkey! Monklet!" Yvon corrected. "Let him go."

But Onésime's legs suddenly stiffened, as if he had convulsed by means of a supreme effort. At the same time he uttered a new clamor, shriller still.

"Oof!" exclaimed Tête-de-Loup. "What's the matter with him? Has he swallowed the anchor?" And in order to resist the sudden weight he felt in his fist, with a thrust of his back the mariner hoisted himself up on to a block of stone higher than the others.

You have all seen on a butcher's stall chaplets of sausages linked together by knots of gut. To the seminarian's legs another individual was clinging, and to the legs of the newcomer, yet another. It was a whole package, collapsed on the ground, that unwound like a cable.

And Tête-de-Loup, writhing with laughter, continued to rise up, lifting the human chaplet.

Let us be clear. We have, then, firstly, Tête-de-Loup; secondly, Fil-d'Acier; thirdly, Petit-Corbeau . . .

Who was number four? And who was number five?

Have I told you that the *Rigolette* had departed from a French port, whose name is immaterial, and was bound for one of our colonies, the name of which I shall refrain from telling you, in order not to reawaken the great colonial quarrel?

I want to propose a riddle to you. What is the article with which France is overflowing, and which she exports, more than any other to the lands that she honors with her protection? Is it silk, cloth, Rouenneries, or even Parisian products like lace or refined sugar?

You haven't got it.

It's . . . functionaries.

What was hanging from the seminarian's legs was simply an ex-sub-prefect who was going to be the governor, or at least the deputy governor, of the colony in question.

A sub-prefect in the blood, a sub-prefect to the bone-marrow, when, by virtue of certain signs aboard the *Rigolette*, he had been informed that there was a strong chance that he would soon find himself facing the Eternal, Hector de Durplastron had immediately thought about the obligations of propriety imposed upon him by that situation.

It was indisputable that God had placed him, in the hierarchical scale, well above a prefect, and even a minister of the interior. Furthermore, it would have been futile to deny that it was a matter for an introduction, because Hector had never yet found himself in the presence of his supreme chief. In sum, there might be ladies there—the Holy Virgin, martyrs . . . There might be music, the seraphim being up to date with the current of modern fashion . . .

Hence the inexorable necessity of donning evening dress.

So Hector de Durplastron had been in haste to put on his black suit and stick his opera hat under his arm so, when the pitiless abyss had seized our sub-prefect in its powerful jaws, at least Hector would have a tranquil conscience and could confront the terrible moment when Saint Peter, opening the gates of Heaven, would announce with full lungs: "*Monsieur le Sous-Préfet* Hector de Durplastron!"

But—and see, young people, how beneficial formal dress is, no matter what those frightful Bohemians might say—

Hector was saved by one of those circumstances that the most fanciful of novelists would not have dared to invent.

Hector had very little hair, even less nose, and tiny eyes. He must have been very ugly, you cry. Error! Hector was ornamented by a pair of fan-like side-whiskers, a marvel. When he went along the boulevard, the café waiters saluted him and his side-whiskers had almost been worth an embassy to him.

In private life, those side-whiskers, carefully curled every morning, expertly fluffed-up and perfumed with a vaporiser, had the allure of wings. In the water, flabby, depressed and spongy, they resembled fins . . . well enough that the fish mistook our sub-prefect for a colleague, all the more so as the cod-tails completed the illusion, and they had carried him gently to the shore.

Number five, the end of the chaplet, had escaped from a novel by Jules Verne.

He was a timid, benevolent scientist preoccupied with treasures buried in the ocean depths: benthodytes, *calveries*, stomias and other bizarre beasties,[1] which, it is affirmed, live under pressures of thousands of kilograms.

A member of a host of scholarly societies, Monsieur Eusèbe Cartilas spent his entire life like a mussel with a closed shell. He only opened up when touched by salt water. That tells you well enough that he was ignorant of all the passions and had never had to reproach himself for the slightest infraction of the code of modesty. That was even his glory and his compatriots—like Léon Cladel,[2] he was from Quercy—had

---

1 Benthodytes are a genus of sea-cucumbers and stomias a genus of "sea-dragons"; "*calveries*" might be a misprint, for *cavaleries*, the intended reference being to sea-horses, although the usual term for such species is *hippocampes*.

2 The novelist Leon Cladel (1834-1892) was born in Montauban, the largest town in the region of Quercy; he wrote a great deal of fiction set in the region. Figeac, the site of L'Eglise Notre-Dame du Puy de Figéac, is not far away.

nicknamed him the Virgin of Figeac: a title that, far from
wounding him, caressed his pride as a scholar disdainful of
earthly things. In his eyes, the smallest univalve was worth
more than all the women in the world.

Of all our characters, Eusèbe was perhaps the only one
who had not experienced any fear when he plunged beneath
the bitter wave. Many a time, when the engines of research
descended into the depths of the sea to the grating noise of
the winch, Eusèbe had dreamed of being attached to a har-
poon and delivering himself in person to the exploration of
the submarine depths. Now that hazard had favored him, he
had fallen like a lead weight, and if he had not reached the
bottom, he had at least had the brief but real satisfaction of
seeing a few unfamiliar species in passing; only he had opened
his mouth in order to indicate their catalogue number, and
from that moment on he had lost the mental lucidity that he
had been able to defend until then even against the tempta-
tions of the flesh.

Tête-de-Loup shook the human cluster, the beads of which
dissolved. Petit-Corbeau fell to his knees, the functionary
flat on his belly, naturally. As for Eusèbe, he collapsed on his
backside, a position that caused him to utter a cry of pain, for,
in his fall, he had crushed a few holothurians with which he
had filled his pockets and whose shells lacerated his inferior
rotundities pitiably.

"Well, my little lambs," said Fil-d'Acier, when he observed
that everyone had recovered his equilibrium, "this isn't the
moment to bark at the crows. I don't know what you have in
your bellies, but I'm dying of hunger and I've been calling the
waiter in vain for hours; I doubt that he's going to bring me
the stew and potatoes that my esophagus needs . . ."

"Personally, I'm going to smoke a good pipe," grunted
Tête-de-Loup

"Fasting is a mortification," objected Onésime.

Hector did not say a word; he was preoccupied with looking sadly at his buttonhole, in which a multicolored rosette usually scintillated. The insignia had disappeared, probably swallowed by some disrespectful fish . . . and when Hector was not decorated, he no longer had any ideas. It had even happened to him one day, in a gallant encounter, when he was at the feet of a grand dame whose support would have been precious for his advancement, that he lost all his means because he perceived that he had forgotten his rosette.

As for Eusèbe, with his eyes chastely lowered, he was considering a mollusk—a colleague, no doubt—attached to his shoe.

"I could eat a horse," repeated Fil-d'Acier.

"I could smoke a cigarette," echoed Tête-de-Loup.

At that moment, Hector uttered a cry of surprise.

"A beefsteak!" cried the gamin.

"A plug of tobacco!" howled the helmsman.

It was quite simply his rosette that Hector had just found, slipped into the gap in his waistcoat. He replaced it respectfully in his buttonhole and then stood up. I ought to say that he still had his opera hat and was wearing his black suit. All that was certainly frayed, but in sum, with that get-up as well as the beneficent kisses of the sun, his side-whiskers were gradually resuming the incomparable fluidity that had acquired the admiration of a charming ambassadress.

Hector, standing erect with the opera hat level with his navel, made the little twitch of the cervical vertebrae that is the equivalent of a bow in good society and said: "Messieurs, don't you think that before any discussion it would be good if we were to proceed with introductions?"

"There's one that'll make me . . . sweat," muttered Tête-de-Loup.

But Fil-d'Acier, who had already measured his man and whose hunger was not fouling his brain, responded with an old régime bow, clicking his heels, with his elbows tucked in; then, in a resounding voice like that of a barker making his pitch at the Montmartre fair, he cried: "I present to you . . ."—and he enumerated the names and titles of the survivors of the *Rigolette*.

"So, Messieurs," said the sub-prefect, who would not have laughed for half a pound of gruyère, "we cannot dissimulate the fact that we find ourselves at the present moment in a critical situation, and we must summon up all our sang-froid in order that our energy responds to the unexpected obligations that are imposed on us."

Tête-de-Loup grunted something.

"Be good enough not to interrupt me," the sub-prefect went on, who had made excellent speeches in agricultural committees. "You will all have the leisure to respond to me, and be sure that I shall respect, for you as for me, the liberty of the tribune . . . I was saying, then, that our situation is critical, and in that I believe that I will not find any contradictors here . . ."

He paused. There were no contradictors. That was a first success,

If Robespierre had been able to explain all his thinking on the eighth of Thermidor,[1] he might still be at the head of affairs today.

"I shall continue," Hector went on. "Critical as the situation is, however, it does not appear to me to be above our courage. For, Messieurs, in this catastrophe I have the satisfaction of observing that we constitute a group in which all the vital forces of society are represented . . . Yes, I declare loudly, where one finds all the bases of society, society cannot perish. Now, around me—and I take some pride in it, I confess it to you without circumlocution—I see those bases.

---

1 8 Thermidor, year II (26 July 1794) was the day of the coup that toppled Maximilian Robespierre, in spite of a defensive speech he made to the National Convention that day, in which the accusations he made against fellow members only cited three names but succeeded in alarming everyone.

"Here is the clergy"—he designated Onésime—"here are the scholarly bodies"—a half-bow to Eusèbe—"here is the navy"—with a semicircular gesture he showed Tête-de-Loup and Fil-d'Acier—"while I myself, and believe that I say this without pride, merely to complete my demonstration, represent the administration . . . Dare I say the government? Perhaps my title authorizes it . . . Where there is a sub-prefect there is France; where there is a member of the Holy Church, there is divine protection; where there is a scientist . . ."

"There is science," the cabin boy finished.

"And where there are mariners . . ."

"There is a navy."

"There is more than a navy, Messieurs, there is an army . . . there is the flag . . . there is national honor. Thus, you have a government, you have science, you have religion and you have an army . . . shall you despair? No, Messieurs, you are French and you will remain worthy of being so! I have spoken!"

And Hector, parting his coat-tails, tried to sit down. But he forgot that the sub-prefectorial armchair was not behind him, and he fell from quite a height on to his backside—an incident without importance, though . . .

"Well, God-muncher," said the cabin boy, addressing Onésime, "do you have anything to say to us?"

Tall, tall, tall and thin, thin, thin in his frock-coat, which was playing the soutane, Onésime took advantage of the blue sky.

"My brethren," he said, "permit me first to abstract myself from the honor that has been done to me. I do not represent our Holy Mother Church, for I do not yet have the ineffable happiness of being anointed by the Lord, only being an unworthy aspirant to the diaconate. However, the Eternal will pardon me if, inspiring myself with the holy education I have received, I invite you to put your fate in the hands of the

Almighty and raise your hearts toward his celestial throne. *In nomine patris . . .*"

"What about you over there, the father of science?"

Eusèbe raised his eyes, blushed, grimaced a smile, and then said: "Deprived of any instrument and devoid of my library—which, I can say without false modesty, contains veritable treasures, I am in the necessity of declining my competence . . ."

"Then you can all die of hunger like seals," howled Tête-de-Loup, "without trying anything! What a heap of idiots! Let's go, Fil-d'Acier, let's explore our rock . . . and we'll be damned if we don't find anything to get our teeth into!"

"Right!" said the cabin boy.

That man must be a socialist, thought the sub-prefect. *Let's keep an eye open and not compromise ourselves.*

*

The rock on which our five heroes had been cast adrift was not one of those pocket-sized rocks, one of those infantile reefs of which one can make a tour in five minutes. It really was a fine rock, as large as one of the properties of the princes d'Orléans, which is saying quite a lot.

Only there was not a single tree, not one plant: nothing but black, gray and green stone with crevices and fissures, all of it slippery, viscous and mossy. But, as Fil-d'Acier declared, there was an absolute lack of wine-merchants.

Going in single file, our characters explored that inhospitable pebble in every direction.

Eusèbe brought up the rear and leaned over from time to time to collect some zoophyte, which he stuck in his pocket.

But of beefsteak, tobacco, gunpowder or carrots, or even simple fish, there was not a shadow.

Take note that in all possible Robinsonades, you see the castaway discover unexpectedly some engine cast up on the shore, some seal that benevolently allows its head to be bashed in, or a few seagulls' eggs. In verity, those individuals are exceptionally lucky . . . which is explicable, because it is only the few that have not died of hunger who have been able to write their stories. I believe that no one will contest that profound observation. But this time, the five Robinsons risked greatly not being able to make the printing-press groan under their account of their voyage.

For they found nothing, absolutely nothing, and the cortege returned to its point of departure, similar to that of Malborough,[1] but with the difference that if the last were not carrying anything, the first were not carrying anything either.

They sat down again in a circle. The sub-prefect, doubtless without meaning to, had placed himself on a stone a little more elevated than the others, which gave him a false presidential air: a small satisfaction that did not prevail against the stomach pangs experienced by the little group.

Even the seminarian, in spite of the habitude he had of various annual fasts, was yawning extravagantly.

Eusèbe made himself very small, as if he would have liked to withdraw into one of his shells.

Hector was dignified, dreaming about the feasts of his sub-prefecture when he had the official député to his right.

Tête-de-Loup cursed between his teeth

Fil-d'Acier was thinking . . . for what is there to do on a bare rock, except think?

Night had fallen, mildly warm. The ocean settled down, with amiable but terribly ironic murmurs, for it harbored

1 The reference is to the popular folk song "Malbrough s'en va-t-en guerre," [Malbrough sets off for the war] which refers to the first Duke of Marlborough, whose death was mistakenly reported after the battle of Malplaquet in 1709.

superb fish in its boating-lake waves that would have figured admirably in front to the castaways with parsley in their fins, but which scarcely seemed to be thinking of such coquetries.

A heavy somnolence weighed upon the unfortunates, who were afflicted by a dull numbness, and the bleak silence was only troubled by Tête-de-Loup's snoring.

But Fil-d'Acier was still thinking . . .

✳

Suddenly, Fil-d'Acier shivered. I'll wager that the reader was waiting with some impatience for that "suddenly" and that shiver. For in sum, born clever, you will suspect that I would not have started writing this little story only to terminate it with the funereal words: "And the five unfortunates died of hunger after having devoured one another."

I want to take the opportunity to remind you of certain facts that you might perhaps have forgotten, the singular resemblance of which to what follows, save for the details, you will understand later.[1]

A few years ago, shipwrecked English seamen were cast up, like our characters, on a desert island. There were half a dozen of them, including a cabin boy, young, plump and healthy. Hunger did its work; there were tears and the grinding of

---

1 The following section of the narrative suggests strongly that the present story was inspired by the *cause célèbre* of the survivors of the sinking of the English frigate *Mignonette* on 5 July 1884, who were adrift in dinghy (not cast up on a desert island) until being picked up on 29 July by another ship. In the meantime, the captain and two crewmen had killed and partially eaten the *Mignonette*'s cabin boy, Richard Parker, who was allegedly dying, having drunk an excess of sea-water. They claimed that they were merely following "the custom of the sea," but they were charged with murder when they returned to England and—to their amazement— were convicted by a panel of judges in November 1884 and sent to prison. The name of the cabin boy echoed that of a character in Edgar Poe's *Narrative of Arthur Gordon Pym* (1837) and was to be appropriated much later, ironically, by Yann Martel in his novel *Life of Pi* (2001).

teeth, and things threatened of ending badly for everyone when one of the castaways presented the following argument to his comrades:

"It's evident that we're all going to die of hunger, without exception. If we're all dead, we'll be no further forward. Well, there's a means of prolonging the existence of the majority which is to eat the minority—which is to say, the cabin boy."

They cast their votes—without consulting the cabin boy, of course—and it was recognized unanimously that the reasoning of the honorable proposer was unassailable.

The cabin boy was therefore eaten.

And that measure was all the more to be felicitated because, on the one hand, the cabin boy was tender, with a pleasant taste of kid goat, and, on the other hand, they hand not had time to consume his last wing when a ship appeared on the horizon and came to pick up the castaways.

As they were found bright-eyed and healthy, they were interrogated on the resources presented by the island in question, and with the simplicity appropriate to tranquil consciences they gave an account of their menu.

There was a moment of surprise, as there is for everything that collides with prejudices; however, when it was explained, it was deemed that the survivors, who would not have survived without that slight infraction of conventions consecrated by routine, had acted wisely.

The interesting gourmets were repatriated.

But not everyone saw it that way. Scarcely had they arrived in their homeland than they found themselves subject to unfortunate importunities. They were accused of nothing more nor less than murder.

To be honest, that was excessive, for, according to their persistent declarations, the person that they had eaten, and to whom they testified the most profound gratitude, since he had saved their lives, had only had five or six hours to live when he had been killed. Judge, therefore: if they had let him die naturally and dolorously, he would have been detestable, while, thanks to that slight thrust of the knife, he was perfectly tender.

In spite of these explanations, the men were sent to the court of assizes, accused of premeditated homicide and ambush.

Ambush! As if it would have been humane to warn the poor lad of the fate that was reserved for him! To take him by surprise was an act of generosity, and it was treated as a crime!

The strangeness of human justice!

The men were condemned, as murderers, to harsh and various penalties, doubtless according to whether they had eaten the fillet or the ribs.

What do you think? Is that justice?

✳

Now, if I have reminded you of that delicate story, forgotten by Brillat-Savarin in his *Physiologie du gout*, it is to prepare your mind to meditate on the problem that will be posed to you further on. You will have to render a verdict, guilty or not guilty.

However, to spare your perhaps-sensitive nerves, I hasten to tell you that Fil-d'Acier will not be eaten, and that none of our characters will be adapted to Sauce Robert. It is a matter of something else entirely, perhaps even graver.

But, as novelists so often say, let us not anticipate events, and return to the previously-written sentence: Suddenly, Fil-d'Acier shivered.

All of you who have read *Robinson Crusoe* will recall the very profound and entirely natural emotion experienced by the solitary castaway when he discovers a human footprint in the sand of the shore. Evidently, that sentiment must have been complicated by a certain disillusionment; for, in sum, being on a desert island does not lack a certain elegance; as soon as there is one foot there will soon be four, as the fabulist says, and all the originality of the situation disappears.

I recall that a young author once sent me, with a request to examine it, a manuscript that began thus:

The theater represents a desert island. People fill the public square . . .

I did not read any further.

But why did Fil-d'Acier shiver?

This is why.

Because, after having spent a sufficient time lying on his back to excuse him turning on to his stomach, he had perceived a glimmer in the axis of his visual ray: a white light, with the darkness rendered as bright as a star . . .

As an individual familiar with the necessary traditions, Fil-d'Acier had therefore commenced by shivering.

Then he had looked more carefully, and that further examination had convinced him that what he could see really was a light.

But there are lights and lights. . .

Perhaps it was a star; however, with the intelligence that distinguished him, Fil-d'Acier understood that if he had not seen the star while lying on his back it was much less explicable that he could see it when he was lying on his stomach, with his chin level with the rock that was serving him as a mattress, His gaze was tangential to the hard stone. Thus, the light in question was on a plane identical to the one on which he found himself. Hence the conclusion that the light was emanating from a fire placed on a rock, a monolith—*lith* if not *mono*—similar to the one on which his friends had run aground. Finally, as he was installed on the edge of the sea and he could distinguish the splashing of the waves quite clearly, the aforesaid light could only be coming from an external source, from which he was separated by a strait of some breadth.

I shall not insult my readers by reminding them that it is recognized in good anthropology that the sole superiority of a minster of education or foreign affairs over an ape is that the one can make fire while the other is deprived by nature of that essentially civilizing faculty. Whoever says "ape" says the being most elevated in the scale of creation, after which it is necessary to pull up the ladder; one has arrived at humans. So, if an ape does not know how to make fire, even less can a seal or a walrus, let alone a herring.

Fil-d'Acier, proceeding thus from deduction to deduction, said to himself that since there was fire, there must be human beings—which proves once again that logic is the science that enables you to commit the worst stupidities. However, that reasoning, unassailable in appearance, suggested the following resolution:

Of alerting his friends there could be no question; it is the rule—is it not?—to keep to oneself egotistically the windfalls that come along; and as Fil'd'Acier said to himself that fire often serves to cook aliments, he concluded that there might be something to eat out there. Now, it might be that the famous adage "When there is enough for one there is enough for two" is true, but there might perhaps not be enough for six. After having made sure that his excellent friends were snoring or breathing evenly in the most profound slumber, Fil-d'Acier decided to go and see for himself what it was.

He commenced by undressing himself carefully, for two reasons. The first was that he did not want to get his garments wet, which had only just dried out; the second was that he wanted to be ready, in case of alert, to slip away like an eel.

And he slid into the water, silently, swimming just under the surface with the mastery of an expert.

But darkness can be treacherous. The light, which seemed so close, drew away as he advanced.

Fortunately, the air was calm and the water warm, and Fil-d'Acier was able, by executing familiar strokes, to go forward for a long time.

Finally, he perceived a black mass looming up in the silvery waves. Above the said mass were slender and delicate outlines that could not be anything but trees; and between the trees was the light in question, which was now magnified into a butterfly of white glare.

As prudent as a sea-serpent, Fil-d'Acier dived, and then, returning to the surface, he caught hold of the shore and hoisted himself up very slowly, so that only his head emerged from the water . . .

And for the second time, Fil-d'Acier shivered.

You might think that was because he was cold . . . or perhaps you suppose, in your overheated imagination, that he had just caught sight of savages ornamented with feathers, eating some unfortunate matelot, roasted over a bright fire by torchlight . . .

Wrong!

He had just observed that the light, the famous light, was quite simply the flame of an oil-lamp. And next to that lamp . . .

In truth, the thing is unbelievable, but you will see that the matter has been proven . . .

Next to that lamp was a back . . . a naked back, with its accessories. The accessories were posed on a block of stone. It was a white, sound, firm back with sinuous curves, shoulder-blades and rotundities . . . a plump, robust, lush back . . . in sum, a creamy egg-white back . . . and a nape, and a head with shiny black hair, a woman's hair. It was a woman's back! A whole woman!

With the boldness that distinguished him. Fil-d'Acier let himself fall into the depths, not without murmuring, profoundly: "Let's make the tour!" That thought had come to him entirely naturally.

Certainly, if it had only been a question of making the tour in question, I would refrain from taxing him with precipitation, but it was the islet that it was necessary to circumnavigate.

Now, it is known that certain islands, like Sicily and Sardinia, are large enough for that exercise to require a long time; but whoever risks nothing . . .

So, Fil-d'Acier who felt entirely fit and full of flexibility, started swimming along the shore. A few paces away—I ought to say arm's-lengths—he discovered an inlet hollowed out in the strand. He went into it. The light still guided him; he distinguished the oil-lamp more clearly. He saw that it was perched on a rather broad base, with a bulky reservoir and a plump glass—and no lampshade!

Finally . . .

Oh, I would willingly implore the muse, but it's so passé . . .

He saw everything,

He had made the tour.

He contemplated the façade of the edifice. What architecture! Neither the Dorian order nor the Corinthian . . . some fantastic composite, with elements of the Egyptian sphinx and the Trajan column . . . To say everything, a superb bust, ornate and rounded . . . very rounded . . . Arms and shoulders . . . !

Enough! Enough!

And the woman, as nude in face as in profile, leaning forward slightly, was delivering herself—an innocent occupation!—to a work of couture, just like *Jenny l'ouvrière* . . .[1]

She was pulling the needle with a gentle gesture of exquisite regularity, illuminated by the lamplight that put warm and nacreous tints upon her skin . . . and that under a splendid sky, framed by plants that evidently had the right to be termed exotic.

---

1 *Jenny l'ouvrière* [Jenny the Seamstress] (1850) was a successful drama by Adrien Decourcelle and Jules Barbier, which conferred iconic status on its heroine.

Sapristi! That's something you don't see every day!

You will admit that in consequence of such an occurrence, one cannot maintain an absolute sang-froid. And you will not protest too loudly on learning that Fil-d'Acier—in the interests of his companions, of course—hastened to leap on to the shore and run toward the vegetation in question.

Now, he was completely naked; and he presented himself before a woman who was no less naked.

She saw him, and uttered a little scream. She blushed from the roots of her hair to the tips of her toes, which one rarely sees.

Fil-d'Acier bowed. "A thousand pardons Madame," he said, "for disturbing you . . ."

"Who are you, Monsieur? No . . . I don't want to know. Go away. We haven't been introduced."

Increasingly respectful. Fil-d'Acier bowed again, deeply; then, straightening up militarily, he said: "I have a diplomatic character."

"Diplo . . ."

"Matic. I'm an ambassador."

"Oh! A savage!" cried the lady, standing up and taking a step backwards.

Fil'd'Acier smiled broadly.

"Madame is in error . . . not savage at all. My name is Cloarek, Yvon for the ladies, cabin boy second-class aboard the *Rigolette* . . . at your service, if able to be of any."

Faced with such distinguished manners, the lady curtsied and said: "My name is Danaé, Madame Lamboursade . . ."

"Damn! The wife of the ship-owner! But I never saw you on board."

The lady lowered her eyes. "My husband made me swear not to present myself to the males aboard the ship. I was faithful to the word given, and this is the first time that . . ."

Yvon did not blink, in spite of the desire to laugh that was tickling his throat. It was the first time that she had presented herself to the crew! Well, between us, hers was a singular choice of costume.

As Yvon seemed visibly fatigued, the charming and shapely Danaé indicated a stone to him on the far side of the lamp, "Sit down, I beg you."

"Madame is too kind."

One might have thought they were in an upper-class drawing room.

"My God, Madame," said Yvon, crossing his legs, "will you be good enough to tell me to what fortunate circumstances you owe your salvation?"

"Gladly, Monsieur. At the moment when the ship sank, I was in my cabin, as usual, in the process of darning Monsieur Lamboursade's socks . . ."

"Your fortunate spouse . . ."

"My spouse. As he feared that I might get bored during the crossing, he had filled a trunk with holed socks—two hundred and thirty-three pairs. I was on the fifty-second pair when I heard the sinister cry ring out: "Save themselves who can!"

"Which you did, in fact, do . . ."

"Moderately. Monsieur Lamboursade, who is a great philosopher, had fortunately developed within me precious qualities of sang-froid. My spouse has for a motto words whose profundity you will easily understand: *Do what is necessary*."

To prove that he understood, Yvon made the victorious gesture of a man sticking his thumbs into his belt.

"Continue, Madam, I beg you."

The lady had resumed her modest attitude and would have been able to sing, over Monsieur Lamboursade's socks, the celebrated ballad *Run, my needle, through the wool*.

"My spouse venerated as a principle that, in the gravest circumstances, it is necessary not to recoil before any sacrifice in order to get out of difficulty. Thus, in the time when he was navigating, he did not hesitate to throw into the sea, in order to lighten a ship beaten by a tempest, two hundred negroes, the brightest part of his fortune . . ."

"Monsieur Lamboursade is a wise man . . ."

"And I flatter myself that I have profited from his lessons. In short, as the water invaded my cabin, I reasoned as follows: I've read that Virginie, the fiancée of Paul, had drowned during the sinking of the *Saint-Laurent* . . ."

As she hesitated to finish, Fil-d'Acier, who knew his literature, added: "Because she had refused to take her clothes off . . ."

"Exactly. Oh, far be it from me not to recognize the sanctity of modesty. Monsieur Lamboursade knows that . . ."

"Ah!" said Yvon, simply.

"So, remembering the precept *Do what is necessary,* I hastened to quit the veils . . ."

". . . That enveloped your beauty."

"And, opening my cabin door abruptly, I allowed myself to be seized by the waves . . ."

"Lucky waves!" said Yvon, with a smile of exquisite delicacy.

There was a moment of embarrassment; Madame Lamboursade would have liked to have had a torsade, a switch to twist between her fingers by way of countenance. She made the simulacrum of that gesture, but it lacked fabric.

"And was the wave amiable?" Yvon asked.

"Oh, what a wave, Monsieur; what delicacy, what politeness! A gentlemanly wave!"

"One of us," said the cabin boy, miming the gesture of placing an opera hat under his arm.

"In brief, it deposited me gently on the reef where we presently find ourselves . . . But what about you, Monsieur?"

"We'll talk about me in a little while, if you wish. First, I'd like to apologize for this slightly scanty costume . . ."

"Oh, what is necessary is necessary! At first sight, I admit, I was shocked, but the sane philosophy of Monsieur Lamboursade returned me to myself . . ."

"I thank you! Now, will you permit me to ask two questions?"

"Certainly."

"Where did you get that oil lamp?"

"It was a gift that Monsieur Lamboursade gave me on our wedding day. It never quits me, and as it is necessary to expect anything, I took a few precautions in view of a possible accident. I packed it in an impermeable box before leaving my homeland. Look!"

She bent down, which caused the excellent Yvon to blink again in the virginity of his impressions, and she drew an oblong box toward her, sheathed with rubber, with a space in the interior for an oil lamp, and a little compartment for wicks and scissors: a marvel of industrial art.

"When I delivered my body to the fury of the waves," she added, "I told myself that I might be obliged to charm by labor the leisure of long evenings, and having introduced into the box a few pairs of socks and everything necessary for darning, I attached the box to my wrist with a piece of string . . ."

"And the gentlemanly wave brought everything safely to port . . ."

"Exactly."

Yvon said to himself that the strong woman who answered to the name of Danaé would have done well to substitute for the socks a calico skirt and, a chemise: a rudimentary costume . . . but he reflected that on a desert island, it is better to occupy oneself in the nude than get bored fully dressed.

"A second question, since you permit . . ."

"At your service."

"Have you dined?"

In saying that, Yvon, eyeing the lush charms of the beautiful Danaé, awarded her secretly a patent for a beautiful fork . . .

"Well, I believe so."

"But what? When? How?"

"A wave . . ."

"The same one?"

"No, one of its colleagues."

"Go on."

". . . Pushed to the shore, moments after me, a crate full of tins of conserves and a few bottles of choice wine. Only bread was lacking."

"Where did all that come from?"

"My cabin. The crate was given to me by Monsieur Lamboursade . . ."

"On your wedding day?"

"Joker! On the day of my departure . . . When I threw myself into the abyss, I had thrown it into the water on the off chance. But now I think about it, perhaps you didn't take a similar precaution . . ."

"I confess that I did not."

"You haven't dined?"

"Nothing! Nothing at all! And since you ask me so amicably, I confess to you that I'm literally dying of hunger."

"Oh, you poor young man. Quickly, quickly!"

Women, even in the primitive costume of our mother Eve, are good souls. Danaé was one of the best. What an admirable housewife she must have been for Monsieur Lamboursade!

Promptly, with cat-like movements, she disposed a place-setting before Fil-d'Acier. He tried to aid her, but it was as if she were still in her own home, serving Monsieur Lamboursade. See what true virtue is! Not the slightest embarrassment. There are women who would have punctuated it with a "Good Heavens" here and a "Oh my God" there, but Danaé, calmly moving around her little islet, arranged everything—jellied partridge and Provençal mushrooms—with exquisite attentions, and with what grace! Her elbow a little high, she poured Yvon Cloarek—who, being the son of his father, did not complain at all—a sparkling trickle of ruby wine.

Fil-d'Acier was delighted. I dare say that he feasted like a little god. The partridge vanished, the mushrooms disappeared and the bottle emptied under the amiable gaze of Danaé—who, between us, had beautiful dark eyes—who tapped him on the shoulder occasionally to engage him to keep going.

But how the slightest imprudence can compromise the best-established situations! Yvon was certainly well-installed; everything was going swimmingly, and he had nothing else to desire, but that devil of a partridge was spicy, and the mushrooms, with their Provençal seasoning, were so hot! The wine descended so adorably into the stomach of the cabin boy, who was getting on for eighteen years old . . . that, in truth, he suddenly felt a little tickling, not disagreeable at all . . . and his eyes glinted . . . and . . .

You get my drift.

As Danaé leaned over to fill his glass, Yvon suddenly reached out a thin and muscular arm, which wound around Madame Lamboursade's waist . . .

Oh, it only lasted for a fraction of a second . . .

Danaé straightened up, her eyes flashing, her face crimson.

"What do you take me for?" she cried. "You're a wretch! Get out . . . I want you to leave!"

When someone expels you from a desert island, the sole means of excusing yourself is to effect a dive, and at the end of a meal, that can be dangerous.

It was necessary to repair the damage.

Fil-d'Acier stood up and then bowed, putting one knee on the ground

"Oh, my benefactress," he said, very humbly, "forgive my youth, my inexperience . . ."

There was a silence.

Danaé was angry—oh, very angry.

"How, Monsieur," she said, "were you able to lose the respect that you owe me to that extent . . . ?"

"I beg your pardon!"

"I am the legitimate wife—legitimate, you hear?—of Monsieur Lamboursade, a serious man who has never let me lack anything . . ."

"I venerate him!"

"And you take me for . . . for what? For a hetaira! For a vile courtesan!"

"Mercy! Mercy!"

"Know this, Monsieur: that no one—no one, you hear!—has ever touched the tip of my little finger except for Monsieur Lamboursade, who has recognized rights. Oh, if he knew what has just happened, he would kill you . . . he would kill you, Monsieur! What am I saying? I would be the first to cry: 'That man has insulted your wife: strike!'"

Yvon prostrated himself in the dust, which showed him the whites of Danaé's increasingly angry eyes.

Yvon made the most humble apologies.

Danaé hesitated; then she remembered Monsieur Lamboursade's precept. Certainly, she should have called out, and had the impertinent fellow thrown out, but on a desert island, forgiveness was imposed. It was necessary to do what was necessary.

"Get up," she said, in a grave voice. "I'll forget it."

Yvon prostrated himself more forcefully, indicating by his pantomime that he would have liked the ground to swallow him. Then, crestfallen and pitiable, he got up and, still bowing, headed for the shore. But there, the wine aiding, his strength failed and he fell full length on a bed of seaweed.

A moment later, only a sonorous snoring troubled the silence of the night.

Meanwhile, Danaé sat down gravely next to the lamp of fidelity, and heroically blocked the holes through which Monsieur Laboursade's powerful toenails had frayed a passage.

Dawn came.

Danaé was no longer darning. She had lowered her head and was profoundly asleep—but she was not snoring.

Fil-d'Acier woke up with a start, blinking, and saw Danaé, who, simultaneously coquettish and prodigal, had placed a leaf from a tree in her hair.

He remembered. The dinner had been good, but things had finished badly. He had committed what is vulgarly called a blunder. Evidently, Madame Laboursade was honest—very honest. If she was also undressed, it was without any seductive intention. One does what is necessary.

Would she retain any rancor against him? That was serious.

Suddenly, a horrible thought crossed Yvon's mind. He had eaten! He had stuffed himself! Let us admit that he had not come off badly. But what about Tête-de-Loup? What about the others?

"Sapristi! What about the comrades?" exclaimed Fil-d'Acier.

Danaé heard his voice. Indulgent, having already forgotten the child's aberration, she ran toward him.

"What's the matter?"

"I'm a wretch!"

Danaé thought it was an allusion. She blushed again. "Don't think about that any more."

"You don't understand . . ."

"What?"

"While I was guzzling mushrooms, the others might have been dying of hunger . . ."

"What others?"

"My comrades . . . castaways like me."

Immediately, Danaé's charitable soul was excited to the highest degree. She demanded explanations.

Fil-d'Acier, his throat dry with remorse, articulated, with

difficulty, the names of his friends: "Tête-de-Loup, Onésime Bardurot, alias Petit-Corbeau, Hector de Durplastron and Eusèbe Cartilas."

And as he named them, he imagined that he was deciphering inscriptions on a tombstone, and tore his hair conscientiously.

"Come on, come on," said Madame Lamboursade, maternally, "it's necessary not to despair like that. Go in search of your friends . . . and make them welcome here . . ."

"But what if it's too late?"

"It's never too late."

"You're an angel!"

And as Fil d'Acier had raised his eyes toward the heaves as he launched that evocation, his gaze passed over the lentisks—were they really lentisks?—that formed a curtain, and he uttered a cry of surprise.

Some distance from the islet, fifty meters at the most, a black mass emerged from the water.

"The *Rigolette,*" he cried.

It was true.

The sea, raising the ship, had gradually pushed it toward the shore and had lifted it on to a sand-bank. The *Rigolette* had seen the daylight again!

But that was salvation! It was life!

Certainly, the crate of conserves conveyed by Danaé's intelligent prudence, had its charm, but how long would it have lasted in confrontation with six formidable appetites, sharpened every morning by the saline wind blowing from the horizon? Whereas the *Rigolette* contained within her flanks mountains of victuals and exquisite wines . . . not to mention tools and building materials . . .

"I'll be able to dress myself!" cried Danaé.

Modesty spoke first; French gallantry replied: "A dress doesn't make happiness."

"Get away, shut up! Come on, tell me, is it better on your islet than mine?"

"No, no . . . here there are trees, a delightful island . . . there it's just bare rock, disagreeable . . ."

"Well, let's not waste a minute. Go and fetch your friends . . . but offer them my apologies because I can't dress to receive them . . ."

✳

The wretch who denies providence will have to deal with me!

Did it not give at that moment admirable proof of solicitude for the unfortunate?

When Fil-d'Acier landed on the rock he was frightened a first. Of the four survivors of the *Rigolette*, two—the sub-prefect and the seminarian—no longer gave sign of life, sprawled on the hard stone. Tête-de-Loup, in a state of frightful excitement, was grinding his teeth and launching furious gestures with his fist at the heavens. As for the scientist, he was making a little packet of underwear, which he had been asked to do.

Yvon ran to Tête-de-Loup, who launched such a punch at him that if it had reached him, Fil-d'Acier would never have eaten mushrooms *à la Provençale* again.

He leapt sideways and shouted: "Pay attention, Tête-de-Loup, we can eat!"

"Eh?"

We can eat . . . and smoke!"

"Damn it! Explain yourself, toad!"

The toad explained. Tête-de-Loup wanted to throw himself into the water right away. Yvon held him back. It was necessary not to be selfish. Onésime, Hector and Eusèbe could not be abandoned.

"Well, let's pick them up then. Ahoy! Hoist!"

Tête-de-Loup took hold of the seminarian by the legs of his trousers; Yvon took the sub-prefect by the collar and, *en route!*

The scientist came as well; he wasn't heavy!

And into the water! We shall willingly leave out the details of that marine odyssey, and arrive immediately at the psychological moment—which is to say, the charming moment when Danaé, advancing along the sandy strand, came toward her guests,

The woman certainly knew how to welcome people. Of course, Madame, it isn't difficult for you, in your drawing room, in the midst of elegant bibelots, nicely draped in a dress from the latest couturier, to show an exquisite grace and distinction . . . but don't forget that Danaé could not devote herself to any showy effect. My word, I wish you could have seen it.

Nothing is more difficult to wear than . . . nothing at all, save for very special circumstances on which my well-known discretion forbids me to insist.

Well, Madame Lamboursade had a simplicity of manner and a calm dignity that many women would have envied. But as she drew nearer, with a smile on her lips and her hand extended, Tête-de-Loup, who was in the lead, having seen that nymph, that siren—who did not end in a fish's tail—uttered by way of a hymn of admiration the dirtiest oath in his repertoire, and *bang!* he plunged, emotionally, along with Onésime and Eusèbe.

"Be careful, old chap!" cried Fil-d'Acier, who made an effort and threw Hector de Durplastron on to the shore. Then he dived again and emerged, bringing back the scientist, who was no longer anything more than a spongy rag.

Tête-de-Loup reappeared, pulling the seminarian.

Finally, all the characters had arrived safely—but great gods, in what a state!

Tête-de-Loup leapt to his feet first, alongside Yvon, who took him by the hand, took a step toward Danaé and proceeded with a first formal introduction.

"Be welcome, Monsieur," said Danaé, graciously.

Tête-de-Loup mangled his words incoherently having no more saliva; his eyes were wide open.

Sapristi! What a beautiful woman . . . !

But the others!

Fil-d'Acier lifted up the sub-prefect. Hector, whose side-whiskers were hanging down along his cheeks like two parcels, saw Danaé. He made a slight movement of surprise; but he had his opera hat under his arm and his unmovable rosette starred his buttonhole. He bowed correctly.

"Believe, Monsieur," said Danaé, "that I am pleased and flattered to receive a representative of the French administration . . ."

Very good, Danaé! Few ministers' wives would have had such chic in the same costume.

Then it was the seminarian's turn. Oh, that one, whom the water had rendered apple-green, passed through all the hues of the rainbow in a second. He had never seen a naked woman before, except for the statues in the Louvre, and it seemed to him, vaguely, that the actual lady was more complete. But timidity! Decency! The haggard Petit-Corbeau was in a pitiful state.

"Monsieur," Danaé said to him, "it is a stroke of luck for me to be able to offer hospitality to a champion of our holy religion . . ."

Onésime interrupted her with gesticulations, multiplying signs of the cross, muttering between his teeth: "*Vade retro, Satanas.*"

The scientist was more correct. His little mouth contracted in an ugly moue, but it had the pretention of being a smile, and he cut short all conversation by picking off a sea-snail that had clung to his knee.

"If these Messieurs would be kind enough to follow me," said Danaé, "I'll offer them a meal that, I hope, will help them to recover from their fatigue."

She was charming.

She turned round like Richelieu showing the route to his king.

Tête-de-Loup was dazzled. That plump torso put shivers in his backbone.

The sub-prefect had leapt forward and offered his arm to his hostess.

A few minutes later, all the castaways were installed around a stone forming a table, and their teeth were quietly doing battle.

Danaé did the honors with an exquisite grace.

After the meal, they held council.

It was now a matter of pushing on as far as the *Rigolette* and taking therefrom everything that might be useful to their little colony.

They could scarcely count on Petit-Corbeau, Eusèbe or Hector, but Fil-d'Acier and Tête-de-Loup were as solid as pillars. They did not lose any time, and before the end of the day, thanks to the coming-and-going that they had established between the *Rigolette* and the islet, they had brought to firm ground a respectable quantity of crates of biscuits, tins of conserves and barrels of pickles, not to mention a veritable cellar of superior vintages—in short, a whole museum of victuals. There was enough to nourish the colony for a year.

There were weapons for hunting, nets and harpoons for fishing, culinary utensils borrowed from the ship's galley, chairs, tables, chests of drawers, beds and mattresses; nothing was lacking, All of it had been damaged somewhat by the sea-water, but that was a matter for the sun, which dried out everything.

For three days the two matelots were prodigiously active. Hector and Onésime had consented to lend a hand, but were not much use.

Let us not forget to mention Madame Lamboursade's trunks, which permitted her to recover her clothes; she hastened to resume her appearance as a woman of the world. In truth, they were so busy that they had scarcely paid attention.

As it was to be feared that the weather would not always remain so benign, it had seemed urgent to make sure of a shelter for bad days. Naturally, the *Rigolette* had furnished the necessary wood and tools, including an abundant supply of axes, saws and other implements.

Tête-de-Loup and Fil-d'Acier had built a kind of long cabin, divided into three compartments. One was the private apartment of Madame Lamboursade, a bedroom that Fil-d'Acier had disposed with an exquisite grace and which the lady, with the innate tact of her sex, had equipped in a marvelous fashion. There were curtains, carpets, a little desk with copper fittings, a low armchair—what do I know? It was a true boudoir.

The second room was the dormitory of the male castaways.

Finally, a third played the part of a drawing room or refectory; that was where they came together for meals.

All that was very solid, well-covered and well-closed.

In truth, one wonders what the castaways lacked, who found themselves in clover.

On the eighth day, the wind blew hard. The sea was agitated for twenty-four hours. The whole society was snugly ensconced, and did not care a straw about the tempest. And when they perceived, the following morning, that the *Rigolette* had sunk again during the night, the ingrates were tempted to wish her *bon voyage*.

Have I mentioned yet that they had discovered a delectable fresh water spring on the islet? Have I mentioned that Tête-de-Loup had plenty of tobacco? Have I mentioned that Eusèbe had found a grotto in which the most oddly-formed sea-creatures accumulated? Have I mentioned that Hector, having recovered a box of paper, had formed a ministry, so that he could spend his leisure writing petitions to himself?

Have I mentioned, finally, that Onésime had to hand a copy of *The Imitation of Christ*, which he first read in the orthodox manner and then read backwards, in order to penetrate the spirit more fully?

I shall pass over such matters, and better ones.

To tell the truth, Île Danaé, as it had been baptized, was a veritable paradise.

In the morning, Danaé prepared a delicious moka, which the exiles drank voluptuously. At midday, the first meal: meat, vegetables and coffee. At five o'clock, dinner *di primo cariello*, with a superb piece of poultry or fish, killed or fished up during the day, and at dessert a few glasses of fine wine. At nine o'clock, a light supper, sandwiches and tea.

You will understand that with that régime, our unfortunates only regretted their homeland slightly. They did nothing, leading the veritable existence of lizards. In the evening, by the light of her lamp, Danaé doggedly darned Monsieur Lamboursade's socks. As a treatise on trigonometry for naval usage had been found in the captain's cabin, Fil-d'Acier read aloud from it.

It was delightful: a life of patriarchs.

It was the fine season: there were only a few accidents, an occasional squall through which they passed well-sheltered.

It was only a matter of being patient; sooner or later a day would come when a ship would perceive the signal placed, in accordance with Robinsonesque custom, on top of a platform at the highest point of the island. But between us, patience was easy.

Eusèbe Carilas, entirely devoted to his biological and evolutionist research—for he was a fervent disciple of Darwin—had never felt so young.

Onésime, alias Petit-Corbeau, was full of unction; his paunch had rounded out and he gave the impression of a plump petty angel purring his prayers quietly.

Hector was handsome, noble and imposing. He pontificated. The idea had come to him to begin a considerable work: a statistical analysis of the reams of paper employed by the administrations of State from the reign of Louis XIV to the present day. He intended to prove by that means the incredible development of wealth and public tranquility. It is true that he lacked figures, as well as the primary elements to establish his accounts, but he had conceived the idea of genius of leaving the figures blank, intending to fill that slight lacuna as soon as the documents came to hand. He drew up superb tables, surmounted by titles in capital letters.

And time passed.

Tête-de-Loup smoked, chewed, hunted and fished, and Fil-d'Acier, in order to maintain the suppleness of his limbs, did gymnastic exercises on the strand.

There were no arguments, not a cloud in the ever-pure sky: it was Eden before the serpent.

Would the serpent appear? Alas, although improbable, it was fated. And once more, it was to prove that there is no perfect happiness on the earth. The storm was bound to break.

That Cockayne-like existence lasted nearly a month. Then, one morning, Tête-de-Loup, getting up suddenly at six o'clock, started uttering all the curses that he had in his vocabulary—and I can assure you that the cargo was serious.

"Why, what's the matter, old chap?" asked Fil d'Acier.

"It doesn't concern you . . ."

"You lack confidence; that's all right. Are you ill?"

"No . . . made of oak, of bronze, of steel!" And he thumped his chest with blows that resonated as if on an iron plate.

"However," said Yvon, "for you to groan like that, there must be something that's going awry . . ."

"Unless," grunted Tête-de-Loup, "there's something that's going too well . . ."

"What are you complaining about? The nourishment is good . . ."

"Excellent."

"The wine's perfect . . ."

"Exquisite."

"You have plenty of tobacco . . ."

"Yes."

"Well, what do you lack?"

Tête-de-Loup looked at Fil-d'Acier with his large eyes, which were shining like black diamonds. He opened his mouth as if to respond, but, shrugging his shoulders, he contented himself with launching a resounding "You're annoying me," and left the cabin.

What's up with him? Yvon wondered.

Curious, the cabin boy emerged stealthily behind him and did not take long to perceive that he was heading toward the sea.

A suicide! thought Fil-d'Acier.

No, it was simpler than that. Tête-de-Loup undressed in two ticks and dived into the bitter wave. He stayed there, splashing around, for half an hour and then came out of the water, dried himself in the wind, got dressed again and returned just in time for breakfast.

Fil-d'Acier examined him from the corner of his eye.

As usual, fresh, rosy and affable Danaé Lamboursade poured everyone the perfumed liquid. Her hand was plump; her rather broad sleeve allowed a sight of her white wrist and the beginning of her forearm. She was tastefully dressed. Her tight bodice modeled the richness of her bosom. She was a truly beautiful woman, with fine flesh, and attractive beyond all expression. And so good! She would not have hurt a fly!

Smiling, she had the chaste simplicity of Roman matrons, and never seemed annoyed in the slightest. She accepted the situation with a sterling philosophy; she rarely mentioned Monsieur Lamboursade, and never expressed untimely regrets. In addition, she ate well, drank moderately and might have been called a good egg.

Having addressed a few amiable words to each of her cast-away companions, as she did every morning, she noticed the slightly-altered physiognomy of Tête-de-Loup.

The fact is that, in spite of his morning bath, his face was congested; his cheeks were red and his eyes a little swollen.

She questioned him gently. But for the first time, Tête-de-Loup seemed peevish, almost disagreeable; he grunted unintelligibly.

"Come on," said Madame Lamboursade, maternally, "we're among friends. It's necessary to tell us the truth, frankly. Are you in pain? No. Then you desire something . . . ? We have nothing to refuse one another . . . I'm sure that these Messieurs agree with me. Whatever they can do to be agreeable to you, they'll hasten to do it . . ." And she added, with a childish inflection: "What does Monsieur lack? Tell the little lady. Oh, the bad boy . . ."

Tête-de-Loup shivered, which might have indicated a commencement of fever—unless it was something else . . .

"Monsieur," said Hector de Durplastron, with his customary correctness, "it seems to me that you can't refuse our amiable sovereign the information that . . ."

"Damn you! Leave me in peace, I tell you!"

Tête-de-Loup had said that rather hoarsely. The remark cast a chill. I cannot even affirm that Onésime did not make the sign of the cross.

But Danaé, who know the world of sailors—hot heads and good hearts—was not a woman to be troubled by so little.

Hector had adopted a stern expression. He, a functionary, had been insulted. He was already looking around, as if to search for a brigadier of the gendarmerie.

"Come on," said Danaé, "I can see that you're suffering. It's necessary to get some air. Go take a walk, my friend."

At this point, Eusèbe Cartilas intervened. "If my feeble knowledge can be useful to you, I'm a doctor of medicine . . ."

"Ah! You're right. We didn't think of that. Monsieur Laramé,"—you will remember that that was Tête-de-Loup' name—"show your tongue to Monsieur . . ."

"My tongue!" howled the helmsman.

"And come here so I can take your pulse . . ." And as Tête-de-Loup looked at him in bewilderment, the scientist added: "The best thing would be to leave me alone for a moment with Monsieur . . ."

Tête-de-Loup tried to protest; but Danaé, desirous of not prolonging the scene, which might have turned sour, made a sign to the others, who went out, leaving Tête-de-Loup alone with Eusèbe.

Only two minutes had gone by before Eusèbe emerged from the cabin precipitately, his arms raised, in an attitude of fear and stupefaction.

"Well, what is it?" cried all the voices anxiously.

"Cold baths! Cold baths!" Eusèbe responded. "There's nothing but cold baths . . . !"

It was impossible to get anything else out of him—professional secrecy, no doubt.

What was the mystery, then? as was once sung in vaudevilles.

I do not want to know what, in that short interview, had terrified the scientist. But I ought to add, to my great surprise, that Tête-de-Loup showed a docility to Eusèbe's advice that, in view of the precedents, would not have been expected of him. He spent his time in the water now, to the extent that it was necessary to make a detour if one did not want to find oneself confronted at any moment by the hairy torso and enormous legs of the former helmsman.

Oh, he was conscientious! He bathed and he bathed!

Whatever his malady, diathesis, idiosyncrasy or pathological state was, the regular treatment worked. Tête-de-Loup resumed his normal physiognomy. Furthermore—an important point—had not been sleeping recently; Fil-d'Acier, who had the next bed, heard him turning over continually, moaning. A heart that sighs does not have what it desires, as the song says. Now, however, Tête-de-Loup slept like a log, snoring like a spinning-top.

Would that amelioration last? A mystery!

✻

One night, Fil-d'Acier, who had taken a little drink at the evening meal, was letting himself drift, while still awake, in the cheerful dreams that youth provokes, when he seemed to hear a scarcely-perceptible movement at one of the ends of the dormitory.

What was happening there?

That was the corner where Onésime slept, whose health did not give rise to any anxiety, for he had never been fresher and more appetizing.

The seminarian had risen in rank. He had been promoted to seraphim.

Curious, Fil-d'Acier did not budge.

The noise recommenced, still faint. It was evident that, whatever he was doing, Onésime was taking every precaution not to be heard.

The dormitory was feebly illuminated by a night-light fueled by seal-oil, disposed in an old pedestal lamp. By that dubious glow, Fil-d'Acier could see something white moving in the place at which he was squinting attentively. That was simply Onésime in a nightshirt.

What was astonishing about that? There are people who have the mania of getting up during the night, and the explanation for that is perfectly natural . . .

Only . . .

Instead of going to the right, as the probabilities seemed to indicate, the white phantom, after having paused hesitantly on the edge of his bed, decided to stand up on his feet and, very slowly, started walking diagonally across the dormitory.

Where the devil can he be going? Fil-d'Acier wondered.

The strangest thing was that the night-light was suddenly extinguished. Evidently, Petit-Corbeau had blown it out.

Hmm. Interesting! Fil-d'Acier was intrigued, and peered into the darkness.

To his great surprise, he remarked a luminous ray that seemed to be springing from the wall and making a line in the darkness. From the wall? Fil-d'Acier immediately devoted himself to a topographical analysis, and realized that it was not the wall but a door . . . and the door was that of the room in which Danaé slept.

But how was the light filtering through it?

The door was closed inside by a large wooden bolt engaged in two grooves. There was no lock, and hence no keyhole.

Now the beam of light disappeared . . .

Immediately, Fil-d'Acier could no longer hold still. In his turn, he slipped out of bed and crept, like a veritable savage, toward the mysterious point.

He arrived, and in spite of the obscurity, he saw that Onésime—the child of the Lord, the future pastor of souls— quite distinctly, bent double, had applied his eye to a hole excavated in the wood . . .

Oh, the dirty swine!

Fil-d'Acier did not try to retain himself. He launched a kick that reached Onésime in the . . . bull's eye, saying to him in a low voice: "*In nomine patris . . .* !"

Onésime did not make a sound. He raised himself up slightly, pivoted on himself, and returned to his bed on all fours.

What the devil could he see? wondered Fil-d'Acier.

And resolutely, he applied his eye to the hole in question . . .

He licked his lips like a gourmet.

What he saw was, however, not entirely new for him; it was a landscape that had struck his gaze when he had first landed on the islet, before having made the tour of it . . .

"Damnation!" sighed Fil-d'Acier. And with that laconic exclamation, which translated his thought accurately, he got ready to return to his bed.

The thing was evident. That rogue Onésime had made a hole with a drill during the day, and he came by night to deliver himself to telescopic exercises . . .

Damn! Damn! Damn!

As Fil-d'Acier turned around he bumped into Hector de Duplastron's bed and, having stumbled, he placed his hands on the mattress in order to retain himself.

Stupor! The bed was empty.

Where the devil was the fellow?

He was not in the dormitory. He was not—*proh pudor!*—in Danaé's bedroom.

Fil-d'Acier was quite perplexed. Was Hector crouching somewhere?

The cabin boy set about making a tour, groping in all the corners, but found nothing . . . until, feeling the door with his fingertips, he found that it was ajar.

Hector had gone out. The functionary had permitted himself a leave without asking for permission.

Well, that was suspicious! Fil-d'Acier opened the door and slipped outside.

Fortunately, the night was mild, perfect weather for taking a stroll in tandem—a stroll that, in any case, was not very long. For—I blush to have to reveal such turpitudes—Fil-d'Acier had perceived Hector at the first glance, in his nightshirt, stuck to Danaé's window, his eye applied to the shutter.

Him too! Did he at least have his rosette? Evidently not. He was lacking in all tradition.

And he was so attentive, plunged so profoundly in a study

that certainly had nothing administrative about it that he did not hear Fil-d'Acier approaching on tiptoe . . .

The cabin boy leaned over and cried into his ear, in a stentorian voice: "Vive l'Empereur!"

Hector jumped, bowed, and then disappeared as fast as his legs could carry him into the cabin.

Faithful to his method of investigation, Fil-d'Acier looked for the drill-hole, found it, and looked through it.

The perspective was not the same, the angle being different, but it was no more disagreeable.

"Damn!" said Fil-d'Acier, who liked interjective language. And, tearing himself away from that contemplation, which required to be qualified by vehement adjectives, he stepped back, raising his eyes to the heaven, as if to take them as witnesses to his virtue.

Between the soil and the sky, however, there was the roof . . . so that his gaze, in its voyage toward the ether, encountered the lid of the cabin . . .

Fil-d'Acier started, murmuring: "What! A monkey!"

In fact, the mass, the black thing that he had glimpsed, had all the appearances of a pithecoid.

A monkey! But it was the first one that had been encountered on the island, and yet it had been explored in all directions . . .

A monkey, lying there on the roof, absolutely motionless . . . ?

It had the form, though . . . but not the color. It was white. Now, a white monkey has yet to be discovered!

Fil-d'Acier was increasingly perplexed. This night was definitely procuring him extraordinary sensations.

What was that animal?

Was it necessary to fetch a rifle and caress its spine with a few lead pellets? It did not seem to be animated by very ferocious intentions, though; its muzzle was stuck to the roof.

To the roof? No—to a small window fitted into the roof, in order to let the light of the sky into Danaé's bedroom . . . Danaé again!

As agile as a monkey, Fil-d'Acier could have competed with the most agile macaque. He did not hesitate. He suspended himself from the edge of the roof by his wrists, hoisted himself up . . . one, two . . . and fell upon the monkey.

The monkey uttered a cry and tumbled down. It was Eusébe Cartilas, the collector of crustaceans and holothurians, the luminary of science, that runt of a man extracted from a bottle, that pickled fetus!

Him too!

And blushing with shame for humankind, Fil-d'Acier returned to his bed.

Nothing was budging any longer in the dormitory.

Pensive, Fil-d'Acier did not fall asleep until morning.

✳

The next day, the day after, and an entire week passed without any new occurrence—except that at meal times, an embarrassed silence sometimes reigned. Where was the flood of words that had seemed impossible to stem?

Hector de Durplastron had read verses—yes, verses!—in which there was question of azure and stars.

Onésime, full of emotion, had attempted to recount the story of Sainte Thérèse, who was, as everyone knows, a glutton for divine love.

Eusèbe, remaining within his specialty, had explained how primitive beings procreated, in spite of asexuality, by binary fission.

Tête-de-Loup had let himself go, after drinking, singing the slightly lively refrain:

Not that Danaé Lamboursade took offense or complained. It is only light women who play the prude. She retained her soft smile on her crimson lips, her calm gaze and her immaculate dignity. She did not see anything, she did not divine anything, either of those formidable appetites, nor those surreptitious gazes, nor those menacing quivers . . .

For in the end . . . what happened, I shall tell you . . .

When one is on a desert island, one might be virtuous for many reasons.

The first, which is sufficient, is that, under penalty of not being deserted any longer, the island in question lacks women.

The second is that, because one eats diabolically there, one does not grow fat and one has no energy to expend for one's pleasure . . .

But here, it was quite different,

The nourishment of conserves and pickles was extraordinarily spicy; the wines were heady and did not only go to the head . . .

And Tête-de-Loup did his best but the cold baths could not prevail against an abstinence of several months . . .

The Imitation of Christ is necessarily stimulating, and it awoke in Onésime sensations that had nothing mystical about them . . .

And Hector had won a candidature for government by six hundred votes by means of getting, in three months, all the women on his side

And even Eusèbe Cartilas studied the mysteries of pisciculture at too close a range . . .

And to say everything in a word, Fil-d'Acier himself . . . !

Let us draw a veil!

*

One day, a commercial traveler returning from a tour of the départements handed his employer an account of his expenses that read:

> Breakfast . . . . 3 fr.
> Dinner 5
> Room 2.50
> Not being made of wood 8
> ————
> 18.50

The employer paid without making any comment.

Well, our heroes were not made of wood either.

And Danaé did not divine it.

She was always there, gracious, unconsciously coquettish: a ripe fruit summoning the teeth.

No, they were not made of wood; and gradually, life became intolerable.

Those five men, whom misfortune had brought together, and who ought to have been brothers, became enemies, Atrides. They exchanged sly, hateful, alarming glances. Knives quivered in their hands; they jostled one another when Danaé passed by; at night five pairs of eyes, as red as those of wolves, were aimed at her door.

A disaster was inevitable. It was evident that the men were going to devour one another.

The most terrible was Tête-de-Loup. He had meat, he had wine and he had tobacco: as Lafontaine says: "Good supper, good shelter . . . and the rest!" But the rest he did not have. And he was exploding in his cutaneous envelope, and seeing red.

One morning, he rushed upon the seminarian, doubtless to strangle him.

An hour later, Hector offered Eusèbe a glass of water in which he had infused old sous, but the cunning fellow, who was a chemist, while grinding his teeth, showed him his lancet, dipped in the fresh cadaver of a seal.

That a man would be dead in short order was not in doubt.

Behold, then, beings whom Providence had visibly protected, heaping them with all those gifts, who were not running any risk of dying of hunger, thirst or cold . . . and yet, there was a lacuna.

Death—murder—was lying in wait for them.

Another week, and there would have been a frightful slaughter.

Is all that possible? "Cold baths! Cold baths!" I would like to hear you shout . . .

It was necessary to make a great resolution. Note that it was the youngest, Yvon, who showed in all this the greatest clarity of mind.

One morning, he asked for an audience with Danaé.

She received him, as always, courteously and affably. She was, as always, darning one of Lamboursade's socks.

"Speak, my friend," she said, with the feminine majesty that had never quit her since their original encounter.

"Madame," said Fil-d'Acier, after a little cough to assure his voice, "the generosity that you have always testified to me has decided me to attempt in your regard a supreme step . . ."

"Supreme!"

"Yes, Madame, supreme. You appear not to be aware that we are all running the greatest peril . . ."

"Really?"

"Madame, five men are at death's door, and you alone—you alone, do you hear?—can save them."

She put the sock down on a little table and listened, attentively and emotionally.

What arguments Fil-d'Acier employed, in what colors he depicted the conflict and with what social, physiological or moral considerations he supported his thesis . . . I was not there, and I cannot tell you.

The conversation lasted for a long time; it required argument. It was a formal consultation. There were serious negotiations, argumentative jousts in which a few lances were broken. But Danaé was a woman of intelligence and courage. She could not allow five men who might still be useful to their country to perish before her eyes by virtue of poorly-understood scruples.

She repeated Lamboursade's famous dictum; do what is necessary.

And when Fil-d'Acier emerged from her room, when the castaways directed flamboyant gazes at him, he simply said:

"Madame Lamboursade awaits the doyen . . ."

And Eusèbe Cartilas went in first . . .

✳

The deportation of that interesting group lasted for another four months, but those four months were paradisal, eldoradic.

All constraint had vanished; the most cordial intimacy reigned between the members of the colony, who were no longer anything but a single family.

It was touching.

Danaé did not seem to begrudge the work of devotion and mercy to which she had so valiantly lent herself. Never capricious, never sulking, always attending to her duties, which she had understood with the serenity of great souls . . . in four months she could never be accused of a single act of nepotism, injustice or irregularity.

Once, Hector had the unfortunate whim of wanting for a moment to make the most of his governmental influence. His shame was of brief duration, and let us render him the justice that he recognized his mistake valiantly.

The clearest impartiality presided over that petty festival, which only ended on the day when a ship was spotted heading straight for the islet . . . it was flying the flag of the fatherland!

It was Lamboursade himself, who had charted a new *Rigolette*, commanded by the same Captain Van Crack . . . for not a single victim of the shipwreck had perished.

And Lambouersade, bounding on to the shore, took Danaé in his arms and only pronounced the words: "My wife!"

The five castaways came to shake his hand, saying to him: "Never, Monsieur, will you know how much we owe Madame . . ."

Well, yes, he knew!

And do you know what he did, that good-for-nothing, that imbecile, that miserable husband?

Did he not take it into his head to accuse Madame Lamboursade, on her own admission, of reiterated adultery!

And he dragged her before a tribunal.

Oh, it was a solemn day when the heroine appeared before her judges, her head held high . . .

She explained her case herself, without prevarication or reticence, with the complete conviction of a conscience that felt itself to be above vain suspicions. Sometimes, she was even able to raise herself to the highest regions of eloquence.

"What, *Messieurs le juges*," she cried, in a peroration that one newspaper qualified as sublime, "according to Monsieur Lamboursade's theory, I should have let those men perish who had testified so much regard to me! I should have witnessed their agony—who can tell?—in a supreme orgy of mutual murder! And that when, in order to save them, it was suffi-cient to . . . I shall not finish. I appeal to all wives!"

Applause burst forth in the courtroom.

The deliberation of the jury only lasted five minutes, and the president, in notifying Danaé of her acquittal, added these words, which will find an echo in all hearts:

"You are free, Madame, and I dare say that you will take away from here the esteem and gratitude of all honest persons." Then, turning to Lamboursade, he added: "As for you, Monsieur, I hope she forgives you!"

THE SATCHEL

> For a long time a desire so strange, so bizarre
> and so extraordinary has been urging and
> tormenting me that I would like to hide it
> from my own thoughts.
> (Cervantes)

I

AMONG the letters that my valet de chambre brought me this morning one struck me, by virtue of the tormented, almost hieroglyphic, handwriting of the address. It bore the postmark of Parcy-sur-Somme, an indication that said nothing to my memory. I opened it with all the others, moved by the unconscious curiosity that makes us divine a mystery, and I read the signature: Gaston Descorval, a former comrade at the *École de droit*, of whom I had lost sight long before; a rather singular fellow for whom I had once felt a keen sympathy, more instinctive than rational.

This is what he wrote to me:

> *If you have not forgotten me and if, in spite of*
> *a voluntary retreat, you have conserved a little of*
> *the amity that you once testified to me, I beg you to*
> *come to my aid. I am, by virtue of my own fault, by*

virtue of my crime, in the most horrible situation in which any human being can find himself—to say all, between suicide and despair.

I need your advice; I need to confess, to be judged by honest consciences. So I am appealing to you; and I beg you to ask Maurice Parent, whose address I don't know, to accompany you. I have not killed anyone or stolen anything; I have done less and worse. It isn't a matter of money, because I'm prepared to give my entire fortune to redeem my folly. I shall say no more. Don't try to understand; only say to yourselves, the two of you, that there is an unfortunate to save from the most frightful despair . . . and can even you do it?

Wire me your response; it's a sentence of life or death that I'm awaiting. Come!

G.D.

Certainly, the journey to which Gaston was inviting me was not one of those that frighten a man, and yet, taken by surprise, I felt scantly disposed, I confess, to respond so promptly to an appeal whose real motive escaped me, especially when I remembered always having remarked in my former comrade a turn of mind inclined to paradox and exaggeration.

However, rereading his letter, probably written in a fit of intense fever, I felt full of pity. Fearful of obeying a perhaps-unjustified alarm, I immediately went to see Maurice. Fortunately, he was at home. I told him briefly what had happened, having the weakness to dissimulate under a rather stupid irony the anxiety that, in spite of all my resistance, was becoming increasingly poignant.

"Have you replied?" Maurice asked.

"No."

"Well," he replied, gravely, "go to the nearest telegraph office; when you return I'll be ready, and we'll depart . . ."

"What! You've decided that, without reflecting?"

"I beg your pardon," said Maurice, "but I have reflected."

I had often talked to Maurice Parent, whose lucidity of mind, near to genius, and quasi-superhuman finesse exercised on all those who knew him an authority that no one thought of resisting. We compared him voluntarily to Edgar Poe's Dupin, and often had recourse to him as a kind of Oedipus for whom no sphinx had undecipherable enigmas. In fact, he had both a passion and a genius for observation, and more often than not he resolved problems by discovering an infinitesimal detail that had escaped everyone else. He was also benevolent and devoted, and loved struggling against the unknown. He only knew Gaston very slightly; but it was sufficient to determine him to intervene that he scented—if I might put it thus—the trail of a mystery.

I did not hesitate, therefore, to obey him, and an hour later we were outside the Gare du Nord, about to take an express and awaiting the time of the train.

I perceived that Maurice carefully avoided talking about the object of our preoccupation. We discussed indifferent subjects, installed in our own in a first-class compartment, until the locomotive whistle gave the signal for departure.

As soon as we had passed the first stations Maurice commenced: "Now, my friend, tell me the story of this Descorval, about whom I know very little and have not seen for five or six years, How old is he?"

"Between thirty-six and thirty-eight years."

"What has he been doing thus far?"

"I can only speak about the six or seven years during which I was acquainted with him in the Latin Quarter. As far as I could understand, he was an orphan whose parents, farmers in the Artois, had left him a rather tidy sum, an income of fifteen or twenty thousand. Having studied successfully at the college of Amiens, he came to Paris to do his law, very assiduously at first but gradually drawn away by the pleasures of a facile and idle existence. I don't even know whether he obtained his license."

"What was his character?"

"Difficult to define—for me, at least. A mixture of eccentricity and reason, sometimes very good, at other times almost nasty, having the kind of cold pleasantry that is often tinged with cruelty."

"Do you think him capable of a bad deed?"

"That depends what you mean. He says in his bizarre letter that he hasn't killed or stolen. I can believe that; for a start, he isn't energetic . . ."

"So be it—but I divine a reticence in your language. Incapable of a crime, possibly—but a villainy?"

"Perhaps the expression would still be too strong. Let's take an example. You recall the episode in *Les Misérables* in which a passer-by, to amuse himself and the gallery, plunges a snowball between Faustine's shoulders . . ."

"He'd do that?"

"Yes, but he'd repent of it a minute later and make any sacrifice to redeem his malevolent action."

"You see," said Parent, "that we're beginning to understand one another with regard to words . . ."

"More, perhaps, than fundamentally," I put in. "Nothing is more difficult, at least for me, than an analysis of character. The examples that come to my mind ring false. No, I've never known him to be cruel, at least in action . . . but this might be clearer: nothing amused him more, in our youthful conversations, than to take a false opinion to its foundation, to affirm an inexact fact, with such clarity and skill of explanation that he often won his case; people agreed with his opinion, and believed in his story . . . and the next day, it was a veritable joy for him to confess that he was making fun of us . . ."

"Fundamentally, a joker . . ."

"Almost. Here's a story that comes to mind. Among our comrades there was a poor fellow, one of those unfortunate for whom poverty lay in wait at the first door of life and would pursue him until the last exit, opening to death. His parents were dead, he only had an uncle in possession of a few sous, but who had declared long ago that he would disinherit him completely. The other was resigned to it; he worked very hard, giving lessons and making ends meet as best he could.

"One evening, at the brasserie, Gaston arrives, sits down, and, pretending not to see Clindot—that was the starveling's name—says in a loud voice: 'Well, do you know that the worthy Clindot is rich now? I've just come from my notary, who is also his uncle's; his uncle has died intestate, leaving forty thousand francs.'

"You san imagine the scene. Clindot, pale, more dead than alive, protests, declares it impossible, that he knows of the existence of a will. Gaston insists, says that he's charged with informing Clindot that he has to go to the notary's office on Monday morning—it's now Saturday evening. In sum, how can his veracity be doubted when, taking a stack of gold coins from his pocket, he offers Clindot an advance of a thousand francs? The poor fellow can't resist the temptation, much less the hope. There were twenty-four hours of mad joy . . . and on Monday he was thrown out of the notary's office unceremoniously. He wanted to kill Gaston, who had pulled his leg by lending him a thousand francs . . ."

Maurice had listened with the greatest attention, and when he remained silent I said: "Well, what idea does that give you of his character?"

"One of our novelists has judged him," Maurice replied.

"Who?"

"Frédéric Soulié. Reread *Les Mémoires du diable*. Among other types drawn from life but forgotten today, look for Ganguernet."

"I remember him. But Ganguernet is cheerful . . ."

"Straight-faced comedians are often more dangerous . . ."

The train sped on, and we soon stopped at the station of Logeneau, from which we were to render to Gaston's property.

II

We found a carriage at the station conducted by an aged domestic, who approached us and put himself at our disposal.

A moment later, we were going along the road at the trot of a fairly vigorous local nag.

It was October; autumn was advancing rapidly. In a fresh breeze, leaves were whirling around us; the sky was gray and sad—as sad as the man conducting us, who looked round from time to time, casting glances at us that were almost tearful.

"You're in Monsieur Descorval's service?" I asked him.

"I was in service with his father," said the man. "I've known him since he was born." Then, without waiting for a new question, he went on swiftly: "You messieurs are physicians, then?" he added, anxiously.

Maurice did not give me time to reply. "Is Monsieur Descorval very ill?"

"Oh, Messieurs, it's unbelievable . . . when he was so fresh and vigorous three months ago. It was a true pleasure to see him striding along the roads, fatiguing the keenest hunters . . ."

"And since then?"

"It was like a thunderclap. Suddenly he began getting thin and pale; no more appetite, no more strength. He no longer went out. One might have thought that he was afraid of setting foot outside. He stayed shut up in his room all the time, not wanting to see anyone. And believe me, who watched over him, when I tell you that I'm sure that he hasn't slept for a month. He tries to deceive me; he disturbs the bedclothes and thumps the pillows, but I've watched him, and I know that he spends every night pacing back and forth in his room, in bare feet so no one hears him . . ."

"And in your opinion," said Maurice, "what's wrong with him?"

"How do I know? I'm no scholar. Only . . ."

"Only what?"

"I don't know how to put it . . . one would think that my master has ideas in his head . . . something like chagrin or regret . . . and fear too. A fever! But you're messieurs from the city, you'll find that out much more easily than me . . . and you'll cure him, won't you?"

"You love your master?"

"Well, yes. He's a good man, something of a joker who likes to tease people, but whenever he thinks he's done harm to someone, he puts his hand in his pocket right away, and he isn't mean, I can tell you . . ."

We did not miss a word of that rambling—which, unfortunately, did not cast any light on the mystery that awaited us. The pensive man was now whipping his horse murderously, impatient to bring his master men in whom he had confidence. The road was long and bumpy, rather poorly maintained, and on a hillside.

"We're here," the man said.

"We had passed the few houses of a village—or, to put to better, a hamlet—when the vehicle stopped outside a sturdy grille beyond which an avenue of chestnuts extended. At the end was a house, white with green shutters, of modern construction, neat and well-maintained, of rich bourgeois appearance.

The carriage stopped before a perron. The coachman got down, took charge of our valises, and preceded us to open the door of a vestibule.

I was slightly astonished, I confess, that Gaston had not even taken the trouble to come to meet us. Rapidly, the man-servant made us traverse two large rooms and then showed us a door.

"He's in there," he said. "Go in—he's waiting for you." And he went away, leaving us alone in the almost bizarre, if not ridiculous, situation of intruders whom no one welcomes.

But Maurice was not a man to pause over such trivia. He knocked, and then, without waiting for a response, we went in.

The room into which we penetrated was plunged in the most profound obscurity; the shutters were hermetically sealed.

"Are you there, Gaston?" I called, amazed.

"Yes, come in," replied a voice whose strange tone caused me an inexpressible anxiety. "You've both come?"

"Yes, Maurice Parent and I have hastened in response to your appeal—and let me tell you that I'm a little surprised by the reception we've received . . ."

"Oh, yes, this obscurity!" the voice said. "Pardon me, but I'm suffering so much . . . only darkness soothes me . . . Wait!"

We heard trailing footsteps, then a rustle, as if tremulous hands were wandering over papers on a desk. Finally, there was the scrape of a match, and the flame of a candle, yellow and flickering, made a patch in the darkness. So indecisive was its radiance, though, that it showed us the gripping and alarming specter of an emaciated man with hollow cheeks and eyes sunk in their orbits: a terrible representation of despair and remorse, already struggling with death.

"Gaston! My dear Gaston!" I exclaimed, advancing toward him with my hands extended. "What's happening, then?"

Maurice, who was cooler, examined him attentively. Like me, doubtless, he remembered the strapping fellow of old, with the slightly doll-like face and the young and vigorous appearance. What a decline!

Meanwhile, Gaston had shaken our hands; then he made an effort to advance chairs; but I had seen immediately that his good intention no longer had any vigor at its service, and I spared him the trouble. "Well," I said to him, "here we are. You see that it's necessary not to despair of amity, and whatever the dolors are that are overwhelming you, I suppose that our presence will render you some confidence."

"Oh yes, thank you. I'm grateful to you . . . profoundly grateful . . . and I'll have further need for you to excuse me because, in truth, I don't know why I've summoned you . . ."

"What do you mean?"

"It was something like an impulse of folly, the stupid gesture of a drowning man trying to hang on to something . . . as if it were possible to save myself."

"We'll try to do that. Why shouldn't we succeed?"

"Why? Because it's impossible."

"You can't have thought so when you wrote to me."

"How do I know? Was I thinking? I was uttering a cry of anguish, of agony . . . without any hope of being heard."

"You're unjust. Our presence here is the proof of it."

"Pardon me," said Maurice, who had not yet pronounced a single word. "Permit me, Monsieur Descorval, since you were kind enough to think of me, to put a little order in our conversation, if possible." His voice, very precise and clear, lent a tone of reason to that slightly crazy dialogue.

Gaston turned toward him. Maurice went on: "I have a very positive mind, which believes in the power of logic. You're ill, my dear Monsieur, ill in body and mind. As we told your domestic, we have been summoned here for consultation, as friends and as physicians. Lament, cry, weep—so be it; but above all, tell me what you know about your malady. In other terms, you have a story to tell us. Why delay? We are not judges, and we do not have the pretention of setting ourselves up as confessors. You are facing men of good will who are ready to attempt anything to relieve you, to heal you. Imprudent or culpable, you do not have to fear reproaches or moralizing phrases. I have observed and experimented with life sufficiently to be convinced that anything is possible. Strange as your case might be, you do not have to fear surprising me. And now, calm down, take your time, use preambles as long as you please, employ any euphemisms and reticences that come to mind. Our duty is complicated by patience and perspicacity. We'll listen you whenever you wish."

Maurice had said all that in a serene, benevolent and persuasive tone. I remarked that Gaston's attitude, whose physiognomy, poorly illuminated by the vacillating candlelight, took on a calmer and attentive character.

"Would you prefer it," I added, "if we postponed the decisive conversation until tomorrow?"

"No, no," he said, swiftly. "Monsieur Maurice is right. I'm like those invalids who know themselves to be doomed but cannot forbid themselves a supreme hope. I lied just now when I seemed to withdraw the appeal that I addressed to you. I don't believe that salvation is possible, but I wanted to attempt that final effort . . . and if I hesitate to speak, it's less by reason of the probable futility of my confession than . . ."

He stopped, as if incapable of articulating another word.

At a sign from Maurice I respected his silence. We waited for a few minutes. I saw the invalid's hands clench and twist; he was struggling against I know not what force that was enchaining him, obliging him to keep quiet.

"The thing is," he said, in a dry voice, "that the confession I have to make is both ridiculous and shameful. I'm dying of not being able to speak the truth out loud, for fear of the atrocious humiliation that awaits me—but it's that confession you must receive. All that a man has of self-esteem, self-respect and dignity, is rebelling within me. When I begin to speak, I blush; I break out in cold sweat. It seems to me that before pronouncing the fatal word I shall drop dead before you . . ."

156

He stopped, doubtless expecting a reply that would lend new impetus to his speech. I had understood that Maurice was desirous that he fatigue himself with his own loquacity. We kept quiet.

Then, after a few seconds, Gaston made a violent gesture of decision. He pushed away the candlestick, so that his face remained in shadow, and it was in a low voice, hoarse with emotion, that he told us the following story.

III

"Three months ago," he said, "I went to Amiens to buy a few books. I was in perfect health, alert and brisk. Having achieved my objective, I was wandering through the town, killing time until I had to catch the train, when hazard led me to go past the Palais de Justice.

"Groups were gathered outside the grille; there was talk about the trial that was being judged therein. It was a session of the assizes. A woman exclaimed: 'Oh, that vagabond will surely get what he deserves!' And, sniggering, she drew her hand across her throat in a significant gesture.

"I looked at the clock. It was three o'clock. I had more than an hour to wait. I went through the grille and, an indifferent curiosity-seeker, my hands in my pockets, I went up the wide stone staircase, arrived in the vestibule, opened a door and found myself in the hall of the assizes.

"The crowd was not very compact. It was possible for me to advance to the front rank, where I stood, examining the various actors in the judiciary drama that was being played out before me.

"As chance would have it, the prosecutor knew me. He addressed a slight bow to me and, summoning an usher, had me conducted as far as the court, where I found myself very comfortably seated.

"Opposite me was the accused, whose interrogation was concluding.

"The man was horrible: an enormous head, with a large protruding jaw, a veritable mouth of a wild beast; on the head, a thicket of red hair, a fiery brushwood whose stiff twigs fell back over his forehead all the way to his squinting red-ringed eyes. The enormous shoulders revealed a colossal strength, and the hands, gripping the bar, resembled the paws of a ferocious beast.

"I shall tell you in a little while what happened within me; for the moment, I only want to tell you the facts in their brutal simplicity.

"The man was struggling courageously—or, rather, crudely—against the accusation. Listening attentively, this is what I understood:

"Two months before, on the twenty-ninth of May, a farmer returning from Craon had been murdered at the junction of the road that goes from Lambès to Suimes. The cadaver had been picked up still warm, with a mortal head-wound. The man had been killed by a single blow to the skull.

"People immediately set forth in all directions, and an hour later a man was arrested two kilometers from the theater of the assassination: Pierre Lhôte, known as Pierre Taureau, who was found drunk at the Trois Mages inn, half way to Lambès. When searched, he had the sum of twelve francs on him.

"He was a beggar, a vagabond of the worst species, much feared in the vicinity. The proof was acquired that on that same morning he had not possessed a centime. Public rumor had already accused him of several acts of violence. His hands were enormous and he carried a cudgel, a single blow from which was sufficient to stun the most vigorous man.

"The antecedents and the reputation of Pierre Taureau were detestable; everything justified the accusation brought against him. It was even proved that on the preceding market day at Craon he had been seen prowling around the farmer he was to kill a few days later.

"The moral proofs were abundant, but what supported the accusation better than any judiciary dissertation was the attitude of the wretch, whose visage sweated crime: an utter drunkard whose mouth was thickened by alcohol, who responded to the president's questions with an unexampled insolence and who, in short, confessed his guilt by his very denials. Several times the jeers of the audience had underlined his brutalities and he had raised his fist toward the back of the room with such a ferocious gaze that cries of sincere fright had responded to him.

"He denied everything, and kept on denying it.

"The witnesses filed past, bringing the support of their observations and their long acquaintance with the accused to the accusation.

"Only one matter remained obscure. The victim, someone had said, at the time of the murder, had been carrying a leather satchel suspended from his shoulder by a strap. The farmer must have taken to the market a sum of at least two hundred francs. The accused only had twelve francs on him and the satchel had not been found, any more than the rest of the money. The most careful searches had been fruitless; it was evident that the murderer had taken the precaution of putting the satchel and the money in a safe place . . .

"It was then that, scribbling a few words in haste on my card, I had it passed to the public minister. The prosecutor looked at me in surprise, addressed an interrogative sign to me to which I responded affirmatively, and charged an usher to give my card to the president.

"I had written these words: *I request to be heard, by courtesy of the discretionary power of the president, in order to furnish information of the greatest importance.*

"My name is known in the locale, where my family has been resident for a long time. In spite of the strangeness of my step, the president, after conferring with the defense and the prosecution, did not hesitate to defer to my desire. I was summoned to the bar.

"This was my deposition . . .

"But before anything else, in order to comprehend its importance, it's necessary that I explain the disposition of the places to you. I have told you that the road to Craon cuts the road from Lambès to Suimes at a right angle. The junction point, where the murder was committed, is known as the Croix-des-Sauts; the crossroads is shaded by trees dominated by a cross once erected in memory of an event now completely forgotten. The transversal road goes eastwards toward Lambès and westwards toward Suimes. Lambès is four kilometers away, Suimes about six. I suppose that explanation is clear enough. The murderer had been stopped two kilometers away in the direction of Lambès, which is to say, to the east.

"'Monsieur le president,' I said, 'my presence here is entirely due to chance; it is, therefore, with a profound surprise that I have observed, on listening to the debates, that I was in possession of information that, I believe, will change the face of this trial completely

"'I have just heard mention, several times, of a satchel belonging to the unfortunate victim of the murder at the Croix-des-Sauts. That satchel, it appears, was of black coarse leather with a copper armature. Now, on the evening of the twenty-ninth of May, at about half past seven, I was returning to my property in Parcy, following the Suimes road. The tribunal and Messieurs the jurors are doubtless not unaware that about five hundred meters from Suimes, on one side of the road, there is an old abandoned quarry, a sort of profound trench more than five meters deep, encumbered with stones, as if there had once been a landslide.

"'I was passing alongside that quarry at the aforesaid hour when my eye perceived a black dot about two meters from the edge. Driven by curiosity, I advanced, leaned over and I touched the object that had attracted my attention with the end of my cane. I succeeded in suspending it from the end of my cane and I saw that it was a black leather satchel with a copper fitting, manifestly empty. Without taking any further interest in that discovery, obviously valueless, I wound it around me cane and hurled it into the middle of the quarry, where it disappeared into the interstices between the stones.'

"Such were the facts that I brought to the attention of the court. The crime had been committed, it appears, at five o'clock. The presumed murderer had been arrested at six o'clock in the direction of Lambès. How could he have carried the satchel five kilometers from the Croix-des-Sauts in the direction of Suimes? I did not insist, delivering the facts to the sagacity of the magistrates.

"Hearing that, Pierre Taureau, with a cry of furious joy, had crushed the bar with a formidable blow of his fist, howling his innocence,

"The prosecutor, extremely vexed by my intervention, insinuated that there was no proof that it was the same satchel, but the accused's advocate, taking possession of my deposition, demanded an immediate investigation, a transportation of the tribunal and the jury to the place,

"The president—whom, I learned later, was not sorry, for personal reasons, to oppose the public ministry—came down on the side of the defense. The situation of the accused, who had not ceased his denials, changed completely. All sympathies were now on his side. The investigation was decided by the tribunal and the debates adjourned until the following day.

"The tribunal was transported to the quarry of Suimes, and there, on my indications, the satchel was found, damp and half-rotten. Someone affirmed that it really was that of the murdered man. The innocence of Pierre Taureau became evident, and the next day, when the hearing was resumed, the

public minister having abandoned the accusation, the man
was freed."

Descorval interrupted himself. We had listened to him
with the greatest care, but I confess that I had not found in
the story any of the clarifications that I had expected. Gaston
had done his duty, and that was all. Whence came his despair
and his shame?

I looked at Maurice in order to communicate my impression to him, but he was already speaking, addressing Gaston,

"Your deposition was false," he said to him.

IV

Gaston had a frisson that shook him completely, and I saw
him lower his head, as if those simple words had been an
expected verdict.

The most singular thing was that I experienced a sort of
disillusionment. The human mind is so made that, on first
indications, it immediately forges a theme from which it
does not intend to depart thereafter. Gaston's terrors, and his
pathological psychological state, had led me to create an entire
drama in which cowardice, treason and all villainies played
the principal role; and—shall I say it?—I was ready to pardon
him by reason of the interesting emotions I hoped to feel.

But that banal story of the court of assizes and that declaration, true or false, left me completely cold, and my enthusiasm had diminished in proportion. The urgent appeal that
had been addressed to us, the strange reception given to us, no
longer constituted for me anything but an almost-ridiculous
stage setting.

Meanwhile, Gaston did not continue his story; a numbing
embarrassment weighed upon us.

Once again, Maurice intervened: "If what remains for you
to say is more painful," he said, "it's better for you to finish it.

Confession is often a cauterization with a red hot iron; hesitation can, instead of a cure, lead to a more serious wound . . ."

"You're right," Gaston said, "but if I experience so much reluctance to speak, it's because nothing in harder for a man confess than his stupidity. You can obtain a confession of a crime from a guilty man more easily than the confession of a stupidity from an innocent one. But what's the point in hedging? My cowardice recoils in vain . . . I want to speak.

"I have always had an incredible penchant for practical jokes; I was well-known for it in the Latin Quarter. Nothing satisfied me more than astonishing an interlocutor by means of some plausible cleverness that my insistence and my aplomb made briefly into a verity . . ."

"I know, I know," Maurice put in.

"Now this, in my opinion, is the principle, at least in my case, of that mental predisposition. In my youth, in my childhood solitude, I had fits of ambition that were almost furious. I dreamed of immense, universal renown. I envied men whose names were on all lips, those whose exploits were recalled by legend through the centuries; one of my joys was to imagine, by a singular abstraction outside reality, that as I passed along the street, all the passers-by might point at me, saying 'That's him!'

"How I progressed gradually from that infantile fever to the stupidity of a grown man wanting to pass unperceived at any price is easy to deduce. Naturally idle, inapt for social struggle, loving repose and comfort, I had none of the strengths or qualities that command attention, nor even any talent of the second order—a superior skill in fencing, equitation, billiards, piquet, or whatever—that might conquer the admiration of a small number. My fortune, as mediocre as all my talent, condemned me not to surpass a certain level, and yet the desire to astonish—I cannot define that paltry ambition any better—subsisted in me, haunting me perpetually. Whenever I had succeeded in provoking an impulse of surprise, I felt proud, as if I had won a great victory. That passion, whose field of action was more restricted every day, took on such proportions within me that, in order to satisfy it, I could no longer spare myself. I became cruel, and had it not been for a natural pusillanimity I would have committed a crime to force attention, Erostratus, with his incendiary cowardice, must have been like me.[1]

"But the game became too dangerous. Several times, in Paris, I was attracted by bad affairs from which I had difficulty extracting myself with my honor intact. Although I understood that my conduct was sometimes odious, when I exercised my malevolent verve at the expense of the weak, and strove sincerely to correct myself, my vicious nature always triumphed. In those impulses of stupid malice, there was a force that seemed invincible. I have often acted badly, very badly.

"One day, despairing of triumphing over myself, I came to bury myself here. At least opportunities would be less frequent. Who was there to astonish here? My domestics, my valets de chambre, my cook? Oh, if I told you everything! In that solitude, I sometimes came to play a comedy with myself, to attempt to deceive myself, to trick myself. It's a folly like any other—unfortunately incurable, I'm convinced of it.

"I won't go on any longer, perhaps, even at this moment, trying to excite in you a sentiment of surprise. To be much scorned is still one of the forms of notoriety . . . You know enough now to understand what happened within me on the day that I'm talking about.

"As I've told you, I went into the court of assizes entirely by chance, without any other design than passing an idle

---

1 Erostratus, or Herostratus, became ironically notorious in history after setting fire to the temple of Artemis at Ephesus in the fourth century B.C. As a punishment, his judges are said to have invoked the law of *damnation memoriae*, forbidding the mention of his name—which ensured that the same, which might otherwise have been forgotten, was not merely remembered but became legendary.

hour. However, I experienced an initial satisfaction when I was introduced into the courtroom. I was not just anyone, a mere passer-by. People had looked at me when I came to take my place near the jury. My flattered vanity awoke the old dormant passion within me. I remember that I suddenly envied the president, dominating the audience with his red robe, the prosecutor, the witnesses, all those to whom general attention was successively attached, including the accused, the stupid murderer whose every response provoked a ripple in the auditorium.

"I felt an imperious need to stand up, to show myself, to make a speech. It would not have taken much for me to accuse myself in order to achieve a *coup de théatre*.

"But suddenly, listening to the debates, I was astonished to observe that, without knowing it, I was involved to a slight extent in the affair. This is how:

"On the day of the murder—of which I was complexly unaware—a few moments after the victim had been found, while returning from hunting, I had passed the crossroads of the Croix-des-Sauts. My foot had collided with something; I had bent down and I had picked up a black leather satchel with a copper armature. It was open, and empty.

"Mechanically, in a manner of banal play, I had suspended by the strap from the tip of my cane and I had gone straight ahead in the direction of Suimes. I arrived at the quarry that I mentioned a little while ago. The idea occurred to me of whirling the satchel at the end of my cane and throwing it as hard as I could into the middle of the stones. I saw it disappear. Then, without thinking about it any longer, I went home placidly.

"Now, that fact, trivial in itself, took on a capital importance in the context of the trial. And in my eyes, how I felt myself magnified! I had the life of the accused in my hands. Either I could tell the truth, in which case I could not dissimulate that I was slightly ridiculous. What else would the man be who, finding a satchel on the road, played with it like a child, carried it off like a trophy and threw it away like a true gamin? And then, if I said that, I would not produce any effect, since I would only be corroborating the accusation, taking away from the defense an argument of which people had already decided to take no account . . . Or I could lie . . . in which case everything changed its appearance. By proving that the murderer had taken the road to Suimes. I would destroy at a stroke the painstakingly-erected scaffolding of the case; I would put one over the magistrature, the court, the entire judiciary population. Like a successful advocate, I would return a murderer to society. There was a mischief on that side that filled me with delight. To trick the law, was that not an admirable triumph for intimate satisfaction?

"But there was something for me better than that Platonic triumph; there was the earth-shattering public effect of my deposition. By revealing the probable presence of the satchel in the quarry, inflicting upon the prosecution a denial without contradiction, I would become the focal point of all gazes; in my turn I would dominate the president, the jurors, the public minister. For a few moments, I would be the master, the *deus ex machina* . . .

"My hesitation did not last long. As soon as I began speaking, I heard the surprised murmur of the crowd, encouraging me with its astonishment, according me the desired importance. I understood that people were asking my name, which ran from the courtroom to the tribunes; I saw ladies craning their necks to get a better view of me. Then the president rendered homage to my impeccable honorability, emphasizing my social and moral situation. I was someone . . . and the murderer was acquitted . . ."

At this point I interrupted Gaston with a disappointed exclamation: "What! Is that all? Certainly, I can see a condemnable mischief in that, and I understand very well that your conscience might reproach you for a fantasy a little too vivid; but in sum, how could you know that the advocate would succeed in having his client acquitted? Less recommendable individuals have probably been saved . . . and your murderer is not the only one who is waking at liberty . . ."

Maurice stopped me with a gesture. "Wait before reaching a conclusion," he said. "I have reason to believe that the story is not yet finished/"

"No," said Gaston. "I haven't said everything yet."

"We're listening."

"Permit me first," said Gaston, turning in my direction, "to register the falsity of your overly optimistic appreciations. You judge me poorly. I have laid my conscience bare before you, and I have hidden none of the vices—the word is not too strong—whose existence I recognize within me: the excess of stupid vanity; the unjustified vainglory; the jealousy, if you like, of those who are above me.

"But on the other hand, I am not a man to lose the notion of the harm I do. When the fever induced in me by temptation fades away, I suffer, really and sincerely from the immediate or possible consequences of the acts committed.

"Thus, the day after the acquittal of the wretched Pierre Lhôte, I experienced a real remorse. He returned to the village of Lambès, reinstalled himself in the hut that served as his domicile, and recommenced roaming through the region, always begging, an object of repulsion and terror for everyone.

"It is necessary not to forget that that man had had the frightful energy to kill an inoffensive unfortunate in order to steal a few écus from him; it's necessary not to forget that he had felled him with a single blow, as a butcher does an ox, the cadaver of which he skins while still warm.

"Certainly, pleasantries are facile. To return a murderer to society, that phrase has a good effect when one does not know what has become of the criminal, when he is lost in the turbulence of a big city; but when the assassin is continually found in the passage of the man who, knowing him to be guilty, has saved him by means of a lie; when one has to fear incessantly that the ferocious beast might awaken and claim some new victim, can you not understand the terrible torture that that constant responsibility—what am I saying? that complicity—inflicts on you? For, when hazard puts him in my path and our gazes meet, I seem to read in his eyes an ironic thanks. He knows that I lied!

"And since that terrible day, I tremble every morning that public rumor might rise as far as me to bring me the news of a new crime. If he strikes again, am I not a murderer?

"I am enduring the frightful torture of sensing, close by, the latent crime, the crime that I have unleashed when the law had reduced it to impotence, the wild beast whose cage I have opened and who is roaming freely. Whom will he kill?

"I have attempted everything to liberate myself from that obsession. I have given him money—a great deal of money—for him to obtain an estate, to establish a commerce. Once sheltered from need, perhaps he might have mended his ways—but he has drunk my money, rolling from tavern to tavern, and once his intoxication has dissipated he has become a beggar and a vagabond again, still menacing.

"Then like a coward, I sought at least to remove that perpetual evocation of the crime from my sight, in order that I would no longer see him, that I would no longer be exposed to hearing the cry of a new victim—and that would have been a relief, egotistical, it's true, but profound. I've offered him a small fortune to expatriate himself, but he refused. The brute has the passion of the parish.

"And for two months I was subject to that anguish, that primal agony of continuous anxiety squeezing my heart by day and by night. If I went to sleep for an instant, I woke up suddenly, haggard and covered in cold sweat, with cries and groans in my ears. I saw the grimacing face of the murderer by my bedside, shaking my sheets with his blood-stained hands.

"However, time passed, and the impression was gradually diminished; there were intermittencies in my nightmares. Pierre Taureau continued his life of a wandering beast, but no plaint rose up against him. It was possible, after all, that the lesson had been severe and that he had profited from it . . .

"Then one morning . . ."

Gaston stopped suddenly, with a tremor so violent that it frightened us. Dreading an accident, perhaps a syncope, I seized the candle and approached it to his face.

He was even more livid than at our arrival; his convulsed features presented an alarming character of horror and super-human despair.

"But what remains for you to tell us?" I cried. "Has that wretch killed again? What frightful crime has suddenly reawak-ened your anguish, your remorse? Speak! Speak, then . . ."

Gaston raised his head, and we saw a dolorous sight: large tears springing from his eyes, the pupils of which were fed with insomnia, trickling down his cheeks in the wrinkles that suffering had hollowed out there.

Maurice, moved himself, took him by the hand. "Finish the confession," he said, "and if it is within the power of man to save you, I swear that you can count on me."

I knew by Maurice's tone that it was no vain promise; and I knew him well enough to know that he would only stop before the impossible.

"Thank you," said Gaston, softly. "This is it. One morning, my domestic told me—with a triumphant accent, alas—that a malefactor had been arrested the day before, and charged with the murder committed at the Croix-des-Sauts . . ."

We uttered an exclamation of surprise.

"Ah! You understand now," said Gaston, coming to his feet, tall and thin, as emaciated as a specter. "You understand the hideous significance of those words. Near the quarry, in a shack, a man lives with his wife and child: a journeyman earning his living with difficulty in ingrate daily labor, hiring himself out here and there, one of those jacks-of-all-trades known as handymen . . .

"Now, unknown to me, from the day when I declared—me, you understand—that I had seen the satchel in the quarry, without confessing that I was the one who had brought it there, suspicion had fallen on him. He had been watched, and finally he had been accused of having committed the crime that I know, personally, had been committed by someone else.

"It was me who had directed the stupid suspicion of the law toward him; I am his accuser, his calumniator . . . and for a month, by my fault, because of my crime, that unfortunate innocent has been groaning in prison, cursing fatality or Providence—what do I know?—without knowing that there is only one name that he ought to curse: mine! Mine . . . !"

And the wretched Descorval collapsed in an armchair, his head in his hands, sobbing . . .

I was terrified. That unexpected twist had fallen on my head like a cold shower. To have saved a criminal—my skepticism had adapted to that antisocial whim; but to be the cause of an innocent man's doom surpassed all measure.

He went on, energetically:

"You know everything now, and isn't it enough? It appears that the gravest presumptions—of which the point of departure is, don't forget, the discovery of the satchel a few meters from his dwelling—weigh upon that unfortunate. Oh, you know as well as I do what tiny details, what combinations of insignificant circumstances, can lead judiciary investigations to deduce. The police, believing that a false route was taken to begin with, have thrown themselves passionately on to that new trail. In a fortnight, a month at the most, that man will come before the assizes . . .

"And me, what will become of me in all that?

"This is my situation. I can keep quiet, remain confined in my lie, which renders me unassailable, and then that man, harassed by the public ministry, by witnesses that will show against him the same passion that they deployed against the other—that man against whom false charges will have been amassed, the combination of which will command conviction—will be condemned . . . to the galleys, perhaps to death, while I, breathless, dying of shame and remorse, brooding my cowardice and my ignominy, will be the prison-guard putting my hand on his shoulder . . .

"Tell me, is that possible?"

We kept quiet; our silence was a sufficient response.

"I can talk . . . that is my duty, I know, I sense it . . . well, listen: I would rather kill myself than endure that shame! Can you see me, before the judges, the jury and the audience, insulting and mocking, admitting that I lied, laying bare the paltriness of my conscience, the idiotic platitudes of my vainglory? That would necessitate a heroism of which I am incapable. I would rather confess to having killed or stolen than reveal that stupid baseness. Besides which, follow the consequences of my confession: pursuit for perjury, condemnation and dishonor. I'd be doomed forever . . .

"Such is the horrible alternative in which I'm struggling. I have a rope around my neck, and whatever I attempt in order to escape from it, the knot tightens and strangles me . . . !

"You know now why I summoned you. For a month I've been suffering to the point of screaming. I needed that confession; only you in all the world know the truth. I don't ask you to judge me, for I've pronounced sentence myself. I've decided to kill myself. Can you save me? I don't think so, and yet I'm interrogating you. Now I'll shut up; it's for you to speak . . ."

His voice died away in a sob.

And we remained silent, crushed by that terrible and unavoidable reality.

For me, Gaston had no other resource than suicide. Like him, I could not admit that he could resign himself to confess, at least while alive. I only thought that, before dying, he must address his declaration to the court, in a sealed envelope. Cadavers are not brought to trial; they would have pity on the madman who had punished himself, and silence would extend over that sinister adventure . . .

"First of all," said Maurice, "let's return to normality, I beg you. I hate nothing more than this material apparatus of despair with which you've surrounded yourself. What does this obscurity signify? What does this theatrical scenery of despair, complicated by an intimate vanity, portend? My dear Monsieur, I regret saying this, but I fear that you're posing before us. Whoever wants to have clear and sane ideas ought to live an ordinary and logical life. If you are mad, this pretention to premature burial can only augment the aberration of your brain. If, by virtue of your sin, you're reduced to suicide, well, look that eventuality in the face. Don't go to ground like a beast fearful of death. And on that note, will you please ring for your domestic and order that dinner be served to us, with lamps and candles, in a room that has nothing sepulchral about it, and prove that some courage remains within you by sitting down with us, like a sensible man who might have weakened, but who is ready for any sacrifice to redeem himself."

Maurice had pronounced those words in a dry, almost imperious voice, and although I could not see Gaston's physiognomy, I understood that the desired effect had been produced.

Gripped by self-esteem, ashamed of his pusillanimity, Gaston obeyed, and half an hour later, before the eyes of the bewildered domestic, stiffening himself against the fear that was clawing him, our host did the honors of the meal as best he could.

We chatted, carefully avoiding the subject that had assembled us, talking about Paris, the latest political and artistic events, so well that Gaston gradually joined in the conversation.

Nine o'clock surprised us still at table.

"I'm exhausted," Maurice said, "and I ask your permission to retire to my bedroom. As for your affair," he added, addressing Gaston in a casual manner that seemed almost shocking, "we'll talk about it at leisure. I only beg you to give me the newspapers that have rendered accounts of the trial; I'm certain that you must have collected them."

Gaston blushed and responded with a nod of the head. He went out and came back a moment later with a stack of newspapers.

"Good," said Maurice. "Now, bonsoir, until tomorrow! Try to sleep, Descorval. Insomnia is a poor counselor."

Maurice and I occupied adjacent rooms.

"Well, what do you think of all that?" I asked him, before quitting him.

"I think," said Maurice, "that if that man is forced to kill himself, there will be one imbecile fewer in France."

V

Left alone, I reflected. I was not under any illusion. Gaston had called us like an invalid condemned to have recourse to empirics.

The situation was no less simple for being original: a murderer freed, an innocent man imprisoned and threatened with capital punishment, all by the fault of a madman—for I could only tax with folly the incredible cerebral fantasy of my former study companion.

Knowing the fashion in which Maurice proceeded, I re-considered the terms of the problem one by one, and having installed myself at my table, pencil in hand, I made notes:

1. Pierre Taureau. What could be expected of him? He had escaped the merited punishment by a miracle, and it was improbable that, having always denied his guilt, he would now consent to tell the truth. I am familiar with the dispositions of the Code by virtue of which one cannot be charged twice with the same offence. It is thus that the murderer of Paul-Louis Courier,[1] once acquitted, was then able to confess his crime with impunity and serve as a witness against his accomplices—but that was a legal subtlety that a brute would never understand. However, it might be an ultimate resource. If he accused himself of the crime, Gaston would be saved, since the innocent man would be liberated. That remained to be seen . . .

2. The innocent man, whom I was obliged to designate as X, not knowing his name. Naturally, he would struggle with the energy of despair. And after all, he might be acquitted. The presence of the satchel in the quarry was not one of those material proofs before which all negations are futile. That the law was eager to follow that trail was natural, but other indications would be required to establish the culpability of the accused. Now, it was improbable that bad luck would pursue that unfortunate to the extent of causing further evidence to surge forth as false as the first item. He might be able to provide either an alibi or some other circumstance that would overturn the accusation, since he was not guilty. Affairs like those of Lesurques or Lesnier are not so frequent as to be

---

1 Paul-Louis Courier (1772-1825) was a Hellenist scholar, Napoleonic soldier and political pamphleteer whose turbulent career—disrupted and transformed by the Bourbon Restoration—concluded when he was shot in a wood near his house. Five years after the event, and in controversially clouded circumstances, two of his servants were convicted of the murder.

multiplied in a century.[1] Whatever prejudices one has against the law, it is necessary not to be ridiculously suspicious of it. It was in the impartiality of magistrates that Descorval's best chance of salvation still lay.

In a few days, perhaps tomorrow, an order of dismissal might return the innocent man to his hearth and deliver Gaston from his anguish at a stroke. He would find the means of indemnifying the poor man for the few weeks of prejudice to which he had been subjected. The affair would be definitively shelved, as they say . . .

But what if that hypothesis were not realized?

I noted in passing the possibility of an escape, but that was uniquely for memory. The capital point remained.

3. Gaston Descorval. What could he do? In that regard, conscience could not hesitate. He could not let an innocent man be condemned, and, in consequence, it was his strict duty to reveal the truth. He had to, but could he? I confess that in his place, although I do not have the stupid vanity that had doomed him, I would hesitate. His confession would be his moral and material ruination. The law would not pardon a trick that had had such grave consequences. He would incur a conviction; humiliated, dishonored and shamed before everyone he would be constrained to expatriate himself after having sold his property at a rock-bottom price. I even believed

---

1 Joseph Lesurques was famously convicted of a murder committed during the robbery of a mail-coach, partly because of a mistaken identification by an eye-witness. The abundant supplementary evidence gathered against him was all circumstantial, and the case eventually became a famous example of the unreliability of such circumstantial evidence, but only after much argument in the press. François Lesnier was convicted in Bordeaux in 1848 of the murder of Claude Gay but the conviction was overturned when another man—who had given evidence against Lesnier—was convicted in 1855 of the same crime, creating a contradiction that had to be resolved. A third trial became famous in French law by virtue of its careful reassessment of the evidence offered in the first two and its reliability.

that I remembered that giving false testimony leads to the deprivation of civil rights. Thus, his situation, if he accepted the shame of the confession, would be atrocious.

I could not see any way out. To have recourse to the highest-placed persons in the land is scabrous and unreliable; Gaston was not sufficiently important that anyone would be disposed to bend social rules for him. It would be difficult, if not impossible, to cover up an affair that had already received so much publicity.

I could see only one resource: that Gaston expatriate himself before the confession, which would still be a sort of suicide. However, we ought to advise that rather than . . . the other.

In sum, he was finished, and Maurice was not wrong to treat him disdainfully as an imbecile.

That mosaic task took me late into the night. I finally went to sleep, and when I woke up it was broad daylight; the weather was superb, streaming with sunlight.

I ran to Maurice's room. He was no longer there—which did not astonish me unduly. I rang; the domestic came. Maurice had gone out early and had said that he ought not to be expected for breakfast, adding that if he had not returned by dinner time, we should not worry about him.

I thought at first that, despairing of rendering any service to the man who had summoned him, he had simply returned to Paris, but that was a gratuitous accusation. All his effects were in their place and nothing in his room indicated a departure. I saw that he had been working a great deal himself, taking cuttings from the newspapers that had been brought to him of everything treating the sad affair.

And Gaston? The domestic declared that he had found him much calmer than usual that morning.

"I don't know what the messieurs said to him," he added, "but he is completely changed. He gives the impression of a man who has made a decision."

What decision? Had the unfortunate fellow accustomed himself to the idea of an imminent death?

There is no position more painful than that of a friend not knowing what practical advice he ought to give, and unable to do so. So I was not in any hurry to find myself facing him. I even thought that throughout the time that he did not see us he was forging illusions worthy of our pity; he surely believed that both of us had set forth in quest of means of saving him; our very absence must seem to him to be a guarantee of our zeal . . .

Fundamentally, all that reasoning could be summarized in an entirely egotistical conception: I preferred to dispense with the embarrassment of a conversation that I judged futile, especially without the presence of Maurice. I resolved, therefore, to make a tour of the surrounding area.

Announcing to the domestic that I was going out, I adopted the preoccupied attitude of a man marching toward a determined goal; that was another fashion of reassuring Gaston if he interrogated his domestic.

The grille closed behind me; I was outside the grounds of the house. I uttered a sigh of relief. The atmosphere of the dwelling had been weighing upon me and I escaped from it delightedly.

I paused momentarily on the edge of the road, not knowing the direction it took and consulting my whim before choosing which way to go in my capricious peregrination.

At that moment, I saw a man turning the corner of the wall and heading toward the gate at a slow pace: a tall figure clad in a worn, much-patched shepherd's cloak; a genuine Callot vagabond. A soft felt hat with a wide frayed brim was pulled down over his head, allowing the sight of a grim hirsute face bristling with red hair. It was not a beard, eyebrows and moustache but a mask cut out in a rough fleece. The effect was singular. That head, human by virtue of the bright eyes—I might even say intelligent—and the thick sensual lips, was a brute in his physical eccentricity.

The cloak enveloped the man entirely; his shoulders were exceptionally broad, suggestive of an extreme vigor. The hand passed through the gap was holding an enormous cudgel, on which the fingers designed claw-like nodes. I also noticed the feet: true canal-barges, as the gamins of Paris say. In fact, he was a colossus, something like a human gorilla, whom I would not have cared to encounter in a corner of a wood.

With his heavy tread, which compacted the earth of the path, he followed the wall, his head bowed, perhaps contemplating some evil coup, but in any case hesitant; that was obvious.

Suddenly, a vision surged forth in my brain. I remembered the portrait briefly sketched by Gaston of the individual that he had snatched from the claws of the law by means of his lie.

A true face of an assassin.

I took a few steps toward him and said to him, abruptly: "You are Pierre Taureau?"

He stopped, with an abrupt shudder, and raised his bestial visage toward me.

"What do you want with me?" he asked. The voice was hoarse and thick, which did not astonish me. It suited the face, and resembled a growl.

"Have you come to see our friend Gaston?" I asked, still in the imperative mode that appeared most appropriate to establish my domination of the individual. It is by brutal audacity that lion-tamers triumph.

He had stopped. As if by virtue of an involuntary and unconscious movement, his hand had knotted round a leather strip attached to the pommel of his cudgel.

I was not afraid. "I must warn you," I went on, raising my voice, "that Monsieur Descorval is ill and cannot receive anyone."

"Ah!" he said. Then, after a pause, he added, tranquilly: "That's unfortunate. I'll come back another time, that's all."

I put my hand on his shoulder.

"I am his friend," I said, "his intimate friend; and however confidential the communication might be that you might have to make to him, I can transmit it to him."

He had stopped, looking at my hand, which, on his enormous shoulder, was reminiscent of a bird's foot. I thought I could detect on his lips a slightly disdainful smile, and, in fact, seeing the smallness and weakness of my hand posed on that mass, I felt embarrassed, almost ridiculous.

"Then you're one of the two messieurs from Paris who arrived yesterday?" he said.

It appeared that the wretch was spying on the house. I withdrew my hand and replied, rather dryly: "You seem to be well-informed."

"It's not difficult," he said, laughing. "I'd already come to speak to the monsieur yesterday evening, and I arrived just as your carriage went through the grille. Then I said to myself that it wasn't the time to disturb him, and that I'd come back in the morning. He's ill—bad luck! It doesn't astonish me, though; I've never had any luck."

He struck the ground violently with his stick.

"You astonish me," I said, looking at him fixedly. "It seems to me that once, at least, you haven't had too much to complain of hazard . . ."

"And when was that?"

"When the unexpected arrival of Monsieur Descorval provoked an acquittal . . . also unexpected, you must admit."

While I was speaking the man began to draw away in the opposite direction to the one he had taken a little while before, and I walked alongside him, needing to raise my head in order to speak to him.

"Oh, as to that," he said, "It wasn't luck. It had to be . . ."

"What do you mean?"

"They couldn't condemn me for that."

"Wasn't the evidence accumulated against you?"

He shrugged his shoulders. "Evidence! Damn! There wasn't a shadow of any. I told the judges that myself. It seemed to make them angry, not being able to condemn me . . . but I wasn't afraid."

He said that in a calm tone, playing conviction very well.

"That doesn't alter the fact that, without Descorval's intervention . . ."

"Oh, I don't say that he didn't do well. He's a worthy man, and if he ever needs me to break a head for him . . ."

I'm softening his language slightly, you understand.

We were still walking; I sensed that the conversation was moving on to fertile ground of its own accord, and I wanted to profit from it. Ideas still vague were germinating in my brain. The man did not seem to me to be so intelligent that one could not reckon with his peasant cunning.

"Tell me," I said resolutely, "you've doubtless come to talk to Monsieur Descorval in order to ask him for something . . ."

"Perhaps . . ."

"Monsieur Descorval has told me a great deal about how you interest him—as, I believe, he had already proved to you. If your request is acceptable, then, you can be sure in advance that he'll respond to it favorably . . ."

"I certainly hope so," he said, in a tone in which I thought I heard the echo of a latent threat.

"Well, although he's ill, I can see him whenever I want to. Tell me what it's about and I'll try to obtain what you desire. It's not easy to talk on the road; isn't there some tavern hereabouts where we can sit down tranquilly, sheltered from indiscretion?"

He turned to me abruptly, as if stupefied that a "monsieur" was talking about going into a tavern with a ragamuffin like him

"It's necessary," I said, more clearly, "and unless you don't trust me . . ."

"There's the Licorne," he said.

"The Licorne it is, then. Is it far?"

"A few steps, when we've passed that clump of beeches." He designated a bend in the road a hundred meters away.

We went on, both keeping silent now. Doubtless he was meditating the best means of conciliating my sympathies; personally, I was ruminating a rather bold plan, especially when I considered the enormous girth—and hence the probable capacity of absorption—of my companion.

The Licorne was empty.

"Why, it's you, Taureau," said the innkeeper cheerfully. "No stupidities, you know! I'll stop you after the third glass." He shut up suddenly, on perceiving me.

I went straight to a glazed door at the back, divining a small room. I was not mistaken; there was a table covered with a waxed cloth, and a few chairs.

"Serve us a bottle of good wine," I said; and I added, borrowing the phraseology of popular novels: "You know, first-rate, with a cork . . ."

The innkeeper hastened to disappear into his cellar.

"Sit down," I said to Taureau, and, following familiar principles, I placed him full in the light, remaining in the penumbra myself.

When the glasses were filled I clinked them in the most natural fashion in the world, drank a swig, and when he had done likewise, I commenced: "Now I'm entirely yours. You see, my friend, in all things, frankness is the best means of reaching an understanding. You need help; we're both ready to render you service, only, for your part, you'll be docile, won't you? That's agreed."

He had thrown his hat on the table and set aside his enormous cudgel, a knotty stick that could have stunned a man with a single blow.

I looked him full in the face. He was terrifying, with his muzzle of a wild beast, his enormous lips and carnivorous teeth. But he did not understand very well where my preamble was leading; he had opened his eyes wide, raising his eyebrows, and I saw that they were very blue, almost soft: a singular contrast with the ferocity of his physiognomy.

"Are you listening carefully?" I said. "Do you know the law?"

"Me, I don't understand anything. Are there laws for poor folk like me?"

"For you as for all citizens; and you'll be convinced of that. There is in the Code—you know what the Code is?—an article that bears the number 360, and which says . . . follow me closely . . . that a person legally acquitted can't be retaken and accused of the same crime. Do you understand?"

No expression could describe the bewilderment—evidently feigned—revealed by the physiognomy of my interlocutor. I might have been talking Hebrew and my language would not have appeared more unintelligible to him. But I am not a man to be discouraged, and I went on. "It's really you, isn't it, who was accused of the crime at the Croix-des-Sauts?"

I saw his first clench. "Yes, yes—lies!" he said.

"Lies or not, you've been accused, judged and acquitted—which is to say that you're free and that nothing remains of the accusation brought against you . . ."

"That did me wrong in the beginning. They were all against me. They wanted to get rid of me. But it didn't hold, because, fundamentally, everyone knows that I've never harmed a fly . . ."

He was on the defensive, as is evident. But I continued, imperturbably:

"Now, suppose that the jury was mistaken in acquitting you; suppose that it were proven—entirely proven—that it was you who killed the man in question . . . well they wouldn't have the right, you hear, to lay a hand on you. Too bad for the law if it was mistaken. You're free and you'd remain free even so . . ."

"Ah!" he said, in an indifferent tone. "That's odd."

"It's a fact. So, you have no reason to be anxious. You can speak in all sincerity, recount exactly what happened at the crossroads of Craon. Look, I'll wager that, fundamentally, you're not as guilty as people believe . . . You might have agued with the man . . . he might have insulted you, eh? Then one gets carried away, and a bad blow is soon struck . . ."

He did not respond, but he looked at me more fixedly with his wide astonished eyes.

"How curious it would be," I continued, "when the other comes to trial—the innocent man who's in prison—to simply tell the truth! First of all, it would be a good deed, a truly good deed . . . which wouldn't cost you anything. On the contrary, for, I tell you, if you save that unfortunate—and you can—well, we'll give you all that you ask . . ."

In a suddenly softened voice, Pierre Taureau said to me, placing his hand on my arm: "But what good would it do me to have been acquitted, if everyone believes me to be a murderer?" And without leaving me the time to reply, he went on: "Look, you don't seem to be a bad man, but I see what you're thinking. You feel pity for the man who's been arrested and, at the same time, you're telling yourself that I was acquitted unjustly. I'd already divined something like that in what Monsieur Descorval had said to me. Now I'll reply to you: I was acquitted justly. I've never committed a crime, that one any more than any other. Now, do you know that you're asking me to sacrifice myself for someone I don't know? That I can't be retaken, possibly, but it's no less true that everyone would know that I was a murderer and that would be to my shame . . . unjustly."

Singularly enough, as he spoke his accent lost its roughness; the form of his language was less rustic. He perceived my surprise and continued: "I'm going to astonish you. Do you know what I am—or, rather, what I once was? I've had good land in the sun . . . oh, not here, twenty leagues away. When I was young, people called me Pierre le Faraud.[1] At thirty, I married. Five years later my wife ran off with a Parisian; then I sold everything and set off to search for her. Oh, I searched it, your city, from top to bottom and from bottom to top. After three years of searching I found the woman at the Maternité; the Parisian had abandoned her, pregnant . . . and she had just given birth. She died begging my pardon. I departed like a madman, and I came to bury myself here, ruined, brutalized, drunken . . . and people call me Pierre Taureau . . . and when men are killed on the roads, they accuse me because I'm a vagabond and a beggar . . . that's my history. I haven't killed anyone . . . it's me who has been killed!"

How can I render the impression of stupor that overwhelmed me? While that unfortunate was speaking, under the influence if the valiant wine of France, which had not intoxicated him, but, on the contrary, had put a warmth of resurrection into his heart and brain, I saw that strange face clear; the eyes brightened with an astonishing softness.

"But why didn't you speak like that to the judges?" I exclaimed

"Why? Those men rebuked me at every word! And then, in prison there's nothing to drink . . . and when I haven't had a drink . . . then I'm a brute . . ."

"Then you swear to me that it wasn't you who struck that man?"

"Why would I have killed him? I had no need of anything. People nourish me hereabouts, I carry out commissions, and the innkeepers pay me in glasses of eau-de-vie. I have no need of money . . . or, rather, I wasn't thinking about it . . ."

____

1 i.e. Pierre the Vain.

184

He stopped abruptly, as if suddenly retaining words that were ready to escape.

I confess that I was profoundly moved; there scarcely remained a residue of suspicion against my own sentimentality.

The last remark put me on guard.

"You weren't thinking about money," I said. "Does that mean that you're thinking about it now?"

"Ah," he said, "that's something else. Perhaps ideas have occurred to me . . ."

"Tell me about them."

"That's why I was going to see Monsieur Gaston this morning."

"I've already told you that you can speak to me as to him."

"It might have been easier to tell you about it, because he's already been generous. He's already given me money . . ."

"To establish a small commerce. You drank it . . ."

"Yes, I know he thinks that . . . but I would have explained . . ."

I had to insist. Evidently Pierre retained some rancor because of my insinuations. However, I pleaded my case as best I could, assuring him sincerely of my interest.

As if weary of resistance, he made his decision. I saw him rummage in the interior pocket of his cloak, and he took out a letter carefully wrapped in a piece of newspaper. He held it out to me and said simply: "Read that."

The letter bore the heading of a notary's office in Paris.

This was written:

> *Monsieur,*
>
> *As I have had the honor of informing you, the young man in whom you are interested, has bought a small fruiterer's shop at 29 Rue des Dames in Baignolles. The funds you addressed to me, eight hundred francs, have served to pay six months rent*

in advance and the initial expenses of installation. Monsieur André is very active and hard-working, however, it will be difficult for him to pay next month's settlement of his purchase. According to what he has told me and my own information, a sum of five hundred francs will be necessary. In accordance with your instructions I have invited him to come back to see me a little later and I am hastening to let you know the situation in order for you to take whatever measures you judge necessary.

    Please accept, etc.

The letter was signed by the notary's chief clerk.

"But what does this mean?" I exclaimed. "Who is this Monsieur André?"

The man, lowering his head as if in shame, replied in a low voice: "It's my wife's son."

That wretch, that savage, that presumed murderer, had collected the child of the dead woman. He had confided him to worthy folk who had brought him up, put him in a boarding school, and eventually, the lad being twenty-two years old, he had used the money given to him by Descorval as the means to establish him—and that via an intermediary who would keep the secret. The child of the dead woman did not know whence those benefits came to him, and he would always remain ignorant.

I was flabbergasted. This was the man who had been ac-cused of an infamous murder! I would have liked to bow my head before that sublime mendicant, that desperate man only attached to humanity by a naïve, exquisite, adorable generos-ity . . .

Mute, I looked at him, and then I understood how dif-ferent men can be from our first impressions. A little while before, thinking about the murder, I had seen Pierre Taureau as abominable, brutal, stupidly bestial—but now that face seemed illuminated by a radiant dawn.

When I was able to speak, I assured him that the sum in question would be poured out to him the next day—what am I saying?—and doubled.

"Oh, no need!" he said. "Only, as Monsieur Descorval had offered me the money to quit the locale, I was going to tell him that, if it was absolutely necessary, it would be very hard, but that I'd do it."

"What's the point?" I exclaimed, "since you're innocent!"

VI

I was profoundly satisfied with myself; I must confess that it was not without some vanity that I congratulated myself on having conducted my investigation so well. Maurice Parent—the Master—could not have done better.

Having separated from Pierre Taureau, I hastened to my friend Gaston's château.

He was waiting for me with an impatience easy to understand, justly surprised that we had both disappeared in the morning without making him party to the reasons for our absence.

I found him in his study, pale and feverish.

With an almost theatrical gesture he showed me the wide open windows letting in floods of light.

"I'm obeying my physicians," he said, in an ironic tone, "but is that any reason for them to abandon me?"

"Maurice hasn't returned?"

"No. Where is he"

"I don't know. He went out before me—but be sure that he's occupied with you."

"Unless he considered from the start that the task is impossible."

"Don't talk like that," I exclaimed. "Nothing is impossible, and I've brought you some good news myself."

"Really?"

"Yes. At table, fork in hand—for that matinal excursion has hollowed out my stomach—I'll prove to you that you're more than half saved . . ."

When we were installed, I said to him: "Gaston, you remember that one of your great concerns was having 'returned to society,' as the popular expression has it, a wretch capable of committing another murder?"

"I did say that, in fact."

"Well, be reassured; that dread is vain . . ."

"Which means . . . ?"

"That Pierre Taureau, so miraculously saved by your intervention, did not commit the crime of the Croix-des-Sauts. In a word, he's as innocent as you or me."

And with a volubility excusable by the joy that I was feeling—which would have been even greater if Maurice had been able to hear me—I made him party to the long conversation I had just had with Pierre Taureau.

I don't say that I didn't emphasize, with a little coquetry, the Machiavellian quality of my interrogation; I owed myself that small triumph of self-esteem, by reason of the service rendered.

Finally, victoriously I set before Gaston's eyes the letter that proved the sentimental heroism of the man that we had considered thus far as a murderer.

"I've engaged myself in your name," I added, "for the miserable sums of which the man has need; and I believe you won't regret it."

"No, certainly not. I've never refused a benefit, and it isn't in such circumstances that I'll begin. But is that all that you have to tell me?"

"I don't understand you . . ."

"Because you doubtless haven't understood yourself."

I was amazed by the indifference with which Descorval greeted my communication, and in truth, I was not far from accusing him of ingratitude.

"What do you expect, then?" I asked, in a piqued tone.

"Don't be wounded," he said, "but I insist on the point that you've completely misunderstood my situation. Yes, as I told you, during the first month that followed my unqualifiable aberration, I was haunted by the idea that Pierre Taureau, freed unjustly—I believed so then—might commit another crime, of which I would be, in a sense, an accomplice, the virtual author. But in sum, as time passed, that anxiety faded away. The man did not give rise to any complaint; he had resumed his ordinary conduct, and nothing proved that he might be drawn into another act of violence like the one that had nearly cost him so dear. I was even counting on the efficacy of the lesson.

"It was then, in that moment of calm, that the new thunderbolt fell upon me: the arrest of the innocent man.

"Now, think. How does the fact that Pierre Taureau is not the author of the murder at the Croix-des-Sauts change the horror of my situation? The man who is presently in prison has only been arrested because the victim's satchel was found in the quarry, a few meters from the shack were he lives. Without that circumstance, which I know to be false, he would not have been troubled. I cannot doubt his innocence, since it is me who created the heaviest presumption that weighs upon him. I have no wanted to make any investigation, convinced that the scaffolding of any deduction rests on the matter of the satchel.

"So, today as yesterday, before as after the more or less decisive establishment of Pierre Taureau's innocence, I find myself in the alternative of allowing an innocent man to be condemned or confessing my moral crime.

"I won't go on. I thank you sincerely for what you have attempted to do for me; I'll be grateful to you for as long as I live . . . which will perhaps not be long, for Maurice Parent's words have dictated my duty. Now, let's talk about something else and wait to see what happens."

No cold shower had ever produced a more refrigerant effect than those words, serenely pronounced in a slightly tremulous voice.

I would have liked to become irritated, to emphasize the importance of my discovery. I had no arguments. It was what is known in theatrical jargon as an utter flop.

Annoyed and discontented with myself I quit Gaston immediately after the meal, uncertain as to what I ought to do. I had definitely been wrong to embark upon the affair, in which I had only foreseen disappointments.

And Maurice had abandoned me! I waited for him all day in vain; he did not appear. I knew that no one in the neighborhood had seen him. On the pretext of an indisposition, I had myself served in my room. I did not want to find myself facing Gaston again, and in the ferocity of my egotism I preferred to leave him to his solitude. Thus, a physician, sensing himself to be impotent, abandons a patient that he cannot save.

I slept badly, with stupid dreams. It was me who had murdered the man at the Croix-des-Sauts!

In the morning, a telegram was brought to me.

I uttered a cry of surprise; it was from Maurice, datelined Paris.

He had gone, then, renouncing the struggle.

Be patient, the telegram said. *Say nothing yet, but hope.*

What could that signify? Was Maurice mocking Gaston and me? What could he attempt in Paris to save him? Vainly, he was trying to fool us. That was bad on his part, and I did not recognize therein the delicacy to which he had habituated me. It was quite simply a desertion.

I sent the telegram to Gaston without a word of commentary. It would have been painful for me to hear my friend's conduct criticized.

What should I do? I would gladly have departed myself, but I did not dare.

VIII[1]

Victory! I do not feel any joy, but it is necessary that I recover all my calm in order to put my ideas in order, to give them substance, and above all to establish the terms—the solution—of the problem in a fashion so clear that no objection will be possible.

I have just sent a note to Gaston containing the words: You are saved! Expect me tomorrow at ten o'clock in the morning.

It is four days since I have seen him. I was wrong, I know, to neglect him like that, but I could not, after Maurice's abandonment, accept the idea of facing the poor fellow, whose recent resignation had devastated me.

I had my valise transported to the inn and I took a room there, not without having sent Maurice a rather stiff telegram in which I warned him that I would only wait for forty-eight hours before taking the return train.

He responded to me with his eternal: *Patience!*—a word so easy to pronounce for those disinterested in your anguish.

I had seen Pierre Taureau again, who had made a thousand protests about receiving the sum, of which he claimed, half was unnecessary. Then he begged me to write to the notary's clerk myself, instructing him to keep the five hundred francs in case of need. The man was decidedly above suspicion, and I had a great sympathy for him. That same evening, however,

---

1 I have reproduced this heading as it is given in the text of *La Magicienne*, wherein there is no chapter VII.

he got abominably drunk; that was his vice, evidently born of the despair that his wife's departure had caused him.

I was embarrassed enough to remain for the time during which I had promised to wait for Maurice—not that I believed in his return, but I wanted to keep my word in full.

It was then that an idea of genius, if I may say so, crossed me mind.

What was the great, invincible obstacle to the salvation of my friend Gaston? It was the man arrested for a crime that he probably had not committed, but for which he was being pursued because of conclusions drawn from premises that we knew to be false.

So I reasoned thus: one of two things must be true: either that man was innocent, which appeared highly probable, or he was guilty—which, after all, was possible. If he was innocent, was that so difficult to prove? We all know that the law has an unfortunate tendency, especially when it believes itself to be in possession of an indisputable point of departure, to accumulate the most insignificant circumstances and attach a value to the least conclusive testimony to reinforce the accusation. Furthermore, I knew that the accused—a certain Jean Brault—was a man devoid of education, and I divined that he was defending himself ineptly, paralyzed, as Pierre Taureau had been, by the ever-alarming apparatus of the law.

I had a sane and logical mind. Not only was I not blinded by unfavorable prejudices but, on the contrary. I admitted *a priori* the inanity of the charges weighing against the man in question. Why should I not deliver myself to a counter-investigation, striving to bring together all the facts tending to establish his innocence?

I said to myself that, even if that innocence were to be proven, Gaston would not be completely free of anxiety; for, in sum, there had been a murder, and one day or another, pursuits undertaken against a new suspect might reawaken his anguish, but that was a detail without importance. In truth, once the man was set at liberty, Gaston could breathe easily.

Thus, I thought, either he was innocent—or guilty.

In the latter case, if Gaston acquired the certainty that the story of the satchel had not been the determining cause of a justly-motivated arrest, if the fact of having placed that evidence in a place where it took on a considerable importance could be regarded as providential, in a way, and then, no more anxiety, no more remorse, but on the contrary, I know not what pride in having obeyed a quasi-miraculous suggestion.

Having made those two points, I decided to go to work, as discreetly as possible, and to find the key to the enigma.

After all, Maurice Parent could not hold it against me that I had, as a good pupil, profited from his lessons.

My research, slowly and carefully carried out, lasted three days. This was the result:

Jean Brault was a local man. His father was a farmer, sufficiently well off, who, toward the end of his life, had gone to the bad. A widower, still vigorous, he attracted to his home young country girls hired as maidservants and installed them as mistresses until, his caprice having waned, he threw them out. The law had been obliged to intervene several times; serious accusations related to the consequences of his relations with the unfortunate girls had been made against him, but had not been established solidly enough to give rise to a prosecution.

The worst aspect of all that was that the wretched father rendered his son, still almost a child, a witness to his debauches, not giving him any education, and letting him hang around with all the idlers of the neighborhood. One can understand why Jean never acquired the habit of work, and when his father died, leaving debts that far surpassed the value of his property, Jean found himself reduced to black poverty.

It was necessary to live, though. Lame, Jean was unfit for military service, but his infirmity did not prevent him from working in the fields, and he began to hire himself out in various directions. He was now twenty-eight years old. People agreed that he was a sly fellow, hypocritical, avid and very violent. Three or four years before, in a brawl, he had injured his adversary badly and had been sentenced on that account to ten days in prison. Since that time he had gone to ground, so to speak, in a hut belonging to the commune, the ruin of a building once serving for the exploitation of the quarry. He was coupled with a beggar-woman of sorts picked up in the road, with whom he had a child, today aged eighteen months.

He worked hard, but without addressing a word to anyone. He did not associate with the other men of the village, and always gave the impression—this is the expression they used—of ruminating some evil deed.

The creature he had attached to his fate, who scarcely appeared to be worth any more than him, almost never showed herself. They lived on a wretched plot of vegetables that had been abandoned to their enjoyment out of pity, like the building, and for which they only paid an insignificant sum in kind by way of rent. They also raised rabbits and a few chickens. It was worse than poverty, it was the filthy dirt of indifference and grim resignation, more apparent than real. What proved that is that when one of their neighbors reproached him for living thus, like a wild animal, he responded: "The others will come to me when I'm rich."

Rich! Was it possible, with his métier of handyman, with no fixed employment, that he could arrive at a relative well-being? Evidently not, and those words had to conceal a plan, as yet vague.

He was arrested as a murderer and these were the circumstances on which the accusation was based:

Jean Brault could not say where he was at the time of the crime; he claimed that he was working on his plot of land, in a kind of shed where he had assembled a few tools and a work-bench. If he mentioned that circumstance it was because no one had seen him in his field. His wife supported his claim, but a terrible charge proved that she was lying. At the timed in question, a peasant had come to ask for him and she had replied that he was absent. Why would she have deceived that man, since, according to her own confession, he was one of those who gave her husband work? She objected that he paid so badly that Jean no longer wanted to put himself at his service—an improbable assertion, since Jean seized any work whatsoever with both hands.

I would not mention, of course, the presence of the satchel in the quarry, if that fact did not attach the decisive proof that established the wretch's guilt. It was not him who had thrown the satchel into the middle of the stones, but, in making enquiries in the neighborhood of the place where it had been found, the police had discovered a hiding place of which no exterior sign revealed the existence, which contained twenty hundred-sou coins.

Where had that sum come from? Was it supposable that those people would be living in black poverty, scarcely eating the necessary, if they had a relatively large sum at their disposal? However, it might have been possible to accept Jean Brault's explanation by positing an excessive miserliness, but, unfortunately for him, he had lacked the most elementary prudence.

Two months after the murder, he had gone to see the notary in Craon to deposit a sum of two hundred francs as a down payment on a small house with a field, which he was in the process of buying, a few hundred meters from the quarry.

It is understandable that in those circumstances, the law had not hesitated to act. Before the crime, no one had ever seen an écu in that man's hands, and now, all of a sudden, he was found in possession of three hundred francs!

If the law can sometimes be accused of obeying unjustified prejudices, this time, no one could blame it for following that track.

At the beginning of my investigation, however, I could not help feeling a certain apprehension. It was evident that without the incident of the satchel, suspicion would never have been directed on to that path. It might be the case that fatality was overwhelming that man by attracting attention to him and putting him under suspicion when his possession of that sum was natural and explicable.

I strove to resist, therefore, the conviction that was already imposing itself upon me, and I deployed more activity in verifying the facts; but my optimism could not resist the crushing revelation that awaited me.

That same morning, one of the witnesses summoned by the examining magistrate had made this fact known to me: the victim had collected in Craon a sum of between two and three hundred francs, part of which was in recovery of a debt that was owed to him by a baker.

Now, in the first trial, the baker, having been called, had neglected to mention the important detail that, in putting together the sum due, he had been obliged to include two forty-franc coins that he conserved like fetishes, having marked them with crosses traced with the point of his knife.

Among the coins given by Jean Brault to the notary in Craon one of those coins was found! His culpability was thus demonstrated! Gaston's stupid imprudence had not launched the law on a false trail. The circumstance of the satchel became secondary, unnecessary. That was salvation.

I was very glad that the affair had terminated thus, for, while recognizing that he had been wrong—very wrong—I could not hold the death of the sinner against him. I was able to sleep tranquilly until the following morning.

IX

What is happening?

This morning, on arriving at Descorval's house, I found him in an indescribable emotion.

My note, which had reached him the previous evening, rather late in the day, had transported him with joy and he was waiting for me with a feverish impatience.

I arrived at his house at seven o'clock in the morning, but someone had preceded me: the postman, who had brought him a summons to appear that same morning, at midday, before Monsieur Michal, the examining magistrate, in Amiens.

Gaston was a sorry sight; all his panic had been reawakened. What need had they of him? In what way could his intervention be useful?

The most singular thing was that the judiciary missive was joined by a brief letter signed by Maurice Parent, only containing the words: *Please ask our friend to accompany you.*

Was Maurice in Amiens, then? How long ago had he returned from Paris? What a singular fashion of acting! Would it not have been simpler, and—let's say the word—more appropriate, to keep us up to date with his actions, so far as he had taken any?

In truth, there are people who surpass mystery!

I hastened to tell Gaston all that I had done; I told him about the evident proofs that had been obtained of the culpability of Jean Brault, outside the discovery of the satchel. In consequence, his own culpability was henceforth discountable.

"But they've just summoned me," he exclaimed, "to renew the declaration I've already made at the court of assizes. What should I do?"

At first sight, the case of conscience was rather subtle, and I did not respond to his question, deciding to reflect during the journey.

It was evident that his deposition was devoid of importance, since the discovery of one of the stolen coins in the hands of the murderer was more than sufficient proof establishing his culpability. Thus, the interests of the accused were no longer in play.

But that was not the point: could Gaston lie again, when we both knew that he was lying? Could he boldly and cynically make a false declaration?

On the other hand, for that simple point of honor, ought he to compromise himself, doom himself forever?

Decidedly, I dared not give him that advice, nor the other.

I would have a hundred times rather not have accompanied him, in order to leave him complete freedom of action; but I dared not let him depart alone.

X

I shall recount now without commentary. You will understand that I have to be quite sober.

At midday precisely we went into the Palais de Justice in Amiens.

I was not a little surprised to encounter in the courtyard Hardouin, the celebrated physician known to all Paris, for having figured in so many sensational cases, as the most illustrious man in the field of legal medicine. He was nicknamed "the Impeccable," a title justified by the clarity and reliability of his observations.

He saluted me with his hand, smiling, and then passed by.

Undoubtedly there was some important case that had required a summons to the court. At another time I would have been interested, but I had other cares on my mind, alas.

Gaston now inspired me with a real pity. He was as pale as a corpse and I feared that the crisis might be beyond his strength, for he was no longer anything but a shadow of himself and the emotion might kill him.

After a few moments of waiting we were both introduced into the examining magistrate's study.

Everyone knows whether studies of that kind are liable to raise flagging morale.

Monsieur Michal, a man of about forty, very cold and correct but with a certain hint of malice in his gaze, invited us to sit down. Then he set about leafing through a dossier for nearly a quarter of an hour, without appearing to preoccupy himself further with our presence since we had crossed his presence. That fashion of acting was horribly enervating; I saw Gaston's hands clenching with impatience and anguish.

Finally, Monsieur Michal raised his head and looked at us. "Monsieur Descorval," he said in a neutral, atonal voice, "I have summoned you in order to obtain a renewal of the very important deposition that you were kind enough to make to the court of assizes by courtesy of the discretionary powers of Monsieur le Président during the affair of Pierre Lhôte."

Gaston listened with his eyes wide open, He resembled a madman,

"If you will permit, I shall read it," said the magistrate, and, without waiting for the slightest sign of Gaston's assent, he picked up a piece of paper and read aloud from it.

It was the little speech previously pronounced by poor Gaston; the clerk had carefully reproduced the slightly pretentious tone of its phraseology; I seemed to be hearing him speak, posing before the court and the public, satisfied with the effect he produced.

"Is that really what you said?" asked the magistrate.

Undoubtedly, he took for an affirmative response the sobbing grunt that emerged from Gaston's breast, for he resumed speaking without waiting any further. "I desire," he continued, "to call your attention to the importance of this deposition, for"—he was emphasizing his words slowly—"the fate of Jean Brault rests on it . . ."

My surprise was such that I could not contain myself. "Pardon me, Monsieur le Juge, but there are many other proofs of Jean Brault's culpability."

The examining magistrate could certainly have reprimand-ed me forcefully for my intemperate interjection, which I would certainly have merited, but he did not seem shocked by the remark and, fixing his stare upon me—in which, in spite of myself, I persisted in detected irony—he said:

"Do you think so, Monsieur? I would be grateful if you would be kind enough to develop your thinking."

"Since you authorize me to do so, Monsieur," I said, with my utmost dignity, "I shall try to be as brief and clear as pos-sible. Of Jean Brault's past I shall only say one word: it offers no guarantees."

"Agreed."

"I will even say that a bad education always bears its fruit sooner or later. But I shall pass over those purely moral considerations to get to precise facts. I do not know whether Jean Brault has justified an alibi. He claims that he was at home. His wife now admits that she declared at the time of the crime that she was absent. I know that she claims to have lied in order to get rid of an importunate, but that thesis is inadmissible."

"I beg your pardon," said the magistrate, "but the visitor has admitted himself that the refusal to see him is perfectly ex-plained by the state of the relations existing between himself and Jean Brault."

That was too much; was I facing an examining magistrate or an advocate? It was, I admit, the first time I had heard an accused man defended by such a mouth.

"So be it," I went on, slightly piqued, "but has Jean Brault found anything to explain that mysterious hiding place evidently intended to conceal the product of a theft?"

"It is established that Jean Brault had once been robbed of the fruit of his small savings. His prudence is not inexplicable."

We were decidedly playing a fantastic scene destined for some comedy of mores.

"And it is doubtless not inexplicable that Jean Brault, deprived of everything, living in poverty and dirt, had amassed a relatively considerable sum?"

"All the less inexplicable," said the judge, "because, with an orderly method rare in a peasant hardly knowing how to write, Jean Brault keeps regular accounts. Those accounts go back five years. No doubt is possible as to their authenticity: the wear and tear of the paper and the handwriting, nothing is lacking for the conviction of the most meticulous experts. For five years, Jean Brault, whatever his wages or the profit of his journeywork, put aside five sous every evening. Calculate, and you will see that in five years, the accumulation of that miserable sum gives nearly five hundred francs . . ."

"Doubtless," I said, sniggering rather disrespectfully, "it was the example of his father that taught him economy."

"To a prodigal father, a miserly son."

"Proverbs are always right—but I don't know what adage borrowed from the wisdom of nations can explain how, in the sum so slowly amassed by Jean Brault, a forty-franc coin stolen from the victim was found."

The magistrate put his hand on a document.

"I have here," he said, "the deposition of a local farmer who recognizes having paid with the sum of forty francs, in a gold coin marked with a cross, an account that Jean Brault had allowed to accumulate."

"But by what entitlement did the farmer possess that gold coin?"

"The most legitimate title. He had received it from the man who died, nearly an hour before, in the event at the Croix-des-Sauts."

I was astounded. Those ripostes floored me. My entire investigation was crumbling. I must have looked very stupid, because the magistrate went on, with a pinched smile: "Pull yourself together, Monsieur. No one is infallible."

He turned toward Gaston and said: "You understand now, Monsieur, the enormous importance your deposition has. All the charges existing against Jean Brault have fallen, one by one, and I would now be ready to sign an order of dismissal if one last doubt did not remain in my mind. The man has refused peremptorily to give the slightest explanation to justify the presence of the satchel in the quarry a few meters from his hut. He claims to know nothing, and to have seen nothing. Now you, Monsieur Descorval, saw that satchel in the place where it was found, a short time after the catastrophe at the crossroads. That precious indication inculpating Jean Brault is the last fact to which the instruction can be attached . . . and we consider it vital. So I am asking you to be kind enough to confirm your testimony by placing your signature at the bottom of this document."

And with a deliberate gesture, he pushed the piece of paper toward Gaston.

The poor fellow stood up, indignantly.

What passed within him in those few seconds? I saw him look with an ardent gaze, an alienated gaze, at the piece of paper, then the pen and the inkwell. He made a gesture as if to take possession of them, in order to accomplish the infamous deceptive action.

Suddenly, though, he uttered a hoarse cry, put his hand to his throat, tore open his collar, and cried, sobbing: "I'm a wretch! I lied! I lied! Kill me now . . . I deserve to die . . . Oh, I'm suffering!"

He tottered and, as he moved away from me, he would have fallen full length if, the door having opened abruptly, Maurice had not caught him in his arms. Doctor Hardouin, who was accompanying him, hastened to help Gaston.

"Nothing to fear," he said, after a pause. "The shock was rude, but a week of material and mental calm will be sufficient to repair everything."

For myself, I no longer had sane possession of my ideas. Gaston's heroic confession established him as guilty of an odious crime. What, then, was the calm of which the doctor was speaking?

Maurice had helped Gaston to lie down on a sofa and I saw him murmur in his ear something that I could not hear. To my great surprise, Descorval's face lit up with a joyous gleam.

"Is that possible?" he murmured. "Oh, thank you! Thank you!"

"Silence," said Maurice, smiling. "We have to conclude this little affair."

Now I remarked that the examining magistrate, in his turn, was a little pale.

"Doctor," he said to Hardouin, bowing, "you have brought me your report?"

"Here it is," replied the physician, handing him a folded piece of paper.

The magistrate unfolded it and read it attentively. His hands were trembling.

"Messieurs," he said, addressing a sad gaze to all of us, "Monsieur has just made a difficult confession. It is my turn to speak, and I want to do that in all sincerity. First, permit me, Monsieur Maurice Parent, and you, Doctor Hardouin, who have answered my appeal so promptly, to address the expression of my thanks to you. My gratitude is not feigned; for, after the dolor of having committed a fault, there is no greater joy than to repair it. My fault, Monsieur Maurice Parent divined at first glance, and I thank him for that. This is what it has been: on the basis of public rumor, in the enthusiasm of a conviction that seemed to be victoriously imposed, I believed without discussion, that the death of Michel Varin—the peasant of the Croix-des-Sauts—was the result of a crime. I required, to establish the state of the cadaver, the intervention of an officer of health, whose report I accepted blindly, so far was doubt from my mind, and I judged it unnecessary to proceed with an autopsy. You, Monsieur Parent, obedient to a method whose logic is incontestable, having the documents of the trial before your eyes, immediately asked yourself: 'Was there a crime?'

"It is rare that we ask ourselves that question. The immediate arrest of Pierre Lhôte gave the accusation a real substance; the man's bad reputation, his habitual drunkenness and criminality all contributed to annul my hesitation, supposing that any had existed. It needed very little for the man to be condemned, and I feel full of indulgence, I confess, for Monsieur Descorval, who intervention prevented a regrettable judiciary error.

"Still relying on the initial medical report, the rigorous exactitude of which we did not think of contesting, we launched ourselves on another track; here the danger was greater, for it was a matter of a man whom appearances alone showed to be capable of an evil act. Jean Brault has always been unfortunate, he has more merit than any other in not having despaired, and, harnessing himself to frightful labor, that man has succeeded in extracting himself from the mire of poverty in which he was struggling. He has been at liberty since yesterday, and for my part I have already repaired as far as possible the harm that I have done him. I assume that Monsieur Descorval will not forget him.

"Finally, I arrive at the capital point.

"On the insistence of Monsieur Maurice Parent, who explained to me certain contradictions in the medical report, I ordered the exhumation and autopsy of the cadaver of Michel Varin. Monsieur Parent immediately departed for Paris and, thanks to him, Doctor Hardouin—whose acquaintance I am honored to have made—was kind enough to proceed with the necessary observations himself . . .

"Here is his report, conclusive even for ignorant persons like me.

"Michel Varin was not murdered. He died of a double pulmonary and cerebral congestion determined by drunkenness. As for the wound in his head, it was quite superficial and was occasioned by the fall of the congested man on the angle of a step on the pedestal of the cross.

"Finally, I ought to add that an important, decisive testimony was lacking throughout the examination: that of a farmer who received from Michel Varin, in a tavern half-way between Craon and the Croix-des-Sauts, payment of a sum due, for which Michel had handed over his last sou.

"Michel, who was very irritated by that reimbursement, was abominably drunk, and set off on foot. The congestion killed him five hundred meters further on.

Unfortunately the farmer had departed on a journey to the south of France and had no knowledge of the trial. He only returned a few days ago, and I received his deposition, from which it results that it was he, shortly before his departure, who paid Jean Brault the forty-franc piece found in the home of the notary.

The investigation was therefore closed; I have made my error known to Monsieur le Ministre de Justice, and Monsieur Maurice Parent has been kind enough to affirm that my position will not suffer too much therefrom.

There remains the case of Monsieur Descorval. I lent myself, in accordance with the desire of Monsieur Parent, to a little comedy whose denouement has turned to the honor of the guilty party, who refused to persist in his . . . inexactitudes. I do not doubt that he comprehends now all the gravity of certain childish acts, and we shall remain silent about all that."

With what lightness we descended the step of the Palais de Justice! I had embraced Maurice, in a crazy surge of joy and gratitude. Descorval, resuscitated, had invited us all to dinner at Parcy, and even Hardoun had accepted gladly.

As you can imagine, we talked about the affair.

"I only regret one detail," I said, "which is that the examining magistrate was so badly mistaken on the count of Pierre Taureau, a worthy and courageous man."

"Hush!" said Maurice. "Pierre Taureau fled with his thousand francs, and he is here in Amiens, leading the devil of a life."

"But the child . . . ?"

"Pierre Taureau has never been married. There is no child . . . there is only a joker of a notary's clerk who lent himself to a trick that has cost our friend Descorval a thousand francs . . ."

I lowered my head, rather vexed. Decidedly, I was not born for investigations.

"In truth," said Descorval, who was visibly reviving, "I don't regret the thousand francs. Only I'd like to obtain from the magistrate that the satchel is returned to me. I'll suspend it in my study and it will always remind me of my stupidity . . ."

"By the way," said Maurice, "that satchel had nothing to do with the affair. Michel Varin was not carrying anything in it; he put his money in his pockets!"

THE STORY OF A NIGHT

I

AM I a hero or a coward? Ought I to despise myself or do I really have a right to self-esteem? And since I have a great desire to obtain a categorical answer to those questions, why am I not making my confession to a third party, a friend? No, I sense that no one, no matter how devoted he might be, and no matter how frank the revelation of my conscience might be, would judge me as equitably as I can myself, for I alone know. I alone can admit to myself what cannot be confessed to anyone else, even the most intimate confidant, even to a priest. In the utmost depths of our being there are secret coverts that the most expert eye, even the best directed by a confession, cannot scrutinize, because an examination so complex requires a long experience that the expert in question would inevitably lack.

Whoever wishes to judge the conscience of another judges in accordance with his own; he will try in vain to disengage himself from his particular personality; egotism is a force that no impartiality can resist, and every man of who is asked: "Given the circumstances, did I do well in doing what I did?" substitutes for it this one: "Would I have done the same in his place?"

But you are not me. There are no two men in the world whose past, character, passions, weaknesses or nobilities, visible or real, are, I do not say identical, but even equivalent.

In the same way that, in exterior form, no two faces, two features or two expressions, no matter how fleeting, can be said scientifically to be identical, it is even more the case that in the anatomical dissection of the consciousness, no two moral fibers, aspirations, desires and wills have the same principle or the same potency.

Human personality is essentially unique. Each of my actions is the result of motives that are only put simultaneously into action by causes whose exceptional coincidence relates to a singular state that can never, except by an extraordinary play of chance, be reproduced in someone other than me.

Is not the identity of acts itself an illusion? Another man might act like me, to arrive at a similar conclusion, without a single one of the motives that directed me having the slightest part in his determination.

That is why, truly and absolutely justly, not recognizing any other judge than my own conscience, it is to that alone that I want to expose my case, after having sworn, for my repose, to tell the truth, and the whole truth. That oath, which made to another, would surely be a lie, by reason of the attenuations and compromises that, with all the good faith imaginable, I would not be able to forbid myself, I am certain of keeping with regard to myself.

This piece of paper, which I have just placed on my desk, and over which my pen inclines, will contain the impeccable witness-statement that will impose the merited verdict upon me. And when I reread it, not finding a single word that is not the expression of the truth, the tribunal of my conscience, before which I am summoning myself, will absolve or condemn me.

Will I have the courage to write everything? It's necessary. I wish it.

My action closes the past but opens the future. The judgment, rendered by myself, will give me the strength to accept that future, to submit to it, to extend and develop it, or, on the contrary, will convince me of my impotence to realize it, as it must be.

In the latter case, I will examine what remains for me to do, and if I must disappear, even die, I will not recoil before the sanction of the decision I shall have rendered.

Courage, then! The excitement that has sustained me until now is dying away. I am and must be calm, and, poring over myself, I shall read myself like a book. Let's go!

II

That night, it was at one o'clock in the morning that I left the house of my friend Ch***, the sculptor. He had invited me at the Bourse, on the stroke of three o'clock, and without any great ceremony I had accepted, for it is amusing at his house, and furthermore, he had announced to me the presence of Sarah Bell. I immediately sent my wife a telegram telling her that I would not be back for dinner.

The telegram was laconic: *Don't wait up for me. Regards.*

Then I went to chat for a while with my broker, regulate a few accounts and give some instructions, and from there I went to Riche's, where I chatted until six o'clock in the best mood in the world with my café comrades. In fact, I was very cheerful, entirely at ease, delighted with myself and enjoying in advance the pleasant evening in prospect.

Ch*** came to collect me at six o'clock, and, arm in arm, conversing gaily, we went as far as his small house in the Rue Fortuny. The weather was superb, perhaps a little warm and slightly enervating. I experienced an intimate agitation that was not unpleasant. What did we talk about during that walk?

Everything and nothing: art, the theater, politics. Out opinions only differed just enough to spice the conversation with courteous argument.

"By the way," he said, "I recommend you to be reasonable with Sarah Bell." And when I laughed, he added: "Don't play the innocent; I'm well aware that she pleases you, and that, for her part, she doesn't look upon you unkindly."

"Isn't she charming?"

"Delightful, adorable, and witty all the way to her fingertips . . . and between us, a true talent. She showed me recently, in her studio, panels that are absolutely successful. She's only wild intermittently—but be careful. If she ever takes it into her head to love you sincerely, seriously, she'll do so with a desolating fidelity. I repeat, be careful; you're a serious man, a financier, the father of a family . . ."

"What! The father of a family!"

"Married, at least, and you have the future before you. Be sensible . . ."

I defended myself, laughing, answering for myself with a caution that my comrade was obstinate in finding insufficient. Really, that Sarah Bell is an exquisite young woman, and when, having arrived, I looked at her blonde hair, slightly tousled, cut in a boyish fashion, and her blue eyes, sparkling with finesse; when I had brushed her round and supple fingers lightly with my lips, in the Regency fashion, I experienced a delectable impression. She has amiable manners that charm me. Joyfully, with a mischievous frankness, she wanted me to place myself beside her at table, and throughout the meal we talked in low voices, like old friends. To say that we did not care about anyone else would be a lie, though; we occupied ourselves with others much more than ourselves.

I felt full of verve, and when an argument started regarding the preeminence of art over literature, I allowed myself to pronounce what was almost a speech, with a facility of elocution and a choice of expressions by which I was both surprised and delighted. Sarah Bell applauded me in her fashion, by applying the tip of her ankle-boot to mine. The painter Laurent responded very wittily. I riposted. Our host intervened, and the skirmish soon became general.

Nothing pleases me more than those passes of arms in which one warms up, delivering oneself entirely, parrying, breaking and advancing, often striking at the right point. Only then do I feel alive, rejuvenated, making infantile gibes and getting carried away like a student.

And that is particularly exquisite when you have an attentive woman beside you. her lips parted as if to breathe in, to drink your words—I mean a pretty woman like Sara Bell, by whom one feels that one is understood and almost admired.

I was taken aside then; did I still have the right to make such speeches, having renounced literature to throw myself into finance? I was sent reports and stock quotations. A deserter of the art, ought I still to permit myself to preach for the god I had denied?

All that was said, naturally, gaily and without malevolence.

I protested, affirming that I have not abdicated any of my ambitions. Only, I do not believe in intuition, in innate knowledge, and I do not want, like so many others, to depict fashionably a humanity that I do not know . . . or, rather, did not know. The Bourse is a microcosm, or rather a menagerie, in which the human beast reveals itself in all its incarnations; I record the roars of wild beasts or the mewling of jackals; I detail in my notebook impudences, audacities, hypocrisies and cowardices. Every vice has its file, every villainy its page, every passion its current account. One day, I shall add it all up, and it will be a book . . .

"Get away!" someone cried. "You talk too much about your book ever to write it."

"A book is a mistress—you're married!"

"Oh, only a little," I riposted, looking at the blonde Sarah, who smiled at me with an unequivocal sympathy.

However, I had the good taste—imitated, moreover, by my friends—not to leave the conversation on that terrain.

A moment later, the music began. A young virtuoso of sixteen, Hungarian by origin and even with a hint of a gypsy complexion, played with a diabolical fervor. Sarah and I took refuge in a little smoking-room separated from the drawing room by a heavy Oriental door-curtain, one side of which was lifted, and there we chatted delightfully.

That woman has unusually gripping features; I stimulated her to talk, taking pleasure in the timbre of her voice, which has echoes of distant bells. She told me about her childhood, when, having been abandoned by her mother on the streets of New York, she had almost died of cold and poverty; then there had been an unexpected adoption by a family from Louisiana, who brought her to France; then a further isolation and abandonment, a consequence of the death of her protectors; and finally, the sudden revelation of an artistic vocation, the slow, arduous, persevering toil, and now—who knows? Perhaps an imminent, decisive success.

I allowed myself to be lulled by the soft murmur of her confidences.

Amity was born between us, cordial and emotional, putting its enveloping note over our previous sympathies, which had only been translated thus far by the exchange of teasing banter.

And privately, I told myself that Sarah would be an exquisite companion, that in traveling with her one would find an intelligent camaraderie, new revelations and unknown sensations.

It would be easy for me to absent myself for a fortnight, or a month. Without dwelling on that thought, I knew that, at home, the announcement of my departure would not even

provoke any observation, by reason of the submissive indolence—or what I called that—of my wife.

Sarah understood me admirably; sometimes, in a
swiftly-launched observation, she divined me, anticipating
my words, slower than the prescience of my own ideas.

The hours passed, and passed. I no longer had any notion
of time. Gradually, our friends withdrew. We remained alone
with our host. I looked at the clock. It was midnight. Ch***
considered us, smiling, and I know not what unexpressed
thought caused Sarah and me to blush.

We got up and took our leave. She lived a short distance
away, in the Rue d'Offément. She took my arm and slowly,
very slowly, we set forth. She leaned on me, and sometimes, if
her hand slipped, I brought it back, closing it, in order for the
pressure to be more sensible.

That conversation had resumed, with nuances of delicate
intimacy.

We stopped for a moment before her door; then, quite
naturally, without either of us making the proposition, we
resumed walking, going back and forth along the sidewalk in
a monotonous stroll that it did not seem to us ought ever to
end.

We did not talk about amour. There was something between us unnamed and more subtle, and apparently indifferent words acquired a harmonic savor on our lips. Our "*vous*"
had the softness of "*tus*."

A few large drops of rain recalled us to reality. A storm was
commencing. There was a flash of lightning. With a fearful
cry, Sarah ran to her doorway, and there I saw her, in the stone
frame, against the black background of the panel; standing
out, white and pink, with the golden nimbus of her hair.

She rang, holding her hand out to me. There was the kind
of frank embrace between us that is both a thank you and a
promise. Then she disappeared.

Crossing the street, I waited momentarily, desirous of seeing a light appear that would be like a last reflection of her. I did not see anything. The rain grew heavier. By an exceedingly rare hazard, having not been signaled, an empty carriage was passing by and the coachman consented graciously to pick me up. I had myself taken to the Café Américain, and there, alone in a chosen corner, I stayed for about half an hour. But the noise soon increased and a crowd invaded the tables. Almost irritated, I left, and, climbing back into my carriage, I had myself taken home.

III

As I was going upstairs, a singular idea crossed my mind.

Since the beginning of the week, it had been the fourth day that I had come home like that, after midnight. My concierge must have conceived a meager esteem for my virtue.

That made me laugh.

I did not want to wake anyone. I took my key from my pocket and turned it carefully in the lock. I went in.

The antechamber and the dining room, which I traversed, lighting my way with a candle taken from a sideboard, seemed to me to be dark and cold. I know not what remorse assailed me, as if I were suddenly ashamed of the bourgeois existence to which I had condemned myself; and in an instantaneous evocation I saw, far away—very far away—under a luminous blue sky, a little house perched on the edge of a lake, with a portico of colonnettes enlaced by flowers framing the charming silhouette of a young woman, blonde and smiling.

I went into my study, where, some time ago, in an alcove fitted with drapes, I had had a bed set up for days like today when I came back late.

I lit my lamp, divining that I would not fall asleep easily. I intended to take advantage of my insomnia to put a few accounts in order.

But before sitting down, I went, as I had the habit of doing, to my wife's bedroom, in order to bid her goodnight.

I did not intend to wake her, tonight above all.

I therefore pushed the door carefully, which slid over the carpet.

In the big, broad bed my wife's head appeared to me, slightly pale; the closed eyes had faintly colored shadows. She was lying at an angle, her body occupying, so to speak, both our places, including the one that I had no longer come to occupy for some time.

She was profoundly asleep, and I do not know what unconscious perversity led me to consider her more attentively. Why not admit it? I was thinking about Sarah, and making a comparison.

My wife has black hair, very thick. She is simply coiffed, and the correct brunette line frames her delicate features, her large eyes and her slender straight nose, very well. In the blonde Sarah there is something light and fantastic—aerial, so to speak—that I do not find in my wife, who is evidently more beautiful but without that hint of originality that is the spice of beauty.

I looked at her, and in that contemplation I experienced a strange, inexplicable sensation. It was really her, and yet I seemed to be subject to the singular attraction that grips you on the threshold of a mystery. Still motionless, she did not sense my gaze attached to her. She was breathing slightly heavily, and sometimes the regular respiration was broken by a longer exhalation that resembled a sigh.

Her lips, young and red, were slightly parted, allowing the sight of the enamel of very white teeth; there was something in that like an attempted smile stopped by a rather dolorous contraction, and the glow of a night-light attached a gleam to the fringe of the eyelashes that resembled the filtration of a motionless and saddened gaze.

Why did I stay there, standing still, my gaze riveted to that pale forehead? I know not what strange thought was haunting me. I would have liked my gaze to have the power of penetrating that little head, which—I don't know why—appeared to me to have acquired an enigmatic character in that slumber.

I would have liked to know, ardently, where that thought was wandering, errant in a dream. It was like an obsession that imposed itself upon me, and which I could not escape. That curiosity had surged forth within me suddenly, without it being possible for me to formulate its object. There were questions on my lips that I would not have been capable of making precise, and, with an anxiety that weighed upon me like suffering, I waited in silence for a response to an interrogation not yet emitted.

No sign indicated that an awakening was imminent, that some instinct had alerted her to my presence.

Why persist in remaining there? Had I the intention, then, of waking her? No. On the contrary, I was enveloped myself by the ambient somnolence of that room, filled with a sweet perfume that I recognized, which had often, in days past, put a kind of intoxication into my brain.

Doubtless that was what was troubling me.

At that moment, and as I turned round with great precaution in order to return to my study, my gaze fell upon a little item of Italian furniture in olive-wood encrusted with ivory, which I had bought in Naples during our first voyage.

Grooves ran across the upper face, framing narrow drawers and two doors that slid under the pressure of a spring.

Suddenly, brutally, my gaze was caught by something abnormal.

Above the doors was a full plinth, on which the artist had depicted a race of amazons, launched forth bare-breasted on horses, with quivers over their shoulders. In the middle of that plinth, cutting one of the figurines in two, I saw something white: almost nothing, merely a line as thin as a chalk stroke.

What was it?

I was under the influence of a sort of neurosis that magnified impressions to the point of giving them an unhealthy acuity. That line, which had never been there before, produced a painful effect on me. Carefully stifling the sound of my footsteps, I went to the item of furniture with the formal intention of getting rid of it, convinced that a thrust of a finger would suffice.

But my hand, on touching it, felt that what I had mistaken for a streak was a resistant body.

I bent down, holding my breath and looked.

This is what I saw:

The extreme edge of a piece of paper had slid from the interior to the exterior. Now, at that point of the cabinet, I knew—or thought I knew—that no cavity or drawer was accommodated.

I had chosen, examined and bought that bibelot myself, and the merchant, opening its various compartments before me, had said to me—I remember it as if it were yesterday— that the plinth covered a solid section. Thus, he had deceived me, or was himself deceived, for now I had proof that there was an empty space there, since the edge of the piece of paper was protruding therefrom.

Delicately, with my fingernails—which I wear quite long—I seized the extremity of the sheet of paper and pulled it toward me, slowly enough for there to be no fear of tearing it.

But then, under the traction, a sliver of wood turned on itself, and I saw that between two planchettes sustaining two drawers above and below, there was a long, narrow space: a veritable hiding-place of which nothing outside permitted the existence to be divined.

And in that hiding-place there were letters.

An indescribable pressure gripped my heart, and at the same time, my blood froze throughout my being: an intimate sensation of chill that was both atrocious and unsavory.

But I did not make any abrupt movement. Without my will playing any part in my action, obedient to an entirely mechanical impulsion that regulated itself, I pushed the sliver of wood, which resumed its place with a dull click.

Then, holding the letters in my clenched fingers, I went past the bed again, this time without turning my head; I reached the door, which I closed behind me, without making the slightest sound . . .

And I found myself in my study, sitting at my desk, with the sheets of paper, which I had not yet unfolded, in front of me under the white radiance of my lamp, invaded for the moment by a cowardice that I did not yet have the energy to combat.

IV

I opened the first letter, the one that had betrayed the secret.

What I experienced, what I did, what roar escaped my breast, what imprecation sprang from my lips, I do not know.

There was a sudden, frightful spasm in all my fibers, followed by a release, like an explosion ripping my nerves, twisting my muscles and penetrating my temples.

My wife is deceiving me! My wife has a lover!

Instantaneously, like a ferocious beast lurking behind a bush, the truth has leapt at my throat, my brain and my consciousness, biting, shaking and breaking my being. I have been surprised, in a cowardly fashion, treacherously, in my confidence, in my placidity, in my complacent security, having never insulted that woman, I don't say with a suspicion, but even with a jealousy.

And just now, emotionally, I was looking at her and almost admiring her!

How I shall avenge myself! I have neither to reason nor to hesitate. I have here, in my hand, the absolute, undeniable proof of an abominable treason. I feel a sharp pain in my heart, which is an insupportable torture.

And have I not a recognized right to do justice: me, the husband; me, who has given my name to that infamous creature for four years; me, who has sacrificed my liberty for her, my youthful dreams, my ardent ambitions; me, who in order to assure her the luxury by which she is intoxicated, devote myself to work that irritates and exasperates me, like a lowering of my intelligence and my will.

I shall kill her, very soon, there, in her sleep, with a single blow.

I have opened the drawer in my desk and taken out my revolver. It's loaded, that's good.

Oh, I don't intend her to suffer. I shall place the cold barrel against her temple; she will not even have time to experience the sensation.

And my finger will squeeze the trigger.

A little noise, a supreme convulsion . . . and I shall be avenged.

In truth, this is horrible.

But what does that woman lack, then? Am I a brutal husband, or even severe? Have I ever refused to satisfy a single one of her desires? And if she had some caprice, would I not have subscribed to it?

There is a hypocrisy in this that confounds me; for, in truth, I have never divined or sensed anything. I have always found in her eyes the same indolent, almost indifferent gaze, on her lips the same complaisant, inexpressive smile. Whenever I entered or exited she always presented her forehead to me with the same calm, extended her hand with the same banal cordiality.

Have I ever sought to quarrel with her stupidly? Have I not left her free to come and go as she pleases, to go into town or remain in the house? Am I one of those ridiculous tyrants who spy on their wives incessantly, obsessing them with mistrust, demanding a detailed account of their least actions, intervening in their amities, constraining them to choose or set aside particular relationships?

None of that. I have always manifested the simple, loyal confidence that is an homage to honesty.

What point is there is arguing, then? Do I, perchance, doubt my right? It is acquired, and nothing can make me fail in it. The felony is patent, hideous. That woman, coldly and shamefully, has betrayed her duty, has dishonored my name, and, rejecting all decency, has fallen lower than the most impure of courtesans.

I shall kill her!

I am no longer feverish; my brain is calm and my hand is not trembling. Let's go!

I have tightened my fingers on the butt of the revolver, and at a firm pace, I am heading toward the bedroom.

But him, the wretch! I need his name.

I have only read—and can I even say read?—one letter, the last, and I have not seen the signature, only the handwriting.

For, if I do not discover that name—the name of the swine that I shall kill after her—it will be necessary for her to reveal it to me before dying.

Oh, she won't refuse me! For a start, all adultery is cowardly; since she has had the cowardice of lying . . . but first I want to try to find out by myself . . .

I have returned to my study. I have put the revolver down, close by, within reach of my hand. It will place itself there soon, at the precise moment when the administrator of justice must strike . . .

Those letters! It requires, in truth, a terrible courage to read them. I shall have it.

The last is this one:

> *Why have you not received me? I have your promise, though. Have pity on me. You know full well that I love you and am going mad in consequence. And you, do you not already love me, a little? For you have said, yes, you have told me that you do not hate me! Tomorrow, no? Tomorrow!*

Then an initial: R.

It's singular, but it seems to me that I don't know that handwriting. Is it disguised, then, counterfeit? Furthermore, my sight isn't very clear at this moment, and the characters are deforming before me. Decidedly, it's very difficult to conserve a relative calm. I'm clenching my teeth as if to break them.

Four letters. Yes, not one more.

Which is the first? They have no dates. But there's an almost sure guide, which is the first word written

That's it.

The first says "Madame." The second begins: *Do you remember, Gabrielle . . .* The third begins: *And you doubt me, beloved!* The gradation is palpable.

> *Madame,*
>
> *I scarcely dare to write to you, and yet it is necessary. I cannot bear the idea that I might have offended you, I who have a respect for you that goes as far as veneration. Yes, I am culpable, yes, I have yielded to an impulse stronger than my will, but you were weeping, Madame, and your silent dolor your suffering supported with such dignity, so courageously, those tears that you tried in vain to suppress: all of that broke my heart I do not know what words sprang from my lips; I have been culpable,*

since you have punished me so cruelly by rejecting me, in forbidding me to pass the threshold of your door, and yet I swear to you once again that not one thought exists in me that is not admiration and respect for you. What have I said? I've forgotten. But if the words translated poorly what I felt, I want at least for you to render me the esteem that is my entire life. What I wanted to say to you, Madame, is that you do not have a friend, servant or slave in the world more devoted than me. I suffer your pain, I weep your tears, and I would give my life to see you happy. Who, then, merits more and better than you the happiness that is so wickedly refused to you? Do you not have everything: beauty, charm, wit, tenderness? Have I not seen you ten times, a hundred times, submitting without a movement of rebellion, without even a shudder, to those abruptnesses that, I sense, cause you real pain, like a brutal blow? The other day, during that anniversary meal, you had graciously arranged bunches of flowers—which one loves—on the table, and, I knew, I sensed that, you were waiting for . . . what? great gods? . . . a word, a smile, a glance: the alms of gratitude that one throws to the most indifferent . . . well, one came in harassed and preoccupied. One announced to you that one had to hurry dinner, that one was awaited. You tried by means of allusions that I understood to recall the day of that date—for which you have, yourself, a kind of religion—but you had not been understood! I saw you, slightly pale, struggling against the chagrin that was constricting your heart. Those poor flowers, one looked at them with indifference. I don't know whether one even made a little joke about that ornamental profusion. I could have remained with you, but I did not want to. I sensed that I would no longer be master of myself; I departed, bearing in my heart a wound that was yours. And you, I know, I divine, spent that evening alone, alone as always, weeping and dreaming of your finished dreams. And you would not want a man of heart to protest against that martyrdom? You would not want someone to feel profound, intimate, absorbing desire, to devote a sincere amity to you, disengaged from any ego-tism? To be your friend! But I do not know any title sweeter, of which I could be prouder! That is what I wanted to say to you, Madame. If I have spoken foolishly, forgive me, and do not condemn me without appeal. For I give you my word as an honest man that, rather than offend you, I would prefer to exile myself far from you forever. You are so good! Will you, then, only be pitiless for me, who has placed you so high that I scarcely dare raise my eyes toward you? I ask for mercy, mercy for the friend, mercy for the slave. God himself is not im-placable. I shall have the audacity to present myself tomorrow evening. If your door remains closed to me, I shall not criticize you . . . oh, no, but I shall suffer cruelly in thinking that, by my own fault, I shall have lost that which is the happiness of my entire life, the adorable conversations that render me better. I await my sentence.

*ROBERT DE S****

The signature is in capital letters. I know the name of that amorous Tartuffe. He is my best friend, or ought to be. It was me who, a year ago, on his return from the Far East, introduced him into my home.

A child, a scamp, with the false naiveties and enthusiasms of an actor. The wretch! And it's with these banal letters, the model of which is contained in the "perfect writing-desks" of all lovers, that these puppets come to throw dishonor into a family, to doom a woman forever, to kill the future of two beings. And these social bandits go unpunished? There is no justice for these dainties of the boudoir, these Judases disguised as troubadours? Well then, I will kill you, you too, but face to face, spitting your infamy in your face. Oh yes, I will kill you . . .

V

The scene to which the traitor makes allusion fixes the date of that letter for me. It was six weeks ago. Yes, the eighth of May, the anniversary of my marriage. I had forgotten it! That was because on that day I had very real, very grave, preoccupations. The sudden fall compromised all my operations, and I was in haste to go to the petty Bourse that evening. Fortunately, the movement was canceled out. What did I do thereafter? Ah! I remember. I went to finish my evening at the home of an old friend, and it was there that I met Sarah Bell for the first time . . .

Four years of marriage! To arrive at this catastrophe!

I still recall the day when I was introduced into the home of the parents of Gabrielle . . . of that woman. They seemed to me to be such worthy people! It was in the country, in a little property near Sceaux.

I had decided to marry. Solitude was weighting upon me, and I sensed that, in spite of my strength of character, I was letting myself be dragged on to a bad slope. I was gambling, giving full rein to the bachelor life, spending money without counting it, with open hands, rebellious to all steady work.

My notary, warning me about the perils of my situation, had spoken to me about marriage. At first I had jibbed, unable to tolerate the idea of alienating my precious liberty. Then I reflected and reasoned, and authorized the first steps.

In truth, that woman was a lovely girl. Her father, a former provincial magistrate, had the amiable and slightly mocking bonhomie of translators of Horace. Widowed for ten years, he had confided the education of his daughter to an aunt—his wife's sister—of a veritably superior intelligence, who conquered me immediately.

I remember what she said to me on my first visit;

"Monsieur, I believe that you could be a good husband. It only depends on you whether Gabrielle will be the best of wives. She has all the delicacies and all the weaknesses of a child. I have striven not to give her any prejudices or any recklessness. She is good, profoundly honest"—yes, yes, she said that!—"she will love to the point of adoration whomever she chooses. But I beg you, do not be one of those husbands who only see a wife as a gracious plaything, with whom one amuses oneself passionately at first, and then neglects and forgets. Marriage is not an act that, once accomplished, has, by itself, virtue enough for an entire existence. For two spouses to be veritably and perpetually united, it is necessary to tighten, often and carefully, the links of the chain that binds them to one another. If it rusts, it breaks. That is up to you. The man who wants always to be with his wife what he was with his bride will be the happiest of husbands. Mistrust habitude; that is what disaggregates the most solid happiness."

I listened meekly, smiling a little privately at those lessons in conjugal experience given by an old spinster.

Gabrielle has changed very little, physically, since that first epoch. I can still see her coming into the drawing room where I had come to talk to her father. She was twenty years old, of medium height, perhaps a little less; she was admirably made, with a finesse of silhouette that struck me. Her black hair, simply coiffed, made the fresh complexion of her face, gently velveted like a spring fruit, stand out. Her wide open eyes had a serene placidity, whose coldness was tempered by an exquisite expression of frankness, also belied by boldly designed and youthfully red lips.

A week did not pass without me being considered as part of the family. No delay had been fixed for what is known as courtship. The aunt, whom I had pleased, was careful not to manifest any absurd suspicion of me. She often came with us on long walks in the country, and more often than not she walked ahead of us, thus leaving us complete liberty to chat and get to know one another better.

Why would I deny it to myself? I was convinced that I had found in Gabrielle the companion of my dreams.

Very intelligent, beneath a modest exterior, I understood that she was ready to give all her love and all her life, to confide herself like a child taking her mother's hand. She needed support; she knew it and said so, knowing herself well enough to measure what she lacked in will-power and initiative. "Promise me always to be my friend and my guide," she said to me, "that's my wish. At any rate, when one is married," she added, smiling, "one is sure of never being alone again."

I loved her madly, and I remember that I was sometimes frightened by the exuberance of my protestations. My speech was vibrant and excited; my passion, imbecile that I was, overflowed in romantic tirades or, by contrast, when we were sitting in silence, on a beautiful summer evening on a bench a few paces away from our indulgent Cerberus, who was knitting obstinately, I would murmur those exquisite words whose force is primarily made of delicacy and charming respect. I could see her large eyes through the darkness, in which a gleam lit up, illuminated by gratitude and hope. And she said to me: "You'll be always be like this, won't you?"

The year that followed our marriage was a dream of happiness. I believe that I didn't quit her for an hour. I no longer had anyone but my wife, better than a mistress, a friend to whom I confided all my thoughts, even the most secret. I admired the rectitude of her mind, the impeccable naivety of her common sense, which was never mistaken. What she experienced for me was simultaneously the love of a wife and the slightly respectful affection of a younger sister. She never acted, even in the simplest matters, without consulting me, if not vocally, at least with her gaze.

Having a very sincere intention of resuming after a brief pause the literary endeavors that I had been obliged to set aside temporarily in order to occupy myself with the reestablishment of my fortune, somewhat depleted, I gave her a part in the studies to which I devoted myself, in order to give my conceptions a solid scientific basis. She was keenly interested in my work, and that was not an obliging pretence on her part. I always liked explaining to her, before putting them on paper, the thoughts that haunted my brain; I have a very clear, very logical mind, and speech is a great help to me in elucidating, for my own sake, questions that present some difficulty.

In those circumstances, I talked to her, and gradually, in her intelligent physiognomy, I saw a light dawn, informing me that I had been understood, while enabling myself to understand better.

That was the best time of my life!

Now, all of that is lost forever . . . by virtue of her crime, by virtue of her ingratitude and felony.

Those memories are killing me, but I don't want them to rob me of my strength.

The deeper the gulf is into which I'm falling, the more I hate those who have precipitated me into it.

The other letters are here. Should I read them? What's the point? Do I not know now that everything is broken, that everything is finished? And yet, I want to climb my Calvary all the way to the cross, to which I shall nail my heart . . . but not without nailing *them* to either side of me, to the gibbet of infamy . . .

VI

Do you remember, Gabrielle, my sister—you have permitted me to address you thus—what you said to me yesterday? As one had got carried away at your home, wanting to lend to we know not who, the volume that one published two years before your marriage, that essay in scholarly romance entitled Small Horizons, *you asked me to look for a copy and bring it to you. I can refuse you nothing, even when, you will admit, the request is not without causing me some concern. I therefore obtained one, not without difficulty, for the publisher has gone bankrupt and all the remaining copies have been sold and dispersed. In brief, I brought you one; you opened it urgently; I do not have the right to lament or to address a reproach to you. Then, in a low voice, in the penetrating tone, simultaneously grave and soft, that is yours, you read out the page that you were slow to rediscover. It was the slightly overlong tirade of Jacques, the hero, when, weary of the violent struggles of an overheated life, he finally poses the thesis of small horizons, which everyone ought to measure to his strength and fill with his reasoned activity. It is, it is true, a paraphrase of the* aurea mediocritas *of the Latin poet, or Candide's "Let us cultivate our garden," but with an entire-*

ly modern note. You let the book slide on to your knees then, and you murmured: "What if two people cannot be content with small horizons?" I did not want to pick up on that remark, which, at that moment, was beyond me; but dear, how just it was, and how I understand it! How crazy are those who, having happiness within their reach, create the tortures of Tantalus for themselves by drawing away voluntarily, as if playfully, from the fruit that they might pick! Dare I tell you that we have known, that the two of us know better than anyone, the small horizon that envelops us and has already given us such sweet joys? It is our amity that has traced it, and there is room within it for our happiness. Do not those admirable evenings when one abandons us, have a charm that embalms our entire life? Perhaps vanity is leading me astray, but when you listen to me, Gabrielle, when I tell you in a whisper my hopes and my desires, when I dare to dream about the tomorrows that prolong shared joys, it seems to me that on your beautiful face, in those eyes as profound as lakes, whose brightness fascinates me and sometimes maddens me—but you don't know anything about that, for I never tell you—I read an encouragement, almost a promise . . . Oh, when I dream . . . ! After all, why lie, to myself and to you? Gabrielle, I love you, I love you madly . . . Is that a crime? I don't want to think that. I only see via you, for you, and the hours that you give me almost every day are my whole life. Do I think, do I exist, when I am not with you? Oh, don't expel me, don't reject me! This confession which is burning my heart I could not hold back. But do you not know, dear, that I love you . . . and not egotistically, for myself alone? That love is the

desire to make you happy, to repair the harm that has been done to you . . . That confession you have read in my eyes, you have heard in the echo of my voice, even when, seeking to deceive one another, I pronounce words that seem indifferent. But you know very well, I tell you, that everything within me cries to you: I love you! I love you! For in the end, Gabrielle, it's necessary to have pity. Have you not understood everything that I am suffering, have you not divined the tortures that are stabbing me, burning me and tearing me apart? Oh, how cruel you are! But no, no, I'm not complaining, I can accept everything, and even more suffering, even more tortures, provided that, like yesterday, you leave your hand in mine for a minute, provided that you permit me to look at you, to contemplate you, to adore you. I promise you not to speak, not to pronounce the words that trouble you, that make you weep. No, I shall just come to sit down at your feet, on the blue cushion, and there, hands joined, docile and happy, I shall fix my eyes on yours, I shall listen to your lips, and I shall take that vision away in my heart, which is my happiness. You won't chase me away tomorrow, will you? Oh, if you knew how I love you! And how I'm really yours, entirely yours!
ROBERT

VII

I read all that infamous and stupid nonsense in a single surge, my mouth dry, my chest breathless. Thus, I have the horrible courage to follow, one by one, the traces of the crime; I see the thought of it born, the plan of it developed, the execution of it in preparation.

So, while I, confidently—stupidly confident—let the hypocritical wife and the lying friend enter my home, into the interior that ought to be respected like a temple, treason rose up between those two beings, bold and impudent.

And I didn't suspect anything! No, in truth, with all my intelligence, I was more stupid than the most stupid of Dandins.

For two months that shameful comedy was being played here, and when I came home, my wife, if I woke her up by going into her bedroom, looked at me with her wide eyes, in which I thought I saw sadness, almost a reproach, and which, an hour before, had been shining with the radiance that maddens that monsieur. The soul of woman is kneaded of lies; it is mud.

And I sometimes experienced a kind of remorse! Yes, really, I had the folly of accusing myself of negligence. This evening, again, I hesitated to render to my friend's invitation. A little while ago, when I felt Sarah Bell shiver in my arms, when my hand enlaced her hand to retain her or ask her to draw me toward her, I resisted. I didn't go with her; I let her door close heavily and separate us.

Triple imbecile that I am!

I'm exasperated by the poor stupidity of these letters. The least of students could have written better ones. Not one original idea, not one impulse that is not banally expressed,

Those false respects, those mutisms of adoration, those plaintive pities—all that is old, worn out, obsolete . . . and women still allow themselves to be taken in by them!

And that stupid individual permits himself to mock me. Yes, in truth, the cunning that forbids him to attack the husband directly and cynically is penetrated by the naivety of his hatred, and above all his jealousy.

What perfidy there is in the slightest words! That book that I requested in order to lend it to someone or other . . .

those difficulties in procuring it, under the insolent pretext of the publisher's bankruptcy and the remaindering of the edition . . . all that is calculated malevolently and insolently.

Where is my copy, then? Oh, yes, I remember . . . at Sarah's who was kind enough to ask me for it. As if I could have refused it to her!

And those sufferings, those tortures, those lacerations! What ridiculous and mendacious phraseology!

That woman, whom I believed to be intelligent, has allowed herself to be tricked by that literature of sentimental hackwork. What poverty!

The third note is short and conclusive. For me, it's a knife-thrust, delivered in cowardly fashion between the shoulder-blades, the blade penetrating all the way to the heart.

So you doubt me, beloved, and you still distrust yourself . . . but why? Are you not mine, as I am yours . . . ?

I wasn't able to finish. A red mist passed before my eyes.

I rose to my feet, my heart wrung by an atrocious grip.

My hand seized the butt of the revolver, and slowly, with an automaton tread, I marched toward the bedroom.

Three o'clock chimed.

I've come in, shoulders forward, looking. What if she were to wake?

Well, am I afraid of her, by chance? Let her wake up, so that I can hurl my hatred and scorn in her face.

No, she's asleep. She has turned on her side now; I can only see her head in profile, her temple and her ear, with the little pearl that I gave her . . . once.

How many times I have watched her sleep thus, in an attitude so gracious that no painter ever found a model more exquisite. There is a ravishing sweetness in that veiled body. Yes, very often, in the early days of our marriage, when I lay awake, following my dreams in the placidity of the nocturnal silence, I leaned toward her . . . and on that pale forehead, unobscured by any shadow, I read a poem of purity . . .

And now that forehead is lying; behind those closed eyelids the gaze is lurking, hypocritical and felonious. And shall I suffer that treason—me? Shall I accept my dishonor and support me own scorn? Shall I be able, tomorrow, in an hour, to recall these odious things, to look at those lips, which have smile at another, those hands, which another has gripped?

No. Let her die.

I have raised the revolver, and slowly, I have lowered it as far as her temple.

A lock of black hair hides the appointed place where the bullet ought to strike. Then, with infinite precaution, my finger lifts it . . . Gabrielle has made a movement. I've thrown myself backwards instinctively, as if I were afraid.

In truth, one might think that I dare not punish.

Why? Have I not every right? Am I not the husband? Has that woman not belied all her promises, all her oaths?

Well, what about me?

What about me?

VIII

I have fled the bedroom. I'm in my study, hunched in an armchair. The revolver has escaped my hand and is lying on the carpet.

Who, then, spoke just now? What was the voice that suddenly threw into my ear that interrogation, which burst forth like the blast of a clarion?

What about me? What? What does that mean? To what is it responding?

I was thinking that that woman had belied all her oaths . . . and those words were pronounced within me, against me . . . like a cry of revenge, a threat, an accusation . . .

Am I going mad? What is this stupidity?

It is when I find out that the greatest of crimes has been committed against me, when I have suffered the worst insult that can afflict a man, when I sense within me the desire and the right to punish . . . that I accuse myself . . . or, rather, that voice, come from who knows where, insults me with an absurd riposte . . .

What! What about me? In truth, it's almost grotesque. Is it me who is the criminal, me the traitor? What insanity!

What is this paradoxical sophism that suddenly comes into my head to break the equilibrium, displace the responsibilities and palliate the undeniable verity by means of a lie?

Have I committed any fault, then? Sarah Bell! Is she my mistress? Do I have two households? Am I one of those men who abandon their interior to give themselves to a stranger? Have I ever refused anything to the woman who bears my name? Have I stolen her share of happiness?

No. I have not sinned. My conscience is calm . . .

Just now I was remembering the first year of my marriage. Was any husband ever more loving, more devoted, more obliging, more submissive? Was that woman not truly half of my soul? I did not have a single thought to which I did not make her party. I did not take any pleasure of which I did not immediately give her the first fruits—the essence, so to speak. I opened every page of my consciousness to her, like a book. I abdicated all egotism, experiencing an ineffable enjoyment in feeling myself live that double life, admiring in that woman a reflection of myself.

How I loved her!

And now sobs are rising to my throat, and tears; yes, I'm weeping like a child, like an idiot.

Was there anything more beautiful than our walks together, when we went at random, awaiting the opportunity, the pretext, for a conversation, the eruption of an idea that, more often then not, surged forth in both of us at the same time? Often, a thought was born in her rather vaguely; she interrogated me and I took pleasure, with a healthy pride of protector and master, in disengaging that inertial conception for her from the fog that obscured it.

A docile and charming pupil, she listened to me with a sort of self-mistrust, as if she were afraid of not being able to understand me sufficiently, but little by little, her subtle mind grasped the truth, the expression of the finest nuances; and if I hesitated to continue, fearing that I might fatigue her attention, she proved with a word her desire to continue listening to me.

That is veritably the best and sweetest of my memories. There is, in the education of a beloved woman, a charm that cannot be compared to any other. And to thank her for having given it to her, I let myself fall to my knees, looking at her, loving her, adoring her . . .

Six months ago, one day when I came home from the Bourse, preoccupied and enervated—I remember it as if it were yesterday—Gabrielle said to me: "Friend, I have a desire . . . a caprice, if you wish . . . in this fine snowy weather I'd like to take a nice walk with you . . . this evening . . . in the Bois de Boulogne, for instance . . ."

And, shrugging my shoulders, I replied: "What a strange idea! Great gods, what poetry! In any case, it's impossible . . . I'm busy this evening . . ."

"You're going out?"

"Yes, and I beg you to hurry dinner . . ."

"But do you know, dear, that I never—almost never—have you with me any more?"

"What do you expect? Business . . ."

"Put it off until tomorrow. Truly, you'd give me great pleasure . . ."

"What childishness! I'll stay tomorrow, or the day after, but today, it's impossible. Anyway, Robert can keep you company. Hurry dinner, won't you?"

And I went into my study.

Was it truly impossible for me to devote that evening to her? What was that business that was so urgent? I made a tour of the boulevard; I went into the Varietés, and from there I went to the club.

I came back after midnight. Gabrielle was in bed, and I saw that she had been weeping. Then rather dryly, I said to her: "What's all this? Tears, now, reproaches? Why? Because I've been retained longer than I thought. It's ridiculous . . . we're no longer children and we can't spend our entire lives cooing like turtle-doves."

She shut up, and I didn't give it another thought.

Come on then, confess, husband!

In the dolorous and heavy anguish that is oppressing me at present, when I sense everything escaping me, when my life is breaking. I'm struggling in vain against a truth that is gripping me, enlacing me and stifling me . . .

The voice that pronounced a single phrase in my ear just now, which made me shudder in my most profound fibers, and which I refused to comprehend—that voice is now speaking so loudly and so brutally that I can't not hear it.

To those memories of the first year, so pure and so charming, which render my present dolor more poignant and more bitter, other memories are opposed, which I try in vain to set aside.

Who relaxed the chain of that intimate union? Who disengaged the threads, one at a time, of that weave? Who wearied of happiness? Who dilapidated the treasure that was there, under his hand?

Well, it was me . . . it is me!

To set oneself up as a judge, to arrogate the right of life and death, is facile. But what magistrate invested with an exorbitant power would refuse to hear, or even to provoke, the defense? Are not official advocates designated for the worst criminals?

That advocate will be my conscience. I want it to speak, I want it to confess. I want it, disengaging itself from the carapace of pride under which it hides, finally to show itself entirely.

And first, I address this question to it, to which I constrain it to respond:

When Gabrielle became my wife, when the young woman abdicated her liberty in my hands, did she, yes or no, give herself entirely, body and soul? Was there some covert of consciousness, mysterious and obscure, into which my gaze did not penetrate? No. That soul was a crystal behind which no shadow was lurking. It had an exquisite chastity, a divine purity, a holy ignorance of life and amour.

In the woman, there was a child, a child who did not know anything, who did not calculate; she was the malleable virgin wax which offers itself, immaculately, to the genius of the artist. Did I encounter any resistance? Was I not the master of fashioning her to the whim of my fantasy? I had the power of the creator, responsible for the creature.

Certainly, I have loved her. I have been passionately smitten with her beauty, her charm and her grace. I have experienced the foolish and delectable vanity of sensing myself the sole master of that virginity, and, placing her on the pedestal of an idol, I have prostrated myself before her, intoxicating myself with the incense that I lavished upon her.

In that excessive amour, is it really her of whom I was thinking? Of the joys felt, is it the case that, sincerely, the larger part did not devolve to me? Was it for her that I loved her, or was it for me?

In raising her up so high, did I reflect on the vertigo that I was putting into her brain?

Every time that I have heard *Ruy Blas*, a thought has haunted me, which is this:

Suppose that it is not Don Sallust, but the queen, who plans to avenge herself on Ruy Blas. She takes him by the hand, raises him ever higher, gives him power, the faculty of developing all his strengths, of realizing the good of which he has dreamed; she follows in his soul the developments of the amour that she is able to inspire in him; she pretends to be touched by it herself, and carried away . . . and, at the moment when "he marches living in his starry dream," she throws this single remark at him:

"You're a lackey!"

What a frightful catastrophe would be produced in the brain of that man! To have believed himself a god, by virtue of the adoration of his faithful followers, and then suddenly to see those respectful individuals, still fearful and prostrate a moment before, standing up to insult him to his face!

The husband, during the early days of his union, lifts his wife to the height of a goddess; she is more than a queen; he proclaims himself less than a subject, he is a slave. Before that intoxicating beauty, he sings hymns and intones prayers. Enraptured, transported to those regions from which no one is believed ever to return, she wants to lift up that kneeling man, of whom she scarcely hopes to be the equal . . .

Then, one day, abruptly, in a fit of ill humor, he stands up and says to her: "Pardon me! Pick up my handkerchief for me."

Surprised, snatched violently from the heaven in which she has lost herself, she smiles, obeys, and for all recompense, requests a smile:

"Oh, let's be serious. It pleased me to play, with the best will in the world, that comedy of the glorification of the wife . . . there's a time for everything. Now I want to occupy myself with my affairs. Pick up your embroidery and don't trouble me."

Today, in confrontation with the irreparable, I interrogate myself; the past three years, excluding the first year, loom up before me, and the infinite pettiness of my stupidity and my cruelty frightens me.

After our long honeymoon voyage, which I would have liked to prolong even further, we returned to Paris.

Gabrielle, raised almost claustrally between a disillusioned father and an aunt habituated to solitude, knew nothing of our overheated life. She often told me that she had only been to the theater once, when very small, and that her eyes were still dazzled by a *féerie* of which she did not even know the title.

It was a delicate and charming pleasure for me to initiate her gradually into the intellectual enjoyments in which Paris is prodigal and in which one is spoiled for choice. In my bachelor life I had few worldly relationships that my wife could share. After the obligatory visits to a few aged relatives we confined ourselves at home, creating delicate distractions for ourselves in which the mind played the largest part.

I devoted a few hours every day to my business affairs, but I spent the mornings and evenings at home, working, preparing materials for the book of which I was dreaming, which have been gathering dust in some corner for two years.

I liked to envelop myself in that intimacy, in which my mind was enlarged, I knew that Gabriele was profoundly happy; she was simultaneously friend, wife and mistress, abandoning herself to the gentle current that cradled her, but putting into that exquisite repose with her feminine intelligence the caressant activity of familial coming-and-going.

By virtue of what sudden alteration, what axial tilt, did I become tired of that happiness? In truth, it seems impossible for me to find the precise point in which the equilibrium was displaced.

I remember that one day, a business affair—a real one—prevented me from going home at the usual hour for dinner;

but I leapt into a cab and came to warn Gabrielle, so fearful was I that she might be anxious. Frankly, I told her how sorry I was to quit her; frankly, she kissed me and asked me not to come back too late. At ten o'clock I came back; she was in my study, reading, lovelier than ever, with the hint of coquetry that expectation gives the beloved.

Then, gradually, I allowed myself to be gripped again by the current of Parisian life.

What is incredible is the degree to which the most philosophical man disdains to apply his philosophy to the things that touch him most closely. I have a very clear intelligence, subtle—not to say sharp—in reasoning; I love to analyze the facts, the least circumstances of incidents that happen around me, but never, never did the idea occur to me of applying that science, if science it is, to my interior life. With regard to my affairs and interests, I never hazarded a step or an action, even an apparently indifferent one, without having studied, weighing the pros and cons, the possible consequences. In my intimate life, I went at random, without reflection, obedient to an irrational instinct, to the whim of the moment, never asking myself what might ensue.

And yet, I sense today, in the frightful crisis I am going through, that it is that science of real existence, of domestic happiness, that ought to be the object, before anything else, of the meditations of a sane man, even if only by virtue of egotism.

Suddenly, without transition, I prolonged my absences, without even perceiving it, in a way, which is explicable because I encountered outside excitations that hastened the march of the hours.

Until then, I had a free mind; I created preoccupations and cares, more often than not for silly reasons, which were mere wisps of straw, but which slid into the wheels of my existence, causing grating frictions there.

After having taken the trouble to come in person to deliver warnings that I would be home late I found it simpler to send messages: notes or telegrams.

Talking a great deal outside, I no longer talked at home.

Working in the study became intolerable to me; I felt an incessant need for locomotion, and scarcely had I come in than I marked on the clock-face the hour of the imminent departure.

Gabrielle was always waiting for me with the same smile, her hand extended; that monotony of affection appeared to me to be tiresome and tedious. The absence of reproaches was more aggravating than if they had been formulated. I was all the more irritated because it was impossible for me to explain the reason for my anger. A door opening or closing, a glass relocated, a stopped clock—such insignificant accidents took on enormous proportions in my eyes.

What had previously appeared to me as charming naivety now seemed ridiculous ignorance; if Gabrielle questioned me, as before, I responded dryly—after all, I was not a schoolmaster.

She had a slight flutter of the eyelids, which became more pronounced when she was animated; once, that intermittence of gaze, augmenting the gleam of her eyes, delighted me, and I like to provoke it. I reproached her for it was an imperfection.

No more kneeling before the idol, no more slow and seductive cradling, no more foolish whispers; of my affairs, my projects, my aspirations, not a word any longer.

After all, of what could she complain? Was I less of a husband than other husbands? Did she lack anything? Was the house not comfortable, and had money worries not been set aside? I had to go out; did I prevent her from going out? Why did we have no relations? Why did we not make visits, why did we not receive them? It was incredible that she had no friends? Why not make some?

The liking for the interior life and for solitude, which I had developed to my benefit for two years I now made into a crime, attributing it to faults of character, to a lack of affability. Truly, that indolence was irritating. Always reading, always dreaming. She was occupied with the interior! But with two domestics, what had she to do? And the airs of a victim . . . !

I was lying. Not once had Gabrielle greeted me with less than a frank cordiality. I saw how happy she was in my presence, how she would have liked to retain me with her; and that happiness and that desire irritated me as a protestation.

I ended up no longer being able to tolerate being alone with her; on the few days when I came home for differ I brought friends, including that Robert whom I introduced as an intimate, a brother, a second self, and before whom, by way of braggadocio, I treated Gabriele with an indifference that was sometimes almost insolent. That woman was mine, I intended people to see that I did not have to make any effort for her. Once, Robert brought a bouquet, and I mocked him so much that Gabrielle started to sob. Furious, I threw my napkin on the table and took Robert to dine at the restaurant.

Then, needing even more liberty because of a temporary liaison, I pronounced the fateful words: "Robert, do me the favor of spending the evening with my wife."

If she asked me to take her to some concert, I excused myself, asking Robert to accompany her. I no longer spoke to her as a lover, no longer as a comrade, but as a churl whom those conversations wearied, and who resigned himself to indispensable dialogue.

That is what I have done. Let's sum up.

For long, long months, that woman was everything for me and I wanted to be everything for her. I intoxicated her with adoration, swearing to her that I could not live without her. Why would she not have believed me? Even if, given my cruel and latent experience as a man of the world, perhaps I knew

deep down that they were only words and that "always" is
only verbiage, did she know it? Did I not want to be believed,
and could I have admitted for a single instant that she doubted my sincerity? If she had testified the slightest suspicion,
would I not have pleaded, with an insistent warmth, to make
it disappear?

But no, no shadow of incredulity had brushed her soul.

She believed in me, ingenuously, recklessly. That conviction—of the eternity of amour—which I strove to impose
on her, she accepted; she received it and was impregnated by
it. How, in any case, could it have been otherwise? Where
could she have learned skepticism? The man who had received
her first kiss represented, in her eyes, the type-specimen of
frankness, of sincerity. Him, lie? Get away! Her security was
doubled by the respect that I had wanted and had been able to
inspire in her. Her faith in my probity was the most precious
guarantee . . .

And then, suddenly, without any pretext, without anything in her having changed, that metamorphosis has been
accomplished in me of lover into husband, of affection into
indifference, of indifference into malevolence. Into that heart,
opened to all future hopes, I have let fall, drop by drop, like
an acid, my disenchantments and my lassitudes.

The "I adore you" has not even left behind the echo of an
"I love you."

And I am astonished that in that darkness, which I have
thickened around her, the slightest ray of amour has put a
dazzlement! In the voice of another, her ear has found the
echo of mine, in the words pronounced, the memory of my
words.

A woman experiences an infinite enjoyment in that music
of sounds, that harmony of murmurs.

Do we not know ourselves that power of modulated words,
do we not abuse it, cruel artists that we are, egotistical charm-

ers, like those hunters who attract birds in order to admire them at first, and then stifle them and throw them into their game-bags?

Until the disastrous hour when that woman has weakened, until the last two months when unhappiness has entered the house from which it ought to have been banished forever, what sin has she committed? For what do I have to reproach her?

Nothing. She has loved me in the plenitude of her abandonment and her sincerity. She had given herself, she had not taken herself back. She was mine and mine alone, and it is me who suddenly did not want her.

And since I am reading, courageously, the utmost depths of my consciousness, do I not find there her mute plaints, her silent and desperate appeals? Have I not seen her, at night, when I approach her bed, suddenly opening her eyes wide and looking at me with an expression of anxious happiness, of gratitude for that return, belated as it might be, with the anxious expectation of a word that might recall the past, an impulse that might recommence the future?

Bored, almost irritated by the necessity of that return home, discontented with the duty from which I dare not yet abstain, I did not see anything, did not divine anything. And when, by chance, she had not wiped away her tears carefully enough. I had difficulty not picking a quarrel with her chagrin.

How she must have wept! Knowing her profound honesty, true chastity and feminine delicacies better than anyone else, I divine the struggles suffered . . . and I shudder.

She cried "Help!" and I did not hear her. To extract her from the danger—which I had created myself—a word would have sufficed, and I did not pronounce it.

In one of those letters—atrocious witnesses to the catastrophe of amour and honor that has fallen upon this house—I see that the poor woman (well, yes, I feel sorry for her now) trying to attach herself to the theories I attributed to the hero of *Small Horizons*. Literary theories!

And yet, my Jacques told the truth. We all dream of the second, if not the hundredth rank in Rome, when we could occupy ourselves with the first in our village. That passion for the beyond kills us; being unhappy is being unsatisfied. But in the woman the propensity is contrary. She accepts the limits of the circle in which the hazards of life enclose her, she only asks to cultivate that garden, whose walls are for her the limit of her universe, and she strives to pick the flowers. We knock down the walls, disdaining the sheltered roses, in order to run in search of free, if not wild, plants.

Through the open breach, despair enters behind us.

I do not have the right to kill that woman.

IX

Four o'clock. Day is breaking, and with its first light, that loss of vigor, that relaxation of the entire being, the discouragement of which sometimes even dominates slumber.

Fever soothes me. I want to reflect further.

What am I going to do? I have denied myself the right of murder, and at the same time the right of punishment. The crime committed is mine. I am the accomplice, if not the perpetrator, the principal author.

I have loved poorly, and I am no longer loved; that is justice. I cannot even invoke in my conscience the law that, in the spirit if not the letter, has imposed duties on me that I have not fulfilled.

I shall go away. I shall abandon everything here that represents my past and depart, never to return.

Thus, in punishing the criminal, I shall punish myself. Equity is saved.

Whether by my fault or not, the first bond that linked us to one another is broken.

It would not be just for me to suffer alone. Even taking account—and I do so broadly—of my personal faults, I cannot demand of myself a verdict of complete absolution. I admit the excuse, nothing more.

In the morning, when she wakes, that woman will find the house empty. I am rich enough, while taking away a large enough sum to facilitate the reconstitution of a future, to leave a large enough fortune at her disposal to shelter her from need. In any case, there is her dowry. I shall draw up the necessary instructions in a few lines addressed to my notary.

Where shall I go? Anywhere. To America, or Australia. I am still young, active and vigorous, and the vicissitudes of a hazardous existence will help me to forget.

Later, when my heart has scarred over, I'll think about divorce.

But what about her? Well, why should I worry? She loves that Robert, she will be his mistress until she can become his wife. That wait, in an irregular situation, will be her punishment. I'm indulgent; no one, I think, could accuse me of pitiless severity.

After all, since it has to be thus!

That isn't true! Again, I'm lying to myself, and I don't want to. It's with compromises of conscience that I've lost my life thus far, and hers. It's necessary that I remain lucid and sincere to the end.

That Robert is a child, with a weak mind, a hesitant conscience.

The day when I allowed him to enter my home, when, having shown myself in the most unfavorable light, I manifested before him more than indifference, almost an insolent disdain for my wife, I extended a trap for his youth and sentimental naivety from which the strongest would have been unable to escape.

I'm pleading his cause. That's unusual, and insensate, but I'm gripped by a need for justice that leaves me no truce. For me, at this moment, no more sophisms are possible; the evidence has seized me by the throat and is forcing me to proclaim the truth.

If one of my friends had taken me to his home, at twenty-five, and confronted me with his wife, adorably pretty, having taken care to indicate to me that her beauty and charm had become indifferent to him, had underlined by means of signals, by the play of his physiognomy, the ennui that he experienced in being in his house, had admitted to me, sniggering, that he was expected elsewhere, that he had responded to submissive, almost suppliant words with those mockeries that wound and kill . . .

Would I not have had pity for that woman, would I not have experienced for her the sympathy that soon becomes love, would I not have paid court to her?

And if that husband, intermittently unconscious, had begged me to offer my arm to that woman, if he had been stupid enough to ask me, as a favor, as a chore, to take her out or to spend the evening with her . . . could I have retained my sang-froid, would I have played Joseph or Scipio?

But once again, that isn't true.

Is it really on the basis of a hypothesis that I'm reasoning?

At the moment I introduced that cherub to my wife, I knew him well; I was aware of his almost infantile sentimentality, his insipid poeticism, his sympathetic naivety. I had already appreciated him such as he is: impressionable, tender and romantic. Was I preoccupied with all that? Is it necessary to spell out the horrible truth? I was content for him to rid me of my wife.

Have I even imposed a few obligations on his delicacy to which he consented? Have I, by virtue of my affection and respect for the woman who bears my name, placed before him limits that he could not pass without felony?

Perhaps he has fought against that amour, born in him by my fault. He's timid, I know that. He lacks initiative and energy. He has let himself go with the flow, stupidly, in a cowardly fashion, and the current has dragged him away . . .

With me gone, disappeared, what will happen to him?

In my wife, the first sentiment will be stupor. I shall not have the ridiculous vanity to affirm that she still loves me, but in the souls of women, whoever they may be, the first love puts down roots too profound for separation not to be a rip.

But admitting that, desperate and panicked, she turns to the man who represents henceforth her entire future, she will bump into another stupor.

At his age, with his situation still uncertain, with his inexperience, he will find himself suddenly in charge of a soul, responsible for the happiness, the future and the life of a woman.

In such circumstances, I have seen the most courageous men become cowards.

If the first husband that we deceived said to us, abruptly: "You love my wife; I abandon her to you; take her," we would flee.

Women do not know us. They mistake for pure gold those manufactured phrases: "consecrate my entire life to you, devote myself to you forever." Conclusion: if lovers were summoned to vote for or against a divorce, nine out of ten would reject it.

So that man will be neither a protector, nor even a friend, for my wife.

What will become of her?

She will remain the abandoned wife, condemned to eternal solitude, for I do not think that she would pursue the lover when the husband has fled. She would be horrified by herself and him. All her innate honesty will rise again to her heart, to her brain. She will experience frightful remorse; she might kill herself . . .

Or she might live; and her life will be a more terrible punishment.

Alone, alone at twenty-three, alone with her beauty, which will expose her to a thousand attacks, alone against the advice of corrupt friends, before unhealthy examples, before masculine strategies.

A day might come when she slips, or falls! I can still hear her, as a girl, saying to me: "Promise me always to be my friend and my guide"—she who, as a young woman, has only lived, has only thought, has only respired through me!

Have I promised nothing, then? Have I not, myself, on the day of our marriage, made an oath? And I do not have the right to say that those were only words. Yes, in the depths of my conscience, I made the engagement to protect and defend her. Does that engagement only have value when it does not have to be executed? Is it charitable to offer small change in exchange for a gold coin?

Certainly, between that woman and me, everything is broken forever. But it not my duty to defend her against herself, to extract her from the hideous consequences of the sin committed. I shall do that . . . How?

X

Five o'clock. Very calmly, my resolution made, I have left the house. I went straight to the home of that man. I take no pride in my courage. It seems to me that at that moment, I was no longer obeying the suggestions of my own will. Something greater, larger and more powerful was dominating me and pushing me forward.

I was obedient to a reason superior to my own; I was the instrument of a justice more just than my own.

I rang at the door to the street and I entered the house; the door closed behind me. I climbed the stairs. I must have been very pale, and yet all my emotions had condensed into a decisive energy.

An Annamite domestic brought back from the Far East by Robert opened the door to me, I escaped from his hands and deliberately opened the door of the room where I was sure of finding that man. At the sight of me he leapt to his feet.

I examined him for a moment. Very blond, the complexion of a child, the eyes wide and ringed with gray; he has the physiognomy of a weakling.

"You! You, here?" he stammered.

"Monsieur," I said to him, "you have understood the matter that brings me. I could kill you . . ."

He did not let me finish. Taking a step toward me, he opened his shirt rapidly, showing me his bare breast.

My hand closed in my pocket on the butt of my revolver, but that was all. I went on, with the same calmness: "I will not lower myself to insult you, or even to reproach you. You have acted as a dishonest man by deceiving not only a husband but a wife. Don't interrupt me. Only I have the right to speak here. You have said and you have written to a woman that you loved her and that you were ready to make any sacrifice for her, to consecrate your life to her . . . now respond to this question: if the husband killed himself, would you marry her?"

His eyes seemed unable to detach themselves from mine. One might have thought that I fascinated him. It is possible, after all, that the extreme mental contention produces a magnetic effect.

He was silent. I repeated my question slowly, emphasizing the words.

"Kill yourself!" he said. "Kill yourself . . . ?"

"It's not the husband that is in question. His life or death must matter little to you. It's the wife that is the subject of preoccupation. When you said that you loved her, you doubtless reflected on the scope of your words. When one addresses such protestations, when one confirms them by letter, to a woman who has not so far weakened, that is to make an engagement of honor to accept all the consequences of one's actions. Of all the possible solutions, a duel is the most banal and the most futile. The man who has killed his wife's lover is no longer a husband but an executioner. The lover who has killed the husband can do nothing for the happiness of the woman he has rendered a widow, for if he marries her, there will always be between them the troubling image of the man they have both killed, the one by her fault as surely as the other with his sword. This is better. The husband can disappear without the wife or the lover knowing that his death is voluntary. In that case, the field is free and the marriage, necessary as the accomplishment of a duty, is possible. That is what I am offering you. So, once again, I ask you whether, the husband having disappeared, you give your word of honor to marry the wife."

I had voluntarily prolonged my tirade, permitting him to recover his self-possession.

"But Monsieur," he exclaimed, "your wife is not guilty!"

"Not one word more!" I said. "Your response proves that you are a dishonest man . . ."

"Monsieur!"

"To the very clear, very firm ultimatum that I pose to you, you oppose an evasive lie . . ."

"But once again, I swear to you . . ."

"I swear to you that you are only experiencing one sole dread, that of being obliged to keep the promises lavished by you on the woman that you knowingly deceived. Consecrate your life to her, you! Sustain her, protect her, when you do not even know how to conduct yourself . . . when, in sum, you are not even free to engage yourself . . . for if I'm not mistaken, you will be returning to the colonies soon . . ."

"In fact . . . I'm expecting the minister's order at any moment . . ."

It required a real courage for me not to slap that wretch.

"That's good. Now listen to me carefully. You are going to sit down at that table and write what I dictate to you . . ."

I had judged him well. He was a child. Doubtless courageous before the enemy—for in Indo-China he had been mentioned in dispatches several times, in a crisis of social life he no longer had any energy or resource. I frightened him, not because I was a man but because I was the husband.

With my hand I indicated the armchair placed at his desk.

He let himself fall into it.

I dictated:

"*Madame, I have been guilty, I have been mad. I have forgotten that I do not belong to myself. I have just received from the minister a formal order to depart for Saigon. I do not even have the time to try to see you one last time. I cannot refuse. My entire future would be ruined. I am returning your letters . . .*"

"But I have no letters!" he cried.

I looked him in the face. He was telling the truth. I continued:

"Omit that phrase, then, and add: '*Burn my letters, for your sake and mine. Adieu, Madame, and forgive me.*' Now sign it.

He had been writing mechanically. When he had finished, he reread the written lines and uttered an exclamation: "But that's horrible! She'll despise me. She'll hate me."

"To believe in that hatred is more pride. The scorn will suffice."

"I won't give you this letter."

"You'd be wrong—for if you don't obey my instructions point by point, I shall go home, and I shall kill my wife. Your letter gives me the right to do it."

"You'd be committing a crime! For she's innocent . . ."

"Once again, silence! You're forgetting that you must be at my orders. I want you to leave Paris this very morning. You'll wait at the port for the order to embark. Count on me; you'll receive it within twenty-four hours. If you write one word more, if you try to see the woman you have deceived again, I repeat to you, it's her that I shall kill. Do you still refuse to obey?"

In that child there was a collapse of the entire being. He hid his head in his hands and wept.

"I'm waiting for your response," I said, without departing from my calmness.

He raised his head again and, looking at me, said: "I swear to obey you . . ."

"Fold that letter and put the address on it. I'll take charge of enabling it to reach her."

When he saw it in my hands, he had a final revolt.

"I've betrayed your amity," he cried. "I'm a wretch, so be it! But by all that I hold most sacred in the world, I swear to you that she is innocent . . ."

"Will you please give orders," I said to him, "in order that you will have quit this house within the hour. I want your disappearance to be a *fait accompli* from that moment."

He wanted to say more, to expand in protestations, but before the glacial expression of my physiognomy, he understood that all speech would be futile.

"In an hour," was all he said, "I'll be ready to quit Paris."

I knew him well enough to understand by his tone that I could be sure of him. In any case, I would keep watch; the battle in which I had engaged was one of those that one does not have the right to lose, for the sake of self-respect.

I put the letter in the post.

At six o'clock, I returned home. When I opened the curtains in my study and looked at myself in a mirror, my face almost frightened me. That night of anguish had aged me by ten years.

And I was only at the beginning of the task that I had imposed on myself.

After having remained for a few moments in meditation, in order to affirm my resolution, I returned to my wife's bedroom.

She was not awake. But on her face, the white ray that filtered through the curtains put a rosy, almost joyful, tint.

I went to the little item of furniture, activated the spring, and slid the letters in. I did not want anyone to know that I had read them.

As I went back past the bed, I enveloped Gabrielle with a long gaze of pity. I knew that today, more than ever, I had charge of her soul.

In my study I lay down on a sofa and remained immobile, not even hoping for an hour of sleep. However, I no longer had the strength to think. It seemed to me that my brain had been exhausted by those slow and sinister meditations. I had a sensation of emptiness behind my forehead.

Gradually, the overexcitement that had sustained me until then died away; nature has unexpected generosities. I fell into a numbness that resembled slumber.

Suddenly, I was woken up by light footfalls.

I opened my eyes. Gabrielle was there, arranging the papers on my desk. Her back was turned to me, and in that first awakening, when the clarity of ideas is still lacking, I gazed at that charming silhouette, the heavy black tresses caressing the nape, that supple waist . . .

But thought returned; memory rushed into my brain.

I uttered an incomprehensible exclamation.

She turned round swiftly and approached.

"What!" she said. "You're not in bed! I was sure that you had worked all night again! That isn't reasonable . . ."

And, leaning over, she extended her forehead to me.

I remembered now. In a second, the flood of thoughts had unfurled entirely. I was lucid again, with my dolor and my anger, but also, clear and positive, my resolution, invincibly made.

I kissed her, paternally, as if she were my daughter.

"In fact," I said to her, "I have been overworking a little lately. Today I feel a little tired; I won't go out."

In truth, she darted an almost joyful glance at me, as if she were rejoicing in an indisposition that would at least retain me in the house. I surprised that gaze, today when it was too late. How many similar gazes I had let escape, when the irreparable had not come between us!

The morning passed without incident. I was slightly pale, but the fatigue I pretexted explained that.

As usual, Gabrielle came and went in her habitual fashion. In the less corrupted woman there is an incredible power of dissimulation. Never, had I not read those accursed letters, would I have suspected anything.

I considered her covertly. She still appeared as youthful as on the day of our marriage. She had the same expression of frank ingenuousness. She seemed, in truth, quite happy with my presence. I had acquired the custom of having breakfast every day near the Bourse; one might have thought that there was a celebration in the house because I did not go out.

In sum, all that appeared to confirm the decision that sometimes, when a dolorous thought traversed my brain, I was afraid of not having the courage to execute.

We sat down at table. I read my newspapers, reading interesting items aloud. Several times, I perceived a movement of astonishment in her features. I sensed myself how incredible that sudden change in behavior must seem, and, thinking about the recent past, I appreciated more fully how stupid I had shown myself to be.

After breakfast, I set about arranging my papers. At about two o'clock, I heard the letters being brought up; Gabrielle brought them to me. Robert's was not there; she must have taken it and hidden it rapidly.

She retired to her room; I waited. It was the crisis.

My heart was beating so rapidly that the pain of the impact was almost unbearable.

She only remained shut in for a few minutes; then she reappeared, apparently impassive, but slightly pale, in my opinion, with a contraction at the corner of her lip. She had not wept. I understood that she had felt nothing but anger. That astonished me; I did not understand and, singularly enough, I was almost wounded by her indifference. A woman, previously impeccable, who finds herself abandoned, brutally, in a cowardly fashion, by a man to whom she has sacrificed everything, ought, it seemed to me, to experience a poignant dolor.

I saw that Gabrielle was preparing to pass, with her needlework, into the small drawing room next to my study.

"You can work next to me if you wish," I told her. "It won't inconvenience me."

Once again I saw her astonished gaze fix upon me

She has come, placid and gracious, and while I am writing, I can hear the friction of the wool sliding in the canvas.

✳

That was a year ago. My house has resumed its old appearance
. . . the old . . . before Him. I have suffered horribly, and
the day when I returned to my wife's room as a husband, I
experienced a mad desire to kill her after having possessed her.
I have not killed her, I have become again the lover of the first
days. She has given herself with a fever of passion in which my
despair divines remorse. There is in the "I love you!" that she
pronounces with all the force of her soul, in desolate surges of
protestation. It seems to me—and I am sure of not being mistaken—that words of confession sometimes rise to her lips,
and that she has to summon all her strength not to cry them.

I do not want her to ask for my forgiveness. I do not want
her to know that I know.

In all the sincerity of my conscience, I have done more
than absolve her. It is me that I have condemned. And my
punishment is to have, in the adoration that I devote to her
and which renders her happy, the terrible anguish of the past,
for which I judge myself responsible.

Now I know that I am doing my duty; I am finally keeping
the oath that I made on the day when she placed her hand in
mine; she does not bear the penalty of what was my crime
even more than hers.

Am I a hero? Am I a coward?

HUMAN LIFE

Among the childhood friends whose memory had always remained dear to me there was one for whom I had conserved a very particular sympathy; we had spent two years together on the school benches, sharing our hopes—our only patrimony, for, both orphans, we had no other riches than those created by our imagination.

It would be very difficult to explain the why and the how of those adolescent intimacies, which put down such profound roots in us that after long years we find them fresh and vivacious under the alluvia of new affections.

Robert, as I shall call him, was destined for the professariat; he had a cool and slow mind. In our student discussions he never emitted his opinion immediately, listening to the other's arguments and gradually coming round to the arguments that happened to touch him; but when all had been said, if he suddenly decided for one thesis or another, he then defended it with a singular tenacity, even when it was not the most just. The most bizarre thing is that once that conviction formed in him, it was absolutely impossible to modify it; he defended it with an almost unhealthy acrimony, even giving proofs that nearly dragged us, many a time, into stupid quarrels.

That was, in sum, only a small quirk, which did not affect our good relationship; fundamentally he was good, and I had observed several times that he tried to repair, within the limits of the possible, on the sole condition of not recognizing them, the wrongs that he had done with regard to one or other of his comrades.

Naturally, I did not analyze his character then with that accuracy; for my part, I was very open and frank by nature, I delivered indiscriminately, under the impression of the moment, truth or paradox, a passionate dithyramb on any subject, but I was as prompt to confess an error as I had been ardent in pleading it.

My character matters little in species, as they say at the palace; I would not even have mentioned that detail if it did not aid me to explain another particularity of Robert's.

When I had uttered, almost at random, one of the mad ideas that rose to my lips, by reason of an irrational impulse, it often happened that, a quarter of an hour later, I had forgotten that whim—to which I had not, of course, attached any importance. Sometimes, when a week or even a month had gone by, Robert would suddenly hurl at me point-blank an objection of which I did not comprehend the meaning at first. What was he talking about? Had I said that? I sometimes denied it energetically. Then, with a stubbornness increased by a truly exceptional lucidity of memory, he would repeat, in my exact words, the flourishes that I had added on the spur of the moment to a theme more brilliant than solid. He had, so to speak, ruminated those phrases for all that time—and thus I observed that he was, in a way, haunted by certain arguments that imposed themselves on him, which brooded for a more or less long time and suddenly exploded at a moment when no one else was thinking about the matter any longer.

The word "haunted" is accurate. Beneath the apparent calm of his mind, a continual labor operated, a reiteration of a single idea, long filtered and examined from every angle, like those musical motifs that sometimes pursue us for an entire day.

There lies the explanation of the studies to which he devoted himself throughout his life, and which, as we shall see further on, necessitated a kind of continual mastication of words.

Two years had thus gone by in a confraternity that nothing had troubled. We liked one another and accepted our mutual faults cheerfully. I was twenty-two years old when an Orientalist proposed to me a post of secretary, which I accepted joyfully, for it was a matter of nothing less than explorations and excavations in Asia Minor. Traveling had been the dream of my entire youth; how could I hesitate? It was an unexpected windfall that I could not allow to escape; and, in fact, I have never had to repent of my resolution, having received, after twenty years of work, almost unmerited recompenses.

It is already twenty years since the day the Robert accompanied me, pensively, to the Gare de Lyon, from which I was departing to go and rejoin my excellent master. We both had heavy hearts and the intelligence not to hide it. A serious and solid bond linked us to one another, and although we were able to convince ourselves then that it would never break, we experienced a dolorous anguish, like an excessive distention. He was returning to Paris. I was not stopping until Smyrna. Where would I go thereafter? There had been talk of Bagdad.

Robert, surrendering himself a little more than usual, told me about his plans for the future. He would pass his examinations as quickly as possible, and while awaiting the *agrégation* he would accept a modest post in the provinces, but his goal was a chair in Paris—and between us, his pretentions were not exaggerated; a dogged worker endowed with a certain verbal facility and an elegant style, Robert cut a good figure everywhere. Have I mentioned that in addition, he had a probity proof against anything?

As for me, I delivered myself at hazard, determined besides not to recoil before any effort to conquer a place, however small, in the sun of science—the only one, whatever people say, that shines for all men of good will.

I remember that at the moment when we separated, I said to him, making allusion to one of his fantasies, to which I was accustomed and over which I had wasted many an evening:

"In the same way that all living beings descend from one unique ancestor, you know, all languages derive from one single word. I shall search for that word, I shall find it, and I shall send it to you."

I laughed; he remained impassive.

We embraced one last time and I departed.

A year passed before I received a letter from him, which reached me in the heart of Mesopotamia.

He was not discontented, working successfully. He thought he would soon be in a position to solicit a professorial post in the lycée of a small town.

His letter terminated thus:

That all languages derive from a single word is saying a lot, and yet . . . !

It took me a few minutes of reflection to understand what that philosophical reflection, thrown out in that singular fashion, signified. It was my last remark that was haunting him.

In those sorts of expeditions, correspondence is neither frequent nor facile. We ceased to write to one another. I did not return to France for five years, and even then my sojourn was to be of very short duration. Nevertheless, I made immediate enquiries about my comrade, and I learned that he occupied a fourth chair in a little town in the center, which I cannot designate more clearly, for it was in that small town that Robert's entire life was to be passed, with its dolorous peripeties.

I wrote to him immediately, offering to make the journey myself to come and shake his hand, but it was him who came to Paris.

Neither of us had any complaint to make of destiny; we each had the good fortune of having delivered ourselves to an absorbing passion, me to the study of Oriental monuments, Robert to linguistics. There is no greater enjoyment for a man than to concentrate all his faculties on a problem that is simultaneously single and multiple, to bring everything to its solution, with the inexpressible and sweet anguish of unexpected discoveries and the passionate triumph of successes obtained. Before an infinitely small confirmation of the hypotheses of intuition, an imperceptible link that gives a chain an unbreakable solidity, the laborer experiences joys that are worth no less than the noisiest triumphs.

As if the last words that I had pronounced on quitting Robert had been an *Open Sesame!* for his intelligence, all his cerebral activities had suddenly been directed to the study of primitive languages. I did not mock, familiar with that self-absorption in a dominant passion.

"The main thing," I said to him, "is that you're happy . . ."

"Entirely happy," he replied, "except . . ."

And as he hesitated, I interrogated him cordially. Had he some embarrassment for which my collaboration might be useful to him?

No, it was only a matter, in sum, of a childishness. People laugh quite willingly at etymologists, who are perpetually under the impact of the famous quatrain: *Equus vient d'alfana, sans doute . . .*[1] In a small provincial town, where idleness is the mother of malice, Robert's preoccupation and their exclusivity, which were translated by distraction, lent itself to mockery; a few dissertations on the Coptic language published by the local newspaper had attracted gibes to him that were

---

1 The "famous quatrain" by Jacques de Cailly, from *Diverses petites poesies do chevalier Aceilly* (1667) actually begins "Alfana vient d'equus sans doute," and continues "Mais il faut avouer aussi/qu'en venant de là jusqu'icy/il a bien changé sur la route" [*Alfana* doubtless come from *equus*, but it is necessary also to admit that in coming from there to here it has changed a great deal on the way]. *Alfana* is the Spanish word for horse, apparently derived from Arabic, and *equus* the Latin.

more malicious than malevolent, but from which, in sum, he suffered, all the more so because the départemental society of antiquaries, fond of old methods, trumpeted that opposition loudly.

"What!" I cried. "Is it possible that you have already become parochial to that degree?"

"I want to be tranquil," he replied, energetically, "and I shall assure my repose, if necessary."

I did not persist, in order not to excite him further. I knew full well that pin-pricks are not the least painful of wounds.

The new separation came, and my travels resumed more ardently; three years had gone by when, having obtained from the ministry a mission to Cambodia, I had to pass through Paris to receive my final instructions.

To my great surprise, I learned that Robert was still in the same town. I enquired at the ministry, astonished that a man of such merit was thus relegated, far from the center of serious studies. People talked about him very favorably. Two *mémoires* addressed to the Académie des inscriptions had been the object of the most flattering comments. He had not requested a change, doubtless absorbed in his research, which were facilitated by the rich library of the town where he resided.

I wrote to him immediately, putting myself at his disposal if it would please him for me to take some step in his favor.

I have his response before my eyes; I shall transcribe it.

> *Friend, your letter did me good; it arrived at one of those moments when one feels, not discouraged, but enervated by the stupidity and bad faith of one's adversaries. These ignoramuses know nothing; if I talk to them about Court de Gébelin or Fabre d'Olivet they smile and shrug their shoulders to mask their insupportable nullity.*[1] *And they*

1 Antoine Court, who preferred to style himself Court de Gébelin (1725-

*permit themselves to mock. Sometime patience is
ready to escape me; as if one could deny that the
word bel, beautiful, is an exact phonetic and intelligent reproduction of the name of Bel, the Sun.
A handsome man is a solar man. You understand
me, but you sense how irritating an opposition is
that is based uniquely on prejudice. You talk to me
about quitting **** in order to come to Paris; no,
that would be to abandon the terrain to my contradictors. It is necessary that they confess themselves
vanquished and that they recognize the filiation of
our languages with the Oriental monosyllables. I
certainly will not yield to them; I shall pursue them
and harass them until they confess my victory and
their defeat . . .*

What could I respond? I found in those few lines all the traits of a character that I knew better than anyone. After all, in the narrow circle in which he enclosed himself voluntarily, he had created an entire society; events only have a relative magnitude. A family quarrel takes on epic proportions for its members sometimes more terrible in their eyes than the wars of empires. There is a universe in a drop of water. Robert, combating for his philological faith, magnified his adversaries to the height of Homeric heroes and insulted them in the manner of Achilles. Why disillusion him? Would not Don Quixote have been the happiest of men if it had not been

---

1784) was a Protestant clergyman and Freemason who was an important precursor of the French Occult Revival by virtue of his interpretation of the Tarot as an ancient depository of arcane wisdom. His unorthodox ideas about the origin of languages and their relationship with mythology would inevitably have appealed to Robert. As previously noted, Fabre d'Olivet (1767-1825) was a Biblical scholar, musicologist and mystic whose hermeneutical analyses and his "translation" of the so-called Golden Verses of Pythagoras were a key influence on several of the leading figures of the Occult Revival.

proved to him that the giants to which he was doing violence were only inoffensive sheep.

I did not insist, therefore, in dissipating an illusion that, at the very least, did not seem to me to be dangerous, and I responded cheerfully, soliciting regular bulletins of victory. Was I, after all, any more reasonable than him, having created an artificial world in the midst of the ruins of all times and all peoples—I who, in the prodigious ruins of Angkor, a mountainous rubble of stones, have wept like a child over the vanished Khmers, and who would give ten years of my life to decipher a single word of their lapidary language, buried in forgetfulness after having been that of a society more populous than our entire Europe?

How the days, months and years fled in those passionate researches!

When I quit Cochinchina to return definitively to France, it was seventeen years since Robert had taken me to the railway station and wished me *bon voyage* and a prompt return. Only one of those wishes had been granted, but I had nothing to regret, having earned my promotions one by one on the battlefield that I had chosen for myself.

To tell the truth, the memory of Robert, during that last long interval had almost faded from me. If he sometimes came to mind, I thought that he must finally be exercising his remarkable faculties in a larger theater more worthy of his erudition. I had had opportunities, if I found myself in a consulate or in the homes of rich compatriots in Indo-China, to consult the official journals, with the very natural hope of finding his name therein attached to some title or honorific function. I did not discover anything, but I imagined that it was merely because hazard was serving me poorly.

On my return, my installation and that of my family—for I was married and the father of two children—and the organization at the Louvre museum of what I had brought back from my explorations absorbed me to the point of expelling Robert from my thoughts. I had not heard his name pronounced, while mine, written a hundred times in journals, must have attracted his attention; the idea wounded me slightly, I admit, that he had not been one of the first to wish me welcome. Was he retained by a hint of jealousy? I was convinced that he should have had nothing to envy me.

Circumstances having brought me to the ministry again, I made enquiries on his subject.

To my great surprise the person to whom I addressed my enquiry made me repeat his name twice, although it is sufficiently uncommon not to be forgotten after being had once.

"He ought to be one of your most esteemed professors . . ."

"Oh, I know my personnel," the other replied, "and I assure you that the name is absolutely unknown to me."

I experienced an impression of malaise; having lived, I had not thought of the possibility of his death.

"Monsieur," I said, "pardon me if I insist, but the man of whom I speak was one of my closest friends, and I attach the greatest importance to any information that you can give me."

I was in one of those situations that oblige the complaisance of the most indifferent functionaries. He put himself at my disposal.

It was certain that Robert did not figure anywhere in the lists of personnel; but how long was it since his name had disappeared?

I recalled the information I possessed; ten years before he had been a professor in the town of ****.

Ten years. It was necessary to have recourse to files already relegated to the archives—which is to say, the attics. I had to retire without having obtained satisfaction, but with the hope of being informed the following day.

I was exact at the appointment.

When I entered, my functionary, who was laughing with one of his colleagues, suddenly assumed a sad and distressed expression.

"He's dead!" I exclaimed.

"I don't know whether he is still alive," he replied, "but he has not been part of the teaching personnel for a long time."

"He handed in his resignation?"

"Not exactly . . ."

"You're saying that he was sacked?"

"I can only refer to this note, which closes his file," said my interlocutor, handing me a piece of paper.

This is what I read:

Individual to be replaced within twenty-four hours. Confidential matter. Ministerial Office.

That laconic document was dated ten years before, about three months after my departure for Indo-China.

I had, as they say vulgarly, a chill in my back.

The compassed attitude of the functionary was not of a nature to encourage me in my investigation; in an instant, twenty ideas surged forth in my mind, not honorable for my old friend, and involuntarily, I felt cowardly. However, I made one last effort of courage.

"Do you think," I said, "that the dossier might be communicated to me at the office?"

"In general," the other replied, "these sorts of notes, which are very rare, refer to matters of an extreme delicacy. It's evidently not a matter of purely professional misconduct. I tell you this in confidence, but it gives the impression of wanting to cover up an affair by virtue of which the administration might have experienced some moral damage. If that is the case, I doubt that even the minister would take it upon himself to give you the details."

"But in your opinion it must concern some indelicacy or a fault against honor?"

The man spread his arms, shaking his head. Everything was possible, but he did not know anything.

Any persistence would have been out of place. I went away, my heart heavy and my head a little low, as if the fault committed by my friend were weighing on my own conscience.

But my curiosity was irritated.

I am wrong only to speak of curiosity. When the first impression, disagreeable primarily because of the indifference of the man who had informed me through clenched teeth, had dissipated somewhat, I felt moved by a profound pity.

I have never admitted the idea that one only loves one's friends on the condition that they are impeccable. It is when one has failed that one has need of amity; otherwise, what does the word signify?

And then, I knew Robert to be profoundly honest, incapable of compromising his conscience. He had no needs and no passions, in the tempting sense of the word. I told myself that in the universitarian world, as in any category of life where competition is intense, there are sometimes executioners and victims; had Robert succumbed to a slanderous enmity? However, he could not have been condemned without an investigation, without allowing him to defend himself. One might have thought, given the tenor of the note, that it was a matter of a *flagrante delicto*, after which all denial or explanation was impossible.

Who could inform me? Perhaps the minister—but I did not have the courage to confront even more painful revelations. I wanted to know, but without anyone knowing that I knew. Our conscience is sometimes Byzantine.

Evidently, Robert had quit the town where the deplorable adventure, followed by brutal destitution, had occurred. Was he in Paris? Momentarily, I had the idea of addressing myself to the police, but going to that extremity was repugnant to me. One final resource remained.

Having obtained initial academic successes, it was unthinkable that he had renounced seeking more; if not, it was necessary to suppose that his name could no longer even be pronounced, by reason of some infamous condemnation—and even then, I had had in my hands memoirs of transcendent mathematics that bore the imprint of a state prison.

I therefore went to one of the best-known linguists, and asked him directly the question that interested me.

"Ah!" he said. "You knew that Robert. He was a man of powerful intelligence; he had a kind of gift of divination."

"You're speaking in the past tense; is he dead?"

My interlocutor looked at me fixedly and replied: "I don't believe so."

"Has he submitted any new *mémoires*, then?"

"Not for ten years . . ."

"Then how do you come by the opinion that he is still alive?"

The scholar's eyes laughed heartily. "Sincerely, I can't respond to you. Admit that I've divined it. It was initially a presentiment, which changed subsequently into a certainty . . . don't ask me any more . . . I need to be discreet."

I sensed that he had a fervent desire to explain more clearly. A light dawned in my mind.

"I understand," I said. "He has published further *mémoires*, but under another name. You've recognized his style and his methods of investigation. Is that it?"

"Precisely. You've also guessed?"

"Then you won't refuse to reveal that pseudonym to me?"

"Indeed I will refuse. It resembles too closely the name of one of my colleagues."

He had said that in one breath, like a secret that he was impotent to retain any longer, and he was so confused by his malice that, although he was an old man, he blushed like a child.

"Damn!" he said. "I won't say another word."

I had the delicacy not to abuse that first success. It was up to me to draw the necessary consequences. I thanked him and immediately went to a specialist publisher, who, at the first words I pronounced, exclaimed:

"Today, the uncontested master of comparative philology, the renovator of the history of languages, the fortunate rival of Max Muller and Pictet, is undoubtedly Monsieur ****, the erudite academician. His *Grammaire universelle*, published two years ago, is a masterpiece, and announced for next January is a *Dictionnaire des racines du langage*, which the scholarly world is awaiting with impatience."

After such a magnificent advertisement, it only remained for me to acquire the said marvels, which I did; then I asked, rather casually: "Was it not here that the *mémoires* of a certain Robert were published?"

The bookseller made a slight movement of recoil. "Indeed," he said, after a pause, "but they're entirely sold out."

"That's unfortunate . . . but as I have an urgent need for them. I'll consult them at the Bibliothèque."

Clients who request treatises on Coptic or Aramaic languages are not numerous enough for the publisher not to experience a real heartbreak at losing a sale. "I'm certain," he said, "that I have one left."

"I'll pay four times the price," I said, looking the man straight in the eyes.

"In fact, they're so rare . . ." he murmured, "but in order to be agreeable to you, I can search . . ."

"Send them to me," I said, handing him my card.

I have already said that the press was affording me a noisy notoriety at that moment.

"Oh, for you, Monsieur . . . !" exclaimed the merchant.

And without further explanation, he disappeared into the back room of the shop. Only it is necessary to believe that those undiscoverable items were not buried very deeply, for scarcely five minutes had gone by when I had the pamphlets in my hand

The bookseller quoted me a price that was almost reasonable, but as I placed my hand on the pommel of my cane, he said: "Monsieur, will you permit me to ask you something?"

"Speak . . ."

"I'd prefer it, if anyone asks you about the provenance of the *mémoires* . . ."

He pointed to them, as if he would have experienced some difficulty in calling them by their titles.

". . . If you didn't say that you bought them from me . . ."

"On one condition," I said.

"What?"

"That you reply frankly to my questions. You haven't seen Robert again for ten years?"

"No, quite sincerely."

"Do you know where he is now? I'm an old friend, perhaps his only one. It's purely by virtue of affection, and for no other reason, that I'm looking for him. If you render me the service I request, you won't have obliged an ingrate . . ."

Now, it is necessary to say that there had been much talk about the publication of my journal of explorations in Cambodia, which I had not yet linked by any contract. The specialist understood my implication.

"I can only tell you that proofs arrive from the town where those books are printed, and that the corrections are in the handwriting that you must know."

A quarter of an hour later I was at home, plunged in dissertations on Sanskrit, Hebrew, the Massoretes . . . what do I know? But what was not in doubt was that Robert was at least the collaborator of the academician. Compared to his *mémoires*, the more recent work was conceived on an identical plan, to the extent of formulae that I recognized.

When I read the name of the printer, I was amazed. The town in which Robert lived was, according to all appearances, the one in which he had been living when I departed, the one where he had been teaching and where destitution had struck him. He had not, therefore, accomplished any dishonoring action.

I returned to the bookseller, who, having become my publisher, had nothing to refuse me. Unfortunately, that was all he knew.

Naturally, Robert's disappearance had not made any impression in Paris. Only the publisher of his *mémoires* had been preoccupied with it, and only for two or three years thereafter. He had only picked up inconsistent rumors. There was mention of a matter of a woman and a quarrel. That was all. Robert had been destitute. What had become of him? No one knew when, suddenly, the unknown philologist having published a short *mémoire*, connoisseurs were slightly surprised to rediscover the method of the famous *mémoires*, which they had not forgotten. After all, the academician had not failed to mention them in his preface and to proclaim their value as so many indications precious for the science. Thus, apart from a few people who were not duped by that clever game, in the first rank of whom was the publisher, no one was preoccupied with anything but the importance of the new works, and Robert was completely forgotten.

He was alive. He was living in France, I needed no more than that. A week later I disembarked at the railway station of ****. I was in haste to know the whole truth, and also to render to my friend, for whom I felt sorry instinctively, all the services that might be compatible with his situation and mine.

I rendered immediately to the printer, who made no difficulty about telling me that Monsieur Robert was indeed the nominated copy-editor of the works of the academician in question. He lived in an outlying district of the town on the far side of the river.

Furnished with the exact address, I set forth, and discovered, not without some difficulty, the rather isolated back-street that had been indicated to me.

I experienced a constriction of the heart.

The quarter in which my friend had taken refuge—that expression occurred to me spontaneously—was only inhabited by poor people, factory workers. There was poverty in the air, hanging in rags from the windows, emphasizing the crumbling of the plaster with black stains.

I addressed myself to a woman who was nursing a baby while sitting on the sidewalk, her feet in the muddy gutter.

At first she did not appear to understand me; I multiplied my explanations.

"Oh, the man in the writings . . . yes, I know. At the very end of the street, in the field."

I followed the indication given.

The street did, in fact, end abruptly, opening on to a vast extent outside the town. A single house was there, as if proscribed, presenting its flat windowless back to the town. If that situation was intentional, it was sufficient to demonstrate an incurable misanthropy.

I felt intimidated. How would I be welcomed? Since Robert had no longer sought to recall me to memory, might not my persistent amity appear indiscreet to him? I could not turn back, though. I went around the house and found myself in front of a little gate.

I rang.

After a moment I heard the clucking of poultry and a woman appeared, surrounded by a crown of hens, to which she was throwing grain. She was old but neatly dressed, her gray hair bound in a blue handkerchief.

She came as far as the gate, without opening it, and said: "You've surely made a mistake, Monsieur."

"I don't believe so. Is it not here that Monsieur Robert lives?"

"You're mistaken all the same," she said, "firstly because Monsieur Robert isn't here, and secondly because if he were, he wouldn't receive you."

"Why?"

"Because no one enters here."

"You're mistaken in your turn. It will be sufficient for you to tell your master my name for his door to be opened to me."

She shrugged her shoulders.

"You won't catch me in default," she said. "I have my orders, and they're not recent. If you were the good God in person, you wouldn't enter here by my doing. The least I can do is to obey the poor man."

She had pronounced the last words with an unfeigned accent of sincerity that touched me profoundly.

"My good woman," I said. "God knows that I would not want you to fail in your duty. You can answer one question, though. Will Robert be back soon?"

"That, anyone can tell you as well as me; at six o'clock sharp, he'll be here."

"In that case," I said, "as it's now five o'clock I'll return in an hour. As soon as he returns, give him my card; I'll present myself at the gate, and if he doesn't want to receive me I'll go away, that's all."

"Oh, that I can do," said the woman, "but don't build up your hopes; our master is stubborn!"

While speaking she glanced at my card; I saw her raise her eyes upon me again with an expression of astonishment.

"You're from Paris?" she said.

"I've just arrived there, and I only took the time to come here."

But her physiognomy had resumed its impassivity. I thought I was mistaken.

"Return at six o'clock," she said. "He'll have seen your card."

I had, therefore, an hour to waste. I had not judged it appropriate to ask in what direction I might encounter him. I decided to kill time by walking straight ahead for half an hour, which, when I returned, would give me my exactitude.

Now, everyone knows that in a provincial town, whichever direction one takes, one infallibly arrives in the most frequented center, the location of the theater or the Hôtel-de-Ville—which it is necessary to attribute to a kind of suggestion that only appears singular because it is poorly observed. The truth is that one follows unconsciously the movement of the inhabitants, in the direction in which they are going most numerously. There is no trace, as in great cities, of the cross-currents that can confuse you; the flow is uniform and regular, and one allows oneself to be drawn by it.

It was thus that I found myself, at five twenty-five, in front of the town's principal café, at a corner of the main square. I decided to sit down for a moment at one of the tables overflowing on to the sidewalk; all things considered, I intended to arrive at Robert's house before he had had time to weigh his decision carefully. Why impose myself if he preferred not to receive me?

I had been there for a few minutes when one of my neighbors, leaning toward the ear of his companion, murmured: "Look! What did I tell you? The chronometer-man!"

The half-hour chimed at the same instant.

"I'll set my watch," said the other.

At that moment, a man of tall stature, but stooped, enveloped in a long black frock-coat went past the café, without turning his head to the right or left.

The gas was illuminated.

It was him: Robert, pale, wan, emaciated and hollow-eyed.

He did not see me, of course. I remained stupefied, as if that apparition—possible, after all, but not foreseen, I admit—had taken on a fantastic character in my eyes.

But that hesitation was of short duration. I got up, threw a coin on to the table and launched myself after Robert.

At first he walked slowly, with a trailing gait.

When I found myself on the sidewalk, two meters away from him, I perceived that his figure straightened and his tread became firmer. His pace was rhythmic, like that of soldiers going into action.

I did not overtake him; it pleased me to follow him for a while, to consider him without his knowing that he was under observation, and in the silhouette that was moving before me I attempted to seize some sign that would put me on the track of the solution I sought.

We followed the main street of the town, which headed straight toward the bridge leading to the outlying district.

The shops were beginning to light up, showing their wares, rendered more seductive by the sparkle of the gaslight.

There were, in sum, many people in the street. It was the beginning of March, and the mild weather favored strolling. Groups of ladies stopped before the shop windows, hypnotized by silks or lace.

Robert had slowed his pace again, to the point that I had great difficulty not treading on his heels. He had raised his head again, and he was looking around, searching the groups with his sharp gaze, his eyes now wide open.

I had passed over to the sidewalk opposite to the one on which he was walking, in order to see him at an angle, and under the intermittent light, the alternating play of which made all his facial features stand out, I was struck by the absolute change that those few minutes had produced in his physiognomy.

A little while before he had seemed to me to be sad, exhausted, indifferent to everything; now he seemed bold, almost provocative. He stared brazenly at all the faces, but no one appeared to see him. It even seemed to me that some turned their heads away and walked more rapidly.

Suddenly, the door of a shop opened and I saw a woman come out, dressed in black, accompanied by a boy who seemed to me to be about fifteen years old. A veil hid the features of the lady, who was very small and thin, and certainly would not have attracted my attention if Robert had not stopped suddenly at the same moment, stepping back against the shop to let her pass, removing his hat at the same time with a theatrical gesture, excessive in its deliberate politeness, and bowing profoundly.

I saw the woman shiver with an unequivocal gesture of repulsion, and, hastening her pace, she drew her son along and passed by.

Robert had not budged, and remained in the same place, hat in hand . . . for two or three minutes.

The crowd continued moving around him, without anyone appearing to perceive his presence.

Finally, he replaced his hat on his head with a brutal, furious thrust, and started running in the direction opposite to the one in which the lady and her son had just disappeared.

I do not know why the thought came to me of a sharp, cruel despair that might end in suicide.

I ran behind him, having difficulty keeping up with him, for he was more agile than me.

We arrived thus in a part of the street that was poorly lit and almost deserted, and already I could scarcely make out in the distance the black shadow of the bridge.

"Robert! Robert!" I shouted, with all my might.

He did not hear at first but, making a last effort, I arrived beside him and placed me hand on his shoulder,

"Robert!" I repeated. "Don't you recognize me?"

This time he turned round abruptly. "Who's calling me? Who are you?" he said, in a harsh tone.

I named myself.

He took a step back; then, suddenly, as if in a relaxation of his entire being, he threw himself into my arms.

"You . . . you, finally . . . oh, how long I've been expecting you!"

"You were expecting me, you say? But how?"

"Haven't you come in response to the letter I wrote to you?"

"I haven't received any letter . . ."

"But I addressed it to the Louvre . . ."

"Ah! The Louvre! I don't lodge there, and your letter must be buried in some concierge's lodge . . ."

"But then, how has it happened . . . ?"

"That I'm here? On my return from the Orient I searched for you . . ."

"And you found me?"

"Not without difficulty: an entire odyssey that I'll tell you about. I've been to your house, where your maidservant told me that it was impossible to see you, but that you would be back at six o'clock, and that if I wanted to risk it . . ."

"Oh, yes," said Robert, nodding his head. "The chronometer-man!"

"You have that nickname, then?"

"I have others," he said. "But in that case, you don't know anything . . ."

"I can respond to you succinctly: nothing at all."

He remained silent for a moment. "Perhaps it's better thus," he muttered, between clenched teeth. "He'll understand me better."

We had passed the bridge, I felt more tranquil.

Furthermore, in his most natural voice, Robert was now interrogating me about my travels, my work; he congratulated me cordially, without my detecting the slightest echo in his voice of jealous irony. His mind appeared to have recovered all its liberty.

Naturally, I abstained from making any allusion to what I had seen a little while ago; it was not my prerogative to provoke confidences on subjects that I sensed were exceedingly painful. I therefore stuck to the only subject of our conversation thus far, until we arrived at the gate of the little house.

The worthy woman was there, as if on sentry duty. When she saw her master open the gate and stand aside to let me pass, she raised her eyes to the heavens.

"Then it really is the monsieur you were expecting . . ." And, turning to me, she added: "Well, you can boast of having passed where no one else has ever set foot."

"Come on," said Robert, "let's shut up, old woman. It's a matter of giving my friend dinner. Carte blanche . . . chicken, rabbit, whatever you wish, as long as it doesn't take long."

"I'll make you an omelet . . . that won't test your patience."

Robert preceded me into the house, and I confess that I was pleasantly surprised when, by the light of a lamp, I observed the extreme neatness of the house. I had been afraid that Robert, by reason of absorbing preoccupations, might have let himself slide into the ranks of those dirty old scholars who, under the pretext of not wasting their time in futilities, renounce the most vulgar obligations of hygiene.

To tell the truth, the entire house was nothing but a library, but well-ordered, with carefully-dusted fir-wood bookshelves. There were a good six thousand volumes there, the majority of which were in-quarto or in-folio; but that had an excellent physiognomy. In each room a long table, occupying the center, bore open atlases, copies of steles or molds of inscriptions.

"You know," he said to me, laughing, "that there's only one word, the type of all languages."

I laughed too at that allusion, which took us back so many years.

"And that word is . . . ?" I asked.

"You know it as well as I do: the *être* the ċ;[1] Armenian has opened superb horizons to me on that subject. The problem is resolved . . ."

"You're still working, then?"

"Certainly, more than ever . . ."

"And you're happy?" I added, stupidly.

He looked at me, and took my hand. "Now that you're here, I can be."

"Believe that I'll employ all my forces in that. Isn't it to put myself at your disposal that I've come?"

"You haven't forgotten me, then?"

"Any more than you've forgotten me, since you've written to me . . ."

He seemed veritably joyful at my presence; his complexion had colored slightly.

"And you're still working relentlessly?" I said

"Oh, the work, my friend, is what sustains me," he exclaimed, "and which comforts me, for without it, without that profound absorption of my entire being in passionate studies, I'd be dead ten times over . . ."

"You've suffered a great deal?"

"A suffering that no one can understand or appreciate . . . but you're here now! What weighs upon my existence is the injustice and egotism of others; but I intend to reckon with them, and it's in order to obtain that victory that I've summoned you."

To what was he alluding? Had he, then, had the desire for ten years to relieve himself of the kind of disgrace that the universitarian decision had caused to weigh upon him? That astonished me, but I did not insist.

---

1 In the original this character is rendered as an italic c with a grave accent, which does not appear to be included in the symbol set of current versions of Word, so I have made this substitution.

In order to change the subject, for I preferred that he come to decisive confidences of his own accord, I told him how the publisher—I only mentioned him—had put me on his track.

He started to laugh.

"I know full well that, behind that ignoramus, the whole world divines me, and I reserve for him, perhaps in a few days, a surprise that won't be to his taste, but which he'll have merited a hundred times over. Oh, the bandit! When I can escape from his claws . . . !"

The maidservant informed us that dinner was served.

We sat down at table. In spite of everything, I felt more reassured; it was impossible that the man who was going to recount to me facts prejudicial to his honor could conserve that attitude of relative indifference.

I was no longer even seeking to formulate hypotheses; I waited, and, as a skillful politician, I brought the conversation back to my travels, which furnished me with the means of occupying the floor, while not appearing to exaggerate my discretion.

"Ah! The language of the Khmers!" Robert exclaimed. "You're still stuck on it, like the others."

"What! Have you deciphered it?"

"My friend," he said, with the most amiable casualness, "whenever you wish, I'll introduce you to people who speak it."

And as I looked at him with a somewhat incredulous smile, he went on, impatiently: "The Khmers! But they're only Kimri . . . K-M-R, you understand, who, in the age of Ram, the standard of the Bull, crushed by the Aryans, fled their ruined cities, are found at the Pont-Euxin under the name of Cimmerians . . . C-M-R . . . then, still pursued, ran aground all over the place, including the land of Wales, formerly Camria, C-M-R . . . where they speak kimric . . . K-M-R and one of whose counties bears the name of Carmaert . . . but you know nothing, you divine nothing! Nothing shows you better than an endless grapeshot of scientific vocables . . ."[1]

"I'll point out to you," I said to him, "that I'm not issuing any pretention."

"But indifference is a fault in itself. You've been to Cambodia and you've seen with your own eyes the ruins of the immense empire of the Khmers, and you haven't seen that you've touched one of the most precious sources of primitive language? But your Khmers, who were the Jews, the fugitives of ninety centuries ago—ninety, you hear!—you can still follow on the map of Europe; I can show you them in the Sarthe, in France, in Lorraine . . ."

"They must have changed a great deal over time," I murmured, almost unintentionally. But suddenly I saw such a contraction of anger in Robert's face that I seized him by the hand. "Are you mad?" I cried. "Are you going to hold an untimely joke against me?"

"One doesn't joke about science," he said, dryly.

"Especially when one is only an ignoramus . . . in certain matters, at least. Come on, I was wrong . . . your hand."

And I held out mine, wide open, over the table.

His face cleared. "From the moment you recognize your faults, it would be bad grace for me to persist. Anyway, I can prove to you . . ."

And for half an hour, head bowed, taking great care to hide my impatience, I was subjected to a veritable dissertation—not without interest, for his faculty of deduction was marvelous, but singularly untimely when, in my opinion, it

---

1 Throughout the nineteenth century, and for much of the twentieth, orthodox cultural anthropology was dominated by migrationist theories—heavily influenced, of course, by the migrationist aspects of the "history" rendered in *Genesis*—equally beloved by Fabre d'Olivert and other unorthodox "historians" like Madame Blavatsky. Migrationist theories were particularly popular in France among Romantic historians and Romantc literateurs; Lermina was very familiar with them.

would have been preferable to occupy ourselves with more immediate matters.

But I rediscovered him as I had left him; entirely committed to his opinions and determined to impose them on others.

I had only one means of escape; I declared myself converted, convinced, and entirely ready to converse in his maternal, or ancestral, language with the first Khmer I encountered on my return to Paris. And in spite of several offensive returns, he finished by accepting my act of submission as sincere.

I had noticed that he was only drinking water, abstaining from coffee and liqueurs, eating very little and not smoking—in sum, not sacrificing to any human weaknesses, which, for my own part, I could not resist; within normal limits, of course.

We stayed there after dinner with our elbows on the table, prepared for intimate effusions, and I was trying to figure out how I could draw him on to that delicate terrain when he suddenly said to me:

"You don't know, then, that I've been expelled from the university?"

I do not like to lie. "I know that," I said. "This is how I found out." And I gave him a brief account of my odyssey through the bureaux,

"Imbeciles!" he said. "Then you must have thought me guilty of some horrible misdeed?"

"I only thought of coming to question you myself."

"Thank you for that."

"So, tell me briefly what great crime motivated that injustice."

"I fought a duel and I killed my adversary."

I started, all the more so because that sentence had been spoken in a singular tone, with a kind of indifference that shocked me.

"You killed a man! You! He must have insulted you very gravely?"

"He did more and worse than that."

"I confess to not understanding . . . but it's better if I let you speak. Tell me everything, without hiding anything. I swear that I'll listen to you with religious attention, with no other prejudice than that inspired by my sincere amity for you. And I won't interrupt."

I had spoken in a grave voice perhaps more solemnly than was necessary, but the idea of murder, even in a duel, had suddenly chilled me.

"Ah! Now you're like the others . . . it wouldn't take much for you to call me the Killer, as everyone here has been doing for a long time. But I tell you, and you won't doubt my word, that it was an honest duel. Wasn't I risking my life too? Couldn't I have been killed as easily as my adversary?"

"Let's not argue, I beg you, especially when I don't know anything. You can't expect me not to feel a perfectly natural emotion on hearing that tragic circumstance mentioned for the first time. I can't criticize you, and I'm not; even if you were guilty, I'd be more disposed than anyone else to absolve you. Let's not get lost in futile preliminaries and get straight to the facts."

"Well, the facts are quite simple; here they are. I'll try to be as brief as possible, but in order for you to reach the same conclusion as me, it's necessary—isn't it?—that I give you the most relevant details. I'm confessing to a friend, as to a priest, certain in advance of absolution."

I was duly warned; I had nothing more to do than listen.

"I'm going back," he said, "beyond these last ten years, even further. You haven't forgotten that, during our last conversation in Paris, I mentioned the veritable persecutions of which I was the victim here. And again, in order better to seize the value of the word, it's necessary for you to enter, so to speak, into my own skin.

"For fifteen years I have been devoting myself to studies in comparative philology, which are unarguably the keys to all the other sciences. In order to throw oneself into that path, so arid to begin with, sown with stumbling-blocks, where illusion and error await you at every junction, it's necessary to armor oneself with a triple breastplate of faith, will and perseverance. From the day when I chose it, glimpsing the grandeur of the goal, I gave myself entirely to the chimera. It was necessary that it respond, or it would devour me. That's enough to tell you how little the banal obligations attached to the post I had accepted weighed upon me.

"Whoever wants to be free must accomplish strictly the duties that his function imposes on him. No one could demand anything from me except for a strict observation of my contract; and I can also declare, without pride, that no one obeyed the universitarian prescriptions more regularly than me. Asking for no favors from anyone—on the contrary—I intended to conserve my complete independence. As soon as my courses were finished, I no longer had any accounts to render. Moreover, it would have been strange for anyone to ask me for any, for I led from then on a cenobitic existence. As soon as I had heard the heavy door of the lycée close behind me, I ran to shut myself in my room, and there I worked to arm myself for future struggles.

"With you I don't have to be modest. What I know would indemnify the libraries of ten academies and, remarkably, thanks to a method personal to me, that encyclopedism is allied with a perfect order and an impeccable memory. My brain is a keyboard in which each key corresponds to a labeled item of knowledge in a special pigeon-hole. I know all known languages, living or dead. In all that I have no other merit than having channeled my energies in accordance with a plan from which I have never strayed.

"I am only emphasizing these points in order to enable you to understand more fully the rectitude of my conduct in the circumstances you're anticipating

"The first duty of the true scholar—I mean the laborer of sane reason and good faith—is to combat error wherever he encounters it. Now, in the early days of my sojourn here, I ran across a few issues of a regional journal calling itself scholarly and archeological, every page of which displayed, with an unconsciousness that became impudence, blunders that would have made the least of schoolboys blush. I could not, in good conscience, allow such ineptitudes to circulate; I went to find the editor of the town's daily newspaper and declared that I intended to respond in his columns, to those ignoramuses, who were the shame of scientific France. He did not understand me at first, although it was a matter of the simplest things, the translation of a stele in the museum of Boulaq. But as soon as I had showed him the revue in question he became more affable and put himself at my disposal, even insisting that I not spare my adversary—which, I beg you to believe, was not my intention. I have learned since that the journalist was the political adversary of the ignoramus, but that was a matter with which I did not have to concern myself. I did my duty, entirely, like an artillerist reducing enemy guns to silence. I extinguished the fire of the revue. In three months, it ceased to appear."

"But your adversary? Did you know him? What became of him?"

"I only know his name," said Robert, with an insouciant gesture. "He's dead."

I glimpsed abysms of ferocity. "Continue," I said, resignedly.

"If you think that the struggle was finished, you're greatly mistaken. Putting no value on a publicity that, in sum, was no longer of immediate utility, my own work being still in a period of incubation, I ceased my collaboration with the newspaper. Two years passed in the most absolute security. I divided my time between the lycée, my room and the library, where I had discovered treasures, stupidly ignored by an idiotic curator, whose dismissal I provoked . . ."

"What!" I cried. "You had the man sacked!"

"Don't feel sorry for him. A wretch who had an entire collection of runes in old baskets—yes, my friend, runes, run aground in that town the devil knows how . . . and who would very nearly have sold them by weight . . ."

"But in sum, didn't he need his post in order to live?"

"I don't know," said Robert. "But let's not dwell on insignificances; we're arriving at the crisis. The antiquaries of the province have a life as hard as their heads, which is saying a lot. I had completely forgotten the old local revue, having put myself in contact with those of Paris, which at least welcomed rectifications with merited consideration, when one morning, I received in a wrapper a brochure of menacing appearance. My instinct was not deceived; it was the *Rediviva*! And to complete the audacity of the new editor, a monsieur I did not know, in a sort of prospectus, pronounced my name eulogistically, expressing the hope that I would sometimes contribute to his infamous publication—yes, infamous, for in that same first number, had not a miscreant taken it into his head to write a eulogistic history of Massoretism . . . Yes, my friend, the crime that has weighed so heavily upon humanity and still stifles it, the rascally work of the Tiberiad school, which has disfigured the work of Moses and poured ridicule on *Genesis* and the rest; they had the audacity to excuse it—what am I saying? to approve of it—and in an issue in which my name was pronounced . . . tantamount to accusing me directly of complicity.

"I ran immediately to the newspaper that had already served me as a tribune, but, to my great surprise, I ran into a formal refusal. It appeared that the new director of the unspeakable thing that called itself a revue was a friend of the journalist. A friend! Are there friends when it is a matter of truth, of justice? In vain I explained exactly what the crime of the Massoretes consists of. He was scarcely polite, and I was obliged to retire. Fortunately, the resource remained to me of a pamphlet. I did not fail to have recourse to it.

"I was not rich, spending almost all my salary on books and having been obliged, in order to pay for an *Oedipus* by Kircher,[1] to renounce breakfast for a month, but I did not have the right to hesitate.

"My pamphlet appeared, as cold and trenchant as the blade of a knife. I had striven to remain calm, but in the last two pages I let all my verve overflow, and I abused everyone in a mastery fashion. You can be proud of me . . . or, rather, I'll let you read my copy, the only one I have left.

"There was a terrible row. The revue riposted . . . what a riposte! I blushed for it myself. I prepared my second pamphlet. This time I intended to launch my whiplashes so well that not an inch of skin would remain on the back."

I could not help interrupting: "Is the editor of the revue dead?" I asked, with the most perfect innocence.

"I don't know," said Robert. "Let's pass on. In the meantime, something rather singular happened. I had a colleague at the lycée who was sympathetic enough to me. He was the professor of music, a young man of twenty-five or thirty, with whom I sometimes had occasion to chat and who appeared to be interested in the miraculous theory of numbers, of which, as you know, music is the most perfect—or, to put it better, the absolute—expression.

"About a month after the publication of my pamphlet, and as I was irritated by the nasty gibes that were being unleashed at me here and there in the local press, the young man . . ." (I shall call this new character, who is, alas, very important to

---

1 *Oedipur Aegyptiacus* (1652-54) by Athanasius Kircher was an important pioneering work of Egyptology, which also refers to Greek and Hebrew sources, and neo-Pythagorean mysticism, in a syncretic spirit.

the story, Monsieur Laurent) ". . . took me by the arm in the street and said to me:

"'Do you know, my dear colleague, that although you have detractors, you also have friends . . .'

"'That proves,' I said, 'that there are intelligent people here. In truth, I was beginning to doubt it.'

"'Friends and admirers,' he insisted, 'even female admirers, and I am coming to you as an ambassador. My wife has a great desire to make your acquaintance, and also a young woman of great merit, the daughter of a former pupil of the Ecole des Chartes, now an orphan, but very well-educated, whom your polemic has enthused.'

"I wondered where that preamble was heading, and summoned him to explain himself. It was a matter of an invitation to a family dinner in the near future.

"I refused categorically. I had neither the desire nor the leisure to mingle in society.

"He insisted with a perseverance that ought to have made me suspicious. I struggled in vain; he reckoned with me by talking about some very curious books, manuscripts that had come to him from a defunct uncle and might interest me. In short, one has these moments of weakness in life. I accepted, and he was delighted.

"When the day came for me to do it, I was on the point of pretexting an indisposition or making some other excuse twenty times over. I wish to God that I had really been nailed to my bed by some incurable malady.

"Finally, at the appointed hour, I crossed the threshold of that accursed house, correctly dressed, without any affectation of elegance. I might have looked like one of those dandies who have no other occupation than measuring the knot in their cravat. Furthermore, I was in a rather good mood; that day I had made some interesting connections between the Finnish and Tamil languages. We too have our white stones.

"In sum, everything seemed quite all right. Monsieur Laurent's wife was a petite creature, thin, pale and insignificant, entirely occupied with her two children, the elder of whom was five years old; she welcomed me with the busy politeness of a housewife. Two of my colleagues were there, the professor of Rhetoric and the professor of German; I had known them for a long time as inoffensive and little desirous of debates in which they knew in advance they would be beaten.

"Finally, there was the other female guest—my admirer, in Monsieur Laurent's words—a rather beautiful young woman of twenty-two, very simply dressed, who would have been sympathetic but for a hint of malice that curled her lip.

"That first skirmish between society and me passed without encumbrance. I was even treated with a cordiality that seemed to me to be genuine, Mademoiselle Félicie . . ." (that is the name by which I shall designate the young woman) ". . . spoke to me about my pamphlet, not without intelligence. In spite of an excusable ignorance, she had an intuition of the truth, and I exercised some pleasure in furnishing her with supplementary explanations that appeared to strike her.

"I departed satisfied. That house did not displease me and, in sum, it provided me, once a week, with an acceptable diversion from my perhaps-excessive claustration.

"For two months, every Thursday, regularly, I went to sit down at the table of Monsieur Laurent and his wife. The inevitable Félicie was present. I had no suspicion of the infamous trick that she was preparing for me. I have forgotten to say that she prided herself on some literature, and that she contributed from time to time to the newspaper that had recently refused me its collaboration.

"Meanwhile, I had put the final touches to my second pamphlet and one Thursday, the day I dined with the Laurents, before meeting the printer at the café at ten o'clock in the evening I had slipped the manuscript into my pocket. I arrived at the house without suspicion and naturally, during dinner, I let myself go in speaking about the volley of green wood that my contradictors were about to receive. It seemed to me that they listened to me with some complaisance, and, I believed, with a certain attention.

"I ought to say that it was a matter of a part of my studies, perhaps the most original and the least common, since almost no trace of that famous pamphlet remains, of which I destroyed almost all the copies.

"Now, lend me all your attention, because, in what follows, the slightest detail has its importance.

"My dissertation was treating the migrations of the Finns, and I demonstrated how, forced incessantly northwards, they had left their traces from the Caspian Sea to the Baltic—traces that are found in the names of towns and villages, in customs that still subsist and in popular Russian locutions whose origin no one, until now, has been able to explain the origin. It was not the most impassioning subject, and I confess that I surrendered entirely to the pleasure of having an attentive audience, in the first rank of which Mademoiselle Félicie figured, who, with inflamed cheeks, never took her eyes off me and who, at a certain moment, as if in response to a signal departing from who knows where, begged me to read a few pages of my pamphlet, the presence of which in my pocket I had been unwise enough to announce.

"I will add that in that study I corroborated each of my affirmations by an entirely new analysis of the Finnish poem the *Kalevala*, which recounts, as you know, the adventures of the hero Vainamoinen, and in which, until now, people have only seen a mythological and poetic cosmogony, whereas it is in reality a kind of odyssey, the geographical and linguistic itinerary of the exodus of that people through the Orient and the Occident.

"The insistence that they put into demanding that reading ended up, indifferent as I am to anyone's esteem, tickling my stupid vanity, and I consented to read a few pages of my pamphlet, which were greeted, as you would imagine, with a unanimous approval. I still did not suppose that that entire comedy might conceal a trap.

"Ten o'clock chimed; I recalled my meeting, excused myself, and hastened to take my leave.

"To my great surprise, Monsieur Laurent joined me on the stairs, wanting, he said, to accompany me to the café. No similar desire had ever come to him before—take note of that.

"We found ourselves in the street, and Monsieur Laurent, after circumlocutions that I did not understand, said to me point-blank: 'Let's see, my dear colleague, I like frankness. Respond to me in a word: have you ever thought about marriage?'

"I was so taken aback by that stupid question that I was utterly nonplussed, bewildered. And as, no doubt, he found that I was not answering quickly enough, he went on: 'Between us, I know that my question is somewhat outside received customs, but we aren't people to use futile ceremonies. I have the most profound esteem for you, and all those who know you hold you to be a man of courage and intelligence. You work very hard, you're alone, you don't seek pleasures outside; you are, in sum, I can say, an indoor man. Well, why not, from now on, install your existence in normal and definitive conditions? I can plead *ex professo* before you the cause of marriage, for I'm completely, absolutely happy, and on that point, let's agree, I'm more knowledgeable than you. Men like you, my dear friend, those who have healthy ambitions in the head and the heart, can't constitute a family too soon. With your tastes for assiduity and calm, your household would be a paradise . . .'

"He talked, but I was scarcely listening. I am so made that my own ideas grip me invincibly and without any intention. I was thinking at that moment about Ilma, who is, as you know, the mother of Vainamoinen, and listening very vaguely to Monsieur Laurent's dissertation, who, naturally, mistaking my silence for an acquiescence, continued singing the praises of marriage and paternity. It's even probable that a movement of the head that is ordinary to me when I study appeared to him to be a sign of formal adhesion to theories about which I cared very little.

"Then, placing his hand on my shoulder, he said: 'Since you aren't defending yourself, as I dreaded, tell me now what you think of Mademoiselle Félicie.'

"There was a silence that extracted me from my reverie. 'Oh, Mademoiselle Félicie,' I said, unconsciously. 'She's charming . . .'

"'Isn't she? And what an excellent heart! If you knew her better, modest, gentle, a mind open to all great ideas, and, as you have been able to judge for yourself, passionate for literary studies . . .'

"'Indeed,' I said, 'the demoiselle comprehends quite well, and if she worked . . . it's only unfortunate that she always gives the impression of smiling and mocking slightly, even when she seems to be praising sincerely . . .'

"'What! You thought that? Oh, how desolate she would be if she heard you. But my dear friend, look more attentively and you'll remark that that slight curl of the lip comes from an imperceptible scar . . . one of those childhood accidents that we all have. No, no, Mademoiselle Félicie does not have a mocking turn of mind; she's a serious and devoted person who would make an excellent wife . . . I'll add that she has a small dowry, forty thousand francs . . .'

"This time I looked Monsieur Laurent full in the face. 'Why are you telling me all that?'

"'You don't understand?'

"'No, upon my word, not at all,'

"'Too modest, my dear! I'll summarize. Marriage doesn't frighten you; Mademoiselle Félicie appears charming to you . . . well, you have only to say the word for Mademoiselle Félicie to become Madame Robert! It isn't regular, I know, but bah! Happiness arrives rarely enough within arm's reach for one to seize it anyway. I'm not charged with asking for your hand,' he added, laughing, 'but I'll gladly serve you as a spokesman.'

"I recovered all my sang-froid; the trap was, in truth, too crude.

"'Monsieur,' I said to him, very dryly. 'I beg you never to return to this subject; I do not want to marry.'

"And with that, I bowed and drew away abruptly.

"In truth, you will agree, that indiscretion, that audacity in disposing of me, of my future, surpassed permissible limits. Me, think of marrying! Me, preoccupy myself with that scholaress who knew nothing! I was furious, but in sum, I had cut short any whim of persistence. Good!

"I had no suspicion of the unexpected consequences that the burlesque scene was to have.

"The printer was waiting for me at the rendezvous and I gave him my manuscript, not without having announced to him that I would look over the proofs myself and that I reserved the right to make corrections until the last minute. I had suffered too much from the wretched misprints that had soiled my first pamphlet.

"All went well; I had made the resolution not to return to Monsieur Laurent's house, in order not to give any further pretext to his matrimonial fantasies.

"A few days had gone by without any incident when, one morning, one of my colleagues, the professor of Rhetoric, said to me, with the most amiable of smiles—the wretch!—'Have you read the *Pandore*, my friend?'

"'What is the *Pandore*?'

"He informed me that it was a weekly revue published by a few young people of the town who had been bitten by the literary tarantula.

"'No, why?'

"'This time,' my torturer continued, 'you can't complain of being misunderstood. God, what eulogies! Read it, and, as they say in Paris, you'll drink a full jug of milk.'

"Hmm! That didn't suggest anything good to me. Why was this *Pandore* occupied with me? I gave my lecture and, as soon as I was free, I bought a copy of the fantastic *Pandore* on the way home. Glossy paper, a pale green cover: a boudoir periodical.

"Already I felt an involuntary chagrin that my name should figure in a similar publication, but, triumphing over that initial prejudice, I cut the pages.

"After a piece of verse on 'stars that are eyes' I fell upon the title: 'An intimate conference,' and below it, the inexplicable words: *A Scandinavian poem.*

"I passed on and continued leafing through; but nothing remained except a reverie under a dolmen. Either I had been deceived or I had committed some confusion myself. It was not in that issue that there could be question of me. However, to acquit my conscience, I went back, and suddenly I read my name. Yes, stuck to redundant epithets: *the eminent professor, the learned man, the powerful laborer* . . . I turned the page swiftly, and found myself back in confrontation with the title that had struck me a moment ago: *A Scandinavian poem.*

"Suddenly I uttered a cry of dolor, and even more of profound desolation. I had been betrayed, mocked, dishonored . . . yes, dishonored. The author of the article, which was signed with Félicie's name, attributed to me, with formulae of hypocritical admiration, a conversation on the *Kalevala*, which I presented—me!—as a Scandinavian poem. Have you understood? And, in order to insist on the stupidity of which I had given proof, in order to gather against me all my adversaries, to give them the right to laugh at my expense, that hateful woman, ingenious in her hatred, made me pronounce phrases like 'the Finns, ancestors of the Swedes,' or even: 'Vainamoinen invokes Odin'!

"I was suffocating. In truth, I do not know how I did not die of rage. I believe that I have never experienced such suffering. I would rather, I declare, that one of my limbs had been torn away with red-hot pincers.

"So, in good faith, unable to suppose the treachery, I had delivered myself; I had furnished the whips that those wretches had steeped in vinegar in order to flagellate me more dolorously! All my words were odiously travestied. With a perfidy that frightened me, details had been copied from an absurd *dictionnaire* that applied to the *Eddas*, and they had been stuck to a few fragments exactly recalling the *Kalevala*.

"It was odious, monstrous, fantastic.

"That is what you get for rejecting girls who throw themselves at your head! She had avenged herself, without wasting any time. It was shame for me, in all its horror.

"Certainly, I could protest, but who would believe me? And I, who castigated others, would be judged guilty of having confused—which a child of ten would not have done— the *Kalevala* and the *Edda*, the Finns with the Scandinavians, Odin with Jumala! Which is to say that my enemies had triumphed, that I would pass for the least of the ignorant, for a beaten donkey! What a victory for those I had reduced to silence! What a revenge!

"The commotion had been so strong, I tell you, that I wept—yes, me, a man! I wept stupidly.

"But energy soon returned to me. I could not admit that those bandits could laugh at me with impunity.

"The hour had come to return to the lycée. Oh, I did not care about my course, my pupils; I had something like smoke in my eyes, my throat was dry, my brain was ready to explode.

"I arrived at the lycée. Hazard served me; at the very moment when I entered the first courtyard, Monsieur Laurent was there, chatting and laughing with the other professors while waiting for the bell to ring.

"He was sniggering. Of course! What was a poor fellow like me, now that the disloyal blow had been landed, but an object of ridicule and nothing more?

"I advanced, shaking the ignoble libel in my trembling fist.

"However, I succeeded at first in recovering my sang-froid. 'Monsieur,' I said to him, showing him the pamphlet. 'Have you seen this?'

"'Ha ha!' he said, in a victorious tone. 'That might change your ideas . . .'

"'Because it pretends that for me, the Finns became Scandinavians . . . ? I engage you not to aggravate the outrage with a misplaced irony,' I went on. 'I beg you to tell me whether you had knowledge of . . . this thing . . .'

"'Obviously,' he said, in a surprised tone, 'the author consulted my memory regarding a few details . . . and I believe . . .'

"'A truce on pleasantries, I tell you; so this is the fact: you admit that you are guilty of this infamy . . . at least as an accomplice . . .'

"'Guilty . . . accomplice! An infamy! What do you mean?'

"'Oh, you're pretending not to understand . . . you doubtless believe me to be too stupid to have pierced your blatant duplicity. No, Monsieur, I am not as stupid as you might suppose . . . and I tell you in front of all these messieurs that you are a lout and a coward . . .'

"He took a step back and went pale. He turned to the other professors: 'Messieurs,' he said, 'be my witnesses . . . I do not understand anything of this unqualifiable scene. It is to be believed, in truth, that the poor fellow has lost his reason . . .'

"He was evidently trying to slip away, to escape.

"I stepped forward and I said: 'Whatever you might think, wretch, I have all my reason, and the truth is that I shall wash your face with this filth . . .' I advanced my arm, brandishing the pamphlet.

"'Ah!' he said. 'Don't touch me.'

"My hand fell on his face. He was slapped, and vigorously, believe me.

"He tried to throw himself upon me, but someone interposed himself: the deputy headmaster, who substituted for the second professor. 'Messieurs, I have been a soldier. These quarrels are not settled by fisticuffs. No scandal, I implore you; the University must not suffer from your brawls. Not a word more here. After the courses, we'll immediately give this affair the sequel that it requires.'

"'The sequel,' I said, 'is slaps, every time I encounter . . .'

"'We'll fight, Monsieur!' cried Laurent.

"'Whenever you wish,' I replied shrugging my shoulders. 'But I'll wager that you're the last of capons.'

"'Messieurs, Messieurs,' said the deputy head, 'once again I adjure you, and, if necessary, summon you in the name of the *alma mater*, to adjourn this dissension. After the courses, I tell you. I'll be there, and everything will proceed promptly . . . to your satisfaction.'

"Oh, I felt better; that swiftly-administered correction had relaxed my nerves. I was conscious of having acted as I had to, finding myself incontestably in the cause of legitimate defense.

"While my pupils listened to the terms of their next assignment being dictated, without reading or hearing them, I reflected on the incredible perversity that had just suddenly attacked me. Was it me who had gone in search of those fellows? Now I understood that it was a plot that had been woven a long time before. They could not reckon with me by honest debate; they had carried out a flanking movement, and I had let myself be caught, like an imbecile

"I was only irritated by my gullible candor. I had divined nothing, understood nothing, and yet, so many signs ought to have warned me: the indifference of Madame Lambert, who had evidently been kept outside those machinations, and who, having no reason to seem interested in my work, had displayed her inattention almost insolently; the exaggerated enthusiasm of that Félicie, who had no other goal but to have herself married, under threat of public dishonor; and finally, the mellifluence of the musician who led that intrigue. Why? By virtue of the dilettantism of malevolence, perhaps.

"But it wasn't over! Ah, I was a clown, a Trissotin to be mocked. We were not playing a comedy; I would be able to show it, and a few pages of preface added to my brochure would prove that the little man was still alive. It would be short but decisive; so much for the mud-slingers.

"I was in haste to get home and set to work.

"As I went out, I was no longer thinking about the manual chastisement that I had inflicted on the traitor, and who for me, in the face of the projected reply, had no further importance. But in front of the Lycée I found the professors who had witnessed the altercation, and, a little to one side, the accursed Laurent.

"The professor of Rhetoric, having approached, said to me: 'Monsieur, even though our step is not regular, we have decided to oblige your adversary. Monsieur Laurent desires to address a few words to you in our presence. He has promised not to depart from the most complete calm. For your part, do you feel sufficient self-control to make us the same promise?'

"Oh, that Monsieur wanted to talk to me. So be it. One lie more or less! In any case, he would not be the honest merchant!

"So, on my consent, the man approached, very pale, like the malefactor he was. 'Monsieur,' he said to me, 'this morning you delivered yourself to an act of violence that I cannot qualify. Doubtless, circumstances of which I am unaware have taken away the notion of your actions. I have shown myself in your regard to be a good comrade, I dare say a good friend. Of that amity I am giving you a final proof by offering you the opportunity to efface the past by means of a word of regret. I am holding out my hand to you; put yours therein and let us explain ourselves like the honest men we are.'

"I interrupted him with a burst of laughter. He was ready to forgive me for the harm he had done me!

"Exactly what I replied to him I don't know, but I made him sense that I was not duped by his hypocrisy or his cowardice. And to put everyone at ease I explained briefly the unexampled treachery of which I had been the victim, and of which that man, his wife and his parasite were the odious instigators.

"'You're wrong to accuse my wife and friend,' the villain replied. 'If errors have been made, they were entirely involuntary, and you're mistaking the intention of those who were only thinking of praising you.'

"'You'll apologize, then!' cried the rhetorician.

"'I refuse,' I said, 'because it's a lie.' And I stung him with a few more vigorous epithets.

"I was dragged away. It was time.

"In the evening, the professor who intervened in the affair came to my home with one of my colleagues and challenged me on Laurent's behalf. It only remained for me to appoint seconds. I was living then opposite the barracks. I sent a request for two sub-officers to come to my house and I said to them: 'I won't accept any arrangement. If anyone talks to you about apologies, refuse them flatly.'

"Those worthy men, trusting me, understood their mission admirably, and the following morning everything was settled. I knew that some impossible conciliation had been attempted. 'Fortunately, we were there,' said the sergeant.

"In sum, we were to fight with foils the following day at seven o'clock, behind the barracks. Foils, sabers or pistols, it mattered little to me. I was convinced that I would kill my adversary, although I had never touched a weapon.

"I did not go out that day, preparing and polishing the article that I was writing against the expected attacks.

"Would you believe that Félicie had the audacity to present herself and have a neighbor ask me whether I would receive her? 'Tell the creature,' I said, 'that I speak as it suits me, and when.' She persisted, it seems, with tears and grand phrases, but she finally had to depart.

"Then she wrote to me. Of course, I knew the anthem. She pretended to prove her good faith, accusing herself of ignorance, offering me the most complete apologies. Monsieur Laurent had absolutely nothing to do with it, etc. . . . I threw the letter in the waste-basket.

"I did not sleep that night, and my overexcitement was such that I could not even work. I did not think about the duel, though, but only about the laughter that the antiquaries of the département were preparing at that moment at my expense. I am certainly not of a violent character, but I felt capable of all reprisals.

"In the morning I was ready when my seconds came to find me. My attitude appeared to please them. One of them gave me some advice: go forward, arm extended. I was scarcely listening.

"We arrived on the terrain first, the others a little later.

"One of Laurent's seconds—not the professor of Rhetoric, whose attitude was very correct—approached me and asked me whether there was any means of arranging the affair; but the other three intervened, and I was grateful to them. What did they take me for?

"The duel was brief. I went forward, arm extended. Laurent fell. I bowed and withdrew with my two seconds, who took me to breakfast. They were very proud of me . . ."

I had not wanted to interrupt the story that Robert was telling me, all the details of which remained engraved in my memory, by the exclamations that I cut short, and which did not trouble him. Never, I admit, had I observed such unconsciousness. He emitted the strangest ideas with a perfect sang-froid. If he spoke of the crime committed—Odin for Vainamoinen—I sensed that for him, the guilty parties were worthy of universal execration. All argument was impossible.

Revolted, however, I cried: "And the poor fellow was dead?"

"Not immediately," Robert replied. "It appears that the blade had brushed the lung. He lingered for nearly a year, and then died."

"But your destitution?"

"It followed the duel within a fortnight. It appears that the story was known in high places. At first they had the strange thought of bringing me before a tribunal, but the entire personnel of the lycée would have been compromised. The professor of Rhetoric was moved and I was dismissed."

"How is it that you did not leave the region?"

"Me! Why? I had work in progress, I wasn't rich; here I had a low rent and could live cheaply . . ."

"But that man who was dying . . . so close to you!"

Robert made an angry gesture. "So I should have deserted the terrain before my adversaries, like a coward?"

"You were attacked, then?"

"They didn't dare!"

In truth, I wondered whether I was not dealing with a madman.

"Is that all that you have to tell me, then?" I asked. "In what way can I be useful to you? It seems to me that you are well able to defend yourself."

My voice had become harsh and ironic.

Robert looked me in the face. "Ah! Are you claiming, by chance, that in all this I have some reproach to make to myself—from the moral point of view, I mean? Was it me who had provoked those people? Had I done them any harm? As for the duel, might I not have been killed as easily as that man—me, who had nothing for which to reproach myself . . . ?"

"Pardon me, but you're giving yourself absolution far too easily. In all that you have told me, I have understood, personally, that the veritable provocateur was you. Since you have appealed to me I have the right to give my opinion. You are very knowledgeable, far be it from me to contest that, but so am I, not to displease you. Well, I would give . . . well, my collection at the Louvre . . . not to have the death of a man on my conscience . . ."

He tried to interrupt me but I went on:

"You don't appear to comprehend that, of all sacred things, the most sacred is human life. All the science in the world is not worth the breath of a living man. Eddas or Kalevala, Odin or Jumala, what does all that matter in the face of the fact that you have made a cadaver of a thinking being? And the poor fellow had attempted everything in order not to risk his life, a life he knew to be useful to his family . . . He held out his hand to you, but your ferocious scholarly vanity was stronger than the vulgar sentiment of humanity, while it is evident, moreover, that in all this there as nothing but a misunderstanding, an error committed by a poor girl who was overzealous, and who might perhaps have loved you! In truth, don't ask me for my approval; I refuse it."

I stood up, thinking that after that formal criticism I ought to withdraw. To my great surprise, Robert did not move.

"We're not on the same plane," he said. "I alone know what those people had made me suffer, and I don't believe in their good faith. But in your argument, only one point touches m, and I beg you to listen again. You have told me that that man's life was useful to his family. That is true. And now, if you care to recover a little impartiality, we shall see whether, from that point of view, I have not done all my duty, perhaps more than my duty, and whether, in sum, it is not me who has the right to complain."

I did not understand. I made him a sign to continue.

"I'll resume my story," he said. "In fact, your opinion has been that of many people here. Since the death of that man I have been treated as a pariah. I have been given infamous nicknames: the Bloodletter, the Killer, what do I know? They have tried to make me quit the town. I have resisted all that. It was necessary that I remain here, because the collection of Oriental books in our library is unique, and also for other reasons, which I shall explain.

"I was no longer thinking about that adventure when I learned suddenly that Laurent was dead. There was a kind of scuffle in the town; the police were obliged to disengage my house. I did not hold firm against the storm; admitting all sentimentalities, I moved, and went to install myself in a remote quarter.

"I did not see anyone. I ate bread and drank water, the butt of many petty persecutions, in spite of everything; even at the library, people drew away from me and the curator scarcely replied to me with politeness. But work has its enjoyments, which enable everything to be forgotten.

"One day—he had been dead nearly six months—the professor of Rhetoric who had served as his second stopped me in the street and said to me, rather harshly: 'I don't understand, Monsieur, how you have the audacity to remain in this town when the wife and children of your victim are dying of starvation.'

"While speaking to me he had assumed a defensive stance, doubtless thinking that I was going to slap him, like the other—another one who did not understand me. I am not stupidly susceptible and am only irritated when the reason is worth the trouble. I asked him for details, which he gave me.

"As a professor Laurent earned two hundred and fifty francs a month, and with his lessons he made almost double that. I've said that he had two children, a girl and a boy, the former three years old, the latter five.

"I thanked him and, having gone home, I started to reflect. At this point I entered another order of ideas, which is also the one at which the tribunals arrive when they acquit a criminal but condemn him to a civil reparation. There had, in fact, been a prejudice caused, and according to the principles of the code, which are found in the Egyptian laws, and even in the Zend-Avesta, it was up to me to repair it.

"The man earned six thousand francs a year; it was up to me to furnish them to his family. Admitting that his wife had something to do with her husband's treason, her role had only been passive. I even admit, in conformity with Hebrew law, as described in the Pentateuch, that the submission of a wife does not give rise to any action against her. In any case, in spite of the wrongly translated verse of *Genesis*—proven by Fabre d'Olivet—children cannot bear the punishment of a paternal crime.

"Unfortunately, I was very poor and I did not know how to get myself out of it, when hazard threw in my path the academician of whom you are aware. He circled around me for a while, and then proposed a collaboration, which I refused flatly. Collaboration is complicity. Can you see me, even without being named, taking responsibility for the blunders of an ignoramus? I would be helping to propagate stupidities. I found something better. That absurd individual is rich and ambitious. I offered him a treaty of which the terms were these: he would pay me a salary of seven thousand francs and furnish me with the money necessary to buy books useful to my research, and in exchange, I would abandon to him all my works, which he alone would sign. But the contract had one condition *sine qua non*, which was that he would never permit himself to change a single word, that I would correct the proofs and regulate the print run. He accepted."

"And for ten years," I exclaimed, "you have delivered your works . . ."

"Don't interrupt me. You've heard the figure: seven thousand francs; this is why: I went to a notary and it was agreed that an annual sun of six thousand francs, disbursed by my . . . scholar, would be remitted to Madame Laurent in trimestrial installments. It was understood that I did not want to appear in all that. I've had enough trouble with that family. The other thousand francs were sufficient for my maintenance."

"But you could work outside your contract."

"I've forbidden myself all publication other than those in question. Anyway, I have enough. I rent this little house, I have an old maidservant who breeds chickens and rabbits; the two of us live quite well."

"But you're suffering; you told me so yourself. And I can understand that; to have surrendered, sold the flesh of one's flesh, the marrow of one's brain . . ."

"Oh, if it were only that! I don't care about that anomaly, which even has something piquant about it. Have you not noticed that my man dare not even speak, dare not hazard a word in public, for fear of committing a stupid blunder? I remember that once, he permitted himself to add a footnote to a passage that had appeared obscure to him: twenty idiocies in fifteen words. I rebuked him so forcefully that I dreaded momentarily having a second murder on my conscience. I assure you that the role of showman holding the strings of a puppet in the wings isn't without charm; and then, you see,

I haven't yet surrendered the whole secret. That triumph, I'm reserving for myself . . ."

"But when will it come?"

"You'll see. Madame Laurent was, it seems, very surprised by that unexpected windfall. She and her two children are living with her aged mother. If I had broken her life, I have reconstituted it. I assume that you won't criticize me . . ."

"Which is to say that I admire you and I humbly beg your pardon for the severe words that escaped me just now! And I taxed you with egotism and insensibility! But what you have done is sublime . . . and very few people—perhaps including me?—would have been capable of such a sacrifice . . ."

I had seized his hands and I shook them vigorously. He disengaged them gently.

"You can't keep within limits," he said. "Just now I was an assassin, now I'm Saint Vincent de Paul. Neither one not the other: a rational man, that's all."

"You have as much heart as reason."

"Let's pass on. Madame Laurent has had the chagrin of losing her daughter, four years ago. I thought momentarily about diminishing the amount of her pension, but I judged that it would be unjust. Her husband, in working, would have augmented her resources himself. And then, a son costs more as he grows. I thought of utilizing my academician and, with a knife at his throat, he obtained a bursary at the lycée for the boy."

"Here? But why hasn't Madame Laurent left the town?"

"I don't know. Her family is local, I believe."

"But will you remain too, riveted to this ingrate labor?"

"No. My treaty expires in a few months and, although I know that the man is disposed to renew it at any price—what would he be without me?—I believe that I'll abandon him to his ignorance. What a fall! No, you can't imagine the tortures that individual has made me suffer. I've been obliged to forbid him to write to me. Each of his letters—he has the pretention to involve me with his works—had enraged me. Perhaps I shall deal with an English publisher for my great work, the synthesis of all my research . . . then I'll donate the capital of the Laurent income and I'll be free. But before all that, it's necessary for me to obtain a certain satisfaction . . ."

"What does it concern? You spoke to me about a suffering that pursues you. If it depends on me to free you from it, believe me, I'll do the impossible . . ."

Suddenly, Robert's face had changed expression; his features had hollowed out as if an invisible claw were digging furrows therein.

"Yes," he said to me, "I'm suffering, I'm suffering horribly. Oh, you'll understand me. It's so difficult for anyone else to . . . how shall I put it? . . . enter into our skin momentarily, to live our life, to think without brain. For each of us, it's our idiosyncrasies that constitute our entire being and which, uncomprehended, leave us unexplained and inexplicable to others."

"I was mistaken momentarily on your account," I put in. "I am not seeing you with the same eyes as before, and your eccentricities no longer frighten me. Speak, therefore, in all frankness. I am certain that I can appreciate even the most infinitesimal details of your consciousness . . ."

He made a gesture of reckless resolution. "Well," he cried, "I'm dying of not being saluted by that woman!"

"What!" I said, with an involuntary start.

"Yes; it's stupid, it's mad, but it's thus! But in sum, by what right does that woman, after ten years, refuse to accord me that sign of politeness, which one accords to the most indifferent? Does she have the right to scorn me? Have I, after all, committed a dishonest action? Certainly, I understand—for I have as much common sense as anyone else—that in the first years following the catastrophe, due more to hazard than to me, she experienced a sort of repulsion for me. It was illogical, since, I repeat, fate alone had decided between her husband and me . . . but in the end I passed over that weakness. But the years have gone by. Has she suffered? No, thanks to me, I've made her existence easier, more secure, than the one she had before. Her son has grown up; all careers are open to him. Well, I say that she does not have the right to pursue me with a hatred and a scorn that I know to be unjust. To everything there is a prescription and I intend to profit from it. It's ridiculous, I concede, for it would be better to remain indifferent, but I can't. Can you see me, when I have just collected my miserable twenty-five francs a month, knowing that I leave her five hundred . . . I encounter her; naturally, I raise my hat . . . ? She, haughtily and insolently, turns away and pretends not to see me. Is that just? I make you the judge of it. After ten years! And then, in sum, I'm not arguing. That woman no longer has any reason to hate me, she no longer has any right to disdain in my regard. I want her salute. So, every day, at the same hour, which is the one when everyone comes out and crosses the main street, I come out too. I don't encounter her every day . . ."

"But sometimes, like today, you go past just as she emerges from a shop . . ."

"You know that!"

"Then you step aside, and slowly raise your hat . . ."

"You've seen . . . and then she passes more rapidly, without a gesture without a sign . . . and I, half-mad with despair and anger, run away like a malefactor. It seems to me that all the scorn and hatred of the town is weighing upon my shoulders . . . it's an obsession of which I can't rid myself. I'm dying of it."

"Will you permit me to make an observation?"

"Speak."

"In spite of everything, in spite of yourself, there's a kind of remorse on your conscience—that's not a word devoid of meaning, I assure you. You haven't committed a crime in the strict sense of the word, but you've violated one of the laws of nature, which wants you to respect the life of your fellow. And for you, that remorse, the shadow of that deviation from the good and the just, has acquired substance, if I might put it thus, has incarnated in that woman. Yes, it's a haunting, which is increasing and developing in being entertained by your tenacious mind. What, in reality, is that woman's salute worth to you? Ought you not, when you see her one the right-hand sidewalk, to pass by on the left-hand sidewalk? Instead of that, you follow her, you seek her out. You've pronounced the word yourself: obsession. Is your brain not powerful enough to triumph over it?"

He lowered his head and said: "No."

"I don't want to preach stupidly. There's a means of liberating yourself."

He raised his head excitedly. "What?"

"It's necessary, as if by virtue of an involuntary indiscretion, for the notary who proves her pension . . ."

He stood up violently, pushing back his chair, which almost fell.

"It's done!" he exclaimed. "Yes, I've committed that pettiness, at the risk of seeing the woman refuse the income . . . Don't hold it against me; you're right, I'm haunted . . ."

"And when she knew that?"

"I went to place myself in her path. I saluted her . . . she turned her head and passed by . . ."

"That's bad," I said, in my turn. "She ought to have appreciated, as I do, your truly exceptional delicacy. Six thousand francs annually, for ten years—you know that that makes sixty, and that no tribunal would ever have allowed such a sum. In your place . . ."

"Don't talk about yourself," he said, rather harshly. "It's a matter of me. Yes, another would have stopped the pension and gone elsewhere . . . but I want to remain in the right and do my duty. But I also want her to do her duty in my regard, and the duty of that woman is to salute me . . ."

"Perhaps she hasn't understood your sacrifices . . ."

"But those details are trivial . . . and then, what's the point of arguing, of commenting? Is what I ask excessive? No! She ought to salute me . . . or else . . ."

"What will you do?"

He did not reply, but it seemed to me that a shadow passed over his face, as if the veil of a sinister thought had been lowered over it.

I reflected. What should I do? It was event that against that haunting, like a possession in which the demon was the *idée fixe*, reasoning remained impotent; the conscience cannot be exorcised. On the contrary; in such a situation logical arguments exasperate the illness. In purely mental afflictions, treatment by contradiction is contraindicated.

Robert had let his head fall into his hands; I could only see his almost-bald head crowned with a fringe of graying hair: a tonsure larger and less neat than that of a monk. I said to myself that that man, too, was one of those social deserters who only have humanity in incomplete sensations and diverted passions.

However, I was gripped by a great pity, all the more poignant because the cause of his pain seemed to me to be less justifiable; and it was complicated by the anguish that one experiences in confrontation with a weeping madman. My duty was to speak, though, if only to distract and soothe him.

"Pull yourself together," I said to him. "I've told you that I understand. I'm sincere, but what do you expect? The case is exceptional, and at the risk of giving you a paltry idea of the promptness of my intellect, I renounce for the evening seeking a solution to the problem. Let's talk about something else, and then, tomorrow morning, the night having brought counsel, we'll see what can be done."

He raised his head and looked at me.

"In fact" he said, "what is a few hours more or less, in the matter of torture?" The irony of his tone hurt me.

"But in sum," I said, "what can I do for you?"

"You call yourself my friend, and you haven't guessed?"

"In truth, I confess . . ."

He got up and started marching back and forth agitatedly. "That's singular! The idea is, however, quite simple . . . as soon as I knew you had returned, it occurred to me immediately . . ."

"Well then, tell me . . ."

"And you'll do what I ask?"

"I promise. Perhaps you doubt me, after what I said to you . . ."

He stopped in front of me, his arms folded over his chest. In truth, his emaciated silhouette was frightening to behold.

He lowered his voice, as if he were ashamed of what he was about to say.

"Let's see," he said. "Can I go to see that woman myself?"

"Do you want to? Oh, I see; how did the idea not occur to me immediately? In fact, it's necessary that someone pleads your case with Madame Laurent. You haven't dared to go to see her . . . in sum, you're right. But I find myself in a very different situation. I can act as an ambassador, pleading your case with arguments that it would be impossible for you to use yourself, putting in the light and making full value of your abnegation, your disinterest. Listen, permit me to act exactly as I see fit, and give me, as they say, *carte blanche* . . ."

As I spoke, his features relaxed; his respiration became more even; he revived.

He took my hands. "I confide myself to you," he said. "I only beg you to succeed."

"It's necessary that I know exactly what you desire . . . from a practical point of view—material, as it were."

"Oh, do I know? I want no longer to have to pale under that woman's gaze. I want . . ."

"You want her to forgive you . . . that's the word. Oh, I sense very well," I added, in response to a gesture that he allowed to escape, "how painful it is for you to recognize an unaccepted culpability, in spite of everything, but to women it's necessary only to talk about pity, and it's from her alone that you can await an end to your agony . . ."

"Then don't question me any longer," he said, "act . . ."

I promised, and the evening ended in the best conditions.

When I returned to the hotel I had obtained Madame Laurent's address, and, in reality, I did not doubt the success of my step.

It had been agreed that I would only go to the lady's house in the afternoon, but Robert and I were not to see one another before my visit; he had urgent work to finish.

It was about two o'clock when I rang at the door of the house, very modest, in which she lived, a short distance from the main square, in a calm street where passers-by were rare, and, doubtless for that reason, uniform and symmetrically arranged houses, the choice of petty rentiers, were arranged to either side.

I had thought hard about the matter, and my mission appeared to me to have every hope of success.

A maid came to answer my ring; I handed her my card and was introduced into a small drawing room, simply but tastefully furnished. In the corner opposite the window there was a piano enveloped in a black cashmere sheath. On the mantelpiece—which astonished me—there was a tobacco jar, with cigarette papers and a box of matches.

The walls were almost bare; only a few frames enclosing diplomas awarding, the name of musical societies, the title of honorary member to . . . Laurent.

There was also a very small frame occupying the middle of a large panel, containing a portrait, or, rather, a pencil sketch, of a young man with untidy brown hair and bright, frank eyes, with a violin in his hand.

I experienced a sentiment of unease; there was no conceivable doubt that it was a portrait of the dead man. I would have preferred to speak without his presence; it did not seem that he ought to hear what I had to say.

I heard a rustle behind me. I turned round abruptly, upset to have been surprised in the contemplation of that portrait. Dissimulating my embarrassment, I bowed, saying: "Madame Laurent?"

"That's me, Monsieur."

With a glance I had examined the woman who was before me, with the stupid vanity of a man who believes, thanks to the acuity of his intelligent faculties, that he can judge his interlocutor instantaneously.

No more insignificant physiognomy had ever been offered to the perspicacity of an observer. Madame Laurent was petite, very thin and flat-chested; her shoulders were devoid of substance, her hands long and thin. As for the face, what can I say? She wore a sort of black bonnet garnished with ruches, which enveloped the face like a nun's head-dress, hiding the hair. The complexion was mat and gray-tinted, the lips colorless, the wings of the small nose were pinched. Over the eyes, of which I could not discern the hue, the eyelids were partly lowered, as if in a perpetual need for sleep.

How old was that woman? According to what I knew, perhaps thirty-five, but she seemed much older to me. If I had been told that she was fifty I would have believed it. Everything in her was aged, effaced, blurred, and her black dress, a kind of sheath, was confounded with the somber furniture.

However, I had been struck by the timbre of her voice, as clear and pure as that of a young girl. In that alone I found the woman beneath the mourning of a widow.

As I had not spoken immediately she glanced at my card, which was still in her hand, and said: "I do not have the honor of your acquaintance, Monsieur. May I know . . . ?"

She remained standing and did not invite me to take a seat. Evidently unaccustomed to visits, she was under the coup of a surprise and a curiosity that she did not seek to dissimulate under affectations of politeness.

I made my resolution and said: "Madame, I have not come here on my own behalf, but on behalf of an unfortunate, whom I have taken the liberty of serving in your regard as a devoted advocate."

"An unfortunate?" she said. "A pauper?"

That confusion embarrassed me. I felt that I had started badly. But alas, with out habits of tergiversation it is difficult to get straight to the point. It was necessary to finish, though.

"No, Madame, If the man whose spokesperson I am is poor in money, he is above all morally unfortunate, and the relief of that dolor, that torture, which almost surpasses the limits of human strength, as I can appreciate better than anyone, being his friend, can only come from you. In a word, I have come to you as a suppliant on behalf of my friend, Monsieur Robert."

She had listened to me anxiously, as if having both divined and dreaded the name that I was about to pronounce, and when it had escaped from my lips—oh, the poor woman!—she did not flinch, did not shudder, did not weep . . . but on the face that I had judged a little while before to be insignificant, one might have thought that a mask had suddenly been placed: a mask of terrible anxiety and bitter distress. Thus it might have been were hands reaching into your breast to wring your heart and you had the courage of an apparent impassivity.

Her eyes were open, and there, in the gaze through which a glimmer had passed—a suddenly-illuminated red star—I read as clearly as on a photographic print a spectral evocation rise up in her brain. And yet, those words cannot render accurately what I saw: neither anger nor despair, but rather the numbing horror put into the soul by the hypnotism of a profound pit.

So, fearfully, I said: "Believe, Madame, that if I have accepted this mission, only grave reasons could have decided me to reawaken memories . . ."

"Do you believe that my memories were asleep?" she responded, with a riposte so swift that one might have thought it prepared, so simultaneously precise and sinister was the phrase. "Sit down Monsieur," she said. "I cannot hold it against you that you are the friend of that man. I will listen to you and respond to you. In any case, it is necessary that an explanation takes place. That crisis ought to be produced. Perhaps I should have provoked it myself. Sit down, and speak as frankly as you desire. I shall not interrupt you."

Was that really the same woman who had previously appeared to me in a grayness of nullity? Now I had before me a courage, an intelligence, a consciousness translating itself in precise ideas and terms, with a sort of audacity drawn from the sentiment of right. I really was an advocate; she was the judge.

That physiognomy, illuminated by an interior fire, seemed to be that if someone resuscitated, emerged from the tomb in response to a summons and now living in all her dolor and all her galvanized anguish.

In fact, I preferred that attitude; I was not short of arguments, and Robert's cause was one that could be pleaded.

She listened to me, her chin supported on her hand, her eyes staring into mine.

I told her about the solitary, desolate existence of the man who, obedient to stupid prejudices, had committed the fault, the crime, that had broken her life. Taking for a point of departure the absurd duel, I showed her the seconds, more determined than the combatants and opposing any conciliation. I made the most of the equal risks run, the surprises of fatality that defied all expectations. How many duels conclude with an insignificant scratch!

I showed the unfortunate scholar plunged in his books, cloistered, wanting to be alone and seeing at every hour the phantom loom up before him that he could not expel. I affirmed that Robert had experienced and was experiencing profound, ineluctable regrets, and I gave for proof that tenacity of remorse after ten years had gone by. That remorse was now translated into the desire for forgiveness, the supplication of forgetfulness. It ought not to be held against him if he sought the manifestation of that pardon, that forgetfulness, in a material sign—tangible, so to speak. I understood that the poor woman was justly irritated by the quasi-pursuit of which she was the victim; I explained it to her. It had no character of deliberate persecution, which would have been monstrous. Let us say that here was a madman—so be it! But ought she not to discover, in that very obsession, and excuse for that species of request for rehabilitation. For my friend, the horror that she testified was a perpetual genesis of his remorse, an incessantly-renewed signification of the judgment with which that he had struck himself.

Certainly, I could not deny that it would have been more natural to go away, that he decided to quit the town; but it was necessary not to judge him as an ordinary person. I had known him for a long time. I explained his age, ripened by his adolescence. In any case, did he have a perfectly sane mind, a man who had risked his life for a quibble, whose insignificance I recognized myself? Furthermore, I had divined, I knew that there was nothing in that quarrel but a misunderstanding. Once again I was not excusing Robert, but analyzing him.

"Madame," I said, finally, "I repeat that it is not to your reason, to your logic, that I am appealing, but only to your pity. You are a woman, more apt than others to appreciate those fugitive nuances of consciousness that differentiate individuals so profoundly. Robert has been guilty, a criminal, but he is only a wretch . . . have mercy! That is what I ask you, only that. The first time you encounter him in your path, humble and suppliant, when he bows to you, have the courage to look him in the face and return his salute. Make that sacrifice, the dolorous grandeur of which I appreciate, and I promise, using my influence upon him, to remove him from your path forever. He'll depart; I'll take him to Paris and you'll never hear his name pronounced again. Oh, it would be a great happiness for me and a satisfaction of conscience, for him and for you, if I took him away with your consent."

She had kept her promise, listening to me without interruption, always looking at me with her fixed eyes, in which I divined thoughts without being able to read them.

When I stopped, she simply said: "Have you no other arguments to present? It seems to me that you've forgotten one."

Was she speaking ironically? I could not believe it. Indeed, voluntarily, I had omitted any allusion to the sacrifices that Robert had imposed on himself in order to subsidize her needs and those of her children. But since she was inviting me herself to emerged from my reserve, I no longer had to remain silent.

I told her everything: how that man, whom in his soul and his conscience, did not believe himself to be culpable—wrongly, perhaps, but having more merit in acting as he had done in consequence—had not been able to bear that, because of him, even as an instrument of fatality, a woman and children should be deprived of resources. Obedient to that instinct of justice, he had condemned himself to poverty, and even more, to obscurity. He has sold more than material goods: his intelligence, his labor, his passions, his ambitions, his vanity as a scholar. He had made money of the lobes of his brain, the fibers of his heart. Had he not repaired, redeemed, the harm that he had done? Could he have done more? Was he thinking of liberating himself from the obligations that he had created for himself? On the contrary, he was seeking to give them a definitive character. And this time I was appealing to both pity and reason, and, I concluded, in addressing Madame Laurent with all the respect that her dolor and regret inspired in me, I permitted myself to remind her there is no criminal so great that he cannot obtain amnesty by expiation.

I shut up. Then, without raising her voice, speaking in a tone that was almost solemn, Madame Laurent said:

"I will not forgive, nor will I make the sign that seems to you to be insignificant but would be a hypocritical sacrilege for me. This is why. Obedient to ideas that I will not dispute, since they are those of the great majority, you have never asked yourself what human life is. For you, to kill a man's wife is to deprive her of sustenance, of a position, to take away the resources on which she has a legal and moral tight to count. And your strongest argument is that that man has repaired, as best he can, the material damage that he has caused. We do not understand one another. It is not my banker that that man has killed, it is my husband, the father of my children, a spouse and an educator. You did not know him; you do not know what he was. Two words: good and intelligent.

Good . . . do you understand? With his cordiality, with his generosity, with his gently and becoming justice he filled this house, still impregnated with him. You ought to have divined who he was when you learned that, superior to prejudice, he went to hold out his hand to the man who had insulted him and, even on the terrain, he asked his seconds to make one last attempt at conciliation. It is not an ordinary man, you'll agree, who rises above the reproach of cowardice.

"Intelligent, I affirm to you, and passionate for his art—music—which procured him infinite joys. I could give you proof of the encouragements he received. Modest, he did not hasten to profit from the propositions that were made to him. He knew that he was young, he wanted to feel solid ground beneath his feet. More knowledgeable and better inspired than many others who had already conquered success, he was still working and trying himself.

"He lived my life; I lived his. This house, where our two children played—I had two then!—was enveloped by an atmosphere of mutual affection and devotion; hopes too, and how beautiful they were! All that goodness, all the exquisite qualities of that consciousness, all its noble ambitions, already partly realized: that is what the man you call your friend has killed. That is what a human life is!

"That man has given money; he has done well. He was afraid of the visible poverty that was his work. Here there is the visible poverty of the absence of a husband and a father. What has he given—what could he give?—to palliate that . . . the irreparable loss that he has caused to fall upon us? What fortune could have compensated the joys of which the poor dead man was frustrated?

"You ask me for pity! Wait. My daughter, my poor daughter, is dead; I shall tell you why. The child had a godmother who lived in a neighboring village. It was a joy for her father to take her there. My husband dead, I took her myself. In returning, the child and I were surprised by a horrible storm. We were well covered; we arrived. The child had wet feet. 'Why didn't you carry me?' she said. 'Father always carried me when it was muddy.' Alas, I was too weak. Because her father was no longer there to carry her, the child died of a fluxion of the chest. It's your friend who killed her.

"You see that a father brings more than money into the house.

"Again, a son remained to me, rather idle, perhaps unintelligent. I was too weak with him, my poor survivor, and I'm guilty of his lack of success. Would it have been the same if his father had been here?

"At every minute, at every step, the absence of the husband and the father is like a black hole, a void into which one slips and falls. The armchair where he sat down is empty; his place at the table, empty; the air that he filled with his voice, empty; our hearts, into which he put confidence, empty; our minds, which he infused with his intelligence, empty. The father gone, there is a kind of blindness in the house. I do not forgive God when he kills a father.

"Human life! You consider it at the moment when it ended. You say: 'It's ten years ago that he died.' I say to you, personally: 'Ten years ago he was alive; ten years in which that heart, that goodness, that justice, that intelligence would have created wealth for himself, for his family and for everyone.'

"Does your friend imagine that he has redeemed all that? He has not killed him once; he kills him every day. Every instant when my husband ought to be here and he is not weighs a heavier responsibility upon his murderer.

"I have taken the money. Certainly—why not? My son has received the greater part of it, and it will aid him to fray in life the route that his father would have opened wide to him. But do you count for nothing the joy that the father would have experienced in guiding his son himself to the age of maturity? All the mental satisfactions that you have stolen from him—is that nothing? There, on the contrary, is the crime: to have prevented a man from living, thinking, devoting himself to those he loves and enjoying the happiness that he owes to them!

"In all that I am making no mention of myself, my tears of yesterday and those of tomorrow, my lost intimacies. Perhaps I could have forgiven that, but I cannot forgive that my husband no longer has the joy of being loved, I cannot forgive that he was taken away from us when he was so happy in being loved . . . look at his piano, in front of which he spent hours of good and healthy intoxication when he was composing; I cannot forgive his unfinished and mute manuscripts, in which he heard future harmonies . . . I cannot forgive the man who killed him, because he loved life and life loved him.

"He expected much anguish in the struggle. He enjoyed in advance the energy of perseverance with which he knew himself to be endowed. Even his battles foreseen and proudly confronted were taken from him.

"That is human life. It is not understood, not respected. Imagine that, at this moment, he might be here, in the place where you are. Against your indifference, which evaluates the life of a man in money, I protest in the name of my desolated love, not egotistically, for it's of the dead man that I'm thinking, the man who was prevented from living. He was forty years old; I'm thirty-five, but I've aged by all the years that he has not lived.

"Once again, Monsieur, I regret not being able to respond to you as you have hoped; the step, the gesture that you ask of me, would be a comedy, a game. One does not play with human life . . ."

I did not respond. I saluted that woman profoundly, whose dolor had made a great social philosopher,

I returned to Robert and I told him everything, word for word. I thought he was going to argue, to resist.

"She's right," he said,

"What are you going to do?"

"Nothing."

"Don't stay in this town. Disengage yourself from all obligations. I'm rich; I'll help you to keep your engagements of conscience and reconquer your liberty. Come to Paris; I'll take charge of your future."

He did not make any decision. I stayed with him for another two days; he was calm, as if resigned to the inevitable. I could not extract a formal promise from him. I departed.

After a month, I received a letter; he was working and had made a contract with an English publisher for a rather large sum.

Another month went by, and then another. I wrote to him in my turn: no reply

I made enquiries. One day, he had been found dead in his study; he had not committed suicide, but since my departure, he had not gone out except to deposit a capital to the credit of Laurent's son.

A week later, the obsession had killed him . . .

Why not say that remorse had destroyed a human life?

A PARTIAL LIST OF SNUGGLY BOOKS

G. ALBERT AURIER *Elsewhere and Other Stories*
CHARLES BARBARA *My Lunatic Asylum*
CHARLES BARBARA *Stirring Stories*
S. HEZOLNRY BERTHOUD *Misanthropic Tales*
LÉON BLOY *The Tarantulas' Parlor and Other Unkind Tales*
ÉLÉMIR BOURGES *The Twilight of the Gods*
ADA BUISSON *The Baron's Coffin and Other Disquieting Tales*
CYRIEL BUYSSE *The Aunts*
JAMES CHAMPAGNE *Harlem Smoke*
FÉLICIEN CHAMPSAUR *The Latin Orgy*
ARMAND CHARPENTIER
    Claustrophobic Madness and Other Stories of Death and Love
BRENDAN CONNELL *Metrophilias*
BRENDAN CONNELL *Spells*
RENDAN CONNELL (editor) *The Zaffre Book of Occult Fiction*
BRENDAN CONNELL (editor) *The Zinzolin Book of Occult Fiction*
RAFAELA CONTRERAS *The Turquoise Ring and Other Stories*
DANIEL CORRICK (editor)
    Ghosts and Robbers: An Anthology of German Gothic Fiction
ADOLFO COUVE *When I Think of My Missing Head*
RENÉ CREVEL *Are You All Crazy?*
QUENTIN S. CRISP *Aiaigasa*
QUENTIN S. CRISP *Rule Dementia!*
LUCIE DELARUE-MARDRUS *The Last Siren and Other Stories*
LADY DILKE *The Outcast Spirit and Other Stories*
CATHERINE DOUSTEYSSIER-KHOZE *The Beauty of the Death Cap*
ÉDOUARD DUJARDIN *Hauntings*
BERIT ELLINGSEN *Now We Can See the Moon*
ERCKMANN-CHATRIAN *A Malediction*
ALPHONSE ESQUIROS *The Enchanted Castle*
ENRIQUE GÓMEZ CARRILLO *Sentimental Stories*
DELPHI FABRICE *Flowers of Ether*
DELPHI FABRICE *The Red Sorcerer*
DELPHI FABRICE *The Red Spider*
BENJAMIN GASTINEAU *The Reign of Satan*
EDMOND AND JULES DE GONCOURT *Manette Salomon*
REMY DE GOURMONT *From a Faraway Land*
REMY DE GOURMONT *Morose Vignettes*
GUIDO GOZZANO *Alcina and Other Stories*
GUSTAVE GUICHES *The Modesty of Sodom*
EDWARD HERON-ALLEN *The Complete Shorter Fiction*
EDWARD HERON-ALLEN *Three Ghost-Written Novels*

www.ingramcontent.com/pod-product-compliance
Lightning Source LLC
Chambersburg PA
CBHW050012120726
47903CB00006B/1733